# CONDITION: TERMINAL

Back in the control room, the secretary had finally reached the QC, who now listened calmly to the urgent message from the head technician. "Sir, we have a Code 6."

"What kind of organ is it?" LeBearc asked.

"A heart," the technician said.

"Call the autopsy area and get whoever is on duty there in forensic cardiology up to the control room right away. And keep this contained. In fact, I want you to clear the control room of everyone else."

"Yes, sir."

The patient was frantically trying to get off the table. He tried again to scream but couldn't make a sound.

Observing the patient via the computer console's monitors, the QC punched his personal six-digit password into the keyboard. He typed the words "Code 6, deactivation" and then the serial number of the heart. The screen then reported a sixteen-digit number.

The QC typed in the sixteen digits, looked up again at the patient, who was now staring into the camera, and pressed the enter button.

The computer then inquired: "Are you sure? Y/N."

Hesitating for only a second, he looked into the patient's face and hit the Y key.

STEPHEN KANAR

# The J Factor

**BANTAM BOOKS**
New York Toronto London Sydney Auckland

THE J FACTOR
A Bantam Book / February 2000

All rights reserved.
Copyright © 2000 by Stephen P. Kanar.
Cover art copyright © 2000 by Alan Ayers.

ISBN 0-553-58079-5

*Published simultaneously in the United States and Canada*

Bantam Books are published by Bantam Books, a division of Random House, Inc. Its trademark, consisting of the words "Bantam Books" and the portrayal of a rooster, is Registered in U.S. Patent and Trademark Office and in other countries. Marca Registrada. Bantam Books, 1540 Broadway, New York, New York 10036.

PRINTED IN THE UNITED STATES OF AMERICA

OPM      10 9 8 7 6 5 4 3 2 1

To Carol Kanar
You make me happy

# Acknowledgments

I always considered myself a loner. I built my own airplane, a vacation house, and my law practice. Along the way I realized that others were always there to help. Nothing demonstrated this more than what happened after my naïve decision to "write a book." From the beginning I received the most important help of all—support—from friends and family.

Lyn Gray, my good friend and assistant of many years stuck with me, encouraged my efforts, and worked tirelessly. I could never have done this project without her.

Todd Wiggins added his suggestions at the early stages. C. C. Lyons (now Sandford) was a positive, credible voice from New York. Bob Laffin did meticulous reviews. Ann Campbell, Dale Hagen, Betty Ivester, and many others provided help, sometimes without even knowing it, particularly several doctors who should not bear any blame for my liberties with medical science.

My agent, Andy Zack of The Zack Company, made this book possible. He took a chance on a first-timer. Without him, it would only be an unread pile of paper in a file cabinet somewhere. He is a strong advocate. I'm glad he's on my side.

I spent a year working with Christine Brooks of Bantam. She acquired this book and then guided me through the extensive revision process. She understood the story from the beginning and helped focus the words to bring it out. She has been just as excited about the project as I have been. Her patience, enthusiasm, and efforts are far more than I ever expected.

My best friend, teacher, mentor, and honest critic, the eminent writer and poet Carol Kanar, was the one who caused me to realize that not only was I not a loner, but also that I didn't really want to be one. I'm lucky to be married to her and she's beautiful, too—what a deal! Carol dedicated her first book to me and I dedicate my first one to her. Thanks for everything, Carol.

# The J Factor

# 1

**The Near Future:**
**GOVERNMENT HOSPITAL, ORLANDO, FLORIDA**

*Dr. David West opened the patient's chest. Slicing the pericardium, he exposed the heart, which pulsed erratically in a pool of warm blood. The heart had to be replaced. Dr. West completed the heart transplant in every detail in less than five minutes.*

Staring out a window into the distance, David's view of the east horizon was obscured by the black clouds and torrential rain of a thunderstorm. He cleared his head, then reopened the patient's chest and completed the procedure again. He would visualize the operation until he'd perfected every detail. When his patient arrived, he would be ready.

The other members of the cardiac emergency team dropped their paper coffee cups into the waste can as they entered the hospital's glassed-in rooftop triage center and eyed the storm. They glanced at West but said nothing to him. Just under six feet tall with light brown hair, longer than usual for a doctor, David looked like an athlete preparing for action, lost in his own world. He was the outsider, the new guy—supposedly a real hotshot—but, to the cardiac team, untested and unproven. One of them had somehow managed to access West's personnel file and print out a copy of a letter, which he had slipped to other team members to read.

TO:      Denis Long, Administrator
         Government Hospital, Orlando
FROM:    Professor J. H. Barnes, M.D., FACS,
         FASCS, Assistant Chief
         Department of Cardiovascular Surgery
         Yale Medical School

I understand you are considering a young heart surgeon, David West. He was a surgical resident at our school until events led to his forced resignation and a transfer to complete his training. From the version of the story given to the general public one might reach an erroneous conclusion. Officially, West was asked to resign because he performed an unauthorized heart surgery while a first-year general surgical resident. He did it while the rest of the E.R. staff stood around wringing their hands. This surgery saved my life.

I suffered a ruptured aorta while on duty in the E.R. as the on-call cardiologist. I had minutes to live. No other cardiologist could have arrived in time to save me. The staff general surgeon refused to operate because of strict hospital specialty rules. When no one else would act, Dr. West opened my chest while I was on a gurney in the E.R. He fashioned a crude Dacron patch for my aorta, sutured it into place, and stopped the blood loss. A few hours later, the chief of our department successfully

performed an aortic graft. Thanks to Dr. West I
was able to be there for it.

I hope this clarifies any uncertainty you may
have harbored because of West's resignation
from Yale. He is indeed a very talented surgeon.

As the team members read the letter, they each stole
looks at David West. One endorsement left them still
unimpressed. They would make their own evaluations in a
few minutes.

They all watched the remote telemetry monitor that
flickered as a lightning bolt popped, waiting for the first
signals that would indicate that the patient, a sailor who
had suffered a massive heart attack while at sea, was in the
helicopter en route to the hospital. But even with the rapid
transport, he might not reach the hospital alive.

David began mentally opening the chest once again, but
this time the patient went into cardiac arrest. Knowing
exactly how to handle such a complication, in less than
five minutes he had completed another virtual transplant.

But in fact this would be his first independent heart
surgery since finishing his residency six weeks earlier. Despite his self-confidence and maverick reputation, he was
nervous. He drummed his fingers on the tan ceramic tile
windowsill, while his gray eyes looked holes through the
clouds as if to catch a first glimpse of the helicopter. All he
could think about in this quiet time of waiting: How many
patients would he be able to save in his lifetime? How
many would he lose? None from being unwilling to act
because of someone else's rules. He'd decided that several
years before.

The rescue helicopter flew eastbound toward its destina-
tion at Port Canaveral, near the Kennedy Space Center, to

meet the Fusion Electric Corporation ship. The storm had moved inland now, and the coastline sparkled in bright sunlight.

The pilot and his paramedic spotted the ship, which resembled a three-hundred-foot-long modified airplane, well out to sea. The ship was literally flying over the surface of the ocean on a cushion of air created by the lift from its stubby wings, but it could climb to no more than half its wingspan off the surface. Behind the ship, visible for many miles, a trail of steam and mist slowly dissipated in its wake.

Still several miles from shore, the ship began to slow; the hydrofoils extended like landing gear. A white flume of water appeared behind the ship as the hydrofoils touched the surface at over two hundred knots. The ship continued to slow and finally settled onto its hull.

The helicopter circled back toward shore and landed just as the ship arrived at the pier. Two crewmen carrying a man on a stretcher bolted through the hatch and ran for the helicopter. The captain of the ship followed closely behind. He wore a hat and shoulder boards decorated with several rows of gold braid. His military bearing seemed not the least undermined by the fact that his uniform included white Bermuda shorts. They displayed a sharp crease above his spotless white shoes.

The crewmen loaded the patient into the helicopter as the captain, looking gravely concerned, hurried up to the pilot and said in a crisp British clip, "I'm Captain Stapleton. See that you take proper care of Martinez. He's a good man. We did all we could for him aboard and you got him here as quickly as possible. But he can't last long, so you'd better be off."

"Is this 'Martinez' British?" the pilot asked as he filled in a form. In fact, many of the employees of FE were British.

"No, he's an American. No problem about payment; don't worry about that."

The captain impatiently looked into the back of the helicopter as the paramedic attached several wires to the telemetry transmitter, then made a circular motion with her hand, signaling the pilot.

"All right, stand clear," said the pilot, checking gauges and flipping switches, preparing for takeoff. The whine of the jets became a deafening high-pitched roar, and the rotor blurred into motion.

Jumping off the pad, then skimming the screaming helicopter only a few feet from the surface of the pier with the nose down and tail high, the pilot accelerated to over a hundred miles an hour while crossing over the bow of the boat; only then did he lift the aircraft higher and continue to accelerate. He set a course directly for Orlando and called air traffic control. "Lifeguard Sixteen is hot off the Fusion Electric pier to Orlando Government. Request priority clearance."

"Roger, Lifeguard Sixteen, cleared as requested. Altitude and course at your discretion. There's a thunderstorm in your route of flight, heavy rain and cloud-to-ground lightning, wind shear level three. Good luck."

His takeoff would cause half a dozen noise complaints, but the time he'd gain would be worth it. He would fly under the storm through the rain rather than divert around it. Grinning at his own daring, the pilot then checked in with his controller. "Orlando Government Hospital, Lifeguard Sixteen inbound with heart patient."

"Lifeguard Sixteen, we're already talking to your backseater and getting telemetry on the patient. You're cleared to land at pad four. Our team is ready. Telemetry shows arrhythmia. Get him in here as quick as you can."

Rain began to dot the canopy of the helicopter and form small lines that radiated back from the nose. Suddenly the drops became a violent roar as the helicopter flew into the full downpour. Visibility was zero and the pilot flew by instruments, ignoring the lurching and sliding that twisted the helicopter in ways he never thought possible. He had underestimated the severity of this storm.

Lightning popped beside the tail rotor and the hairs on his arms stood up from the induced static electricity. He struggled to keep the copter stable.

As suddenly as it had started, the roar of rain ended as they emerged on the other side of the thunderstorm.

The pilot could see the ugly concrete hospital tower in the distance. A heavy wind preceded the thunderstorm producing wind shear that could cause the helicopter to drop precipitously, with no warning. Normal procedure was to head around in a square pattern, approaching the rooftop landing pad slowly and flying into the wind to reduce risks, but this pattern was time-consuming. The pilot boldly flew directly toward the landing pad. He pulled hard on the collective and raised the nose as the helicopter passed over the top edge of the building. He then applied full power, miraculously slowing the copter down, and gently touching down as the momentum and braking force equalized in a perfect landing. He could not repeat that touchdown in ten tries. Pretending not to notice the trembling in his hands, he took a deep breath and began turning off switches in the cockpit.

When he looked over his shoulder he saw that the hospital team had already removed the patient and were working on him even as they pushed him into the hospital. If he lived, the risk would have been worth it. Just then the storm reached the rooftop and the downpour and lightning began again in full force.

"Hey, you just about dumped me out the back door," the paramedic kidded while reorganizing her equipment.

"Well, somebody said we were in a hurry," the pilot quipped. He completed his form and began prepping the helicopter for his next call.

Martinez realized that one of the blue-suited people walking beside the gurney was actually talking to him, not merely about him. "Sir, can you hear me?"

"Yeah."

"I'm Dr. West. I'm a cardiovascular surgeon, a heart doctor. You've had a heart attack."

"Yeah, no shit! Am I gonna make it?" Martinez struggled to reply.

"That's why I'm here. I'll hook up a temporary mechanical heart to help your own heart and then I'll see how much damage there is, and what we can do about it." When they reached the operating room, someone put a mask over Martinez's face and began counting backwards from ten. The last number he heard was seven, which sounded as if it had come down a long hall, vibrating and echoing off the walls. A nurse began downloading his personal medical records for UNIMED. The administrative nurse watched the UNIMED computer screen at the control panel in the O.R.

*Now it's for real,* David thought, and glanced around the room cluttered with equipment and electronic monitors. The intense operating lights ensured that the tubes and wires cast no shadows. Half a dozen people busied themselves around the sailor.

"All right, people, let's get him hooked up quickly; we're out of time here," West ordered, taking charge. His anxiety vanished.

"Just a minute, Doctor. The UNIMED authorization isn't up yet," the administrative nurse said, watching the screen.

"What's the problem?"

"I don't know. They're busy, I guess. But you can't start until the approval is posted."

West glared at the screen, then looked at the patient and clenched his jaw. Still no authorization. "The hell with this." Taking a scalpel, he made an incision a half-inch long just at the base of the rib cage. Then he inserted a laser cutter, which looked like a set of pruning shears left partially open. A blue laser arced between the tips. Slowly he moved the cutter up along the center line of the patient's chest, cutting a thin line through the skin, muscle tissue, and breastbone. The laser cauterized the tissue as it passed through, leaving a wisp of smoke and the distinct odor of burning flesh but virtually no blood.

"I wonder if I'll ever get used to that smell," West commented to no one in particular as he inserted a chest splitter and pulled the breastbone apart at the incision, exposing the pericardium encasing the heart.

"I'm putting in a valve on the ascending aorta and then on the superior vena cava," West said. Talking to himself was a habit he'd acquired at med school, where the professors required it so they would know what the resident was about to do. "Give me a count from my mark and clamp the pulmonary veins. Ready. Now," he said to the nurse.

The assistant did as directed and West made an incision in the aorta, opened it with his finger, and inserted a plastic valve. An outlet on the valve provided an attachment point for the mechanical heart.

He applied Medibond, a medical equivalent of Super Glue, to the edge of the artery wall; it immediately bonded to the plastic valve, forming a seal.

". . . seven seconds, eight, nine," the assistant continued to count.

"Okay, looks good. Valve is set for normal flow."

". . . sixteen, seventeen."

"Release the clamp. Let's check the seal," West directed. The assistant eased the clamp off to allow blood to flow through the heart and into the artery again. Blood squirted out of a small leak. "Reclamp it," West said. "Give me a count."

He repaired the bond in twelve seconds.

"That was the critical one. It seems to be holding the pressure now." West flexed his fingers, blinked a few times, and looked up at the clock. As he did so, he saw

Virginia Pruitt, the UNIMED coordinator, looming above. She was scowling at him from the observation gallery, impatiently holding a telephone that was connected to the intercom in the operating theater but could only be activated from West's side.

Virginia Pruitt was a thin, dark-haired woman in her late forties with a stiff, officious attitude, a shrill voice, and unquestioned authority. West had been introduced to her during his orientation. He realized immediately that she considered her position of utmost importance. It was her function to authorize or deny any nonroutine medical expenditures and to make certain that all necessary certifications and other administrative requirements were met before any medical services were provided. Government administered, the Universal Medical Hospital and Pharmaceutical Care System—better known as UNIMED—paid for birth-to-death health care for most Americans. The UNIMED coordinator held the purse strings and therefore the power of life in her hands. Pruitt now gestured angrily at the telephone receiver she held.

"Somebody talk to her," West said irritatedly. The administrative nurse reluctantly picked up the O.R. phone.

"Let's get the other valve in and get this man closed." West frowned up at the observation area and saw that Pruitt was animatedly gesturing while chewing out the nurse West would rather have had in attendance at the table.

"Doctor! Something's wrong. There's blood on his heart." As one of his attendants spoke, the alarm on the heart monitor went off with a piercing bleat and another nurse exclaimed, "We're getting arrhythmias and random pulses!"

"His heart muscle is separating," Dr. West said. "It's about to blow out. Here, give me your hand," he said to the first nurse, pulling her hand toward the left ventricle from which there was now a heavy pulsing flow of blood. He felt her resist.

"What are you doing?" she demanded with a horrified expression.

"I want you to hold his heart, help support the muscle and keep it together while I insert another valve so we can get the mechanical heart hooked up."

"But if I do that his heart will stop. I've seen it happen before," she pleaded. She clearly didn't trust the brash young surgeon.

"Of course it'll make his heart stop. That's exactly what I want to happen. I don't want to use medication because of the damage he's already suffered. If this heart keeps beating it will rupture before we can get the valve in and he'll die. Now, don't argue with me. I don't want to have to justify everything in advance."

He carefully guided her hand and placed her fingers around the left underside of the organ.

"Give me a count and cool the heart with nitrogen—but keep it off her fingers—while I get this valve in," he said to the surgical nurse, and immediately made an incision in the vessel leading into the heart. He inserted another plastic valve into the vessel and applied the same bonding agent. He worked quickly but carefully. Except for the continuous flatline drone of the heart monitor and the hiss of the liquid nitrogen—more than a hundred degrees below zero—being directed onto the heart itself, there was total silence in the operating room.

"I want that count," West snapped. The nurse jumped with a start and reported the digital readout on the heart monitor. "It's at forty-five seconds, forty-six, forty-seven."

"What the hell's her problem?" West asked the nurse who had finally hung up with Pruitt.

"She says you can't hook the patient up to a mechanical heart without prior approval from her, and she demands to speak to you immediately."

West attached more tubes leading to the heart machine. "Well, it's too late for that now, isn't it?" he said, as he reached across to the mechanical heart control panel and pressed the start sequence button. "What was the count?"

"Two minutes and twenty-three seconds. We have good vitals and no interruption of brain wave patterns."

"Now," said West. "Turn on the intercom and let me talk to that woman before she has a stroke and becomes our next patient." The nurse, amused but afraid to smile, flipped the intercom switch. "This is Dr. West. What can I do for you?" he asked.

"Don't give me that," snapped Pruitt. "You know what I want. You had no authority to connect a mechanical heart. Prior approval is required and you didn't get it."

"We had an emergency. I had no time to get prior approval."

"That's exactly why I'm here. I have to determine if a mechanical heart is justified under the circumstances. I didn't have time to study the details about this patient. I can't make that decision until I've got the facts."

"Well, it's too late now. He's already hooked up. What do you want me to do, disconnect it?"

"I would, provided I didn't have to get a court order first," she snapped back. "Which, of course, only adds to the expense involved. I can assure you this matter will be brought to the attention of the administrator. You'll have to explain yourself to the medical committee."

"Turn her off before I say something I'll regret," West directed, and the nurse snapped off the intercom. Pruitt continued on punctuating every unheard word with her hand, clicking her manicured nails against the glass like a caged cobra trying to strike. Suddenly West noticed the nurse still holding the patient's heart clenching her jaw muscles and blinking back tears.

"You can let go now," he said. "Let's check your hand." He eased her hand out of the patient's chest and moved away from the operating table. He removed the glove from her fingers, which had turned blue from the subzero cold of the liquid nitrogen. Removing his own surgical gloves, he gripped her hand between his and massaged her fingers. "Can you move them?" he asked her. She tried and they moved slightly. "Good. Your hand will be okay. But go get it checked out now. We'll finish up here," he said as he resterilized his hands in the Steri-Quick and reached for a replacement pair of surgical gloves. "Oh, and Ms. Coffin," he added, reading the name off her operating gown, "I guess you know you saved that man's life."

*"I'm* not the one, Doctor." She looked at him pointedly, then left.

Afterward, in the operating room office, as he stopped to discard his surgical clothes and gloves, the receptionist said, "Dr. West, a couple of things: Administrator Long was here with the UNIMED coordinator. He wants you to come to his office, and he said to tell you, 'right now.' "

"Okay," West said, rubbing the back of his neck, which became stiffer with the thought of that meeting. "What's the other message?"

"Mrs. Martinez is outside in the waiting area."

"Who's Mrs. Martinez?" he asked.

"She's the wife of the man you just operated on. I told her you would talk to her as soon as you came out of the O.R. Shall I tell her you'll see her after you see the administrator?"

"No, I'll see her first. I've got a feeling I'll be with the administrator for quite a while." Still massaging the back of his neck, he walked into the messy waiting area and looked around trying to find someone he thought might be Mrs. Martinez. He saw a teenage boy attempting to comfort a woman in her early forties. She looked like his idea of a southern lady, well dressed and carefully made up, but her eyes were red and she was gripping her purse with both hands as if it were her last contact with the real world. He asked, "Are you Mrs. Martinez?"

"Yes. How's my husband?" she asked as she stood up. The boy stood beside her and steadied her.

"Who's this?" West asked.

"He's our son, Jorge. He drove me over here. I was much too nervous and upset to drive myself."

"Mrs. Martinez, your husband has suffered a heart attack."

"That's what they told me when they called from the ship. Will he be all right? When can I see him?"

"It was very serious. It started with arrhythmia—irregular beating of his heart which interferes with pumping of the blood. Supposedly he fainted while they were at sea. The ship's doctor ordered medication to stimulate your husband's heart until he could reach the hospital. Without lidocaine and epinephrine he wouldn't have survived, but the treatment is very hard on an already malfunctioning heart and only lasts for a short while. Before your husband came in, I had planned to connect him temporarily to a mechanical heart so that we could stabilize him and install a pacemaker.

"But while I was doing the surgery, your husband's heart ruptured, and the only way we could keep him alive was to stop his heart and bypass it entirely for a mechanical heart. We then repaired the rupture, but the organ is extensively damaged. For now, he is totally dependent on the mechanical heart."

Mrs. Martinez broke into tears. Her son tried to comfort her, glaring at West as though the doctor was at fault.

"Mrs. Martinez, your husband is a fairly young man and is probably a good candidate for a transplant, so don't lose hope. We'll get the process started. You'll be able to see him in a couple of hours. He'll look awful, but he's stable now. I'll see you again this evening after I've checked back in on him."

The conversation with Administrator Denis Long opened more politely than West had expected. "I left a message for you to come up here immediately. Do you mind telling me where you've been?" Long looked like a large bullfrog. Only his head and narrow shoulders were visible above the top of his oversized desk, and he wore round, thick glasses that made his eyes seem huge.

"I've been with Mrs. Martinez."

"Who's she?"

"She's the wife of the patient that I just operated on."

"Hmm." Long paused, then continued. "Perhaps we missed something in your orientation, Doctor, concerning the regulations in this hospital. This isn't a university teaching hospital. We don't implement expensive procedures here without first obtaining approval from UNIMED. They pay the bills and they have rules that simply must be followed." Long's show of patience was only partially forced. He was a deliberate man. He folded his arms on the desktop with his fingers interlaced, palms down, elbows out.

West took a deep breath. He already resented the bureaucracy of medicine, and it took considerable effort to keep his voice calm. "I took care of my patient in the way I thought best. I thought that was my job."

"My job, Dr. West, is to take care of all six thousand patients in this hospital. I can't do that unless the bills get paid. And the bills don't get paid unless UNIMED says they get paid. You and I may not like that, but that's the way it is." His words resonated in David's ears.

"What the hell was I supposed to do?" West snapped. "Just let him die?"

"Let's explore that for a moment. Forget the question of whether you should have gotten prior approval from UNIMED or whether they'll even pay the bill, and let's look at what's going to happen to your patient now. Do you think his heart will ever be good enough for you to take him off the mechanical heart?"

"Doubtful. He'll need a transplant."

"There you have it," said Long. "Is he qualified for an IORC transplant? What is his Justification Factor? What are his financial resources? Is he even a good candidate for a transplant?"

West clenched his teeth. "How am I supposed to know? I only saw the patient for two or three minutes before the emergency surgery."

"Exactly. And as you know, unfortunately not everyone is eligible for a heart transplant. And now we have another problem: Once we've hooked someone up to a mechanical heart we can't disconnect without a court order, which amounts to sanctioning the killing of the patient. Meanwhile, the family gets put through all kinds of trauma. All this expense is incurred only to have the person die in a few weeks anyway."

"I can't watch a patient die because you're worried about the bill!" West snapped, his face reddening.

"You have missed the point," said Long, ignoring the outburst. "The very reason that every person in the country is required to have a personal records crystal implanted in an earlobe is so that vital information can be quickly accessed. UNIMED downloads the information while the patient is being prepped for surgery. As it turns out, right now Martinez's Justification Factor is considerably short of that needed for an IORC heart transplant, and under such circumstances a mechanical heart is never authorized by UNIMED. You should have determined this before hooking him up."

"There must be exceptions," said West, regaining his composure. "This was an emergency, after all. I couldn't wait until UNIMED downloaded the records."

"There are no exceptions at IORC. That's the whole point of the Justification Factor system. If your J Factor is high enough you get the transplant; if it's not, you don't. IORC never makes exceptions."

"I assumed that we would have to find a heart from a donor and do it here ourselves if he wasn't qualified. We do transplants here all the time. Not every heart belongs to IORC."

"Yet meanwhile your patient lies in the hospital living on a mechanical heart, hoping that a suitable transplant turns up that we don't need for another patient already on a waiting list in a planned transplant program. All of which we must do in the time period UNIMED allows for maintenance on a mechanical heart. And that, Dr. West, is three weeks, as I think you know."

"It's worth the chance. I couldn't just let him die."

"You'll have the opportunity to explain all this to him and his family if we don't find a heart within three weeks. I know Martinez is your first solo patient, and frankly I admire the work you did today. Everyone in the hospital is talking about it. I don't think anyone ever thought of stopping the heart intentionally by simply grabbing it and squeezing."

West ignored the compliment and waited.

"I'll do what I can to help this time, but you can't afford to call in too many favors on one patient. I'll explain to the medical committee that I had not made clear to you the regulations about authorizing a procedure such as using a mechanical heart. Maybe I can satisfy our UNIMED friend by assuring her that I have counseled you, that you will study the procedures manuals carefully and endeavor in every way, et cetera, et cetera. David, you've got to remember that there is a lot more to practicing medicine today than simply being able to treat your patients. Besides, you mustn't start off here by violating UNIMED policies and making an enemy of the coordinator. Not with your record."

As David rode down on the elevator, he realized how difficult it would actually be to deal with the bureaucratic side of medicine. He had taken the Hippocratic oath; it was his duty to care for his patient. How could he ignore that because of red tape or some system of health care allocation? He then thought of his father, who had been allowed to die of a myocardial infarction because his J Factor was not high enough. Someone had entered an erroneous number in his records, which couldn't be corrected in time. David had decided that day to be a heart transplant surgeon. He had thought perhaps he could prevent the same thing from happening to someone else, but now it seemed a daunting task.

Everywhere there were constant reminders of the Justification Factor, the basis of organ allocation established by the International Organ Replacement Corporation—the IORC. Advertisers marketed food products on the basis of their healthful properties which, the advertisers claimed, would improve a consumer's J Factor at the next mandatory biannual physical examination. Subtle and even blatant urgings prompted people to fulfill their civic obligations, support their children, obey the law, observe the speed limit, and even avoid absenteeism at work in order to maximize their J Factors—since *everything* counted. Warnings of adverse J Factor consequences appeared on cigarette packs and alcoholic beverage containers. Even fast-food restaurants were required to warn customers that the fat content of their products could adversely affect the customers' J Factors. Such control over people and their ultimate survival had been implemented gradually and was no longer even questioned.

David resented the fact that decisions about medical

care were no longer in the hands of the doctors who were qualified to make them. Instead, a private company that seemed as autonomous as the government had the power to control the life and death of everyone, doling out medical resources according to its own agenda.

# 2

**Ten Days Later**

A man in his early fifties wearing tennis shorts got off the elevator and walked very unsteadily into the basement parking garage. The parking attendant wondered whether to suggest a taxi.

"The red Porsche," the man slurred, pointing across the parking garage to the classic 935 turbo.

Opening the car door, the attendant noticed that the interior smelled of fresh leather even though this model had not been built for decades. *A restored car like this costs a fortune,* the attendant thought, as he eased the Porsche alongside its owner and stepped out.

The owner flipped his tennis racket onto the passenger seat, pulling the door shut with a *clump* and offering neither tip nor comment.

A grinding crunch, several quick jerks, and the drunk man sped off with a squeal of his tires and the unique whine and hiss of his Porsche's air-cooled turbocharged engine.

The attendant saw a round four-inch enameled placard on the rear of the car next to the license plate. Looking closer, he saw that it was the green emblem of the IORC with "M.D." printed in the middle. *An IORC doctor and no tip.* "Hey, Doc, check out the posterior aspect of the third digit of my right upper extremity!" yelled the attendant, gesturing. *There should be a J Factor formula for owning such a cool car; that jerk wouldn't make it,* the attendant thought.

The car was fast, no doubt about it. Dr. Richard Thomas liked fast cars. He crunched the gears again and winced. *Maybe too much to drink,* he thought, but a little adrenaline would solve that. He accelerated away from the car behind him, shifted to third gear at sixty miles an hour, and pressed the accelerator to the floor. Reflections of the streetlights and neon signs flashed across his windshield, faster and faster. The car shot forward, the beautiful scream of its engine echoing off the buildings that lined the narrow downtown street.

A GM electric subcompact pulled out of a parking space a few hundred feet ahead of him, and before he could even react he hit the side of the car at the driver's door. He had a fleeting impression of the driver looking into his eyes a split second before impact, and then his air bag inflated with a bang as his world spun lazily around him in a hot white cloud. As the car finally came to rest, he noticed the tennis racket in his lap and thought that must have been what hit him in the jaw.

He tasted the saltiness of his blood seeping between his teeth. He sat for a moment, dazed, then began taking a mental inventory. He felt a numbness in his left wrist and heard nothing but a ringing in his ears. He checked his legs—thankfully, they worked. He squinted at the streetlight reflected through the cracked glass, hopelessly trying to adjust his blurred vision. He looked around at the cockeyed passenger seat and could tell that the dashboard on that side had been pushed back into the floor. Nothing seemed to make any sense, and he shook his head trying to remember exactly where he was and where he had been going before the accident. How much time had passed before someone was leaning over him with a stethoscope, he wasn't sure.

"Hold still, I'm a paramedic. Tell me what hurts," said a male voice.

"My vision is blurred and my wrist hurts. What's cut? There's blood all over."

"Looks like something hit your face. It doesn't look serious."

"Why can't I see right? All I see is a bunch of lights."

"The air bag gas does that. It only lasts a few minutes. You been drinking or doing drugs?"

"How bad is the car?" Dr. Thomas asked.

"It's completely trashed, like it exploded. Nothing much left. It's been a long time since I've seen anything like it. How fast were you going, anyway?"

"What the hell you mean, nothing much left! This whole side of the car seems okay."

"I meant the other car. That's the one that took the beating."

"I'm worried about my Porsche. The other car was just an Electro. That can be replaced."

"Well, the guy driving it can't be replaced. He's dead." The paramedic clenched his jaw as he responded. "How much have you had?"

"I'm a doctor."

"Yes, sir."

"Help me out of here."

The paramedic gave Thomas a gauze pad for his cheek and helped him out of the car. Blood dripped down the front of his shirt and his face hurt. "I want you to call IORC. Do it now. Tell them where I am and ask them to send somebody over here," he ordered.

"You'll have to take that up with him, *Doctor*," the paramedic replied, spitting out the title as he pointed to the black police officer heading toward them. The cop's huge muscles bulged and he had the swagger of a former football player.

"What happened here?" Officer Burrows demanded.

"That idiot pulled out without any warning whatso-ever."

"How fast were you going?"

"I don't know. I had the right of way. He pulled out. He could have killed me."

"Have you consumed any alcohol or drugs?" The police officer became suddenly formal.

"I asked that, and all he said was he's a doctor," the paramedic said. "He's not hurt very bad, just a little cut on his face. We're going to take what's left of this other guy over to the hospital."

"I am a doctor, and I want you to call IORC right now," Thomas said to Burrows.

"I don't care who you are. You don't give orders here," Burrows replied. "I'm now advising you that you must submit to a substance analysis. If you refuse, reasonable force will be used to obtain the analysis. Do you under-stand this notification and warning?"

"I'm not submitting to anything. I want you to call IORC or you'll be in more trouble than you can possibly imagine."

Everything happened suddenly. The police officer didn't look as if he could move that fast with all of the parapher-nalia hanging from his belt and attached to his jacket, but Thomas found himself facedown on the fender of his Porsche with his hands restrained behind his back. He yelped in pain.

"Sir, I'm now going to insert your finger into a sub-stance analyzer unit. When I insert your finger you will feel a slight prick from a sharp point. That's the analyzer extracting a small blood sample. Everything that's happen-ing is being videotaped." He put Thomas's finger into a small plastic device, waited until he saw a flashing light, and then removed the device from Thomas's finger.

Officer Burrows stepped back and said, "You may stand up and turn around now." He looked at the digital readout on the analyzer and then said in a formal manner, "I must now advise you that the analyzer shows your blood alcohol level to be in excess of the legal limit. You are under arrest. Anything you say now may be used against you, and I repeat that it is being recorded and videotaped. You are charged with vehicular homicide with alcohol aggravation."

"Take the damn handcuffs off. My wrist may be broken. I told you I'm a doctor. I want you to call IORC right now."

"The handcuffs stay on. You're being charged with vehicular homicide. And, I ain't your secretary." Officer Burrows began filling in a form on his clipboard. "You can call whoever you want when we get to the station."

"What are we waiting for, then? I don't want to stand out here on the street. My face hurts, my wrist hurts, and I need to take a piss. Let's go."

"Look, you still don't get it, do you? You're not in charge here. I'm going to complete my investigation, and that may take an hour or two. Then I may get around to taking you to the station. Now get into the patrol car and shut up."

Thomas glared at the officer. "Do you know what will happen to you when IORC gets finished with this? Your J Factor will be *below* zero. Do you understand what that means?"

"The IORC can't just change J Factors. There are laws about those things."

"You actually believe that?" Thomas replied. This cop needed to be put in his place. He needed to understand who he was talking to.

Clearly becoming angry, Burrows switched off the tiny video camera attached to his jacket shoulder. "Look, don't threaten me, you piece of shit. You killed that man. You threaten to mess with my J Factor again and you're going to have an accident yourself before we reach the police station. Got it?" He then turned the switch back on, jiggled the camera and said, "It seems to be working again. Like I said, sit in the car and I'll get back to you when I'm finished."

Thomas trembled with frustration. Usually when he told people what to do, they did it. But this cop not only refused to do what he was told, this guy might even hurt him. Thomas was beginning to sober up and, yes, he was getting scared.

.

The ambulance driver walked back to the Electro to help his partner. "Holy Jesus, look at his head!" He grabbed more gauze pads to wipe away blood and tissue that had already begun to dry and harden.

"I can't find his records crystal; I've looked through all this mess. Hell, I can't find his ear," the paramedic said. "Let's get him to the hospital before we lose the organs. Since there's no records crystal, we'll take the body to Government," he said.

"Maybe he's donated his organs to IORC," the driver replied.

"No records, no IORC. They get enough organs. Let's give somebody else a chance."

Dr. Clarence Byrd, a silver-haired, barrel-chested sixty-two-year-old black man, was the pathologist on duty when they arrived. He made a careful search of the victim's body and x-rayed the head to locate the records crystal, but finally concluded that it must have been lost at the accident scene.

It was immediately clear to Dr. Byrd that the victim had died from massive head injuries, but a full autopsy was still required. The victim's chest was disfigured by a surgical scar along the midline. Hesitating only a moment, he then electronically scanned the body. As he expected, an IORC identification number on the man's heart showed up on the scanner as a small green blip followed by a sixteen-digit number readout.

He had to make a decision quickly. All IORC organs were equipped with an electronic module encoded with a serial number. Legally, the body should be transferred to IORC, who had full rights to all of the victim's organs. But a recent administrator's memo had advised everyone in the hospital about a patient on a temporary mechanical heart who would soon be disconnected if a replacement heart wasn't found.

The idea that one company should have a near monopoly on organ transplants frustrated Dr. Byrd. As far as he was concerned, a life was a life, and when an organ became available, the first person who needed it should have it. Dr. Byrd would soon need a kidney transplant, so he secretly hoped a fellow doctor of like mind would do the same for him when the time came. But even aside from his own needs, he despised the J Factor system on principle and was committed to an underground organization called Equal Access, which sought to provide organs to all those in need, regardless of one's J Factor.

Dr. Byrd turned the video recorder on and began talking in his professional monotone. "After determining cause of death to be a severe trauma to the head which resulted in brain death, I will now open the body with the normal Y-shaped incision." He worked in silence, secretly holding his breath until locating the heart in the chest cavity. "The heart is observed and appears undamaged and is being removed now to be preserved for transplant." He would have liked to remove the electronic device attached to the outside of the left ventricle of the heart, but his colleagues in Equal Access had learned that removal usually caused irreparable damage, rendering the organ useless. He had no choice but to leave the module in place. Unless someone was looking for it, though, the tiny device would probably not be seen.

He completed the removal of several other organs and then did a tissue sample and size analysis to determine whether the heart was compatible with the requirements spelled out in the memorandum. Though a little small and not a perfect match, it turned out to be well within acceptable limits.

# 3

A call from the IORC Southeast Quality Control Manager was not an expected or pleasant interruption of the dinner party attorney Wilson Hoffmeister's wife was hosting on this particular evening. The "QC" was the top administrator of an entire IORC district. Something of a cross between a chief executive officer and a member of the board, the QC answered only to Central Management.

Andre LeBearc, a Swiss, was the QC of Southeast. Like most QCs he held an M.D. degree, but a formal education was only one of the necessary credentials. This job required an astute business sense and an ability to make instant decisions that affected the lives of many people.

"Andre," said Hoffmeister, trying to sound more pleasant than he felt, "I suppose this is important." Wilson Hoffmeister had represented distinguished clients in important legal matters for thirty years. He served on the boards of directors of a major bank, an investment firm, a university, and his church. Although he was a senior partner in a private law firm, he now devoted his professional services exclusively to representing IORC in Florida.

Hoffmeister's deep, booming voice commanded attention and respect. Tall and graying, a devoted fitness enthusiast and avid traveler, he exuded power, authority, and self-confidence.

IORC's legal business rarely involved emergencies—Hoffmeister personally saw to that. A legal emergency usually means that someone has made a legal mistake. Legal problems are, for the most part, foreseeable and therefore avoidable. It is much easier to prevent a potential problem than to face a crisis that has developed.

"Can you take care of one of our doctors being held at the Central Police Station?" said LeBearc without preamble.

"Sure, I'll send someone right away. What's the problem?"

"I want you to go yourself. This is a very sensitive matter. A senior transplant surgeon, Dr. Richard Thomas, had a motor car accident a few hours ago. The other driver died and Thomas was apparently intoxicated. He also seems to have urinated in a police car." LeBearc's tone made clear that he resented having to deal with such base matters.

"How far do I go to get him out?" asked Hoffmeister.

"He's one of our surgeons. We want him here, proper time in the morning. Whatever is necessary to get the charges dismissed or reduced, do it. We'll compensate the victim's family, of course. I'll deal with the doctor myself and assure that this doesn't happen again."

"Okay, I'll go right down there." He heard a click on the other end of the telephone line. Not even a thank you, just the sound of the QC hanging up. Arrogance, a regrettable yet necessary attribute for this type of person, generally made QCs unpopular.

Hoffmeister called his office. His firm paid one lawyer from a rotating list of young associates to remain available twenty-four hours a day in case an urgent matter arose. Tonight was Michael Evans's turn.

"Good evening, Mr. Hoffmeister."

"I want you to go down to the Central Police Station

and start getting the paperwork together on a guy named Dr. Richard Thomas, an IORC doctor who is charged with vehicular homicide. I'm on my way to the station, and I'll see you there. Meanwhile, get someone to draw up papers to set the bond for Thomas; arrange to see the night duty judge and get a bondsman down there. Tell him it's for IORC. *Now move.*"

"Yes, sir."

Hoffmeister went back to the dining room, made his apologies to his wife and their friends, and went upstairs to put on one of his blue suits.

When Hoffmeister arrived at the police station, he wasn't exactly sure where to go. His type of law practice had never involved trips to the police station for clients. In fact, he'd never even been to the station before.

As he got off the elevator, he found himself in a large room where several clerks talked to people from behind a worn glassed-in counter. He grimaced at the dirty vinyl-tiled floor and trash cans overflowing with discarded coffee cups and candy wrappers. Several unsavory characters sprawled in plastic chairs. As he oriented himself, Michael Evans, carrying a stack of papers, walked up to him.

"Mr. Hoffmeister, I have most of the information you wanted right here. The officer's name, details about the victim, and so on. There's no formal report yet. The officer is working on it upstairs. They're waiting for you before they ask Dr. Thomas any questions. They have him up on the fifth floor in an interrogation room. He's got some injuries and a nurse has just gone upstairs to check him over."

"How serious?" Hoffmeister asked.

"Not very."

"Have you seen him yet?"

"No, I thought I had better wait for you, since he's

IORC. The papers for the bond have already been filed. We're just waiting for the judge to get to them and sign an order."

"Good. Let's go see him."

The elevator opened into a small anteroom. A Plexiglas-protected receiving window on the far wall allowed the uniformed receptionist to screen anyone coming or going. She spoke into the microphone asking, "Are you the lawyer?"

"I'm Wilson Hoffmeister. I'm here to see my client, Dr. Thomas. This is my associate."

There was a buzzing sound from the door. "Please sign in. Officer Wayne Burrows will be right here."

Within moments a police officer stepped up to them and asked, "Are you the lawyers?"

"Yes, I'm Wilson Hoffmeister. This is my associate. We represent Dr. Thomas." The policeman looked him over, glanced for a moment at the young lawyer with him, and then said, "I'm Burrows, the arresting officer. Follow me."

He led them down a corridor to a small shabby room. Dr. Thomas sat sideways in a straight chair at an old, scarred table. A nurse moved Dr. Thomas's hand back and forth at the wrist. Dr. Thomas winced. "Stop that!"

"I don't think it's broken, but I can arrange to have you taken for X rays at the hospital to make sure," the nurse said.

"No, I'll wait until I get back to IORC. They can check my wrist when they stitch my cheek. I wish we could get on with it," Dr. Thomas replied. He turned to look at the newcomers in the room as the nurse left. Bloodstains covered his shirt, his tennis shorts, and the large piece of gauze taped to his face. "You're the IORC lawyer, aren't you? Williams or something, isn't it?"

"I'm Wilson Hoffmeister and I do represent IORC, but I'm here tonight as your lawyer. This is my associate, Michael Evans. How are you doing?"

"How does it look like I'm doing? I've been sitting here

for several hours bleeding all over the place. The cop here wouldn't take me to a restroom, so I ended up pissing in the back of the police car. On top of all that, the smart-ass threatened me, too."

Burrows glared at Thomas and made as if to step toward him, but Hoffmeister quickly intervened.

"Officer Burrows, I'd like to have a minute to talk to my client alone, if you don't mind." Burrows stared at them for a moment longer, then turned without a word, walked into the hall, and slammed the door behind him.

Thomas stood. "I told them to bring me some clothes when I called my office. I don't know where in the hell they are." He paced for a moment and then turned around sharply. "I want you to find out what happened to my car, and I want to get the hell out of here right now."

"Sit down and shut up," Hoffmeister said. Alone with his client, he expressed his exasperation more freely. "You're in big trouble, and you had better quit acting like a damn fool or you're going to make it even worse. You can worry about your car and clothes later. Right now I want you to tell me exactly what happened and about this 'threat' business."

Thomas looked stunned but nonetheless recounted what had happened. "I left the Metro Club in my Porsche, and some guy pulled out of a parking space right in front of me and I hit him. I didn't have time to put on the brakes or swerve, just—smack—I hit him. He had one of those cheap little cars and I guess the guy died.

"Then this big cop showed up and started pushing me around and threw me onto the front of my car and took a blood sample. After that he said I was under arrest for alcohol homicide or something and claimed my test showed that I was over the legal limit."

"Had you been drinking?" Hoffmeister asked.

"I had a couple of drinks after tennis but I wasn't drunk."

"What did you say to the policeman about your drinking?"

"I didn't say anything to him about it at all. Look, the guy refused to call my office, and finally I told him what IORC would do if he didn't get in touch with them."

"And what was that?" Hoffmeister asked, dreading the response.

"I told him we would reduce his J Factor."

"You *what*?"

"In fact, reduce isn't all. I told him we would reduce his J Factor to zero," Thomas said, looking pleased with himself, pushing out his chest and emphasizing the "zero" with a nod of his head.

"I wouldn't have thought you were that stupid," Hoffmeister said to him.

"What did you say?" Thomas demanded, incredulous.

"I said, I wouldn't have thought that anybody who was smart enough to get through medical school and work for IORC as a surgeon would be stupid enough to say such a thing, even if he were falling-down, knee-walking drunk. Maybe you don't understand how serious what you've done is. Go on and tell me the rest of it. I'm almost afraid to hear it."

"At that point the smart-ass cop began to threaten me. First he turned off his video camera—you know, one of those little miniature ones the President ordered hooked to the shoulder of every cop—and then he said that I might have another 'accident' on the way to the police station."

"Well, who could blame him?" Hoffmeister thundered. "I can't wait for the QC to hear this." How on earth could he prevent this from becoming front-page news? With the growing furor being raised over equal access allocation of organs, all IORC needed now was a big story that a company doctor had threatened to alter someone's J Factor. He would have to do something, and do it fast.

He turned to his associate and said, "What you just heard about the J Factor, you forget, as of now. You didn't hear it. He never said it. Go find out the status of the bond. I want to get Dr. Thomas out of here before he makes things worse than they already are."

Burrows knocked on the door and stuck his head inside. "There's a woman downstairs with clothes for Thomas. Is she with you?" he asked Hoffmeister.

"She's from IORC," said Hoffmeister. "May she bring the clothes up here?"

Burrows left without a reply. Hoffmeister turned back to Thomas, his voice hard. "Let's go over a few things. I'll tell you what you're going to do and what's going to happen. First of all, you will never repeat what you said to Officer Burrows about his Justification Factor. You will keep your mouth shut. You will not say one word to anybody tonight until I tell you to. You will answer no questions that the police ask. You will make no statements and you will get in no more arguments with Burrows or anyone else, understood?"

Dr. Thomas's face colored. For years, people had spoken to him with respect and deference. Suddenly everyone thought they could tell him what to do and treat him as though he were a subordinate. "Now, you wait a minute—"

"No," Hoffmeister boomed, "you wait! This isn't a subject for debate. You'll do exactly what I tell you to do. Don't think, don't speak, and maybe, if you are very lucky, you'll get out of this without going to jail. Whether you get fired or not is up to the QC, but I wouldn't want to lay odds on it. If you don't do what I say, I can guarantee that you'll be fired in about two minutes and you'll be entirely on your own."

Burrows knocked on the door then stepped in again, this time carrying an unzipped garment bag which he had clearly already searched. "Here are his things. I'd like to get on with the questioning," Burrows said.

"Officer Burrows, I wonder if the doctor could use a shower to clean himself up before he puts on his clothes.

He's been through a lot, and I think things will go a lot faster after that," Hoffmeister requested in his most cooperative tone.

"Yeah, I guess he can do that. Come on down this way. I'll have to stay with him, though," Burrows said.

Burrows led them to the police locker room and showers. Wooden benches stood empty between the lockers. The place smelled of dirty socks and disinfectant. The old tubular fluorescent lights cast a harsh greenish glow that added to the dingy atmosphere. Voices echoed off the bare concrete floor.

Burrows threw Thomas a towel from the stack of clean ones at the end of a bench. Thomas stripped off his bloody clothes, piled them on the bench, and stepped into the shower stall. Burrows leaned against a locker and examined his fingernails while Hoffmeister paced a few steps and got his speech ready.

"That guy's a real jerk, isn't he?" Hoffmeister remarked.

"No comment, Counselor," Burrows said.

"Still, he must be a pretty good doctor since he's working for IORC. They take only the best. He does heart transplants . . . probably saved a lot of lives. I suppose it's a high-stress job."

"That's no excuse for getting drunk and killing somebody," Burrows said.

"I couldn't agree more. Nothing's an excuse for that, and I'll tell you he doesn't have any sympathy from me. The problem is that this situation will be an embarrassment to IORC and that's bad for everybody." Hoffmeister paused before playing his next card. "He says you threatened him."

Burrows stopped checking his fingernails and stood up straight, then crouched slightly like a boxer ready to go into action.

"Look, the guy's an arrogant smart-ass, telling me what to do and trying to order me around like I was his flunky.

Then he said he would screw with my Justification numbers. He tells me this just after I've seen a man's head smashed in as a result of the accident *your client* caused. So yeah, I got kinda hot and maybe I said a couple things to him that I shouldn't have, but that was all talk."

"What's this about you turning off your video camera?" Hoffmeister asked.

"You know, I did happen to experience some, 'technical difficulty' with my equipment," Burrows said with a smirk.

"These 'technical difficulties' didn't happen by any chance when he was talking about your J Factor, did they?"

"I don't remember."

Hoffmeister paced a few times. "It seems to me that this whole business about the J Factor and the threats back and forth and the 'technical difficulties' really don't have anything to do with the accident and are a needless complication. The IORC is the only one this hurts—except maybe you." Hoffmeister held his breath.

"What do you mean, me?" Burrows asked, becoming more irritated.

"Well, you'll look pretty bad when the doctor says that you turned off your video camera and threatened him. Regardless of what you say, people will think you're trying to cover up something."

"How's IORC going to get hurt?" Burrows asked.

"Well, you and I both know that they can't arbitrarily change anybody's J Factor, or at least they can't reduce it. But if this gets in the newspapers and on television, all it'll do is upset a lot of people, particularly older people who are hoping to get a transplant. They'll be worried that the rumors are actually true."

"You said they couldn't reduce someone's numbers. Can they raise them?"

"You applied for an IORC job, didn't you?" Hoffmeister asked. It was a wild gamble but the chances were very good that Burrows, like most police officers, had applied for an IORC security job because the pay was much higher and the benefits were better.

"What's that got to do with any of this?" Burrows asked, now on the verge of belligerence.

"Simply that one of the benefits of IORC employment is an increase in your Justification numbers. Did you get turned down by IORC Security?"

"No, I didn't get turned down. I'm completely qualified and I'm even on the waiting list."

"That's good," said Hoffmeister. "You know they're one of the biggest companies in the world and very powerful. They like people who do favors for them."

"You mean maybe I should drop this case and they'll give me the job?" Burrows sneered.

Carefully balancing between bribery and the pretense of ethics, Hoffmeister shook his head and said, "You couldn't if you wanted to. But you don't have to hurt IORC, either. Have you checked the video to see what's there?"

"No, I haven't had the chance. It's still in my machine."

Hoffmeister suddenly had a twinge of nerves. "Is it on now?"

"We don't use them in the station." Burrows reached up, flipped open the small video camera and pulled out a microcassette. "This is the tape. I'm supposed to turn it in with my report, which I can't finish until I talk to the doctor."

"Well, Officer Burrows, I don't think the doctor will have anything to say. In fact I won't let him," Hoffmeister said. It was decision time. He waited in silence but Burrows didn't reply.

"It's very simple," continued Hoffmeister in his most confidential tone. "You help me out and I'll put in a good word for you at IORC. Otherwise we'll go to court and I'll bring up this whole business of threats and 'technical difficulties.' "

Dr. Thomas stepped out of the shower.

"Decide," Hoffmeister told Burrows. "Now." Their eyes locked. Burrows turned and looked at the doctor who, unaware of the conversation, dried himself off a few yards away. Burrows turned back, tossed the microcassette onto the pile of bloodstained clothes, and walked out of the locker room. Watching Burrows retreat, Hoffmeister let out a breath.

"Bring your stuff, Doctor," Hoffmeister said after waiting for Thomas to dress. Thomas glared at him. He grabbed his dirty clothes and tennis shoes, wadding them up into a ball with the video tape unseen among them, and followed along after Hoffmeister. When they approached the door, Hoffmeister pointed to a large trash bin nearly full of paper towels, pasteboard boxes, and soft drink containers. "Throw that stuff away," he said to Thomas.

Thomas stopped. "I thought you just said I should bring it with me."

"Now I say get rid of it."

"Screw you, too," Thomas seethed as he tossed everything into the trash.


Burrows didn't know whether he had done the right thing. To ease his conscience that he had accepted a bribe he convinced himself that the metal detector at the visitors' exit door from the squad room would probably pick up the tape anyway. He thought it would be very interesting to see whether this fast-talking lawyer could explain having a police videotape in his pocket. He sat down at his desk and finished entering his report into the computer, noting that the suspect had declined to make any statements on advice of his lawyer and that a bond had been posted. He then took a blank microcassette out of his desk drawer, put it with the computer disc containing the report, and handed both to the clerk as he left. After all this excitement, he still hadn't finished his shift and had to go back to his regular beat.

# 4

Virginia Pruitt breezed into Mike Martinez's hospital room, forcing an abrupt end to the family's conversation without saying a word. As if in a pantomime, she opened a leather portfolio and, with a flourish, removed a gold pen. She consulted a memo, and only then did she look around the room. "You are Martinez," she pronounced.

"I'm Michael Martinez. This is my wife Betty and my son Jorge. Who are you?"

"I'm the UNIMED coordinator for this hospital." She then recited a canned speech. "I'm here to talk to you about your future care. Undoubtedly you don't understand the expense for the mechanical heart you're using and the cost to take care of you while it's still in operation." She talked slowly, as if to a class of young children.

"I thought it was covered," replied Martinez. "Besides, I have a company supplement."

"It's only covered for twenty-one days, and your supplement only covers your deductible and is for the same period. Meanwhile, the cost"—she consulted her notes for a moment—"is about the same amount for each day as you make in two months."

"Dr. West said I would stay on the mechanical heart until a transplant is available," Martinez said.

"Dr. West is new. He just finished his residency. He's inexperienced in the practical matters of the hospital and has yet to understand that neither money nor facilities are unlimited." She snapped out her words impatiently, resentful of the interruption.

"It's my job to inform you of the realities. Of course you're not qualified for an IORC transplant, not with *your* J Factor." Her lip curled a little as she spoke. "You're overweight, you have high blood pressure and a history of smoking cigarettes, and your genetic analysis apparently reduced your number as well.

"A non-IORC transplant is quite unlikely. Because of IORC's program to give Justification points to people who agree in advance to donate their organs to them, there are few organs available outside of IORC.

"Even if a heart did become available that IORC didn't have the rights to, it probably wouldn't match your tissue. And if it did, UNIMED only covers a portion of the cost of a non-IORC heart transplant anyway. Your portion of the cost for a transplant like this—minus, of course, your company supplement—would be much more than all the money you have," she said, again consulting her records. "In order to pay for this operation you'd have to deplete your entire savings, mortgage your house, and have your wife get a full-time job. And even that might not be enough."

Martinez blinked several times and his wife began to cry, but Pruitt seemed unflappable.

"I'll leave a form with an explanation booklet you should consider very carefully. It's a consent to disconnect the mechanical heart."

"Only a judge can make him do that," Jorge snapped.

"Quiet, son. She didn't say she was making me do it. She said I had to think about it, and that's what I'm going to do: I'll think about it," he said.

"Witnesses are required. Just let someone know when

you're ready to sign." She flipped her portfolio closed with a plop and left.

"Dad, I don't care about college," said Jorge angrily. "How would I feel if I went to college with money that you could have used for a transplant?"

"Son," his father said, "you've got to learn that life is full of hard choices."

"I'm ready to go back to work anyway, Mike," his wife said, trying to blink back her tears. "I sold real estate before and I can sell it again. With that, plus what you make, we can pay off a second mortgage on our house. And besides, if you don't get the transplant I'm going to have to go back to work anyway, so I'd rather do it for a good reason."

Martinez felt pain in his chest. He sighed. The entire discussion had sapped him of energy. He closed his eyes. "You two go on home. We'll talk later," he said without opening his eyes to see them leave, slumped in defeat.

A few minutes later David West came into Martinez's room, saw his patient's closed eyes and pained expression, and said, "What's the matter?"

"I'm afraid a transplant would bankrupt my family. I can't do that."

"The UNIMED coordinator's been here, has she?"

"Yeah."

"She has an unpleasant effect on me, too. Don't worry about that now." Changing the subject to calm him, David asked, "You work on some kind of special boat, don't you?"

"Yeah, it's special. We operate back and forth to the Fusion Electric Master Control power station that's three hundred and fifty miles offshore."

"What's your job?" David asked, seeing that Martinez

was now smiling, enjoying telling someone about his work.

"I'm a machinist's mate, first class, and what that means is that I'm in charge of the engine room—well, not really in charge. An officer monitors everything, but he sits up in another part of the ship watching a computer and lets me do my job. Anyway, I look after the ion engine."

"We'll get you back to your ship just as soon as possible," David said.

West liked Martinez. But how would he tell him if a heart was not forthcoming?

Martinez watched the young doctor leave. Thinking back to his own twenties and thirties, he realized how different his experiences had been from what this man's future held. Still, West would have to deal with death every day. Martinez had also seen his share of death, but it had been different. Twenty years ago he had been involved in a special security operation to protect the newly formed Fusion Electric when it was targeted by terrorists. He had seen more death than he cared to remember on that mission, but because of his skills he had also saved lives—even Captain Stapleton's. It was a time he would never forget. He touched the commemorative tattoo on his shoulder and felt a deep pride.

Now Fusion Electric owned exclusive worldwide rights to provide energy by nuclear fusion. From its earliest days, the company's growth had been unprecedented.

Because all countries needed its product—very cheap electrical energy—Fusion Electric had developed a treaty protocol, functioning as if it were a sovereign country itself. Any country that didn't use FE's cost-efficient electrical energy would have been at an impossible competitive disadvantage. From every country, FE had demanded and had been conceded extraordinary power. The company had sovereign authority over the production, transmission, and sale of its energy, and the legal and actual power to protect its interests.

Hearing early on about the great job security and benefits provided by FE, Martinez had taken the job offer with Captain Stapleton as machinist mate. It was not until he was already on the ship that he realized that the fusion process was nearly self-sustaining, and that the most critical duty in the company was the protection of FE's Master Control power plant. That master plant coordinated the production of electricity through hundreds of local induction generators throughout the world. Now he ran the unique ion engine on the fastest, most powerful and sophisticated ship in the world, a ship that looked like a fancy ferry but was really devoted primarily to protecting Fusion Electric, a ship run by Captain Ian Stapleton. Like the ship itself, Stapleton was more than he appeared; he oversaw the most capable security force in existence, known simply as the SSG—the Special Services Group.

Martinez had no complaints . . . no regrets. In his world there were no excuses, no time for hesitation, and decisions often involved life or death. Now he had to make such a decision. He pushed the call button and waited for the nurse.

When West arrived at the administrator's office he knew right away that the news would be good. Behind his desk Administrator Long leaned back in his chair with a satisfied expression. "Well, Doctor," he said, "we've found you a heart." He was obviously proud of himself. "A car accident victim last night. Crushed head but good heart. Byrd in pathology says it's okay. Tissue and size are within limits for your patient."

Even though he was pleased, West was about to launch into a complaint about the UNIMED coordinator's morning visit to Martinez. But Long continued before he could speak.

"There's more good news," Long went on. "After I found out about the heart, I called the captain of Martinez's ship at Fusion Electric. Those people look out for their own. In ten minutes he arranged a grant for you that will cover all of the costs of the transplant not covered by UNIMED, as well as the costs for the follow-up care."

"I don't know what to say except thank you," David said, surprised. It seemed that all he'd gotten from other people since arriving at Orlando Government was hell.

"I told you I would help you. This time. But from now on I want you to follow the procedures." David swore to himself that he would try his best. What else could he do?

David left to make the arrangements. First he told the clerk to schedule the operating room for a six-hour block of time for that afternoon.

Once scheduled, the transplant team for the surgery had to be ordered. The team included anesthesiologists, inhalation therapists, various technicians, operating room nurses and, in this case, the pathology department responsible for transfer of the organ. David called Dr. Byrd himself.

"I understand you have a heart for me to transplant."

"Everything is ready to go. I haven't observed many transplants so, if you don't mind, I'll bring the organ up personally."

"That's fine. Thanks," David said.

A nurse eventually responded by intercom to Martinez's call. "Your light's on. Your vital signs are fine. What's the problem?"

"I need some witnesses."

"Pardon?"

"Witnesses. I need some witnesses for me to sign a paper."

"We don't have time for that. Ask your wife to check with Administration. We're nurses, not witnesses."

"I'm just doing what the government lady said, the UNIMED lady." Apparently he hit on the magic word.

"We'll be right there."

The charge nurse, a trim, crisp, gray-haired woman of sixty, and two younger nurses, one man and one woman, arrived within a minute. Martinez held the form and strained to reach a ballpoint pen on top of the mechanical heart control box. The charge nurse handed it to him and pushed the food table over so he could rest the form on it to sign.

Martinez looked at the three nurses. The young ones averted their eyes, but the charge nurse silently watched. Martinez looked over at the mechanical heart machine, its rows of digital numbers and symbols blinking brightly, glowing red. He looked over to where his wife and son had sat not long before. He would never see them again.

Once again he looked at each of the nurses, tightened his lips into a straight line, and scribbled his name on the form. Each nurse then signed on the appropriate line.

"Now what?" he asked.

"Do you know what you signed?" the charge nurse asked.

"Of course," he growled.

"Tell me so there's no mistake; no question."

"It's to allow you to turn off the heart machine."

"And do you understand what will happen when it is turned off?"

"Yeah. I'll die."

The charge nurse nodded at the others and they left, getting momentarily tangled together as each tried to be the first out the door.

Alone, the charge nurse turned to Martinez, took his hand, and said, "Mike, are you sure?" Her eyes filled with tears, and she blinked several times.

"I have to. I can't put them through any more. Just

waiting for a heart and then bankrupting my family. It would mean no college for my son. Yes, I'm sure. Let's get on with it."

"Do you want them here?"

"No way."

"If you're sure . . ."

"Yes."

She picked up the telephone and called the UNIMED message center. "We need a Code 80 in Room 72840. Patient is Michael Martinez. The form's complete. He wants the code right away." She listened a moment, then hung up. She took Mike's hand again and stood silently, staring out the small window at the bright Florida day outside.

The message center notified Virginia Pruitt within thirty seconds. She called in an order to the Cardiac Center for a team to implement a Code 80—removal of life support. "This order is stat," she pronounced, like someone playing doctor or someone who had seen too much television, but really only reconfirming to the Cardiology Department staff that she was a pompous bitch.

Ms. Coffin, the nurse who had assisted in the surgery, was on duty when the order came in. She was stunned. Impossible. No way was this going to happen. Dr. West couldn't know or he would have issued the order, not UNIMED.

"Come on," the senior nurse said to Coffin. "You heard. It's 'stat,' " she smirked. She released the brake on the stainless equipment cart and marched out. No nurse wanted to kill a patient, regardless of UNIMED orders.

Coffin hesitated for only a moment, then grabbed the telephone. She knew Dr. West carried a beeper. She punched in West's number to page him and recorded a message. Then for good measure she dialed the number that permitted a public address call in an emergency. The call would probably cost her her job because it violated hospital rules and was sure to anger UNIMED. The line beeped, cleared, and announced: "Proceed with emergency message at the tone . . ."

Then she heard a beep and paged David West.

The E-mail David transmitted ordering the transplant team a few minutes earlier was on the monitor, but had gone unnoticed in the Code 80 flurry.

David sat alone sipping coffee, enjoying a quiet, satisfied moment before telling Martinez the good news. He felt pleased with his place in the world. When the pager on his belt vibrated, he glanced around the brightly painted snack bar for a telephone. He was too new in the hospital to know where the phones were. Then he saw Mrs. Martinez and Jorge huddled over a table talking in whispers. Jorge's face was red with emotion and Mrs. Martinez was red from crying. Ignoring the need to answer the buzz he walked over to them.

"What's wrong?"

"Mike found out about the cost of a transplant."

"I know, he mentioned that, but I've got good news. Fusion Electric has offered him a grant, and we have a heart for him!"

"All right!" Jorge shouted and shot his fist into the air, attracting several stares.

"Dr. West, Dr. David West, report to room 72840 immediately for a Code 80," the PA system blared.

He looked at Jorge and Mrs. Martinez and they suddenly looked frightened, as if they had seen a ghost. They should have been elated. "What?" he asked.

"That's Mike's room number."

He should remember the codes from Orientation. What was a Code 80? Code 90 was a call for resuscitation. Code 80 couldn't be good. Code 80 was . . . "Oh, my God!"

Seven floors and two hundred yards of corridors. Should he call? Too slow. By the time he worked through the automated phone system, it would be too late . . . if it wasn't already.

Never again would he ignore his pager. He ran out of the snack bar at full speed and turned a corner, sending an orderly sprawling. "Sorry. Emergency," he shouted over his shoulder to the man as he kept running. David wiped at his nose, which was now spurting blood.

Elevator or steps? He paused for a second and punched the elevator call button repeatedly. One elevator was three floors above, the other on the 18th floor. Too far, too slow. He slammed open the stairway door and bolted up the first set of steps, already out of breath.

Pruitt arrived at the Martinez room a few seconds before the cardiac team.

"Give me the form," she ordered. The charge nurse handed it over. She checked the signatures and then declared, "It's in order. We can proceed." She glanced at Martinez, then at her watch, and tapped her foot impatiently. The cardiac team, minus Ms. Coffin, pushed into the room with their cart just as the announcement for Dr. West was made on the PA. Pruitt, stunned, asked the cardiac team, "Who made that call? That's not authorized. Dr. West is not required here."

The two team members glanced at each other and shook their heads.

"Very well. Proceed with the Code 80." She held out the signed form for their initials.

Ms. Coffin rushed into the room as the two team members noted the time and began arranging the tubes on the heart machine in preparation for shutdown. They had to stop all blood flow to prevent damage to the machine. "Wait! Dr. West is on his way. Wait for him," Ms. Coffin pleaded.

"Did you make that call?" Pruitt asked Coffin.

"Yes, I did. He's entitled to know and to be present."

"That's unnecessary and you are out of line."

"What's going on here? God damn it, get it over with," Martinez snapped, watching the turmoil. He was now just a spectator.

"Finish your job," Pruitt demanded, looking again at her watch.

"We're going to let your heart take over now," the team leader said kindly, and she clamped the tube that took in the blood from Martinez's body. The mechanical heart would then pump the blood in the lines back into his body, and then the pump would be turned off. If his heart lasted long enough, it would make the process much easier. It would be as if his heart had just given out, rather than her actually killing the poor man. But it was all a pretense. When she pressed the shutoff sequence button Martinez would die.

Martinez looked on and felt his heart speed up trying to maintain normal blood pressure. He tensed and waited for death to take him.

*Be calm,* David told himself. *You're a doctor.* He ran even harder, pumping up the stairs, fourteen flights, two per floor, eleven complete, three to go. He had reached a physical exertion level at which the pain stopped and he felt calm and strong. It must have been endorphins, natural drugs, the body's way of assuring survival; but somehow he was running even faster. His breath was even and his legs followed some automatic command. His mind was already in the room.

The nurse was reaching for the button to turn off the pump just as David pushed through the door.

"Stop," he said quietly, and she pulled her hand back.

"I have a signed form," Pruitt said. She reached for the button herself.

"And I have a replacement heart," David said. Stepping in front of the machine, he unclipped the tube to allow blood to flow through the pump again.

"I didn't authorize that."

"You don't have to. His employer provided a grant."

Just then Mrs. Martinez and Jorge burst into the room and rushed to Mike. Mike looked around and clasped his chest in pain.

David turned on Virginia Pruitt. She stepped back from him. "I was just following procedure. I have a job to do, rules to follow. I have to protect the public interest," she said.

David held out his hand for the form, which she slowly relinquished. He tore it up and put the pieces into his pocket. Then he put on his stethoscope and listened to Mike's heart. But he had a feeling that it was his own heart, pounding in his ears, that he was actually hearing.


The operating room where West would perform Mike Martinez's transplant was one of the newer and more sophisticated facilities available. All of the people on the team wore operating suits and hoods attached to a vacuum system—much like old-fashioned diving suits. Even though air could be drawn into the gown through microscopic pores in the fabric, no air could escape, keeping the staff's skin and hair cells and bacteria from sloughing off and contaminating the patient.

Video cameras projected various views of the surgery on screens along the wall, including a lens mounted on the end of a fiberoptics cable. This miniature camera could be inserted into the new heart, once placed inside the body, and kept in place during most of the attachment process until the doctor made the last few stitches to ensure the best possible attachments. This reduced the chances of blood clots forming at the seams of blood vessels and arteries, which could cause a stroke.

One of the nurses caught West's eye. "Ms. Coffin," he said, smiling. "I didn't see your name on the team roster."

"I asked to be substituted. I hope you don't mind."

"I'm glad you're here." He smiled and they maintained eye contact for a moment. Then he turned to include the rest of his team and said, "Well, let's get on with it. Let's cool him down. Start the timer." The mechanical heart had a built-in refrigeration unit that would cool the blood circulating through it to sixty degrees.

The cooled blood flowing back into Martinez's body caused the brain-wave line on the monitor to decrease until it showed no activity. He entered a state of hypothermia—a breath from dead—with all bodily functions virtually stopped. The mechanical heart would continue to pump the blood through Martinez's body for most of the surgery. His body lay at a tilt with his head well below the level of his heart to ensure a better blood supply and to prevent brain damage.

Dr. West repeated the incision process that he had done eleven days before, trying to follow the same line with the laser cutter. But this time his technique was slower and more deliberate.

"All right, everybody, full hypothermia now. We're ready to remove the heart; I'll completely close off the valves, isolate the heart, and begin disconnection."

He closed the valves and watched the monitors to make sure that the blood flow and blood pressure for Martinez continued in the normal range.

He made an incision in the aorta between the plastic valve and the heart itself and began removing the damaged heart. Just then, Dr. Byrd came in with a small refrigeration unit containing the replacement organ.

West said to Byrd, "Bring that over here. When I remove the old heart, I want you to hold the transplant heart in place while I begin the reattachment. That is, if you want to assist; otherwise, one of the nurses can do it."

"No, I want to," Dr. Byrd said, relieved that he might be able to hide the IORC module with his hands during the procedure.

West removed the injured heart from Martinez's chest and placed it in a stainless steel dish held by one of the nursing assistants.

A freezing mist escaped as Byrd opened the box. He reached inside and carefully picked up the replacement heart. He positioned it in the chest cavity, holding it in place. West glanced only briefly at the heart, noticing that the color was good and feeling as he touched it that it was very cold. He began the attachment procedure—first, the blood vessels and arteries, and then the supporting tissue.

"Why don't you take a break?" said West.

"No, I'm fine. I'm just used to working on dead people," Byrd said, with a forced smile.

West chuckled. "Technically speaking, this man is dead."

"He's not a corpse," Byrd replied. "There's a difference."

West began connecting the nerves that control the heart, a new technique. Until recently, transplanted hearts had no nerve connections and depended upon blood chemicals for signals to the heart. He installed two temporary pacemaker leads in order to maintain the heart's rhythm until the nerves healed.

As he completed his work, West leaned his head back and swung it from side to side, trying to relieve the pressure in the back of his neck. No wonder old surgeons had a permanent arch in their backs. Hours of surgery without relief tended to deform the neck muscles.

"Now we find out if we made good connections." West opened the valves to allow a small amount of blood to flow through the heart. Several seconds passed, during which nothing seemed to happen. Then a small dark trickle appeared in the semiopaque plastic valve in the aorta, so that he knew blood was actually flowing through the heart. Though the heart wasn't beating yet, there were no leaks.

"Okay, we're going to gradually increase the flow," West said as he eased open the valves further allowing the full blood pressure being produced by the mechanical heart to flow through the new heart. He let the blood flow freely through both the organ and the mechanical heart for several minutes to clear out air bubbles, and then raised the blood temperature to 98.7 degrees, thus gradually raising the temperature of both the heart and the brain.

"Okay, here we go," West said, and he touched the computer screen to activate the newly attached pacemaker. The computer indicated that the sequence was complete and that electric pulses were being delivered to the heart, yet nothing appeared to be happening. West administered a stimulant to the heart and increased the pulses to thirty per minute.

In a few seconds he noticed a slight contraction at the edge of the heart—a twitching, really—but it seemed to be in sequence with the pacemaker pulse on the monitor. The heart began at first spasmodically, and then with a more normal rhythm.

"Okay, looks like we've got a good pulse."

West began closing the auxiliary valves and then shut down the mechanical heart. It ceased pumping for the first time in eleven days. Martinez's blood pressure temporarily dropped and fluctuated, and then returned to normal.

Michael Martinez had a new heart. Bryd's face broke into a giant smile.

West directed the technician to scan the site of the transplant with a multiscanner to make sure that all attachments were complete and that no instruments or foreign objects had been left inside. The multiscanner used wide-spectrum sensor—X ray, magnetic resonance, proton emissions and Doppler, microwave and thermal radar—and consolidated all data on a computer screen.

"Doctor, there's something strange here," the technician reported. West was shaken out of his temporary calm, and he looked at the scanner screen above the patient. There was a green splotch on the image of the new heart. On the screen was a 16-digit number.

"What is that?" the technician asked, pointing at the left side of the heart.

"Let me look," West said. He bent down, trying to check the heart without touching it. Only then did he see the small aspirin-sized device attached to the heart where Bryd had been holding it, so small as to go unnoticed unless one were looking for it. He knew such devices existed but had never seen one before.

"Dr. Byrd, did you see that?" West demanded.

Byrd motioned David aside. The two doctors walked over to the edge of the operating room near the door and removed their plastic masks. When they did so, the microphones built into them were disconnected. A vacuum pickup at the door prevented contamination of the patient.

"What in the hell's going on?" West demanded. "That's an IORC heart, isn't it? I thought it was against the law to retransplant their organs."

"You needed a heart for your patient and you got one," said Byrd quietly.

"Goddamn! I could be fired for transplanting that heart. IORC could probably sue me for malpractice on top of that. Hell, I could probably be arrested."

"There's no such thing as a malpractice suit anymore," Dr. Byrd said, evading the issue.

"You know what I mean," West snapped. "We had no right to transplant that heart."

"Look, I'll take full responsibility for supplying the heart. It's there on the videos. There's no way you could have known about it until now."

"Damn," West muttered. "I'm already in deep trouble

because of this case. The UNIMED people didn't authorize the mechanical heart, and the Administrator went out on a limb to bail me out. I'm busting my ass trying to follow the rules. When Long finds out about this I'll probably lose my job."

"Look, you did a beautiful job on the surgery," Byrd said angrily. "You had nothing to do with furnishing the heart. This man was dying and you did what you had to do. You saved his life. You can't just take the heart out again."

West turned around and looked at the technicians, who were watching the two doctors. They knew something was terribly wrong. Byrd was right, of course; West had no choice. He put his hood back on and returned to the operating table, glaring at Dr. Byrd, who returned to the other side.

West began, "Let the record include here that there are no instruments left in the patient, no foreign objects. There is an anomaly on the computer screen but it is part of the heart itself. Surgery is completed. We are closing the patient." West then proceeded in silence, restapling the wound and then personally checking to make sure all vital signs remained stable. He used every bit of control that he possessed to concentrate on his work. He didn't have time now to think about the consequences. He owed it to Martinez to keep his mind on his current responsibilities.

He left the operating room without a word, tearing off his gown and gloves as he charged through the preparation room. He slammed into the swinging doors, banging them against the stops. Dr. Byrd lagged behind West, who was practically jogging down the hall.

"Dr. West, wait!"

West stopped and whirled around to face him.

"Calm the hell down." Byrd sighed as he reached David, then leaned in conspiratorially. "This is not the first time that an IORC organ has been retransplanted. These 'mistakes' have to happen if we're going to save lives. We don't advertise it, but no truly ethical doctor can overlook the obligation when it presents itself.

"Now don't worry about a thing. No one can blame you. I'm the one who provided that heart and it's my ass on the line, not yours. You just forget about it and take care of your patient." Byrd then turned and walked away.

On his way to the waiting room, West tried to reconcile the fact of restricted medical care under UNIMED and the IORC's rules with what he believed were his duties as a doctor. He had wanted to change the system ever since he had learned about it.

Still in his own thoughts, he came upon Mrs. Martinez and her son. They saw him at the same time and stood up.

"The operation went well," he said, trying to sound cheerful. "You can see him in a few hours, when he wakes up."

Seeing the delight in their faces, David couldn't help but think of his father. Nobody had been willing to act against the rules to save his life. Helping people stay alive was the only thing that really mattered.

Given the same circumstances, he'd do it all over again, illegal heart and all. But, he was afraid that there still might be a heavy price to pay.

# 5

LeBearc watched from his top-floor office as an IORC C-5 transport plane lifted off the runway. He could see the entire IORC facility he presided over, several square miles of it adjacent to the Orlando International Airport. He admired the gardens, which had become a tourist attraction here as at other IORC centers. They broke up the stark form of the steel framework buildings, erected from replaceable modular-built rooms, and the gigantic airplane hangars connected by tunnels to the hospital and office areas. Even the genetics and pharmaceutical research center was nestled among exotic plants and trees.

LeBearc glanced at his watch. It read 7:55 A.M. Hoffmeister and Thomas had an 8:00 appointment and should be in the reception room now.

That room contained only a dark wood desk for the QC's secretary, with nothing but a computer terminal on it. The walls were bare of any paintings or other decoration. The QC did not need any chairs in his reception room; he accepted few appointments, and those he did schedule he saw on time. The IORC demanded the same punctuality from everyone, including doctors. Keeping a patient waiting more than five minutes resulted in an unfavorable notation on the doctor's evaluation report; more than fifteen minutes meant a heavy fine, deducted from the next paycheck.

IORC transplant physicians received high pay, many times higher than had physicians in private medicine in years past. Elite IORC research physicians were paid even more. By contrast, government physicians working for UNIMED received a salary equal to that of a high school principal: all part of cost control.

But IORC was first and foremost a corporation, not a government. And compensation of management-level IORC employees was commensurate with that of other businesses. While rumor had it that QCs were some of the most highly paid people in the world, only Central Management knew the actual salaries.

At exactly eight o'clock, a secretary admitted Hoffmeister and Thomas into LeBearc's office. In front of the comfortable chair occupied by LeBearc, a computer terminal on a small table took the place of a desk. Several chrome-and-black-leather chairs arranged in a semicircle faced the QC's work space.

No one offered coffee or refreshments.

"Have you succeeded in getting the charges dropped?" LeBearc asked.

"We're working on that," Hoffmeister responded.

"There shouldn't have been any charges in the first place. It wasn't my fault," Dr. Thomas said. The QC looked at him but did not respond.

"We have a bigger problem, QC," said Hoffmeister. "I wanted you to know about it last night but you were unavailable."

"Did you tell the receptionist that you needed to speak to me immediately?" the QC asked.

"No," Hoffmeister said, "it really wasn't an emergency, or at least not a time-sensitive emergency, and it may already be taken care of anyway. Dr. Thomas, it seems, told the police officer that if he didn't do what he asked, IORC would reduce the cop's J Factor."

"I see." LeBearc looked at Thomas who squirmed in his chair. "Is that included in the police officer's report?"

"I don't think it will be," Hoffmeister said. "Still, it wasn't easy. I had to indirectly promise the cop a job."

The QC touched the screen on his computer terminal. "Security Manager," he ordered. There was an immediate answer from a speaker. "John, there's a city police officer—what's his name?" the QC asked Hoffmeister.

"Wayne Burrows."

"His name is Wayne Burrows. Hire him."

"Sure thing. We'll check his background right away and get an application to him. Will he be calling in or what?"

"I didn't say check his background, did I? I said *hire* him." The QC touched the screen to break the connection.

"Wilson," the QC said to Hoffmeister, "Dr. Thomas will do whatever you say and cooperate in every way. You do whatever is necessary to get the charges dismissed and have this matter over with. Our people will take care of compensating the family of the victim directly. I don't want this business of threatening to change a Justification Factor to ever become public. If you must, you can advise the judge or the police that we will monitor Dr. Thomas on a daily basis for any substance abuse. Get this resolved immediately." It was a dismissal and the visitors stood to leave.

"You stay, Dr. Thomas," LeBearc said, staring at him coldly. When Hoffmeister had gone, he continued, "You are suspended from all transplant procedures. You will report to the autopsy department until I change your assignment. I will adjust your pay accordingly."

Thomas's face went white. It meant a reduction by two thirds, but more important it meant a complete change in his status within IORC. However, he did not dare object.

"Let's understand each other, Doctor," said LeBearc, smiling. "If anything like this happens again, you're through." LeBearc waved him away as he might flick away an insect.

Thomas's hand shook as he turned the knob on LeBearc's door. Did LeBearc mean he would prevent him from practicing medicine? No. It would definitely be much worse than that.

Reluctantly, LeBearc placed a call to the managing director.

The managing director, one of the twelve members of IORC Central Management located throughout the world, was currently visiting an IORC-owned country estate on the northwest coast of Ireland. The managing director had ordered a wrought-iron table and chairs set up for him near the edge of the rugged cliffs overlooking the North Atlantic Ocean. On the table sat a portable telecomputer with built-in satellite interface.

The managing director spoke with an unmistakable Boston twang. While finishing his afternoon tea, he was talking to a QC in Washington, D.C., through his terminal.

"I don't talk to anyone outside the company in my official capacity," said the MD. "You know the policy. Central Management remains anonymous. It's *your* job to convince the Senate majority leader that we get complete autonomy in pharmaceutical distribution. Why should IORC have to go through the FDA for approvals? We have better testing facilities. Hell, we do most of the work for the FDA ourselves! Tell him we can't tolerate a situation in which we have to get approvals from every country in the world. It's too costly and too slow."

"He says that other drug companies are squawking and putting up millions to block our exemption," replied the QC. "He says the press is getting interested and he doesn't think he can keep his party in line. He also thinks the House will probably defeat it even if he can persuade the Senate to approve."

"Bullshit. Tell him that we'll do it as a treaty if we have to. Tell him we'll spread some money around, not least to his reelection campaign. Tell him the President has an IORC heart; he knows what will happen if he doesn't do what we say. Remind the senior senator about his wife's IORC kidney."

"You mean threaten the Senate majority leader?"

"Don't be stupid. Be subtle. Use tact, of course. But make sure he knows the score."

Just then, the MD's telecomputer beeped loudly. "Hold on a minute, I've got another call." With the press of a button the display split into two screens to reveal the MD's administrative assistant looking alarmed as usual.

"What?" the MD demanded.

"Southeast U.S. QC. He's reporting that a staff doctor got drunk and threatened a cop with a J Factor reduction."

"Take care of it," he snapped at the D.C. QC. Then the managing director punched a key on his telecomputer so hard it jiggled the heavy iron table. "What!" he shouted as LeBearc's image replaced his assistant's face on the screen.

"We had a problem last night."

"I heard. Why are you bothering me with this?"

"I wanted to make sure you heard it from me first."

"I don't want to hear about it at all. I especially don't want to read about this in the papers, Andre."

"It's under control, sir."

"It better be." The managing director slammed his stubby finger on the disconnect button and, muttering an oath, turned and glared out across the water, wondering why no one seemed to be able to get the job done without him.

David couldn't concentrate. Nothing was as it should be. His mind kept returning to his past. He had dedicated his entire career to his father. Now, suddenly, it was in jeopardy.

David had known since early childhood that he had been adopted. His parents told him that they had chosen him above all others. In fact, he had always felt wanted, was close to his mom and dad, and had never had the slightest interest in learning the details of his biological family. These feelings had never changed even after his father died. In fact, to try to seek out his so-called "real father" now was not an option for David. To do so, he felt, would show disloyalty to the man who had been the most important person in his life.

His father had owned a successful printing store in Connecticut. He liked to say that he wasn't rich because he owed too much money; doctors and people who owned oil companies were rich. But he socialized with the powerful elite and expected David to follow suit.

David's father was an avid golfer. He pushed David, from early childhood, to take lessons, practice endlessly, and spend Saturdays at their Connecticut country club learning and playing golf and meeting the people who, as he put it, would be running things when David grew up.

In college his father's urging intensified. David played on the golf team and planned to turn pro. He had superb eye-hand coordination, and his five-foot-eleven, 170-pound frame was perfect for the game. Then suddenly, late in David's junior year of college, his father called him home and told him that studies must come first and that David should consider a more intellectually challenging career—perhaps as a doctor. He should not build his life around golf, an endeavor that he had been pushed into and that would result in someone else controlling his life.

This complete change in his dad's attitude was a shock, although David had been growing disenchanted with a golf career anyway. He didn't want to disappoint his dad, but he had already decided that living the life of a pro golfer was not the future he wanted. And David was just as comfortable in the classroom as he was on the links.

After finishing his undergraduate studies with high honors, he was admitted to Yale Medical School and made the transition with ease. Early in his first year of medical school, just as he was leaving for classes one morning, David got a call telling him that his father had suffered a heart attack and had been denied a transplant due to his unusually low J Factor. He had died an hour later. David returned home and found that his dad, true to his normal pattern, had made all the necessary arrangements to ensure David's education and had provided a small fund to get him started. He had also provided for David's mother. But not even six months after his father died, huge secured debts had been called for payment, forcing the sale of the business, and severely reducing the family wealth.

David's eyes teared as he thought of his dad, who would never get to know him as a doctor or enjoy his son's success. David wished he could talk through his current mess with his dad, to get his wisdom and perspective. He missed him.

The events in the operating room the day before now threatened to change his life again. He decided to escape to the golf course to clear his head, something he had done all his life.

When David arrived at the public golf course, the pro had already arranged a game for him. "You'll be playing with Janette Compton," he said.

"She any good? I like to play fast."

"Janette's not bad. She won't hold you up."

David, new in town and also new to the course, really had no choice. He couldn't very well refuse.

He started down the steps to the practice range, where he found himself face to face with a woman in her mid-twenties who was carrying several golf clubs. She was gorgeous in a clean-cut way. Her light brown hair was streaked with blond, and her eyes were as gray as his own.

She had long shapely legs with every muscle defined, full breasts, flat stomach, tight rounded hips, and long tanned arms.

David took all of this in as she smiled at him and said, "Hi." She continued up the stairs two at a time, moving with ease and confidence.

Turning his head, he watched her ascent, nearly tripping on the bottom step.

At the range he hit all but three of the practice balls. He took those remaining balls to the putting green and stroked back and forth a dozen or so times, to get the feel of the grass. Then he headed back to the pro shop.

The woman he encountered earlier was sitting at the snack bar reading a newspaper.

"Hi, again," she said, "I'm Janette Compton. Are you David West?"

"Yeah."

"I guess we'll be playing together, if you don't mind," she said.

"Not at all." Suddenly he didn't.

When they got to the first tee, David suggested, "Why don't you hit first."

Janette teed up her ball on the men's tee, made a couple of practice swings, walked up, and settled herself in position. With a smooth, effortless swing that looked as if it wouldn't hit a ball more than a hundred yards, she hit the ball with a *crack* and it shot out in a drilling arc. It seemed to hang in the air forever, beginning to curve to the left just slightly as it started down. The ball landed 245 yards from the tee and rolled another 25 yards to a stop. David was stunned. She had made it look so easy.

He teed up his ball, suddenly self-conscious. He swung the club too hard and hit the ground, robbing his shot of power. The ball wound up in a bunker less than two hundred yards out.

They got back into the cart and she drove to his ball. David was at his best when he was in trouble. Swinging smoothly this time, he popped the ball out of the trap. It was an impressive shot and Compton said, "Very nice."

With another swing that seemed too good to be true and too easy to be powerful, she struck her ball again. It landed on the green six feet from the hole, then stopped dead.

"That was a great shot," West said.

"Thanks," she said. Each time he looked at her, the golf game seemed to lose its importance. He hadn't met many interesting women since coming to Orlando, and he wasn't about to overlook this unexpected opportunity.

Janette told him she was a government lawyer, two years out of law school, working for UNILAW. Under the UNILAW program, the federal government provided lawyers to citizens who needed legal assistance and the fee was paid by a tax-funded insurance program. This legal program was similar in structure to UNIMED's program for medical care. Private lawyers were increasingly only for the elite, the extremely wealthy, or major corporations, the only clients who could pay the high fees levied for legal services.

Janette noticed David looking at her several times and decided she liked it. By the seventeenth hole he had asked her to dinner, and she had accepted.

When they had finished the game, she had beaten him on five holes; he had beaten her on one, and they had tied the rest.

"I'm glad you asked me to dinner earlier, before we got finished. My adoptive mother keeps telling me I shouldn't expect to be asked out by somebody I beat on the links," she said, smiling.

Her adoptive mother had said more than that; she had said, "You're too damn perfect. You should try to be more human if you expect to attract a husband." Janette had ignored the woman, only a few years older than Janette. She was uninterested in anybody that she had to pretend incompetence or vulnerability to attract. Still, she was pleased to find that David's ego wasn't bruised in the slightest.

"I'm impressed," he said. "How did you learn to play golf like that?"

"I'll tell you about it tonight at dinner. Here's my address." She wrote her address on a napkin, including her phone number.

*Thank goodness she has no patronizing false modesty,* David thought.

He folded it carefully and put it in his pocket. "Eight o'clock?"

"See you then."

He watched her walk out of the snack bar.

The club pro smirked when David went to check out. "Did she manage to keep up?"


When David picked Janette up that evening, she was wearing slacks and a sweater that fit her personality—sporty and feminine at the same time.

"So how did you get so good at golf?" David asked, as they took their seats in a small Spanish restaurant Janette suggested. Only locals knew of the family-owned place that served authentic food in a restrained, comfortable atmosphere. A guitarist played quietly in a far corner.

"You didn't do so bad yourself. Did you play in college?" she asked.

"I played on the golf team at Yale, and at first I hoped to be a pro after college. Then in my junior year my dad turned up the pressure to concentrate on my schoolwork, and he urged me to consider becoming a doctor. I still enjoy golf but it's more like an escape than anything I would do as a job. How about you?" David asked.

"I grew up from age six intending to go professional. My father hired the best instructors. After college golf, I went to the LPGA qualifying school and got my card. I did okay for a rookie and I planned to try out for what used to be called the men's tour—before it went unisex several years ago. The women who play the Big Tour don't win very often, but they don't have to. They make a lot more money if they finish in the top ten than they do winning a women's event. Besides that, I thought the Big Tour would be more of a challenge.

"Anyway, to make a long story even longer, I tried to hit a shot that I had hooked into some bushes during a practice round. Instead of just chipping it out, since the score didn't matter, I swung at the ball as hard as I could; I even hit a pretty good shot, but my club snagged one of the bushes and I tore the ligaments in my left wrist. That put me out for the rest of the season.

"I couldn't really practice or hit the ball as hard as I needed to and I didn't get my card back. After the second try I decided I had better find something else to do for a living—so, like they say, instead of getting a job I became a lawyer."

"Your wrist didn't bother your game any today," he said.

"It actually has kind of a dull ache right now. It's okay if I only play two or three times a week for fun, but that's not the same thing as playing on the tour. I practiced eight to ten hours a day, every day, rain or shine. I couldn't do that now. In fact, I wouldn't want to anymore. Looking back I think the pro golf career was mostly my adoptive father's idea."

It wasn't as simple as that. Adopted at infancy, she had been a trophy for her dad. Janette never considered him as her real father. Her constant childhood questions about her biological parents met with his stern rebuke that confused her and left her even more curious and in doubt of his love. Nevertheless, he basked in her golfing talent. He taught her to practice missing shots deliberately, presenting it as a challenge. He would clap when she would miss a putt by fractions of an inch, playing her own game. After she became good at it, he began setting up games at his private club, teaming up with her and winning golf matches by only a stroke. He thought she didn't understand that he was winning huge bets against the rich suckers, but she *did* know and didn't like being used.

When Janette was fourteen, she had a bitter argument with her father in which he forbade her to seek out her birth parents or even mention the subject again as long as she lived under his roof and he supported her. In response, at the next of his arranged golf games, she played to her limit. She beat all three of her opponents by nine strokes. That ended the games and was the last time she played golf with her father. She vowed then to find her real parents when she finished school and was on her own.

After he cooled off, her father turned her career over to hirelings and went back to his luxury car dealership.

Since then she had been independent in every way but financially, except that she was under a contract for management of her golf career. The injury had provided an ideal way out of that.

True to her vow, when Janette graduated from law school and was on her own, she hired an adoption search agency to find her birth parents. Although the agency was quite thorough in determining the time and place of her adoption, they came to an abrupt dead end. It was as if Janette had never existed prior to that day, and they advised her to give up the search. Occasionally she renewed her investigation on the Internet, but gradually came to believe that she would never find her real parents.

She realized that her mind had been drifting into the past and David was waiting patiently, smiling at her.

"Enough about me. Tell me about doing transplants. It must be very exciting," she said.

"As a matter of fact, I did my first solo one yesterday."

"You're kidding."

"No, I did a lot of them while I was a resident, of

course, but then another doctor was actually in charge. It's really different when it's all my responsibility."

"I know how I felt when I did my first case by myself. When I stood up before the judge I had this feeling that it was really somebody else or that I was just pretending. For the first time I realized that I didn't have the right to think about myself, because I was doing this for my client."

"That's it, exactly," he said. "In fact, I need to go see my patient later tonight. He's never off my mind."

"Could I tag along?"

"Sure, if you want to, but I won't be able to get you into CCU. It's restricted."

"That's okay. I'd just like to see where you work," Janette said with a shy smile.

David had thought he might ask her about the legal penalties for retransplanting an IORC heart, but he couldn't be too obvious. "Listen, tell me about the law concerning IORC. I learned about it in med school but I'm starting to think that I didn't learn all that much."

"I don't have any contact with IORC, but I took a course in law school about sovereign corporations and their treaties. We studied Fusion Electric, IORC, and Nippon Transportation Corporation, along with several of the smaller multinational food conglomerates. The big three operate more or less the same way. They're really nothing but giant corporations that do business in all of the countries of the world. They're so powerful because we want their products so much that they have been able to force governments to enter into treaties with them to give them special privileges—sovereignty really. These treaties are like contracts with each government."

"What's to keep a government from changing its mind?"

"Legally, under the treaties, the International Court. That started after Fusion Electric defended its sovereignty and won. A well-organized group backed by several Middle East governments that were losing their oil-based power attacked the FE power control platform. FE defended itself by force as the superpowers teetered on the brink of war. The International Court decided that FE had acted within its rights, and the world balance of power adjusted itself to accommodate the new order.

"But actually what prevents a government treaty default now is that Fusion Electric could simply turn off all our electricity or IORC could stop doing transplants. They'd be putting their monopolies at risk, I guess, but you can bet that if that were to happen, the public would throw out any government that had caused it. The treaties work because we're all dependent on these companies.

"I'm not up on the details of IORC policies. I prosecute criminals, I don't get into contract or treaty disputes at my office. All I know is that IORC has the right under its treaty to make the U.S. government pass any laws necessary to implement the treaty, and a lot of laws have been passed."

"The IORC retains ownership of any organ that it transplants. I just can't see how that could be legal, but that's what I've been told. How can some corporation own part of a person's body? How could I check on that?" David knew he was on shaky ground but Janette seemed up front so he took the risk to ask.

"I can research it for you, if you want. Why? Do you have a problem with IORC?" she asked.

"No, no not really," he said too quickly. "I've been invited to interview with them and I want to be informed on their policies before I go." She searched his face. David could tell immediately that she hadn't bought this flimsy excuse.

When they arrived at the hospital after dinner, Janette and David saw Betty Martinez and her son in the critical care waiting area. They were playing an electronic chess game.

Several other people were sitting around in worn orange vinyl chairs set between tables of outdated magazines and informative brochures. An old TV with bad reception sat on a wall bracket hissing out static.

"How are you holding up?" David asked Mrs. Martinez and Jorge.

"I'm okay. They say Mike is fine, but they won't let us go in except for five minutes every hour so he can rest. He's wide awake anyway," she said. "He's awfully swollen up and he says his mouth is dry."

"That's normal. We expect that to happen. He's just fine," David assured Betty and then continued, "This is a friend of mine, Janette Compton. Janette, this is Betty Martinez and her son Jorge."

"*Buenos noches,*" she said, having picked up on the Spanish pronunciation of Jorge. She immediately fell into a conversation with him in Spanish. David motioned that he was heading in to see Martinez as Janette chatted on. *She'll be a hit,* David thought, and he walked through the swinging doors to the nurses' station.

David checked the chart for Martinez, then went into the Critical Care Unit. The entire CCU area was surrounded by glass walls and doors. It seemed hopelessly crowded with equipment. There was one nurse for every two patients. Among the clutter of electronic sensors, monitors, tubes, wires, and exotic machines, the important element was this nurse, who never left the bedside between the two patients.

Every few seconds the nurse manually checked and recorded vital signs and readings from several monitors, a discipline intended to keep the nurse alert to the patient's condition. The nurses in the CCU had the most responsibility of any in the hospital. All the patients were on life support, so the nurses were literally keeping them alive; they would tolerate nothing that interfered with their primary task. They guarded the patients from everything, even the interference of careless doctors. They welcomed the family for short periods because it made the patient feel better and more optimistic. But after five minutes the family was required to leave.

It took a trained eye to evaluate a patient soon after a transplant. They all looked absolutely awful: swollen, gray, trembling from the medications, and breathing hard. But these were normal signs. Families were generally forewarned, but were still shocked when they first saw their loved ones in that condition.

Martinez was awake and the breathing tube had been removed from his mouth. He recognized David immediately. "Hey, Doc," he said. "If I'd known it was going to feel like this, I'm not sure I would have agreed." But he was smiling.

"What hurts is not your heart but having your breastbone cut open again so soon after the first operation. Don't worry, though, it'll get better quickly."

"That's okay," Martinez said. He clutched a small yellow heart-shaped pillow to his chest. It eased the pain when he coughed, and his nurse encouraged him to use it. A volunteer organization made and donated the pillows. Recovered patients took them home as souvenirs.

A few minutes later, Betty Martinez and her son and Janette got up when David returned to the waiting room. "He's doing just fine. I've told the nurse to let you both go in to see him for a few minutes, then you should go home."

"No, we want to stay right here," Mrs. Martinez said.

"That's not necessary. He's in good condition and, frankly, it's worrying him that you are both sitting out here and not getting any rest. So consider it a doctor's order. Go see him for a few minutes, then go home." Mrs. Martinez looked relieved. The stress and fatigue of the events of the last several days had taken their toll.

Some of the other people waiting in the room listened while pretending to read their magazines. They were all going through similar experiences, more or less. The ap-

pearance of a doctor, the reassurances and the directions
to return home gave them vicarious faith that their loved
ones would also be all right. The droning of the unwatch-
able TV and the wall clock that seemed to work at half
speed would be their company for the night.

A few days later, Janette Compton thought of her evening
at the hospital with David West. The thoughts came while
she was reviewing a file in preparation for a court hearing
on a motion she was to handle right after lunch. Like all
younger lawyers, she had to handle routine hearings in
more serious cases, such as this one: vehicular homicide
with alcohol aggravation. And, as usual, she didn't get the
file until a couple hours before she was to be in court.

She thought of David because the defendant in this
case, a Dr. Richard Thomas, was also a heart transplant
surgeon. He worked for IORC, and from looking at the
file she could see he had a problem both with drinking and
with authority.

She read over the motion filed for the doctor, which
Wilson Hoffmeister himself had signed. The motion asked
the court to exclude the evidence of the alcohol test. She
reviewed the police report and saw that there was a videotape in the file.

She tried to play the tape, but the only thing that appeared were thousands of dots of various colors moving
around in random patterns across the screen. Static. Someone had erased the tape. She felt her pulse race and looked
at her watch. It was already ten o'clock, and without the
arrest tape there was little time to do anything in preparation before the hearing.

Janette called the police department to speak to Officer
Burrows. The police department informed her that he now
worked for IORC.

*Too convenient,* she thought. Should she consult her

boss? If she couldn't handle an exclusionary motion, how could she expect to be given a really complicated trial? No, she would work it out herself without going for help.

She skipped lunch, studying the file to piece the case together and researching the law.

At one-fifteen, outside the courtroom, she saw a large black man in an expensive suit who appeared to be looking for someone. "Is your name Burrows?" she asked him.

"Right. Are you the lawyer?" he asked.

"I'm Janette Compton, the prosecutor on the case. Let me get right to the point. The arrest video has been erased," she said, watching his reaction.

"That's impossible," he said, his face neutral.

"Care to look for yourself?" she said. Janette led Burrows into a witness room equipped with a video player. The same mass of moving multicolored dots filled the screen.

He shrugged. "Like I said, it's impossible."

"Then exactly what are we watching?"

"You can't erase those tapes like a regular VCR tape. That looks to me like a brand-new tape."

"Well, whatever it is, it's not the tape of the arrest."

"No, I guess it isn't," he said with mock concern.

"Just exactly how do you explain that?" she demanded, getting irritated.

"Looks to me like the wrong tape got in the file."

"Right. What I want to know is, how could that happen?"

Burrows sighed. "A lot of things can happen. There was a lot going on that night. It must be that somewhere along the line a new tape got put in the file instead of the one that was made at the time of the arrest. What's the big deal, anyway? I can testify about what happened."

She looked at her watch. "I may have to go into this tape problem with you during the hearing."

"No problem," he said, unruffled.

Wilson Hoffmeister was already inside the courtroom

sitting with Dr. Thomas and an associate lawyer. All three wore expensive tailored suits. The judge was in his early sixties, moderately overweight, and looked bored.

After the opening statements, Hoffmeister said, "The defense calls Officer Wayne Burrows, the arresting police officer." Burrows came forward, and after swearing in, sat down on the witness seat. He gave his account of the arrest, and Hoffmeister concluded.

"Did you have any technical difficulties, Mr. Burrows, with your video equipment?"

"Yes, sir."

"Are you sure that all of the arrest was videotaped?"

"I'm not actually sure. I've never seen the videotape, so I don't know."

"Your Honor, at this time the defense would request that the prosecution produce the videotape of the arrest so that it may be shown to the court," Hoffmeister asked.

"Apparently the defendant's counsel already knows that the videotape has been erased, Your Honor," Janette said.

"What do you mean, erased?" Hoffmeister said. "I don't know anything of the kind."

"I don't believe that for a moment, Judge," Janette said.

"Wait just a minute, young lady, let's all settle down. Now do you have the tape, or don't you?" the judge asked.

"We have a tape as part of the police file, but there's nothing on it," Janette said, ignoring the sexist remark.

"Then you don't have the tape," the judge said.

"We don't have the tape of the arrest at this time, Your Honor," Janette said, gritting her teeth. Every muscle in her body tensed with fury.

"Judge, that throws a whole different light on the case, doesn't it?" Hoffmeister said. "Officer Burrows, do you know anything about an erased tape?"

"You can't erase a police tape. They're not made that

way. Once a tape is recorded, it's always recorded, like an old-fashioned movie film."

"Can you account for the fact that the one in the police file *seems* to have been erased?" Hoffmeister asked.

"Like I said, it can't be erased. I told her before the hearing, that's a new tape that she showed me. That's not the one that was made at the time of the arrest."

Hoffmeister elected to stop while he was ahead.

Janette Compton stood up, not exactly sure where to begin. She hesitated a few seconds and then decided that a frontal attack was the best approach. "You've been referred to as 'Officer Burrows.' You're not Officer Burrows anymore, are you?" she asked.

"No, I'm not."

"You work for IORC now in their security department?"

"That's right."

"You got that job after this accident happened, didn't you?"

"I applied for a job with IORC a long time ago. The pay's better. I've been on the waiting list over there for a long time. It just happened that I got called right after this accident."

"Does that have anything to do with the disappearance of this tape?" she asked.

"We object, Your Honor. This is all highly improper, and there's no basis for her to accuse this man of anything," Hoffmeister said.

"Do you have any basis for this suggestion, Ms. Compton?" the judge asked.

"I don't have any actual evidence right now, but—"

"Then you will discontinue this line of questioning. I sustain the objection. You stick to the facts you can prove."

"Your Honor—"

"I've made my ruling. Now get on with your cross-examination."

"Mr. Burrows, is there the slightest doubt in your mind that you gave a warning to the defendant, that he understood it, and that you were required to use reasonable force to get the blood sample?"

"None whatsoever," Burrows answered.

"I have nothing further," Janette said, sitting down.

"I just have one more question," Hoffmeister said. "Is it possible for someone to get a recorded videotape out of the police building without its being detected?"

Burrows realized then that he had been completely outsmarted. This lawyer had probably known all along about the metal detector. "Not, really. There are metal detectors at the visitors' entrances. If somebody tried to leave the police department with a tape it would set off an alarm, they would be searched, and then they would have a lot of explaining to do. So I'd have to say no, it's basically impossible."

"I have nothing further," Hoffmeister said, flashing Compton a smug grin.

"Okay, you can call your next witness," the judge said.

Hoffmeister said, "Your Honor, under the circumstances, we have no other witnesses."

The judge turned to Janette Compton. "The prosecution may proceed."

Janette thought for a few moments, then asked the bailiff to call the paramedic to the witness stand. After he was sworn in and had told the court about his arrival at the accident scene and inspection of the vehicles, Janette sat down and Hoffmeister took over.

"Isn't it true that the doctor complained he couldn't hear and couldn't see and there was some discussion about air bags and gas?" Hoffmeister asked.

"Yes, that's true," the paramedic said. "All he really said was that he was worried about his car. He didn't seem to care a damn about the man he had just killed."

"Your Honor, I object to the witness saying he just killed this man," Hoffmeister said.

"Well, I objected to him killing the guy," the paramedic said.

"You will confine yourself to answering the questions, sir," the judge growled at the witness.

"Yes, sir."

"Did you see the police officer give any of these alleged warnings?" Hoffmeister asked the man.

"No, I got so disgusted that after the cop came I just left."

"No further questions."

"That's all the testimony we can offer today, Your Honor," Janette said. "We just found out about the blank tape late this morning, so we were surprised and unprepared to deal with this matter."

"Why did you just discover that the tape was blank today? This case is almost two weeks old," the judge said.

"The file was just assigned this morning. We expected the videotape to show the arrest as it's labeled. The prosecution wants to go into the question of how a blank tape got into the report, as well as the matter concerning Burrows going to work for IORC."

"Ms. Compton, the court has advised you that issue is improper without there being some evidence to back up your accusation. There's no evidence before this court that there was any impropriety, only an error. The defendant has shown that there is serious question about the circumstances of the blood test. Once a question of the propriety of the test was established, that switched the burden of proof to the prosecution to show it was proper, and you have failed to carry that burden. It's the court's ruling that the evidence supports the conclusion that the defendant was incapacitated from the accident and therefore, either because he couldn't hear or because his vision was impaired or he was otherwise in shock from the accident, he was unable to make a knowing response to the warning and request that the police officer made. It is inconceivable to this court that an IORC physician would defy a police officer at the scene of a fatal accident, or that he would walk around in a daze unless he were incapacitated in one way or another. The court will exclude the evidence of the alcohol test, and the court will entertain a motion by the defendant to dismiss all criminal charges in this case. It looks to me as if this was just an automobile accident, although a very unfortunate one."

"Your Honor, the government objects to that," Janette said. "It's premature for a motion to dismiss the charges in this case. There is other evidence available. We believe that the parking attendant where the defendant picked up his car a few minutes before the accident will testify that the defendant was intoxicated, and we believe we will be able to obtain evidence from the club where he consumed the alcoholic beverages. If a motion is to be filed we want it to be filed with a reasonable opportunity for us to do some investigation."

"Very well, but you should do your investigation before the hearings," the judge said.

"And as to this matter of what Burrows did with the tape—"

"Ms. Compton, I don't think you've been listening to what I said. That matter is closed. You had your chance. That's not to be mentioned again in this case, and if it is the court will hold you in contempt. Mr. Hoffmeister, file your motions."

The judge got up and walked out of the courtroom. Dr. Thomas grinned broadly. Janette gathered up her papers, still stunned by the events, and feeling very self-conscious as a result of the judge's comments. She started out of the courtroom, but Wilson Hoffmeister caught up with her.

"Ms. Compton, I have a suggestion. After the court's ruling, there's no way in the world you're going to be able to prove that Thomas was drunk. It's just like the judge said: This isn't a homicide case, it's an accident case. Why don't you reduce the charges to speeding. The doctor's company has already compensated the victim's family. He will plead guilty to speeding and that'll be the end of the matter. Believe me, he won't ever do anything like this again. The damages to his car alone are so much that I would be embarrassed to own a new car that cost as much as his repair bill," Hoffmeister said dismissively.

Outraged, Janette said, "You've got to be kidding—and it's not a joking matter. This whole thing smells. There's no way it's over, not as long as I'm the prosecutor. Videotapes don't just disappear. Contempt or not, I'll get to the bottom of this."

"Ms. Compton, let me give you some advice from thirty years' experience as a lawyer. Sometimes it's best to settle a case and go on to the next one. Keep your perspective. Don't ever try to prove something that you're not sure you can prove, and don't ever try to prove something that you'd be better off not proving, as you did today. That's a short course in practical law. You're in over your head. Leave it alone." He turned and walked away before she could tell him to go to hell.

# 6

Dazed from the hearing, Janette knew her face was glowing red because it felt burning hot. It was her fault for not checking the tape earlier. The system was slow and inefficient.

Still, the judge's ruling was outrageous. How could a judge and a police officer be so uncaring? Didn't they remember that someone had been killed? Did they think it was perfectly all right to let the doctor off when everyone in the courtroom knew that he was guilty? She would not accept this, no matter what, nor would she accept that pompous Hoffmeister's intimidation.

She stormed into the UNILAW building and waited impatiently for the elevator. Another lawyer also returning from the courthouse started to make some small talk, but seeing the expression on her face, thought better of it. She tapped her foot angrily, exasperated at waiting for the elevator. She had to calm down, but she didn't want to.

Ordinarily Janette was a loner. She had never once asked her dad for any kind of advice, and the only "advice" she had gotten from her adoptive mother was criticism. She could make her own way and take care of herself. But, with age, she had learned that in certain arenas some people were better trained than she was to get certain information, and that it never hurt to seek out an expert's advice.

She went straight to the research department, entered one of the glassed-in offices, and banged the door behind her. Warren Jeffries looked up from his computer terminal.

Though Warren Jeffries was a computer techie, he was anything but a nerd. He owned and flew his own airplane, rode a motorcycle, and had been known to sky dive. At a lanky six two, he was a meticulous dresser who sported a carefully trimmed beard. His black hair was flecked with gray and his eyes danced mischievously. Jeffries was one of the best-informed people Janette knew. At UNILAW he was the head of computer research.

"To what do I owe the pleasure of your company?" he asked, pulling his half-glasses down to the tip of his nose and looking over them at Janette. Warren liked to flirt with her, even though he was happily married and had a teenage daughter.

"Warren, I've got an interesting problem for you." Janette explained what had happened in court and during her interview with Burrows. "I'm trying to figure out some way to investigate what I'm supposed to accept as just a coincidence."

"No such thing as coincidences," Jeffries said. "I can prove it to you mathematically if you like. Even the occurrence of random events is not coincidence."

"Get me some evidence that it's not a coincidence, then. Where do we start?"

"I can't get into IORC's records. They're as secretive as any of the intelligence agencies. Still, we can look at the Department of Labor records on hiring, and the police department records of officers who have gone to work for IORC." He took notes on his computer as they talked, keeping track of his ideas. "We can search all the case records to find every instance where a tape was mishandled. We might turn something up. I'll go to work on it. I'll need the case number to account for my search."

"Well, actually I'd like to keep this off the record for the moment. I've been chewed out already today by the judge. Maybe I shouldn't get you involved in this at all."

"I have a lot of leeway here," he said. "I'll write it up as a performance check on the system."

"Thanks, Warren, I appreciate it," she said.

"Any time."

She left Jeffries's office and went across the hall to the law library. She thought of David's questions as she pulled out a book on IORC. After flipping through the volume on treaty law, she called him at Orlando Government. The electronic system answered, and it took Janette several minutes to work her way through the pyramid structure of telephone menus. Everyone assumed that such systems were more efficient than having a human actually talk to a caller. Janette thought it was just an excuse to sell more elaborate telephones.

"It's Janette," she said, when David finally picked up.

"I'm glad you called," he said. "I had a great time the other night."

"I did, too, especially the visit to the hospital. I thought of you today when I was doing some research. I have a book on the IORC. I thought maybe you'd like to talk about it."

"Definitely," he said. "When are you free?"

"How about Friday? There's an Italian restaurant we can try."

"It's a date."

David watched as Janette slid into her chair. Then he sat and smiled silently at her.

"What?" she asked, returning his smile.

"Just thinking how much we have in common. It's

strange, isn't it? We are both almost pro golfers, and I'm adopted, too."

"Really . . ." Janette's voice trailed off as she looked into David's unusually gray eyes—startlingly similar in color to her own.

"Have you ever met your birth parents?" she asked.

"No. I never wanted to. My adopted parents treated me as if I were their own and were so caring that I felt disloyal even thinking about who my real parents might be. How about you?"

"I've always wondered about mine. I tried to find out about them but got nowhere. For some reason, my dad was very much against it."

"I always thought finding birth parents should be a simple process," said David.

"It used to be, because of the need to get medical histories and to find transplant donors. But genetic mapping and the IORC have made that need obsolete," Janette said. "I tried the Internet and found inquiries from several other people like me who had had no luck finding either birth parent. One was a famous baseball player, and another was a violinist who had become an international sensation at age fifteen—both special, successful people who wanted to share their accomplishments with their biological parents and discover their backgrounds."

David wondered how hard it would be to find his own biological parents if he ever decided to, but feeling a twinge of guilt, he dismissed the idea.

"Did you ever contact the baseball player or the violinist?" David asked.

"No. There was no point. I didn't know anything about their families. But there were others too, quite a few actually, so I'm not alone."

David smiled at her and they shared an intimate moment as they waited at their table.

The Italian place Janette had mentioned had been a standby for three generations for the locals in Apopka, north of Orlando. Rustic Italian was the decor; good food and wine were the attraction.

"I did some research on the IORC," Janette said.

"What have you found out?" he asked, as the waitress opened a bottle of Chianti for them.

"Read this," she said, and handed him a photocopy of a section from a book on IORC's treaty with the U.S. government.

## IORC-USA TREATY
## ARTICLE I

### Section 1

This treaty between the International Organ Replacement Corporation, hereinafter IORC, and the United States of America, hereinafter USA, shall supersede all constitutions, laws, rules, regulations, decisions, administrative orders, rules and rulings or any provisions whatsoever that are in conflict herewith, nor shall anything in the future that is in any way in conflict herewith be effective until and unless this treaty is amended in accordance with the provisions hereof.

David skimmed sections of the treaty on court interpretations, taxes, property matters, diplomatic immunity, amendments, language, and the like. Then he read the section on transplants.

## ARTICLE II

### Section 1

IORC shall have perpetual exclusive rights to provide organ replacements, provided that organs from terminally ill or injured persons not otherwise assigned to IORC may be transplanted by others.

Section 2

The USA agrees to prohibit by law any competition with IORC except as provided in Section 1 of this Article II.

## ARTICLE III

Section 1

The IORC may establish rules and procedures for the Justification Factor of USA citizens and residents in order to establish priority in the entitlement to replacement organs from IORC, based upon such criteria as it deems appropriate from time to time. IORC shall maintain the records of and conduct any tests applicable to Justification Factors.

Section 2

IORC and its officers, agents and employees shall be absolutely immune from any claims for negligence in connection with any of its activities. IORC and its officers, agents and employees shall not be subject to regulation of its or their business or professional activities in any way.

Section 3

The records and documents of IORC of whatever nature shall be exempt from any requirement of disclosure.

"Pretty powerful stuff," David said.

"Actually, that's just the beginning. The treaty has been in effect for about twenty years now, and many court decisions have interpreted it to make IORC autonomous. For example, local governments wanted to issue building permits and make inspections on IORC building construction. Court decisions ruled that IORC was exempt. In fact, inspectors were not even allowed on the property. Those interpretations led to questions of whether the police could go onto IORC property and enforce the laws, and that one ended up in an appeal to the International Court."

"Something tells me it didn't go well for the police."

"Nope. The International Court says that the police must ask IORC to turn over any suspect who has violated local law but, as if in a foreign country exercising sovereign extradition rights, it's up to IORC whether they will do so or not. If they don't, the police can't go on the property to arrest anyone. That was the ruling."

"So why are you interested in the IORC? I thought your work didn't involve them."

"There's a computer tech at my office. He and I are doing some extracurricular research."

David felt a twinge of jealousy. She sensed the unstated question and said, "It's not like that. He's happily married."

"What are you researching?" David asked, visibly relieved.

She explained what had happened in court. Then, hesitating, she added, "This is confidential and I probably shouldn't have mentioned it. I'd appreciate it if you don't say anything to anybody else about it. I'm not accusing IORC of anything. I just want to look into the facts."

He raised his hands and smiled. "Trust me. I won't say a word." He wanted to tell her that he was no fan of big powerful organizations that make their own rules at everyone else's expense, but he suddenly remembered that he had told the white lie about interviewing for a job with IORC. However if their dinners continued to go well, he'd find a way to let her know that they were of like minds on this subject.

# 7

Monday mornings were never pleasant in any law office, and that was particularly true this Monday for Janette's boss at UNILAW. Charles Henderson was mid-forties, fat, balding, and bitter from unattained political aspirations. He was lodged behind a government-issue wooden desk— a decorating touch reserved for division chiefs—but crowded in among dented file cabinets that lined the walls of his office. He had just received a call from Police Internal Affairs.

"Just what in hell are you people up to over there?" demanded the police captain.

"What do you mean?" he asked.

"Your computer people have been poking through our records without telling us in advance what they intended to do."

"We're authorized to access your records; we're all on the same side, aren't we?"

"I'm not talking about authorization. I'm talking about interagency cooperation. I can look into your records, too, but I won't do it without calling you first. I'm pissed about this. If your people think there's anything wrong I want to know. It's my job to investigate officer misconduct. It seems these searches pertained to an Officer Burrows who was recently cross-examined in court by one of your lawyers, a woman named Compton."

"I'll look into it. I'm sorry we didn't give you a call before the records were searched."

*Damn it! Why would Compton do a thing like that? And what is Warren Jeffries thinking about, tapping into Internal Affairs without notifying them?*

Henderson told his secretary to summon Compton and Jeffries.

At the same time, across town, Hoffmeister had just received a call, too. It was no more pleasant for him.

"Wilson, I was given to understand that the Thomas case was a closed subject," LeBearc said.

"It's not completely closed—some minor paperwork still pending, you know. But the judge said it was over. He told the prosecutor to drop the accusations she was making about some alleged missing evidence. He even said that if she didn't, he would find her in contempt of court," Hoffmeister boasted.

"UNILAW has been attempting to access our computer records. One of my security techs traced the inquiry to Burrows's file. I'm told they got nothing, but I want this matter concluded once and for all," he said, and hung up before Hoffmeister could respond.

Hoffmeister sat thinking; then he called Charles Henderson.

"This is Wilson Hoffmeister. You have a prosecutor named Compton working for you."

"That's right, Mr. Hoffmeister."

"I had a case with her last week. A missing police videotape surprised her because she hadn't prepared, and she kept asking the arresting officer, who no longer works for the Orlando Police Department, accusatory questions after the judge sustained objections to them. Finally he told her to drop the matter or he would hold her in contempt. *Now* I've found out your computer people have

THE J FACTOR 91

been making inquiries at IORC about that very man: Wayne Burrows."

"I'm sorry, Mr. Hoffmeister. I'll tell her to do as the judge ordered."

"I will report this to the judge if the case isn't dropped immediately. The IORC doesn't like this, and the judge probably won't, either."

"As I said—"

"Listen, Henderson, I want a telephone call from you by noon today confirming that this matter has been concluded." Hoffmeister hung up.

Two minutes later Jeffries and Compton were standing in the division chief's office.

"Why the hell are you two snooping around police and IORC databases? Warren, let's start with you."

"In the first place, I don't work for you. I work for UNILAW. I'm a civil service employee and I'm head of my department. You're a division chief. I'm not answerable to you and I resent your tone," Jeffries replied.

"I don't care if you're head of the whole damn agency. There are procedures to be followed."

"Look, we run tests frequently to find out what information we can pull up and what we can't in an effort to improve our research methods. Compton mentioned something to me that caught my interest, and it seemed like a good thing to do a test on."

"Did you find out anything incriminating?"

"It depends on what you mean by incriminating. It's certainly suspicious, in my opinion," Jeffries replied.

"What exactly do you mean by 'suspicious'?"

"The hiring of this police officer didn't fit the normal pattern. It all happened too soon after the lost tape."

Turning to Janette and motioning Warren to leave, Henderson said, "I want to talk to you about this. You didn't tell me the judge had threatened you with contempt of court." She started to say something and he held up his hand to interrupt her. "It's not up to you to decide what you'll use the taxpayers' money for. What the hell were you thinking?"

"I think it's my duty as a prosecutor to look into criminal activity that comes to my attention. That's what it says in my job description," she replied, not backing off an inch. Janette never had backed off in her life. She had always been good at whatever she did and had earned the right to stand her ground.

"Bull. It's not your job to harass the important people of this community. You went off on a tangent because you got surprised in court. Now you've started trouble over at Internal Affairs and at IORC, and you've gotten Jeffries into trouble by talking him into doing computer research that he wasn't supposed to do in the first place. None of this shows good judgment."

"It's not my fault cases are assigned too late for preparation. I believe the police officer was bought off. I think he intentionally destroyed the tape, and I think we can ultimately prove it."

"You're entitled to your opinion, but you're not entitled to keep expressing it publicly without any basis. Now I want you to listen very carefully. You are to drop the matter. You are not to use any resources of this office or UNILAW for any further inquiry. It's over. Finished. The charges will be dropped this morning. Do you understand?" he demanded, red-faced.

"I understand, but I don't like it."

"For the moment I'm going to reassign you where you can't cause any more trouble. I want you to report in the morning to the UNILAW-UNIMED Medical Benefits Section."

"You mean I have to do those piddling administrative hearings to decide whether people get disability benefits?" she asked, incredulous.

"Maybe you'll learn some good judgment there."

She was tempted to quit on the spot, simply resign her position and tell him to go to hell. Instead, through a monumental effort, she held her tongue and turned on her heel and stalked out. *There's nothing wrong with my judgment,* she thought. *He caved in to curry favor with someone. It isn't that easy to get rid of me. A new job, maybe, but I'll still be around and I'll watch the IORC.*

The next morning Janette reported to the section director for her new assignment. The director, Ms. Moss, had already heard the rumors about Janette's transfer. She resented the fact that people considered a transfer to her section to be a demotion. "I expect people in my department to stand up for their beliefs and I'll back them when they do," she said to Janette. "Here's your travel authorization. You're off to Washington for four weeks of training. We need you here now, but I want you up to speed. Enjoy yourself and come back ready to work."

Martinez enjoyed an uneventful recovery. Three weeks after his surgery he was released from the hospital to rest at home. A week later he returned for tests and final release so he could go back to work.

"Doc, I'm really not very good at saying things, but I've got to thank you for all that you did," he said, as tears formed in his eyes. He was a big, burly man and this display of emotion embarrassed him.

"I'm just as happy as you are. You're in great health. Here's a form that will admit you back to work. Maybe someday I'll get to ride on your ship," David said as he put his arm around Martinez's shoulder and ushered him out of the room.

The next morning Martinez got up early, showered, and dressed in his uniform, which was now a bit baggy. He drove himself down to the harbor and reported in at

Fusion Electric's land-based office. He told the secretary that he was returning for work and handed over the form that Dr. West had signed.

"Welcome back," the secretary said. "I'll let the operations manager know you're here."

The manager emerged from his office and shook Martinez's hand. "Welcome back, I'm glad to see you're doing so well."

"Yeah, I'm ready to go to work. I thought I'd go out today if that's okay," Martinez said.

"It's okay for you to go out, but the rules say that before you start back to work you've got to be examined by a company doctor and released for duty. Why don't you ride out to the platform and see the doctor there. He can fill out the papers for you and then if everything is in order, we'll assign you crew duties starting tomorrow. How's that?"

"That's just great. I want to thank you for everything the company did for me. I really appreciate it. There's no way I could have gotten the transplant otherwise."

"Don't thank me, it was Captain Stapleton. He called headquarters and arranged it; actually he just told them it was going to happen. He didn't ask. He said he owed you."

Martinez left the office and walked over to the ship. By the time he arrived the word had spread throughout the crew that he was back, and he found two lines of white-uniformed sailors facing one another, forming a corridor along the pier leading to the gangplank. He couldn't really tell whether they were being serious or were kidding him, but whatever they were doing, he was damn glad to see them all. Brilliant white in the Florida sun, the ship sat poised like a missile ready to launch. He walked toward the ship, straightening his shoulders and pulling down the blouse of his uniform. He walked straight between the men and up the gangplank. When he got to the hatch he saw Captain Stapleton standing at naval attention. Martinez stopped and, in accord with naval tradition, turned first to the right and saluted the ship's flag, then back to the left and saluted the captain. "Permission to come aboard, sir?" he asked.

The captain snapped back a salute and countered, "Permission granted, and with pleasure." He broke into a wide grin and shook hands with Martinez. "You're a passenger today, Mike. Would you like to ride over on the bridge?"

"Well, if it won't hurt your feelings none, Captain, I'd much rather be in the engine room," Martinez said.

"You can be wherever you want on this trip. You're the guest of honor."

"Captain, I've just got to thank you for all you done for me," Martinez said, his eyes again beginning to tear.

"I don't know what the hell you're talking about, Martinez," the captain said, and walked away, even though he was still smiling.

Martinez took the easy route down an elevator and along a corridor. When he got to the engine room he looked over all the polished machinery that was as familiar to him as the furniture in his living room. He knew every valve and every control. His assistant, whom he had been training for several years, stood at his post watching Martinez as he inspected the machinery. After a few minutes Martinez turned and said, "You done good, Paul. It all looks shipshape. You done good."

"Thank you, sir," Paul said.

"I'm no 'sir,' Paul. You know that." He walked around with his hands behind his back, admiring the spotless room and enjoying the aroma of oil and polish.

The captain then called from the bridge and ordered the starting sequence on the engine. Paul didn't move or respond. Martinez looked at him. "What the hell are you waiting on? Captain said 'start sequence,'" Martinez said.

"I was waiting for you to give the order," Paul said.

"You're in charge down here. I'm a passenger," Martinez said.

"Yes, sir—uh, yes, uh, whatever," Paul said, not quite sure what to do.

"Did you get that order, engine room? I said begin start-up sequence," the captain repeated.

"Aye, sir, start sequence is being initiated," Paul radioed back. He flipped switches and watched the gauges as the magnetic fields of the ion engine began to build.

There was a hum of electricity, and the hair on their arms vibrated slightly. It occurred to Martinez that the magnetic field of the engine might affect his heart, but he set that worry aside, remembering that the engine was well shielded and only the merest hint of magnetism was actually created inside the engine room.

For an hour Martinez watched the young man going about his duties, adjusting and fine-tuning the engine. Too soon for Martinez, they arrived at the power control station.

More than a mile square, the power platform contained the fusion generators and laser heat exhaust system. Somewhat like an oil rig platform but larger, it was a small city where several hundred people lived. It generated electricity by nuclear fusion energizing induction generators at distribution centers worldwide.

Martinez went aboard the platform and made his way to the medical center. The doctor greeted him. "Martinez, isn't it? I was notified you were coming. Good to see you. I understand you've had a heart transplant. How are you feeling?"

"I'm feeling a hundred percent, Doctor, and I'm ready to go back to work. The doctor who did the transplant signed me off yesterday and said I'm doing just fine."

"Well, let me check you over and let's see what we've got here. You know, we don't get many transplants and I have to make sure I'm following the rules."

He examined Martinez thoroughly. When he scanned Martinez's chest with a standard multiscanner, he saw the

IORC marker and the numbers, which did not surprise him.

When he finished the examination, he said to Martinez, "Let me have the form from the transplant doctor." Looking at it, he opened a manual, read for a few minutes and then told Martinez, "You'll have to get signed off by IORC before I'm authorized to let you go back to work in the engine room."

"Why do I have to do that? The doctor who did the transplant signed me off."

"The company rule says that when IORC does a transplant they have to sign off the patient before they can return to work."

"But I didn't have an IORC transplant; it was done at Orlando Government."

"Well, it's an IORC heart. You can see it on the scanner. The number's right there, so wherever you had the surgery, you still have to get checked off by IORC. That's the rule. You're working with some very sophisticated equipment and a lot of lives are in your hands. The company has rules and we have to follow them."

"Well, I'm fine," said Martinez. "But if that's the drill, I guess I got no choice."

Two days later Martinez went to IORC. He paused out front and looked up at the imposing structures. The glass buildings reflected the early morning sun and so appeared to be made of dark red copper. Everything was new, fresh, and clean.

He was soon registered, processed, and sent along. When he arrived at the designated area, several dozen people were sitting in a comfortable waiting room, and he took his place among them. He waited for only two or three minutes before he heard his name called and an assistant ushered him into a small examination room. A male attendant in a green uniform sat down with him in the room and explained the procedure.

"This is a routine examination. Scanners do most of the work. I'll have to take a couple of tissue samples; then you'll be asked to undress and lie down on the examination table. Several machines will scan your body and you will receive directions over a speaker. Please follow those directions carefully. If you have any questions at any time, you may ask them and an attendant will answer. While the tests are going on, please try to remain as still as possible. Some of the tests may involve the introduction of a painless and harmless chemical that will help outline various organs in your body for the scanners. An air injection system administers the chemical, so if you feel a slight pinch in your arm or your hip, that's what it's all about. Don't be alarmed. If you become uncomfortable at any time, please say so and someone will assist you. Do you have any questions?"

"No, no questions," Martinez said. It reminded him of being inducted into the U.S. Navy as a young man: lots of directions to follow, things going on he didn't understand, and a total loss of personal autonomy and dignity. Devoid of any furniture, except for a fold-out seat and built-in examination table, the room was made of ivory-colored plastic and contained no sharp corners. Drawers let into one wall, and a small countertop protruded outward. Taking an instrument, the attendant scraped gently along the inside of Martinez's cheek and transferred the sample into a container. He then drew blood from Martinez's left arm and inserted Martinez's finger into an electronic device, where it remained for about two minutes.

The attendant then said, "Undress and lie down on your back on the examination table." Martinez complied and the attendant touched a laser pen to the records crystal in Martinez's ear. The laser self-aligned, and in about five seconds beeped, indicating it had downloaded the records from the crystal. The clerk told Martinez to stay on the table and to make himself comfortable. Then he left the room.

Martinez thought to himself that it wasn't very easy to get comfortable lying nude on a plastic examination table but he tried his best. He hated that he felt completely vulnerable. At least the temperature felt good and he could hear some nondescript music playing. He lost track of time until the next thing he heard was a hollow voice on the speaker asking him a question.

"What was that? I missed the question," Martinez said, startled.

"I asked about your transplant. There's nothing in our records about your surgery."

"I had the transplant four weeks ago."

"Okay, just a minute," the speaker said.

In a few more minutes, another question: "Where did you have your transplant?"

"At Orlando Government."

"You didn't have it here or at another IORC hospital?"

"No, I told you I had it at Government."

"Okay," the voice said. The clerk was looking at the information from Martinez's records and trying to understand the discrepancy of an IORC heart and a non-IORC transplant.

The technician stared at the computer reading from Martinez's records crystal and the information on the heart that the scanner had identified. According to the IORC records, the heart had been transplanted into another man three years before.

The technician had heard of such things and they were, of course, provided for in his procedures program, but he had never personally had a Code 6. He pressed the Help button on the screen of his computer and asked for directions. "Upon suspicion of a Code 6 take no further action and notify the Quality Control Manager immediately. Keep the patient under continuous observation and do not allow him to leave the examination room under any circumstances."

He gave his ID number and asked to speak to the QC immediately.

As he expected, he met resistance from the first operator, who advised him that the QC was not available to speak to technicians and that he should follow normal procedures. He then invoked the Code 6, the operator checked her list for the code, and then his call was transferred to the QC's personal secretary. She told him that LeBearc was out of the building, but that she would call him and to hold.

While the technician waited, he saw Martinez saying something, so he turned on the intercom. "Yes, Mr. Martinez, what can we do for you?"

"I need to take a leak," Martinez said.

"Beg your pardon?"

"I need to piss. You know, urinate," Martinez said, angry now.

"Oh, just a minute," and he flipped off the communications switch and turned to the junior technician sitting at an adjoining console. "Get down there with a urine bottle right away. We can't let this guy out of the examination room." The junior tech picked up a specimen bottle and headed into the exam room.

"Here, you'll have to use this," the junior tech said to Martinez, holding out the specimen bottle with a gloved hand.

"Like hell," said Martinez. "Just tell me where the restroom is and I'll come right back." He stood, reaching for his trousers.

"No, sir, you can't do that. You've got to stay in the examination room once the examination starts."

"Bullshit," Martinez said, pulling on his trousers.

"No, you can't leave, sir," the technician said while turning around to speak into the camera in the corner. "I need some help down here."

Martinez looked up at the camera and then at the technician.

"What the hell's going on? What do you mean, help? I think I'm going home," Martinez said, and zipped up his pants.

"No, sir," the technician said, reaching out and grabbing his arm. "You have to stay here."

"Hands off, asshole," Martinez said, shaking the man's hand off his arm and facing him squarely. Martinez was much larger and stronger and the technician backed away.

"I don't know what the fuck is goin' on around here, but I'm leaving. Now get out of my way," Martinez said, stuffing his underwear in his pocket, and pulling on his shirt. Just then, two more technicians came in, one of them considerably larger than Martinez.

"Now, sir, just calm down. You're getting upset and excited and that's not good for you. These tests cost a fortune, so we need to just keep you here in the room until they're finished," the smaller of the two new technicians said. The big one simply stood between Martinez and the door, with his arms folded.

"Yeah? Well, I do mind. I'm leaving. I'll take care of this at Orlando Government." He started for the door. The large technician moved a step forward and put his hands on Martinez's shoulders.

"Sir, you have to get back on that examination table," he ordered.

Martinez tried to push by him, without success.

"Give him an SCL," said a voice through the loudspeaker. Martinez stopped and stared at the speaker.

The first technician reached into a drawer and took out a bottle and an air injection syringe. He attached the drug to the air needle and Martinez began to struggle, now in a panic. He tried to move away but the large technician pinned him in place. He pulled one arm free and punched the junior technician, sending the man into the wall and onto the floor. The man with the syringe held the nozzle next to Martinez's arm and pulled the trigger. Martinez heard a slight hiss and felt his muscles go slack; then he lost control of his bladder.

"Now just calm down, sir. We have to finish the examination and you're getting yourself all excited. If you don't be still, you'll hurt yourself." They put him back on the table and removed his shirt and trousers. Unable now to move his arms or legs in any coordinated way, he trembled and felt his limbs go numb. He could hear and see perfectly and he knew what was happening, but his muscles simply would not respond to his commands. He was fully conscious, but completely paralyzed.

Back in the control room the secretary had finally reached LeBearc who now spoke with the head technician. "Sir, we have a Code 6 here and we've had some trouble with him. We gave him a succinylcholine injection to keep him quiet."

"What kind of organ is it?" LeBearc asked.

"A heart," the technician said.

"Call the autopsy area and get whoever is on duty there in forensic cardiology up to the control room right away. And keep this contained. In fact, I want you to clear the control room of everyone else."

"Yes, sir." He turned to the other people in the room. "Okay, everybody out. Shut everything down and forget this ever happened."

Within a few minutes, Dr. Thomas entered the control room. "I'm here from autopsy. What's the problem?"

"There's a Code 6 in the examination area and the QC's on the way."

LeBearc walked into the room five minutes later. He approached the console and flipped a few switches, replaying the digital recording of the last few minutes at high speed. Everything that was on all monitors was constantly recorded. He watched the struggle, the administration of the drug, and then turned back to the monitor. He brought up Martinez's personal records and the data

showing the supposed recipient of the heart in question.
He pressed several other buttons and a scanner extended
on an arm out of the ceiling of Martinez's exam room and
passed over the man's chest. LeBearc noticed Martinez's
eyes following it as it slowly passed back and forth above
him.

Martinez was frantically trying to get off the table. He
slowly regained minimal use of his hands and feet as the
drug wore off. They twitched and jerked as he tried to
control his muscles and escape. He tried again to scream
but still couldn't make a sound.

The QC verified the green numbers on the second scanner screen. He had no doubt whatsoever. Hesitating for a
few seconds, he noticed that Dr. Thomas was in the room.
"What are you doing here?"

"I got a call to come up from autopsy."

"You can go," the QC said to the technician.

Looking back at Martinez one more time, the QC entered his personal six-digit number into the computer as a
password. He typed the words "Code 6, deactivation" and
then the serial number of the heart. The screen inquired
his authorization. He typed in Code 6, and his personal
number again. The screen then reported a sixteen-digit
number. The QC typed in the sixteen digits, looked up at
Martinez, who was staring into the camera, and pressed
the enter button. The computer then inquired, "Are you
sure? Y/N." Hesitating for only a second, he looked into
Martinez's face, and hit the Y key.

Located in the ceiling above the examination table, a
transmitter sent a microwave signal to the IORC electronic module attached to Martinez's heart. Martinez's
body stiffened. The heart monitor showed that the organ
was beating in an arrhythmic fashion; when one chamber
began to contract, another would also contract, with the
result that no blood was being pumped. In a few seconds,
Martinez's back arched high into the air. His entire body
trembled and convulsed a few times and then fell back

onto the table. The QC checked the monitor display of Martinez's vital signs picked up by sensors above the examination table. He saw the blood pressure had fallen to zero, respiration came quick and shallow, and the heart fluttered without effect. He watched for three or four minutes more until the heart itself, deprived of any blood, ceased beating altogether. Sometime during the process he switched off the alarm, which indicated that Martinez had died.

He turned and looked at Thomas. "Have the body moved down to autopsy. Remove the identifier module from the heart and bring the module to me directly after the procedure. Make out a death certificate showing the cause of death as sudden heart failure. Make a video of the autopsy except the module removal. Make sure the tape's good, then cremate the body, heart included. Meanwhile I intend to track down the doctor who transplanted that organ." The QC turned around and walked out of the room.

Dr. Thomas tried to catch his breath. He looked around but nothing registered. He had seen patients die, of course—even during surgery on a few occasions—but he had never witnessed anything like what had just transpired. He knew that IORC policy prohibited retransplant of an IORC organ, ostensibly for purposes of quality control due supposedly to the high incidence of complications. Intuitively he had suspected that a Code 6 could lead to something like this—and now he knew for sure. LeBearc had treated it as routine.

He also realized then that he could be in Martinez's place; LeBearc was capable of anything.

He looked at the monitor and saw Martinez's body lying on the table. In a few minutes the technicians would remove it and take it to the autopsy room. He'd better protect himself; he didn't trust LeBearc. Thomas removed a blank video microcassette from the supply cabinet, put the cassette in the video system, and made a high-speed copy of the events that had just taken place in Martinez's room. LeBearc had been careless. He had not turned off the automatic recording. The copying took approximately fifteen seconds. Thomas popped out the microcassette and put it in his pocket, wondering how he might even use the tape to his advantage.

Later that afternoon, as Thomas was leaving the hospital, he had forgotten that the videotape could not be carried off the premises without detection. As he got off the elevator and passed into the reception area, a monitor at the security desk beeped and a security guard said, "Sir, could you step over here a moment?" The guard immediately recognized Thomas.

Thomas recognized the police officer, Burrows, immediately, too. He had forgotten that he was to be hired by security. "What is it?" Thomas asked.

"You have something in your pocket that tripped the scanner." *Oh shit! Of all people to catch him smuggling.* Thomas reached into his pocket and took out the videotape, mentally cursing his own negligence. He should have remembered the rules and gotten the tape out some other way. Now he had to ditch it or risk the consequences. Burrows would not do him any favors, that was for sure.

"I forgot to leave this upstairs," he said. "It's worthless now. In fact, you might as well just throw it away." He tossed it on the desk and walked out of the building.

Burrows looked at the tape. Nothing but junk, he thought, probably some medical lecture, but decided to take a look at it anyway.

He inserted it into his console's video viewer. The tape began with a man taking off his clothes.

*We'll, I'll be damned, we've got a pervert on our hands here,* Burrows thought, smiling. *Think I'll hold onto this.* He kept watching and in a few minutes saw a technician go back into Martinez's room carrying a specimen bottle. He watched with growing fascination as the other technicians filled the room. By the time the tape ended, the grin had disappeared from Burrows's face.

"My God," he whispered to himself. His hands trembled as he ejected the tape, placed it on the desk, covered it with a piece of paper, and then looked around to make sure no one was watching him. He would have to think this one through very carefully.

Burrows was in a public area, but he would have to go back inside to change out of his uniform to go home. And before he could leave his station to go change, his replacement would come.

As Burrows watched the people coming and going through the front doors, he struggled with the problem. Only a few minutes of his shift remained. He knew he would have to take a risk. He took out his sunglasses case. Opening it, he put the micro-sized tape behind one of the lenses. Then he laid the case down next to the console. He spread his procedures manual on the desk in front of him and pretended to study it, waiting for his replacement. When he arrived, Burrows pretended to be startled. He jumped, dropped the book, and knocked over a cup of coffee. "Shit," he said as he reached into the desk drawer for some paper towels.

"Hey, man, you're not supposed to be reading when you're on duty. You're supposed to be watching for terrorists or something," laughed the guard. Burrows dabbed at the coffee he had spilled on his pants. He hoped he wasn't overplaying it.

"I'm supposed to go to a basketball game tonight and I was trying to get some of this studying in so I wouldn't feel so guilty about it," Burrows explained. He gathered up his book, threw the paper towels on top of the desk next to the glasses case, and walked back inside to the locker room.

The replacement sat down, threw the paper towels in

the trash can, and immediately saw the case. "Hey," he called, but Burrows was just passing through the door to the employees' locker room. He'd wait and give Burrows the glasses as he came out. Burrows changed his clothes quickly, and headed out by way of the security desk. The guard held out his glasses case. "You forgot these. You need to go back and put them in your locker."

"I don't have time now. If I go back in I'll miss the start of the game. I'll just take them with me." He held out his hand.

"You can't do that; it's against the rules," the guard said. "You're not allowed to take company property off the premises. You know that."

Burrows's heart was up in his throat. "How about hanging onto them for me until tomorrow, then. Just leave them here at the desk and I'll pick them up when I come in."

"You're going to have to learn the way it works around here. If you leave these glasses here, they'll be gone by tomorrow and then you'll have to pay for them. Here," the guard said, tossing the case to him. "Take 'em with you, but next time try to keep all your shit together." The guard switched off the metal detector and motioned Burrows to pass through.

"Right. See you," Burrows said, putting the case in his shirt pocket. He walked out the door to the parking lot. He wasn't sure what he would do with the tape, but at least he had it.

An IORC psychologist, whose only job it was to inform the families of patients who died, contacted Mrs. Martinez. The method of notification was carefully calculated to reduce any animosity the family might have toward IORC. Considerable research showed that in virtually all instances of death of a surgery patient, the family had a psychological need to blame someone, even when no one was at fault.

Mrs. Martinez broke down in tears. Jorge Martinez shouted in anger that the doctor had lied to them about his father.

It would be the next morning before Mrs. Martinez could gather herself together enough to call David West and tell him. By then, Jorge's hostility was beginning to rub off on her.

"Dr. West, I suppose it won't be any big surprise to you, but I thought I ought to tell you that my husband died yesterday," she said.

"What!" said David, his blood freezing.

"As if you didn't expect it," she said. "They said his heart just quit."

"That's impossible," he groaned, his mind racing. "I saw him just a few days ago and he was in excellent condition. I released him to return to work. There wasn't anything wrong with his heart. There's got to be some kind of mistake."

"There's a mistake somewhere, that's for sure," she said bitterly. "Why didn't you tell us the truth? We would rather have had some warning that he might die."

"I did tell you the truth. He was no more likely to die from a heart attack than anyone else—probably less likely, in fact. Tell me what happened."

"He went in for a physical examination that the company required before he could go back in the engine room. From what they told us, he had sudden heart failure during the examination, and he died right there, on the examination table. The autopsy showed that his heart stopped. There's no mistake."

"Where did this happen?" West asked, a shudder passing through him. He was afraid he already knew.

"It happened at the IORC hospital," she said.

He took a deep breath. "I'm very sorry, Mrs. Martinez."

"Well, I'm very sorry, too. I suppose it's not your fault; you did everything you could for him. I just wish we had known that he might die like this. Jorge and I are just so upset we don't know what to do. They even cremated him without asking us."

"The cremation is routine. The IORC is entitled to use any transplantable organs and to cremate the remains; that's part of their program. If there's anything I can do, please let me know."

"No, there's nothing anyone can do now," she said, and hung up the phone.

# 8

David sat by the telephone with his eyes closed, trying to calm himself. He refused to accept what he intuitively knew had happened. He needed another explanation. *The IORC saved lives; it didn't murder people.* Perhaps there was something about IORC hearts that caused complications when they were retransplanted or some secret pharmaceutical was necessary to keep an IORC heart functioning. Maybe it was just denial, but David was certain there was nothing wrong with the transplant surgery itself.

But the fact remained that the patient was dead. Could David have screwed up somehow?

Later he went through every word of Martinez's hospital records looking for any mistake or oversight. The only unusual thing was the electronic device attached to the IORC heart, which appeared to have no effect on the organ but was simply an identifier. This same heart had apparently been functioning perfectly in the accident victim.

West tried to telephone Dr. Byrd, but was told that he no longer worked at the hospital.

He called IORC. "I'm Dr. West at Orlando Government. A patient of mine died there yesterday and I need to review the autopsy you did on him." David was given an access code that allowed him into a limited part of the confidential area of IORC's Web site. He was able to review the autopsy on his own computer at Government. It stated the cause of death as sudden heart failure but gave no further explanation.

"Access to the video of the autopsy cannot be granted without a release from the next of kin," an automated voice from the Web site informed him.

David decided that he had better see the administrator.

"I've got something bad to tell you. I probably should have done this when it first came up, but for whatever reason, I didn't. Anyway, you need to know about it now. You remember Martinez, my heart transplant patient?"

"Of course," Administrator Long said.

"He died yesterday, supposedly from sudden heart failure."

"I'm sorry," the administrator said.

"There was a problem during the surgery." West didn't know how to go on without implicating Byrd or appearing to be blaming him. Nevertheless, he had to tell Long everything.

"The heart we transplanted was an IORC heart. I think that may have something to do with Martinez's death."

"When did *you* find out it was an IORC heart?" Long asked.

"I didn't find out until I scanned the heart when the transplant was complete. Then there was nothing I could do. I couldn't remove the heart, so I had to close the patient's chest. But there was nothing wrong with the organ as far as I could tell."

"And Byrd gave it to you," Long said, rather than asked. "Did he know it was an IORC heart when he delivered it or did he discover it when you did?"

"I think you ought to ask Dr. Byrd," David said.

"I did ask Dr. Byrd," the administrator said with no pleasure in his revelation.

"When did you find out?" David asked, now feeling like a fool. He was on trial, apparently.

"I found out yesterday afternoon when I got a call from an IORC official who told me a patient had died during an examination. They were nice enough not to make a note on the autopsy that it was an IORC heart. I assume you know it's against the law for us to retransplant an IORC organ."

"I had no idea we were doing that until too late."

"Well, Byrd did. His view is that there's no reason not to transplant an IORC organ if it will save a patient's life. It's a complicated moral and ethical question, of course, but not difficult legally. The only thing I could do under the circumstances was to dismiss Dr. Byrd. In the meantime I've been trying to figure out what to do about you."

"Have you decided?" David snapped.

"Look, David." Long leaned forward over his desk. "I believe you when you say you didn't know. The worst part is that the poor man died after all this."

"He was my patient. I know how bad it is. That's why I wanted to talk to you. Something doesn't add up. The antirejection drugs that are used are hard on the patient and the organ, but those problems usually develop the first few days after the transplant. Martinez showed no signs of complications. I examined him several times after the transplant. The last exam was four days before he died. There wasn't anything wrong with the heart, or the transplant procedure; I'm sure of it. It's possible that there is something about IORC hearts that causes complications if they're transplanted a second time."

"What are you suggesting?"

"I don't know exactly. I guess I'm not sure it was an accident."

Long sank back in his chair. "Would you like some advice?"

"What?" West asked.

"We try to help everyone we can here, but sometimes it just doesn't work out. I think you ought to try to forget about Martinez. I don't think any of it was your fault."

"Is that just advice or do you know something I don't?"

"It's just advice, but it's good advice. I hope you'll think it over," Long said and stood up, indicating that the meeting was over.

That night David sat in his dimly lit apartment staring into the shadows. He saw Mike Martinez's face as it looked when he'd tried to thank David for his new heart. "Maybe I'm in the wrong profession," David said to the shadows. "Or maybe it really isn't my fault."

If IORC killed Martinez, David would expose them. They would not get away with it. But first he had to exclude any other explanation, including his own sense of guilt.

He spent all of his spare moments during the next several days glued to a computer terminal researching medical journals. He looked for any clue that could scientifically explain what had happened to Martinez, but without success. The closest he came was a footnote in an article written ten years before in which the author hypothesized that there might be difficulties with a second transplant of an IORC organ.

Janette called David from Washington the next day. "I got your calls on my answering machine and I wanted to let you know what was happening. I got transferred to another department and sent to Washington for school."

"Transferred? Will you be living in Washington now?" David's voice expressed his disappointment.

"No." She laughed. "I'll be back in Orlando in a week or so."

"Why a transfer?"

"It wasn't my idea. Apparently I upset IORC and they slapped me down for it. It's complicated and part of the job, I suppose. You remember I told you about the drunk IORC doctor case?"

"Funny you should mention IORC. You remember my transplant patient Michael Martinez? Well, he died a couple of days ago. At IORC."

"I thought he was okay after the transplant," Janette said.

"He was. That's what's strange. It doesn't make sense. The IORC seems to be turning up everywhere."

"You said you were going to interview with them. I hope you decide against a job there. You're not their type, and besides, I don't trust them."

"Why? Do you know something?"

"Just be careful. Call it a bad feeling or whatever you like."

"Thanks for your concern." Her comments sent a ripple of apprehension through him. She was a very perceptive person and not someone whose opinion he would ignore.

That same week he received a letter from the IORC Medical Personnel Office inviting him to visit the Orlando center. The letter said that the visit was part of the interview process and would give him the opportunity to see the facility and meet some of the personnel and consider a position with IORC.

He made the appointment, but not to seek an IORC job. He no longer trusted the IORC, and had no intention of going to work for them. The invitation sparked a plan in him: He would visit the facility and see if he could prove anything more about his theories regarding IORC hearts. He would get to the bottom of Martinez's death.

When Dr. Thomas went into the QC's office, LeBearc was sitting in his chair at his computer terminal. "The doctor who made that transplant is a man named David West," LeBearc said. "Ironically, he's been under consideration for a position here. He's quite special."

Thomas said, "Well, from what I saw during the autopsy, his work is good—considering the limitations at Orlando Government."

"He's recently completed his residency and is in his first few weeks of actual practice. He was forced to resign his first surgical residency at Yale because of an unauthorized heart operation—another irony, don't you think? I believe he has his own ideas about how things should work in medicine and follows his own rules. He will undoubtedly be touchy about his patient's death. As it turns out, he didn't know he was transplanting one of our hearts. A pathologist who is involved in the Equal Access movement provided it to him.

"This West is someone I want to start off as a researcher. I want you to show him around, answer his questions, up to a point. Find out how interested he is in us. We're ready to offer him a job, but we need to make sure there'll be no problem from this Code 6 incident. Other aspects of his background make him particularly interesting—but potentially dangerous. Schedule a heart transplant during his visit and let him observe." LeBearc waved Thomas out. It was his way of letting Thomas know he was back in good graces and to reward him for following orders. Then he called the security manager and ordered electronic monitoring of West.

Cost being no object, the IORC monitored all its employees and had special, more powerful programs—copied from the U.S. Defense Intelligence Agency—to monitor specific persons of interest, now including David West.

Despite his intention to spy, David couldn't help being impressed by the IORC facility. In the huge, modern buildings, everything was clean and in a state of perfect repair. The gardens lived up to their reputation as a famous showplace. Pathways flanked by exotic plants meandered through junglelike growth.

Following directions he had received from IORC, David entered the organ transplant building. He identified himself to the security guard, who looked first at the photo of David on his screen, then back at him. "Welcome to IORC, Dr. West. You'll be entering the employees' section, and we have certain security procedures that are mandatory for all visitors.

"In a minute someone will be here to take you to the locker rooms. You're required to change into an IORC uniform and leave all your personal items in a locker. Your identification number today is zero six five and you must include the zero. You should remember it: zero six five. You may be required to give that identification number, and it also will be the combination on your locker." The guard touched a spot on the computer terminal and a laminated plastic pass bearing the computer-generated photograph of David ejected from a printer. "When you put on your IORC uniform, attach this badge to the left pocket."

A clerk led David down the hall and into a locker room. David changed into the uniform, similar to most hospital scrubs, and emblazoned with the IORC insignia, tested his combination, and then closed the locker.

Dr. Thomas entered, wearing a green uniform similar to David's but well tailored and made out of a heavier, more expensive material. "Hi, my name's Richard Thomas. I'm one of IORC's transplant surgeons. You must be Dr. West," he said as they shook hands.

"Yes, David West."

"Well, come on and let me show you around," he said as he opened the door for David. "We have a lot of security rules around here, but they're all necessary. We have to be careful that patients' records remain confidential. The lives of a great many people depend upon us. You get used to it."

Dr. Thomas first took them into a control center where a block of patients' rooms were monitored.

"We've developed our antirejection process so that the drugs are only needed for about a week instead of the normal three to five weeks. We get the patients up and out and back to their normal lives much quicker."

"How long does it usually take before you can release them?" David asked.

"We're usually able to send them home two weeks from the day of the transplant," Thomas said. "You've been working under completely different conditions at Government, I'm sure. You'll see what I mean."

They left the area and walked down a hall into a room that overlooked through a glass wall what David thought was an operating room. More than a dozen computer screens were arranged above a console of switches, and one large screen in the center was approximately four feet square. A large padded captain's chair was situated directly in front of the big screen.

"This is a transplant procedure area," Thomas said with evident pride.

"The actual operating room looks very small," David observed. "How do all the support personnel and doctors fit in there?"

"That's the patient area you're looking at. We do the operating from in here."

"What do you mean? How do you do that if the patient's on the other side of that glass?" David asked. He was looking at the array of instruments and mechanical arms positioned above the plastic operating table.

"I have a surgery scheduled in an hour and I'll show you how it all works, but basically, we've eliminated virtually all direct physical contact with the patient during the actual surgical process so as to reduce contamination and infection and control the quality of our surgical procedures."

"You mean you operate on the patient by remote control from in here?" West asked, incredulous.

"Exactly. We do everything by manipulating the computer controls from in here. I can do surgery a hundred times more precisely this way than you can with your hands. There's a series of video cameras and fiberoptic lenses that can see inside the heart and arteries until the last couple of staples are set. These images are digital, full three-D holograms. I control the instruments by moving my fingers or a stylus on the large screen you see there. It's a touch-screen computer control. I select what instruments I want, magnify the image to the extent I need, and then simply point where I want the incision or staples to go."

"What if something goes wrong?" West asked.

"Our procedures have been perfected through thousands of transplants throughout the world. The protocol is identical at each of our facilities whether it's in Orlando, Paris, or Tokyo. Things don't go wrong very often. When they do, however, I'm much better off with the computer controls here. In fact, built into the system itself are procedures for every complication that has ever arisen. I simply call up that complication—if the computer hasn't already done so—and then the computer leads me through the proper steps to resolve it."

"This is truly incredible," West said. He was overwhelmed by the technology and by the idea of doing a heart transplant without actually touching the patient. Everything Dr. Thomas said made complete theoretical sense. But it was all secret. He had never heard of any of this.

"How long does it take for you to do a heart transplant?" West asked.

"We routinely do them in less than two hours. If the patient's young and everything goes smoothly, I've gotten them down as short as an hour and twenty minutes," Thomas said, with no attempt to conceal his pride.

"It takes me longer than that to remove the old heart and hook the patient to a mechanical heart."

"Well, as you'll see, we only use a heart machine to cool the patient down. It's attached to the femoral artery. By using hypothermia, plus a couple of pharmaceuticals we've developed to speed the effect, we turn off the mechanical heart after cool-down. Of course we have the mechanical heart ready in case there is a problem. The way we do it, there's less than twenty minutes during which no blood is being pumped to the brain, and our patients experience no brain damage," Thomas said. This part of the process always amazed new doctors.

"That seems impossible. I've never heard of such pharmaceuticals. We use hypothermia, too, but it takes much longer and we need the mechanical heart full-time. Are these drugs written up in medical journals?"

"Our pharmaceuticals are proprietary; we don't disclose anything about them. What I'm telling you and showing you now is all considered confidential. We have an entire division that does research and development of pharmaceuticals. But since our procedures are so different from the ones used in public hospitals, our transplant drugs would be of no use there."

"I was just about to ask you how I could get some," David said, understanding their great value. "Do you have any special drugs that are necessary to keep a heart working after transplant?"

"No, once the transplant is completed there is no need for special drugs for the hearts. They function perfectly." Thomas narrowed his eyes and looked at West. "Why do you ask that?"

"Well, I had a problem recently with a patient. I guess it's no secret that we inadvertently transplanted a heart from one of your patients who was killed in an accident. I didn't know it was one of your organs until the surgery was completed and we were ready to close. Then we scanned the heart and found the electronic module. Anyway, the operation was a complete success and the patient was doing fine. I sent him home, clean bill of health. The next thing I know he's dead. As a matter of fact, your name sounds familiar. Do you do autopsies here?"

"You must be talking about Martinez. As it happens, I did do the autopsy. There are no special drugs needed for our hearts. I think your problem was that this heart had been transplanted once before. We don't think that works reliably. We won't transplant a heart a second time because of the likelihood of complications."

"What kind of complications?"

"Sudden failures."

"Did you find anything wrong with the transplant?"

"No. Everything I found is right there in the autopsy report. It appeared to me that there was sudden heart failure. He started having arrhythmias and expired in the examination room before anything could be done. I checked over the surgery you did and it looked okay to me. Those valves were rather crude, but I know that's the procedure sometimes used in the public hospitals during transplants and I really didn't see anything wrong. No, I think he just had heart failure as a result of a retransplanted heart."

They completed their tour and then returned to the operating room after stopping off for coffee. As they entered the control room, two technicians at computer monitors awaited Thomas. West could see through the observation glass that the patient had already been brought in and was on the table. Mechanical arms extending from above and below the operating table were articulated in several places. The arms were painted refrigerator white, and the joints and moving parts were of brushed stainless steel. Each arm had at its end a number of tools and appendages.

Two technicians inside the patient area wore plastic

suits. The patient appeared to be a man in his early forties. His skin looked blue.

Thomas snapped off some orders and sat down in the chair in front of the control panel. He manipulated several of the controls. A readout of the patient's vital signs scrolled across one screen. It showed his body temperature to be sixty-five degrees Fahrenheit. A mechanical heart pump attached to the patient at the femoral artery on his left leg maintained a blood flow while the preparations got under way.

Without a word, Thomas pressed several more computer controls and the large color 3-D screen in front of him lit up with a high-resolution video picture of the patient's chest. On the computer screen icons depicted dozens of different instruments. The readouts showed that the patient's temperature had now dropped to sixty degrees.

Thomas pressed a button to the right of the computer panel and a green border surrounded the screen. In a window on his screen in the upper right-hand corner, text began slowly to scroll and an announcement came over the speaker indicating that the heart transplant program had begun.

West watched in fascination as the computer took over. It calculated the depth and type of incision to be made based upon information it had gathered from X rays and sonograms, and then requested an order from Thomas to proceed.

He touched the "OK" spot on the screen and the laser immediately began cutting open the patient's chest. It did so at a high speed—faster than was humanly possible—completing the incision in about three or four seconds. Two arms opened the chest and placed tubes in the appropriate locations without any further direction from Thomas. During a pause of about thirty seconds, the computer monitored any changes in the condition of the patient. Then an announcement indicated that it was time to begin installation of the new heart. Thomas again pressed the "OK" spot, and one of the mechanical arms removed the new heart from a receptacle and placed it, with all the gentleness of a surgeon, next to the patient's own heart within the chest cavity. Then the robotic arms severed the connective tissue, loosened the patient's damaged heart, and lifted it free, though it remained connected to the arteries and blood vessels. The replacement organ was slipped into place and would be connected to the arteries and vessels one by one, allowing a more precise graft.

"I'll take over manually," Thomas said. He pressed the red button on the computer console and a loud buzzer sounded for several seconds. The borders around each of the screens changed from green to amber and a flashing title at the top of the main screen read "manual override." The text in the upper right-hand corner stopped scrolling, began flashing for a few seconds, and then stabilized in an amber glow. In larger letters the title changed to "next procedure," followed by a description in writing and an announcement over the speaker. Thomas's left hand could touch any of the instrument icons and also the areas of the screen marked "increase" or "decrease." The robotic arms matched the tracings of his finger precisely and instantly.

He moved his finger around a few times to make certain that the arm was following it, then selected a laser scalpel. The moment he did so, the computer blared out, "Warning! Blood flow not stopped," and a red flashing border appeared around the screen. Thomas touched a clamp icon and pressed a spot on the screen to magnify the image of the ascending aorta to six inches across instead of its actual size of just over an inch. He then moved his finger to a portion of the artery, adjacent to the heart, held it there and pressed a button with his left hand. A mechanical arm placed a clamp on the artery at that point. Thomas repeated the procedure on the superior vena cava, the large vessel through which blood returns to the heart from the body. Next, he turned off the mechanical heart, stopping blood flow altogether and selected the laser scalpel again. The red flashing light stopped and the scrolling in the upper right-hand window continued. He increased the magnification again and slowly traced his finger along the ascending aorta above the coronary arteries. As he did so, the mechanical arm made an incision with a laser scalpel and severed the artery in a fine clean line, exactly duplicating the movements of Thomas's fingers. Because of the great magnification on the screen, Thomas could precisely control the location of the incision. He repeated the process on the superior vena cava, completely severing the heart from the patient.

David could hardly believe what he was seeing. In a few minutes, through use of the robotic arms, Thomas was able to accomplish what took David more than an hour of careful, painstaking work. Thomas noticed that he had duly impressed David, and pressed the automatic button allowing the computer to take over the rest of the procedure. As soon as he did so, the border on the screen changed from amber to green and the computer announced it was correcting an uneven incision and proceeded to do so at almost blinding speed, removing all of the tiny irregularities inherent in Thomas's manual efforts. The patient's own heart was quickly removed, the transplanted heart fixed into place, and the arteries and vessels sutured and bonded in a matter of less than five minutes.

The computer proceeded through its program, occasionally asking for approval to move on to the next step, which Thomas gave by simply pressing the "OK" spot on the screen. David noted that Thomas watched but made no attempt to concentrate.

As the program progressed, West saw, without fully understanding its sophistication, that the computer constantly measured the size and shape of the patient and of the transplanted heart and made appropriate adjustments to accommodate those differences. On several occasions the screen showing the patient's vital signs indicated that certain drugs West did not recognize had been administered. The patient's body temperature remained in the hypothermic range and the brain and new heart were inactive.

The computer indicated that it was ready to begin raising the body temperature and activating the replacement heart. Thomas touched "OK," and the pump attached to the artery in the patient's groin began pumping again to warm the blood. A slight trickle appeared on one of the incisions, but almost before West could see it, the computer had responded and the mechanical arm had applied additional bonding adhesive and some sort of plastic film to the area. Less than a teaspoon of blood had escaped. The process took about ten minutes, and as the patient's body temperature rose above seventy degrees, the brain wave pattern resumed and some muscle contractions in the heart began.

The computer somehow stimulated the heart, and it began to beat. There were no wires leading to a pacemaker, which puzzled David. In a few seconds and without any further outside stimulation it was beating steadily and strongly. When the mechanical pump shut off, the blood pressure never wavered. The computer requested permission to close the patient's chest, Thomas pressed the "OK" button, and the wound was closed almost as fast as zipping a zipper. When that procedure was concluded Thomas stood up, stretched, bent his fingers backward, and suggested that he and David have lunch. The technicians seemed equally nonchalant. For them, it was just routine. In fact, they were already moving the patient out of the operating room as the clerks in the control room began to shut down the various monitors and consoles.

David and his colleagues outside of the IORC functioned at a primitive level of technology compared to what he had just seen. It was like comparing what he did now to the efforts of doctors a hundred years before, who operated without X rays or any means of monitoring the patient.

"I really can't tell you how impressed I am. The failure rate for these surgeries must be very low," David said.

"For all intents and purposes, it's zero. At first, though, we did have surgical deaths. But I'm not aware of any surgical failures in the last, oh, at least three years. Even though we're dealing with the uncertainties of individuals, we almost never have any complications during surgery, and when we do there are programs and procedures that immediately go into effect to correct any complications. I'm not saying we don't ever lose patients, but it's usually later, if other organs begin to fail because of the stress. Hence J Factors. We choose people for heart transplants whose other organs are in good shape and who have a high probability of success. Otherwise, we would simply be wasting the organ."

Before the IORC tour, David believed the company may have killed Mike Martinez. But what a place it was; they were years ahead of anyone else. It was hard to believe they would deliberately kill anyone. Yet he couldn't shake an instinctive sense the place was overwhelmingly sinister.

David was invited to a party at LeBearc's house for the following evening, and he felt compelled to attend. Maybe he could learn something more in a social setting. He decided to call Janette and invite her to go along.

"I'm glad you're back."

"Me, too. What's up?"

"I've been invited to a party tomorrow night and I thought you might like to go. I ought to tell you, though, it's at an IORC big shot's house. I know you're not fond of IORC after what happened in court, but I thought you might be curious enough to come along anyway. It might be interesting."

She did not want to have anything to do with IORC, but after going for a month without seeing David she was afraid that if she turned down the invitation it might be the last one she would get from him. "Why not? Maybe I'll try killing them with kindness, now," she said, summoning up much more diplomacy than she felt.


David drove through a neighborhood of multimillion-dollar residences and found his way to LeBearc's address. As he came around the last curve, he saw a modern architectural version of what in other times might have been an English country estate. The house was enormous; it looked more like a luxury resort, with fountains and bubbling pools, shady paths running through lush tropical growth, and several auxiliary buildings. In front was a parking lot with more than a dozen cars, almost exclusively European-made.

A tall elegant Frenchwoman in her early forties met them at the front door. In a thick accent she introduced herself as Charlotte LeBearc. She was wearing black slacks, an ivory silk blouse, and a string of pearls. Clearly comfortable in the role of hostess, she treated David and Janette as if they were old friends. Within thirty seconds Charlotte asked all the right questions and she had learned what Janette did, where she worked, and what her connection was to David. But Charlotte's animated movements seemed planned and vaguely exaggerated. Her hands and arms drew pictures in the air.

Janette and David both were awestruck by the house. To the left, an open spiral staircase reached from the lower-level pool up through the first floor, and then rose to a third floor and finally to an observation dome on a fourth level. The staircase wound around a central glass chandelier that was three stories tall. Sparse contemporary furniture dominated throughout. Recessed lighting panels illuminated the rooms. In the fireplace, real logs more than six feet long blazed. Outside the windows and beyond the swimming pool, a lake reflected the distant lights of downtown.

Both David and Janette were having difficulty listening to Charlotte LeBearc while at the same time trying to take in the view of the house and its surroundings. The affluence in which they had both grown up had not even prepared them for this level of opulence. Charlotte escorted them to a group of people and then she began a story about getting a speeding ticket. She pantomimed the traffic cop.

Charlotte's audience was captivated. But Janette was distracted. She found her mind wandering as she looked around the room. In the sea of strange faces, she caught sight of a familiar one: Wilson Hoffmeister stood near the glass wall overlooking the pool, surrounded by several people who were apparently enthralled by what he was saying.

She noticed that David seemed to find Charlotte LeBearc's story amusing.

After politely laughing at Charlotte's tale, David said, "Let's try to find our host. He's in charge of IORC for this entire region."

David glanced at Janette. She was stunning as usual tonight, dressed in a low-cut black gown; his body was already responding to the sight of her. Maybe they should get out of here and find somewhere more intimate. He was about to suggest this when she looked away.

"Damn," she muttered.

"What's wrong?"

"That's Dr. Thomas over there—the doctor who killed that man in the car accident, the one I prosecuted. Just my luck, he's here, too."

He then saw Dr. Thomas coming their way.

"Oh, shit!" grated Janette.

"Hello, David," Thomas said, and shook his hand. "And who is your friend?" he asked, narrowing his eyes in a hint of recognition. "I think I've met you, haven't I?"

"We met in court," she said.

Dr. Thomas hardly missed a beat. "Of course. I just didn't recognize you in a different context."

"Context is everything," she said.

"I hope there are no hard feelings."

"We weren't playing games, Doctor. Feelings don't have anything to do with it."

"I think you both should change the subject." It was Wilson Hoffmeister, standing behind them and frowning. "In fact, I insist on it," he said in his deep, commanding voice.

"This is Dr. West. He's a transplant cardiologist. He's looking over IORC. The QC invited him." Thomas was obviously uncomfortable around Hoffmeister, afraid, even.

"How do you do? Excuse me for intruding, but a lawyer is not supposed to discuss a case with the opposing party. At least not without the other lawyer present."

"I think that restriction relates to pending cases," Janette replied. "I understood that Dr. Thomas's case was suddenly dismissed."

"You're absolutely right. I stand corrected. But I don't want Dr. Thomas discussing the case with you anyway."

Before the following silence could become any more awkward, a distinguished man in his mid-fifties, wearing a meticulously tailored gray suit, appeared beside Hoffmeister. "A healthy discussion of the parameters of the law is always interesting. I am Andre LeBearc. Dr. Thomas, would you introduce the lady?"

"The lady is the lawyer who prosecuted my accident case. I don't think we had gotten as far as names. She's with Dr. West."

"My name is Janette Compton."

"I am pleased to meet you. As long as you are in my home, you may discuss anything with anyone you want." He looked pointedly at Hoffmeister. "Dr. West, I am happy to meet you and delighted that you could come, especially with such a lovely and obviously knowledgeable companion."

"Thank you," David said, thinking to himself how gifted LeBearc seemed at easing the mounting tension between his guests. He had expected Thomas to be there because the doctor was, apparently, David's contact with IORC. But it was too strange a coincidence that Thomas was also the man who had caused that horrible car accident Janette had told him about. He noticed that Janette's smile seemed forced.

"I hope you found your tour of our facility interesting. We are proud of it."

"It was impressive. The equipment you have is years more advanced than anything I've ever seen."

"The only other places that have such technology are other IORC centers. My job is quality control and IORC considers that paramount. We can save many lives with the instruments and procedures we have. It all depends on having the best doctors and creative people."

"But it seems to me that your procedures are so carefully detailed that creativity would be counterproductive."

"Ah, you have a point. However, for us to establish the best possible procedural guidelines and routines, we must have people constantly coming up with new ideas. There's always room for improvement. We try to find innovative doctors and research scientists—usually American, by the way."

"Why are they usually American?" Janette asked.

"We have tried people from other cultures. Some are brilliant in their own way, of course, but usually less creative. I think it's because America seems still to be a melting pot, despite all the efforts towards multiculturalism. In a few generations, there is no more cultural diversity, only generic Americans whose heritage is irrelevant. We Europeans are careful to maintain our separate national identities and cultures. Never mistake a Frenchman for a German, for example. Both would be insulted! My wife is a good example. Everywhere else, she dresses, acts, and even speaks French. But here, she takes my son to McDonald's and can order an Egg McMuffin without blinking an eye. Now that I think about it, maybe McDonald's is really the reason for America's ability to assimilate diverse cultures. A war wasn't needed to convert the Russians: you only had to open a McDonald's in Moscow."

There was polite laughter. For now the group seemed calmed, and LeBearc drifted away, replaced by his wife. When she came over, Thomas and Hoffmeister took their leave and she introduced David and Janette to several other people from IORC.

LeBearc rejoined Hoffmeister and Thomas. "The best way I know to keep a woman interested in a topic is to tell her she can't talk about it—especially when you can't actually prevent her from talking," LeBearc said to Hoffmeister and Thomas.

"Don't underestimate her," Hoffmeister said.

"I'm not. I want the entire thing over, and there is no sense in antagonizing that woman. I also want to hire West, and it doesn't help if we insult and embarrass his date. When you showed him around, was he interested in anything in particular?" he asked Thomas.

"No more so than you would expect any doctor to be. He did ask about the autopsy."

"What autopsy?" Hoffmeister asked.

"Would you excuse us, Wilson." LeBearc waited while Hoffmeister, at first taken aback, regained his composure.

"Of course," he said, and walked away.

"What did he ask about the autopsy?"

"He wanted to know what I had found; he asked about defects in our hearts and about special drugs. I think he believes that there may be something about our hearts that makes them nontransplantable a second time. I let him more or less figure that out for himself."

"He is not ready for the real explanation yet; he simply would not understand and accept the issues that necessitate our rules. Let him see the autopsy tape if he should ask," LeBearc said. He also made a mental note to add Janette Compton to the electronic surveillance list.

As they were driving home, David tried to soothe Janette, who was still steaming from the reminder of the Thomas case.

"Charm doesn't get it when you are covering up a crime. Those people *are* charming, I'll admit that, but they're also unscrupulous. I wouldn't put anything past them. In fact I think they're dangerous."

David would like to have voiced his agreement, but he still couldn't risk telling her about his suspicions concerning IORC. Nor could he tell her that his visit to their facility was actually an attempt to prove them capable of murder—he had a feeling that might put them both in jeopardy. For a person as direct as David, remaining silent was not easy. He decided to change the subject. "I don't suppose tonight would be a good time to show you some of the secret things we learn in medical school, would it—secret things we show only to special friends?"

"Somehow," she said, not smiling, "I'm just not in the mood."

# 9

When Janette arrived at her new office, she saw Betty Martinez waiting in one of the gray molded plastic chairs arranged in rows on the painted concrete floor.

"Why, hello," Janette said recognizing Betty immediately from her visit to the hospital with David several weeks ago. "What are you here for?"

"My husband died after the transplant."

"Yes, I'd heard through David—Dr. West—about your husband. I'm terribly sorry."

"I was told that I might be entitled to some benefits."

"Have you already been assigned to a lawyer?" Janette asked.

"No, I just came in and they gave me these forms to fill out. Nothing else has happened yet."

"I'll get your case assigned to me—that is, if it's okay with you."

"That would be wonderful. This is hard enough already. It would be a lot better if I could talk to someone I know."

Janette took the forms, and they went inside. She then showed Mrs. Martinez into her eight-by-eight office, which had glass walls and a door. Once they were settled, Janette began her formal UNILAW routine.

She explained in depth the system for benefits under circumstances like Betty Martinez's. When the UNIMED system went into effect, medical malpractice cases were outlawed. The UNIMED system includes a no-fault compensation program to pay for medical failures. A medical failure might occur even though there's no fault on the part of the doctor or the hospital, simply a failure in the medical care. In lieu of a jury trial, a case goes to an arbitrator, an impartial person appointed by the government, and all that's necessary is to prove that there has been a medical failure and then the benefits are available.

"There's no payment for any pain and suffering you've had, but there is compensation for the loss of income and for the other expenses, and there are certain benefits for spouses and children. Do you understand?" Janette asked.

"I understand, I think. My husband did die of what you said, you know, a medical failure. He got a heart transplant and the new heart quit. It must have been a medical failure."

"It's not that simple," Janette said. "You don't get the benefits if your husband died of natural causes, but only if his death was a result of some failure of the medical system. I think we will have to prove that something went wrong during or after the surgery that caused his heart failure. From what Dr. West told me, he doesn't know why it happened. I'll have to speak to him and see what he would say if he's required to testify. We're going to need his help."

"He told me that he would do anything he could. He's really a wonderful person," Mrs. Martinez said.

"I know, but when a doctor is asked to testify that something he did was a medical failure, he's usually very reluctant to say so."

"I don't mind calling and asking him," Mrs. Martinez said.

"No, let me do that," Janette said. "That's my job."

Janette placed a call to David and they agreed to meet in the afternoon at the golf club's snack bar.

David was twenty minutes late, and Janette had decided he wasn't coming. She was getting up to leave when he finally came in.

"I'm running late. Sorry. I hope you haven't been waiting very long."

"Only a few minutes," Janette said, looking at her watch.

"Sorry," David said again. He forced a smile and shrugged his shoulders to say he couldn't help it.

"I saw Betty Martinez today. She came to UNILAW. She wants to apply for benefits because of her husband's death."

"Well, I hope she does. I'll do anything I can to help."

"I'm glad you said that. I may need you to testify for her."

"Of course. No problem." He smiled at her, his gray eyes sparkling now that there was something he could do.

"It's not that simple. I want to make sure you understand exactly what's involved. This is really awkward, knowing you as a friend . . . What we will be trying to prove is that there was a medical failure. That's what we have to show for her to get the benefits."

David West's eyes narrowed. "Exactly what do you mean, a 'medical failure'?"

"What that means is that Martinez didn't die of natural causes. He died of something that had to do with his transplant."

"I didn't do anything wrong in the surgery, if that's what you're getting at. That's what I'll say if I testify."

"I'm not saying that you did anything wrong. But we have to prove that there was a complication and that he didn't just die of natural causes. What do you think happened?"

"Well, I talked to the doctor who did the autopsy and he agreed there was nothing wrong with the surgery." He sat back, breaking his flow of speech, and sighed. "I have some things I should explain to you since you're her lawyer now." David stared at the tabletop and organized his thoughts. The muscles in his jaw tightened.

"There's something that Mrs. Martinez doesn't know that I've decided might have to do with what happened. At the end of the surgery and before I closed Martinez's chest, we made a routine multiscan to make sure we hadn't left an instrument or anything inside. The scan showed that the new heart was an IORC heart. This was a total surprise to me. The hospital pathologist had supplied the organ. He knew it was from IORC, but he didn't tell me. He is in the Equal Access movement, and he told me that he believes we shouldn't let a patient die just because an available heart is supposed to be turned over to IORC."

"But you *know* IORC has a legal right to reclaim it," Janette said. "We talked about that. Is that why you asked about it before?"

"Yeah, that's why. I didn't do anything wrong, but the pathologist violated the law, no doubt about that. Anyway, the heart was already transplanted and I had to decide whether to leave it in and close Martinez's chest or remove it and let him die. That was an easy decision. I suppose he was sent to IORC for his permission-to-work exam because someone discovered he had an IORC heart."

"That might be enough to be a medical failure if it had something to do with his death," Janette replied.

"That's the problem," David said. "The heart looked healthy and tested within acceptable limits, so the fact that it was an IORC heart should have had nothing to do with it. Of course, legally, it was a problem, but it was not from a medical standpoint the cause of death. Unless there's something we don't know."

"Like what?" she asked.

He lowered his voice. "I don't know yet. But something's wrong. People don't just die spontaneously, particularly people who have had a heart transplant; that's not the way it works. Usually they get sick and there is some sort of rejection; they progressively get worse until they die. I don't know of any case where there's been sudden heart failure after a transplant. I can't prove anything now, but I think there might be something wrong with IORC hearts that we don't know about."

"Like what?"

"Well . . . I had some suspicions at first. But when I visited IORC I was so carried away by how amazing the facility was that I began to doubt my suspicions. And now I'm not sure what to think."

She took his hand. "David, what are you really saying?"

He thought for a moment, and then nodded. "Okay, here's the way I figure it. There are three possibilities and I can't prove a damn thing in any case yet, but here goes.

"Number one, there could be a special drug that is required to maintain an IORC heart after transplant that nobody but IORC knows about. Number two, the heart was flawed and couldn't withstand a retransplant. Number three—which I'm having trouble accepting—is that they did something deliberately to Martinez because he had illegally received one of their hearts. It's hard for me to believe IORC people are capable of murder. Still, as a scientist I can't rule it out."

Janette stared at him. "I can believe it," she said.

"The truth is, I've been struggling with this since the minute I found out he died. I have no medical explanation for a sudden death like his. I've tried to analyze whether I'm going through denial or have convenient paranoia. I can't actually believe that IORC deliberately killed him.

But I can't rule that out until some other explanation comes along. I suppose it's probably more likely that I made some kind of mistake." He bowed his head and looked at the table, making rings with the condensation on the bottom of his glass.

"Hey," she said, squeezing his hand in an attempt to rally him. "Don't be so hard on yourself. Maybe it's because I'm a lawyer, but I think deliberate homicide is a definite possibility. Something about the IORC gives me the creeps; everything they do is supposed to be so perfect, yet it's an ultrasecret organization. What are they hiding? If they are doing something like killing people, the public has a right to know and to stop them. Exactly how *did* you find out it was an IORC heart?"

He explained the electronic module attached to the heart.

"Maybe that had something to do with it," Janette said.

"I doubt it. It seems to be just an identification device. Anyway, the IORC won't talk about any of their equipment. When I visited their facility they were very secretive about everything."

"This is really scary. The more I know about them, the less I like them," Janette said.

"They do save thousands of lives every year."

"And get paid accordingly," Janette said.

"That's true enough, but I don't see anyone complaining about that. If you could see the equipment they have, you would understand why they have to charge so much money for what they do."

"Maybe this whole thing is about money," she said.

"I can't accept that. If they killed Martinez, it's got to be for some other reason."

"Like what?"

"I don't know yet. Look, I'm going to review the autopsy records again and see if I missed something."

"Good. Remember that there's a widow here, and a son with no father. We owe it to them to find out."

"That's exactly what I intend to do," David replied.

The next morning, after completing his rounds and his other routine duties, David called Dr. Thomas.

"Good morning, David."

"You recall my patient, Martinez?"

"I remember," Thomas said.

"His wife has applied for some benefits. I'm going to be called as a witness. I want to do what I can to help her. They asked me whether he died of a medical failure. I'm not sure exactly what that means in law, but I need to know as much as I can before I have to testify."

"I wish we could just stick to practicing medicine and not have to get involved in legal matters. It takes too much time and it's very distracting," Thomas replied, clearly hedging.

"I'd like a copy of the autopsy tape," David pressed. "Since I did the surgery, maybe I can see what went wrong."

"I don't think it was a medical failure," Dr. Thomas said.

"That may be true. Then I'll have to say that, even if it doesn't help the widow."

"I can't make a copy of the tape without the wife's approval, but I'll authorize you to come over here and take a look at it as his treating physician if that's what you want to do."

"I'd like to come over now, if you can arrange it."

"Consider it done. If you've got any questions, ask the clerk to contact me," Thomas said.

After David changed his clothes and passed once again through the tedious security process at IORC, he was escorted to the medical records section. The clerk gave him a quick course on using the equipment. There was a notation on the screen that he was allowed access to the autopsy report and tape for Michael Martinez. No other access was permitted.

David reread the autopsy file, which now contained the microscopic slide reports which showed several trace chemicals, spectroscopically analyzed but not named. He watched the videotape of the autopsy, then rewound it and watched it a second time. Still, he found nothing to explain Martinez's death.

He decided to call Thomas and ask him again about the drugs.

"Hello, David. Are you down in medical records now?"

"I am. And I'm wondering, is it possible that there was something that I should have given to Martinez that would have prevented this heart failure?"

"No, nothing I know of."

"I noticed the other day that you don't use a pacemaker to get the heart started after a transplant," David said.

"That's probably getting into some of our confidential procedures, but since you were cleared to see the procedures anyway, I suppose it's OK. Yes, in fact we do have a pacemaker—it's built into the identification module installed on our hearts. We use that to get the heart started, sort of a jump start. It's usually only necessary to use it for a few seconds."

"Could I look at one of them?" David asked.

"I'm sure the company considers those confidential."

"There's something else interesting," David said. "I noticed that the actual size of the heart was smaller than I ordinarily see. And I know this may be a stupid question, but I assume your hearts are human, aren't they? Not from primates or anything?"

That question brought on a roar of laughter from Thomas. "You really are reaching, aren't you, David? Experiments with pig, sheep, and ape hearts have proven to everyone's satisfaction that nonhuman hearts just won't work well as transplants. That heart wasn't particularly small. I think you're seeing things."

Having struck out with both the tapes and Thomas, David went back to Government and took out the notes he had made before going to IORC. They included his list of possible causes of Martinez's death. He had left them in his locker while he had viewed the tape. Only then did it occur to him that someone might have looked at the notes while he was gone. It had been an incredibly careless thing to do. If he was going to engage in spying, he would have to develop a better sense of self-defense. The IORC wasn't stupid and he'd better not be either.

After David's departure, the IORC security director was going over his copy of David's notes with LeBearc in his office.

"He's pretty smart, isn't he?" the security director for Southeast noted.

"Of course he's smart. That's why we want to hire him." He pushed the button on his communications console. "Get Dr. Thomas up here right now," he said to his secretary. Then to the security director he said, "I don't know if he's figured out what happened, but it's an even chance that he will."

Thomas came in, unsure why he was called.

"Did you see Dr. West while he was here?" the QC asked.

"No, but I spoke to him by phone while he was viewing the autopsy video. He had some questions."

"What questions?"

"He asked about drugs again, and he asked if our hearts were from humans," Thomas chuckled. "He also asked about the heart module."

"What did you tell him about that?" the QC asked.

"I didn't tell him anything, really, only that it was an

identification module and that we also used it as a pacemaker to start up the hearts after transplants."

"Well, that'll probably be enough for him to figure it out," LeBearc said. To Thomas he said, "We wouldn't have a Code 6 or someone snooping around if you hadn't killed that driver. Remember that." He glared at Thomas who took the comment as a welcome dismissal and bolted out. Then to his security director he said, "This isn't over yet. Dr. West is smart, but no good to me if he insists upon sharing what he's learned about Martinez with others. Continue to follow him and note who he is seeing."

David called Janette that evening. "I looked at the autopsy; still nothing. I don't think it's drugs, either."

"Given that, if I ask you at the arbitration what in your opinion caused Martinez's death, what are you going to say?" she asked.

"I would have to say heart failure."

"Natural heart failure, or medically related heart failure?" she asked. "What would you say under oath?"

He hesitated and became very formal. "I have no evidence that the heart failure was other than natural, but I would say that in my opinion it was possible the heart was faulty."

"It's very important to know whether that's a possibility or a probability," Janette said. "Your decision on that question will mean the difference between whether Betty Martinez gets any benefits or not. You know that, don't you?"

"Don't talk like a lawyer. I know it. All I can do is give my honest opinion and I'm not certain. I'm not willing to accuse IORC of murder without any proof."

"Let me be skeptical for a minute. Now, is it more likely that the heart failed or that the heart was perfect?" she asked.

"Well, when you put it like that, I think I would say it's more likely that the heart was not perfect, that it failed somehow."

"That's all I need," Janette said.

"I guess I don't understand the law," he said.

# 10

The Benefits Arbitrator, Edith Spangley, a retired real estate broker in her mid-sixties, supplemented her income by serving in this position. Sworn to be impartial in every case, she worked very hard at it and was generally considered fair.

David was sitting in the hallway of the courthouse on an old wooden bench polished shiny by use, when a clerk called him inside. The arbitrator smiled at David over half-glasses. "Are you Dr. West?"

"Yes, I'm David West," he answered.

This was his first time as a witness, and an unexpected knot formed in his stomach. David immediately knew the arbitration would be unpleasant. Virginia Pruitt, the UNIMED representative from the hospital, sat across the table.

"Ms. Compton, you may proceed," the arbitrator said.

"Dr. West, we have all seen the medical records for Mr. Martinez, including the written autopsy report from IORC. We know from those records that you were the doctor who operated on him, so I will skip the preliminaries.

"How did the transplant go; that is, was it successful?"

"Entirely successful. Martinez recovered just as would

be expected. He left the hospital in good health, and I released him to return to work. The first time I knew anything had gone wrong was when I got a phone call from his wife who told me that he had died."

"Did that surprise you?"

"I was totally surprised. I had just examined Martinez a few days before."

"Something about the heart was not routine; isn't that correct, Doctor?" Janette asked.

"Correct. It turned out the organ that had been supplied to the operating room was actually an IORC heart. I didn't find out until the end of the procedure. When we scanned the patient's chest before closing the operation site, we picked up an identification number on the scanner."

"Do you think it medically probable that the heart was faulty; that is, do you think it more likely than not that it was faulty?"

"I think it's probable that something made the heart fail."

"I have no further questions," Janette said with a smile, as she sat back in her chair and put her hand on Mrs. Martinez's, which was clenched around a tissue.

Virginia Pruitt glared at West and began, "Dr. West, isn't it true that you installed a mechanical heart on the patient Martinez without my permission to do so?"

"Objection, Your Honor—or Madame Arbitrator—excuse me. That's got nothing to do with this proceeding," Janette said.

"I think you're right. Let's get on with the real question, shall we?" the arbitrator directed.

"This was your first transplant by yourself, wasn't it, Dr. West?"

"Yes, it was."

"You're not exactly an expert on transplants, are you?"

"I'm enough of an expert to be internationally licensed and Board Certified to do transplants, and for Orlando

Government Hospital to hire me to do them. Yes, I think I am an expert on heart transplants," he said.

"The point is, Dr. West, you were very protective of Martinez and of his family because this was your first transplant, isn't that true?"

"I suppose so. I did feel a special attachment to Mr. Martinez and even to his family. But I'm not sure it was because it was my first transplant. I expect I'll feel the same way about all of my transplant patients. Anyway, yes, I felt particularly close to him."

"Let's stick to the issues," Spangley directed.

"You'd like to find some medical reason that explains what happened to him, wouldn't you?" Pruitt continued, ignoring Spangley.

"I certainly would. I don't believe that I did anything wrong."

"Can you tell us exactly what was wrong with the heart?" Pruitt asked.

"No, but something definitely went wrong or it wouldn't have stopped. It happened too suddenly and un-expectedly. Maybe it had something to do with the fact that the heart had been transplanted before."

"Are there any other possible explanations?" Pruitt asked.

"I object," Janette said. "There may be a lot of other explanations, but the doctor has given us his opinion."

"I think UNIMED is entitled to find out what other explanations are possible and to go into whether some of those might be equally probable," Pruitt shot back. She was experienced in these hearings and was not going to give up when she thought she had made a crack in the claimant's case.

"Very well, you may proceed, but I don't want to keep at this all day. I have another arbitration after lunch."

"I don't think I remember your exact question," David said.

"Are there other explanations as to why this heart

failed, other than its being a faulty heart?" Pruitt said in a patronizing tone.

"Of course, there are many other explanations. I suppose a lightning bolt could have caused it; lightning has been known to induce current and cause sudden heart failure," David said.

"Other than lightning, Dr. West, what further possible causes are there?" she pressed.

"It's possible that he might have required some sort of special pharmaceutical to maintain this IORC heart, but I've asked IORC about that and they deny there are any such drugs."

"Anything else, Doctor?"

"Other than a sudden coincidental heart failure or some sort of a deliberate act, I can't think of anything else."

"What do you mean by 'some sort of deliberate act'?" Pruitt pounced on the comment.

"I object. This is getting so speculative now as to be simply engaging in an academic discussion of the possible causes of heart failure. I suppose we'll have to list gunshot wounds and shark attacks and go through the whole litany before we're finished," Janette said, her cheeks burning.

"I think we've gone far enough in this area, too. Unless the doctor has some evidence that something intentional was done, I think we are ready to move on to another subject. Do you have any evidence that anything intentional was done to this man?" the arbitrator asked.

"I don't have any actual evidence of anything intentional," West said after a hesitation. They all looked at him and frowned, because the way he had answered the question indicated that he suspected as much.

"Do you have something more on that subject, Dr. West?" the arbitrator asked.

"You're grasping at straws now, aren't you, Dr. West?" Pruitt demanded.

"I'm not grasping at anything. My opinion is that something went wrong with his heart. You're the one who started going into all other possible causes. I merely answered your questions."

"All right, that's enough. We'll go on to another subject."

"May the witness be excused?" Janette asked. "Are there any other questions from UNIMED?"

"No," Pruitt said.

And David left. But he went only as far as the bench in the hall. Filled with a mixture of relief and frustration, he paced up and down the hall and back to the bench without noticing what he was doing. The experience had been entirely unpleasant. It seemed to him as though he hadn't been able to say quite what he wanted because of the way the questions were put. He had a feeling that he had not made himself clear.

He felt lucky to be a doctor rather than a lawyer. How could anyone stand to do this every day? After nearly an hour, everyone filed out.

"You didn't have to stay," Janette said.

"I wanted to know the outcome."

"We won't know anything for at least an hour. When the decision is entered, it will come up on my computer terminal at my office."

"Damn," said Janette.

She, David, and Betty Martinez sat in her office, staring at her computer screen, reading the arbitrator's decision that had been filed electronically into the public record. The first few paragraphs of the decision merely summarized West's testimony; only the last paragraph interested them.

I find that there has been insufficient evidence to
show that the cause of death resulted from a
medical failure. Likewise, I do not find that the
evidence was sufficient to show that there was
not a medical failure. The parties may submit
additional evidence within thirty days. Benefits
are denied subject to any new evidence.

(Signed)
Edith Spangley
Independent Arbitrator Service
United States Department of Justice

"And what does all that mean?" Betty Martinez asked.

"We lost," Janette said, disappointed. "I thought we
had given her enough evidence."

"I don't think we ought to give up yet," David said.
They both looked at him. "It says that we can submit
more evidence. I intend to find out what happened."

"How can we get more evidence? The body was cremated." Janette didn't want to give up, but saw no further
possibilities.

"Maybe I can talk to Dr. Byrd, the pathologist who
supplied the heart. He may know something."

"Maybe we should also talk to Warren Jeffries," offered Janette, brightening with David's infectious resolve.
"He's a wizard when it comes to research. Since Betty is a
UNILAW client, we can get Warren's department to do
any research that might help."

She called Warren and was told that he was at work on
a computer simulation and could not be disturbed. Janette
insisted, and, reluctantly, the secretary interrupted Warren. Within thirty seconds, he had picked up the phone.

"We need a special number for you, or a code word.
I'm always willing to have you interrupt me," he said.
"How's it going with the new job?"

"Warren, I've got a client here in my office. We just had

a hearing that didn't work out very well and we need your help."

"Janette, I'm right in the middle of a simulation and I can't stop it short of the building catching on fire. Tell you what, I'll meet everyone at one-thirty."

At exactly one-thirty, Warren Jeffries, who took great pride in punctuality, walked into Janette's office. He studied David's unusual gray eyes and then Janette's—startlingly similar. After the introductions, Janette said, "Warren, the last time I asked you to do something for me, I got you in trouble. This time it's official." She handed him a completed authorization form.

"That crap doesn't bother me. I don't take orders from the jerk you used to work for," he said, but nevertheless, he picked up the form and slid it into the manila folder he had brought with him. He sat down and Janette explained the entire situation about Martinez, the heart transplant, and everything right up to the hearing and the decision. Her ability to quickly sum up complicated matters in only a few minutes impressed David.

"That's really a tough one. Have any of you got any ideas about where we might start?" Jeffries asked.

"The pathologist at the hospital told me other doctors had used IORC organs before," David said.

"Then let's try to find out what happened to the other people. See if they had any problems. That's the obvious first step," Jeffries said.

"The pathologist, Dr. Byrd, was fired over this. I'm sure I can find out where he is, though. Whether he'll tell me any details about other transplants is another question."

"If there's something wrong with these organs, maybe we'll see a pattern among the other people. Janette said there's some sort of a serial number that shows up on the hearts. How does that work?"

"When you turn on the microwave scanner, you see a series of numbers projected on the computer screen—an identification number generated from an electronic module embedded in the organ. Also, I learned that the module acts as a pacemaker when IORC does the transplant itself. They normally use it to get the heart started after the transplant, but we didn't use it at all."

"Can we get one of them?" Jeffries asked, stroking his beard absentmindedly.

"Doubtful. They're used only at IORC. No one else has access to them. I asked the IORC doctor who did the autopsy if I could see one of the modules, and he said they're very secretive about their technology."

"We need to see one of those modules."

"I'll run some medical research requests through to try to find out what I can," David said.

"Sometimes things like that are written up in electronic technical journals. I'll check, too," Jeffries said, and made a note.

"Let's also check out those trace drugs that were reported in the autopsy," Jeffries said. "When we've found out what they are, we can run a search on the drugs and see if they have any connection with heart transplants or failures."

"We only used ordinary anesthesia, as we always do for transplants."

"Pardon me, Doctor. I'm sure you're right, but I'm a researcher and an engineer, and I like to look at everything, not almost everything."

"Hey—it's your time, and I won't argue with your logic," David said.

David got Byrd's particulars from a reluctant clerk in personnel. The address was in Asheville, North Carolina, where Byrd now worked for the medical examiner in a local hospital.

As part of his inheritance when his father died, David received the printing company's Beechcraft Baron twin-engine airplane—along with the mortgage on it. David had learned to fly while in college. He had no legitimate need for an airplane, and he certainly couldn't afford one. As a result, and on the advice of the company's longtime accountant, he had leased the plane to a charter service in Connecticut that took care of the payments and other costs.

He had learned from his father that sometimes using a private plane made more sense than using the airlines when trying to get quickly to and from places off the beaten trail. David had never been to Asheville, North Carolina, but he soon found out that it wasn't on the major airline routes.

First he called Dr. Byrd to arrange a meeting. The elder man, surprised to hear from him, agreed reluctantly to meet with him Saturday afternoon.

David then telephoned the charter service in Connecticut that operated his airplane. The owner, Julian, was also the chief pilot who had taught David to fly. They chatted for a few minutes and then David asked, "What does the flight schedule look like for Saturday?"

"We don't have a trip scheduled."

"I need a ride from Orlando to Asheville, North Carolina. I thought it would be worth the trouble to get someone to come down here and pick me up. Maybe I could fly a little on the way."

On Saturday morning, when David arrived at midtown Executive Airport, the plane was idling outside the general aviation terminal.

"Why don't you fly left seat to Asheville?" Julian suggested.

David's flying skills were rusty, so he had to correct his headings and altitude regularly for the first few minutes. He had decided to hand-fly the airplane rather than put it on autopilot, and it required his full attention. When done properly, flying an airplane, like playing golf, forces the pilot to forget about other things.

David learned from reviewing the charts that Asheville was located in the mountains, with the airport in a valley. When the clouds were low a plane landing there would have to descend, without being able to see the ground, to an altitude below that of the surrounding mountains. It's a procedure that, when done correctly, is quite safe, but is unforgiving of mistakes. Several scarred, bare spots on the mountains in the vicinity of Asheville attested to that fact.

As David followed his instruments, he slowed, continued to descend, and suddenly broke out at the base of the clouds where he could see the flashing lights of the runway ahead of him, approximately three quarters of a mile away. He heard the clattering of ice breaking off the propellers and hitting the plane's fuselage. He ran through the final checklist, making sure that the landing gear and flaps were down. Then he rounded out the plane's descent as he came over the end of the runway and touched down smoothly.

"Couldn't have done it better myself," Julian said.

The ground temperature was cold, but David noticed perspiration on his upper lip. He taxied the plane up to the terminal and shut down the engines.

In less than twenty minutes, David had followed Dr. Byrd's directions to the old hospital. In the pathology department, down in the dark basement, he noticed a strong odor of industrial disinfectant. Dr. Byrd greeted him, still dressed in his white operating gown. He pulled off his rubber gloves and shook hands with David.

"Just finishing up an autopsy."

"Don't let me interrupt. Go ahead and finish."

"No, I've done all I need to do. The technician will finish it out from here. Come on into my office," he said with a twisted smile on his face. He opened the door to a small conference room and library where papers and books littered the floor, several chairs, and most of the tabletop. An antique microscope sat on the edge of the table next to a number of slides and an open textbook. Byrd sat down in a chair next to another pile of files, propped his feet up on a wastebasket, and waved his hand toward one of the other chairs. "Put those files on the table there. We have to do our reports up here on paper. They still don't have electronic filing at the court. And don't blame all this mess on me. These are mostly my predecessor's things. He died a couple of months ago, but no one has gotten in here yet to clean them up. I try to work around everything for the time being."

"How are you getting along up here? How do you like it?" David asked, looking around, embarrassed to be asking the question but not knowing exactly how to open the conversation.

"Well, frankly, I'm not too thrilled. I got fired because of that heart, but of course I knew I was at risk from the beginning. I have no regrets about it, though my J Factor was reduced—even lower than it already was. I've got bad kidneys and I've been working very hard for the last several years trying to get my Factor up high enough to get a transplant. Even though I can't prove it, I think my involvement in Equal Access has kept it low for years now. But I'm not a healthy man and need to work on all my options. Never mind how much I object to the whole thing, I've exercised, dieted, stopped drinking, and done volunteer work. I thought I had enough points to get the transplant whenever I needed it, but my records got 'confused' again after your transplant, and now I'm down to less than half of what I need. I'm trying to get it straightened out but that's a bureaucratic nightmare that can take forever, which I don't have. It's dialysis for me for now, maybe for good. I started that last week. Otherwise, I guess things are great."

"I'm sorry."

"So am I. But I'm not sorry about the heart, and that's what's behind my firing and my J Factor troubles."

"I had nothing to do with you getting in trouble over this. I was not the one to tell the administrator that you delivered an IORC heart."

"I wasn't blaming you for anything. Like I said, I knew what I was getting into. I'm committed to Equal Access; have been for years. But I'm very reluctant to talk about it anymore, even though I haven't changed my mind about what's wrong with the J Factor system. I resent having to conform to some company's idea of how to live. For now, I want to be left alone to get my own situation straightened out and make it to retirement. I like being in the mountains. This is a good town and the people are super. But that is a discussion for another time. Tell me about your patient's death."

David told him everything.

"I doubt the heart was defective. It looked perfectly okay to me," Byrd said.

"It did to me, too, and I couldn't see anything wrong with it when I looked at the autopsy tape, except its small size, which was within limits, but of course something was wrong."

"And all of this happened right at IORC," Byrd observed.

"We want to check other people who have had an unauthorized IORC organ transplant. You said this had been done before."

"I don't want to talk about that. I absolutely will not go into other cases. It's not fair to the patients. Besides, I've gotten into enough trouble with this one."

"Don't give me that. What more can they do to you that they haven't already done? I know—" David held up his hand, "I know that's harsh, but I'm afraid that none of this is a coincidence—and I think you believe that's true, too. We can check on these other people without involving them directly." David could sense that he wasn't getting through, so he tried another tack. "You can't just ignore this; you wouldn't do that, unless I have misjudged you. I'll need names, addresses, dates of transplants."

"What do you really think happened?" Byrd asked.

"I don't have any evidence, but one of the possibilities we have to rule out is that something deliberate was done at IORC."

Byrd took his feet down off the wastebasket and sat up in the chair. "Like what?"

"Maybe a drug, maybe a shock—I don't know. Maybe something else."

"You really think they'd kill him?"

"You're the expert on IORC and Equal Access, aren't you? What do you think?"

Byrd lowered his voice. "Frankly, I've suspected it all along, but then I'm old and beginning to get paranoid." He hesitated a few seconds. "I'll get you the names but I hope you won't involve the patients. I doubt any of them know that they've got an illegal organ."

"I don't want to involve the patients, either. We just want to check their records and see how they've done after the transplants. One of the doctors at IORC said that you can't transplant a heart a second time successfully. But it seems to me that that's what you've been doing all along— and those people are surviving, as far as we know. You're the only source of information I have."

"Okay, okay, you've convinced me. I told you I'd give you the names. But you know, I'm beginning to wonder if my phone's tapped. In fact, this room might even be bugged, if they really want to take the thing to its limits." He chuckled, and David was glad to see that he could still smile.

"Since you're in a mood to be cooperative, there's something else you might be able to do."

"And what would that be?" Byrd asked.

"Help me get my hands on one of those modules."

Byrd's expression darkened instantly. "You're working for the IORC, aren't you? Is that why you're here?" His face had a frozen expression, but anger seemed to seep out around the edges.

David held up his hands. "Absolutely not." Byrd stared at him for a few seconds more and then relaxed, apparently convinced.

"Okay, come over here." Byrd reached onto a shelf and took down a box of 35mm slides. Inside was a foil envelope that had contained two Alka-Seltzer tablets. Byrd opened the envelope and poured three tiny modules out onto the table. One of them was split in two halves and was held together by an internal wire that connected the parts.

"I've been looking at this damn thing under that old microscope for the last couple of weeks. I sent off a photo of the circuits to a friend of mine, but he can't make anything out of it, either. You take them." He picked up the modules, dropped them back into the foil envelope, and handed it to David. "Find out what the hell's going on. These people are dead serious—pardon the pun—and there's something malevolent happening. You know the joke about the old paranoid, don't you? He may be paranoid, but that doesn't mean that somebody isn't really trying to kill him. From what my friends have told me, I think you're going to find out that your patient is not the only one who died after a transplant like his. Do you have any sort of a toxicology report that was done with the autopsy?"

"Yeah. I've got it with me."

"I doubt it's going to show anything anyway because it was done by IORC and they would sanitize it, but it's worth taking a look. Maybe some clerk slipped up and told the truth."

David handed the report to Byrd, who read it through.

"There are some trace drugs here." He studied the printout. "One is an anesthetic drug, but it shouldn't have been in his system this long after the operation. If there's some way you can find out more about these chemicals or get a copy of the actual spectroanalysis, you might have something to go on."

"We'll check into that. When can I get those names and addresses?"

"I'll fax them down to you. I don't trust E-mail on something like this. Give me your number."

David gave him his apartment fax number. He didn't think it would be safe to receive the information at the hospital.

The IORC had some difficulty tracing David's movements since he used a private plane on his trip to Asheville, but once back in Orlando, he went directly to Orlando Government where he had a message to call Andre LeBearc immediately at IORC.

"Good afternoon, David. We want to proceed with the next phase of your interview if you're interested. Also, I think we need to dispel any idea you might have that there's some defect in our hearts. Dr. Thomas shared with me that you have some concerns. We'd like to show you around one of our organ facilities."

The hair on David's neck prickled. Word got back to LeBearc so quickly.

"I'm interested," he said, *in more than just a job*, he thought.

"You'll need to be away for three days. I'll be accompanying you. I've made arrangements to leave today if you can work it into your schedule."

The short notice posed a problem.

"I'll have to get approval. I'm new here and I'll need someone to cover my rounds. Can I call you back in an hour and let you know?"

"Of course. Please tell your administrator that I would consider it a personal favor if he could arrange to accommodate us. My schedule is very busy and it might be several weeks before I could reschedule."

David went to see Administrator Long and explained the situation.

"Provided your rounds are covered, we don't care about your being away—within reason. I know you want a position at IORC, of course, and I don't blame you. We're really a training ground for them when it comes to transplants. Anyway, I owe the guy a favor for overlooking our use of their heart."

David called back to IORC and was put through to LeBearc's secretary.

"Dr. LeBearc has asked that I take a message. Will you be able to join him for the trip?" she asked.

"Yes, I'm all set here. When should I come and what do I need to bring?"

"Our security rules don't allow cars to be parked here for several days without a lot of complications, so we'll send a car to pick you up. You don't need to bring clothes or any other personal effects with you. We'll furnish you with everything you need."

"I'll be ready," David said, but this last fact made him even more uneasy; he could not even bring his own clothing with him. He wondered if this was really for security reasons, or more about keeping outsiders off guard.

He then called Janette and told her about his trip to North Carolina to meet with Byrd. He chose not to mention the foil envelope with the modules inside that he had hidden in the glove compartment of his car.

"I'm going on a trip with IORC this afternoon. I'll be gone for three days. I'll get the information from Byrd to you as soon as I get back."

"Why are you going?" Janette asked, incredulous.

"I want to learn more about them. They consider it part of a job interview."

"After all that's happened, you're thinking of working for them?"

"I said *they* consider it part of a job interview."

# 11

*Going to face Goliath,* David thought as he walked to the front entrance of Orlando Government to meet his ride to IORC. He chuckled briefly to himself but was then sobered by serious thoughts. If IORC had deliberately killed Martinez, they certainly wouldn't want people to know about it. And given IORC's penchant for control, they would presumably react strongly if anyone even asked questions. The logical extension was unavoidable: David was making inquiries and expressing opinions. If they were willing to kill Martinez, why not him? Was it wise for him to go to some secret IORC facility? He might never be heard from again and if people inquired, what could they do?

Lost in his imagination, David didn't notice the green IORC Volvo wagon drive up to the hospital entrance. He didn't see the athletic-looking man in a blue blazer get out and walk toward him. David was looking at some undefined spot in the shrubbery when the man touched his shoulder. It felt like an electric shock. David's entire body recoiled from the touch, and he had a prickly feeling as his hair follicles responded to the adrenaline. He whirled to face the stranger. "Dr. West?" the man asked, surprised at the reaction

"Right. You from IORC?"

"Yes. I didn't mean to startle you. I'm sorry. I'm here to give you a ride. Are you ready?"

"All set," David replied as he briskly moved toward the car, feigning confidence.

At IORC he went through the now familiar security procedures, leaving his clothes in the locker. This time they furnished him with street clothes, including a blue blazer identical to the driver's. As he dressed he noticed that the brand of underwear they provided was the one he used. Of course it could be coincidence. How could they know what brand of underwear he wore? He had to quit thinking like that or the trip was going to be a nightmare.

Moments later, with a keystroke on her computer, the secretary admitted him into LeBearc's office. LeBearc motioned David to a chair. Before David could take in the details, LeBearc spoke.

"Dr. West, we'll be leaving at two o'clock. I want to explain our rules and then you must sign a confidentiality agreement.

"You're going to one of our principal operations centers. We have technology that we've developed at very substantial expense, and the company considers it imperative that we maintain strict secrecy, thus this agreement. It's very simple. The rule is that you will not disclose anything you see, hear, or learn while at our facilities to anyone under any circumstance without prior permission of IORC. No exceptions. Agreements like this are simple and everybody can understand exactly what's required. We want to be able to show you everything so that you can make an informed decision about joining our company. Without this agreement we admit no one to our facilities."

David kept his thoughts to himself. *Why should information about organ preparation be so secret? I already know about that from medical school.*

LeBearc saw David's hesitation. "Do you have some problem with the rule?" LeBearc asked, raising one eyebrow as though he were surprised that anyone would question it.

"I suppose not."

David read over the one-page document. He saw nothing about the consequences of violating it or its duration. *Well, to hell with it,* he thought, and he signed his name.

David and LeBearc passed through more elaborate security checks and into a tunnel that led to an IORC airplane hangar. David thought that the level of security seemed absurdly complex—as strict as it would be in a place where nuclear weapons were stored.

The enormous airplane hangar could house two giant airplanes and several smaller planes. A C-5 sat motionless inside the hangar, and a small business jet was parked right in front of the tunnel.

The wings swept back at a very acute angle and the engines, mounted close under the fuselage, had large square air intake openings. With his aviation knowledge, David surmised that the plane was capable of supersonic speed.

LeBearc climbed directly into the small jet. David followed him.

The inside didn't look at all like an airplane. Four comfortable chairs and a small wooden bar occupied the passenger space. A hall led to the aft of the aircraft. Opposite the passageway, David noticed two restrooms and beyond them a small bedroom. The crew compartment and cockpit occupied the forward section of the aircraft.

For a moment David couldn't put his finger on what was wrong with the plane, but then he realized the cabin had no windows. It was simply an aluminum tube painted IORC green on the exterior and covered with fabric on the interior. David had never been in an airplane without windows and he didn't like it. The feeling was oppressive.

Maybe there were no windows for structural reasons. Supersonic business jets generally had been built based upon the design of military jet fighters, but with a larger fuselage. The engines could accommodate the larger fuse-lage because of the aircraft's lighter weight in the absence of weapons.

"This plane looks like it might be supersonic," David said.

"I think it is, yes," LeBearc said, without interest.

"Why no windows?"

"It's not intended for sightseeing."

"Where is this place?" David asked.

"The actual location is something that I'm not at liberty to disclose."

"Why so much secrecy?"

"You'll see when you get there."

David waited for the pilot to come on the intercom and give directions to the passengers but that never occurred. Instead, soft classical music played over the sound system. A low-pitched hum built into a shrill whistle as both of the engines started. The plane immediately began taxiing and, without even stopping, turned onto the runway and accel-erated. David swiveled his chair to face forward. LeBearc did the same.

Without windows, the sensation was very different from anything David had experienced before. Suddenly the plane lifted off; the floor angled up at twenty degrees and remained that way for several minutes as the plane climbed, then leveled. David felt the aircraft shudder as it went supersonic.

Once the plane was level, LeBearc turned to David and said, "I want to speak to you about something. We have learned that you have expressed the opinion that some-thing went wrong with one of our hearts."

David was surprised that LeBearc knew about the bene-fits hearing testimony. What else did he know? Here he was, aboard an IORC jet going more than the speed of sound—to who knew where?—and LeBearc gets right to the point. Maybe he *was* facing Goliath. Okay. Fair enough. That suited him. "Yes, I did say that."

"One of the main reasons for taking you on this trip is to let you learn more about our organs. I think what you see will persuade you that our hearts aren't defective. I know it's difficult to lose your first patient, but it's important to our company that we maintain quality and that we prevent any rumors about faulty hearts. We have literally millions of patients. We can't afford the loss of public confidence."

"I was called into court and questioned about possibilities. I asked questions, too, and the answers I got were inconclusive. I'm not starting any rumors."

"If you had any questions, Dr. Thomas should have answered them. Did he not?"

"He did. In fact he answered all the questions I asked."

"Then how did you come up with the idea that the heart was faulty?"

"Thomas said there was heart failure. He didn't explain why or how. I concluded that one possibility was a faulty heart. I'm sure that there was nothing wrong with my procedure. Thomas agreed. I gave my opinion. Besides, I don't justify myself to anyone."

LeBearc did not react outright to this challenge. He merely paused and then changed his tack.

"Well, this visit will give both of us a chance to learn how committed you are to saving the lives of your patients."

"What do you mean? Isn't that obvious?"

"Not so obvious as you may think," LeBearc said.

LeBearc continued after a moment, "I should tell you a little more about IORC, I suppose. The company has a central management whose identity is confidential, as is most of our business. One of the main reasons for confidentiality is to protect management from possible kidnapping or terrorist activities."

"Where is this central management? Where's the headquarters for the company?" David asked.

"There is no single headquarters, and central management is not 'central' in the physical sense. They communicate from various locations throughout the world.

"Your host—my counterpart where we are going—is a bit of an eccentric, and I want to forewarn you about him. Actually, he doesn't fit into the normal pattern of our QCs. They are usually more or less stuffy, compulsive people like myself," LeBearc smiled. "His name is Cal Yoshida. He uses the name Cal because his first name is unpronounceable by Westerners and because he is obsessed with America—particularly California. Don't let any of that fool you, though. He has a PhD from UCLA in mechanical engineering, a very unusual background for a QC, and doctorates in zoology and genetics. Apart from that, he decided that since he was dealing with medical doctors all the time he needed to know about medicine, and in the course of about six months he read all the textbooks that are used for a full medical degree. He's quite brilliant. He needs to be, in his position. He is a committed pragmatist when it comes to his job and IORC." David wondered exactly what that meant.

David had heard nothing from the pilot or any crew member. He wondered for a fleeting moment if the plane was being operated by some robot like the ones used in IORC's transplant surgery. Without any warning or directions to put on a seat belt, David felt the plane slow, then pitch up. He heard the landing gear extend and *clump* into place. He felt a gentle bump as the plane touched down and a loud roar as the thrust of the engines was reversed. The plane taxied to a stop and they climbed out.

David looked around blinking in the bright sunlight, trying to get his bearings. They had arrived at a private airport with a long, wide, single concrete runway and several small hangars, much smaller than the one in Orlando. The surrounding area was flat and sandy with scrub plants and no trees. On the aircraft parking ramp, a steel door in a concrete entryway led to a tunnel.

The sun felt hot and the air temperature felt like the low

eighties. David caught the scent of the ocean. Off in the distance he saw some buildings that looked like luxury resort hotels. He had no idea where he was.

A blond woman dressed in green shorts and a T-shirt waited by the airplane. She was quite attractive, with a remarkably good figure. She could have been an exercise instructor on TV. One of the pilots came down the steps of the airplane carrying two suitcases. He walked over to a green four-passenger golf cart and loaded the suitcases. David said to him, "That was a nice ride."

"Thanks," the surprised man said politely, and walked back to the airplane, which was already being refueled. A rumble in the distance made everyone turn and look. Something approached at high speed down the taxiway from the other end of the airport. As they watched, it resolved itself into a motorcycle and the noise grew louder. The motorcycle headed directly for them and finally slowed. As it got nearer, David saw that it was a very old air-cooled Harley-Davidson, painted bright red, with black leather saddlebags hanging over the rear fender. The rider, an Asian man, wore a backward baseball cap, Levi's jeans, black leather boots, and a T-shirt that read, "I did it first in Venice." Under that, in parentheses, smaller letters spelled out "CAL."

The motorcycle came to a noisy stop right in front of them, and the rider pushed his glasses back up on his nose, took off the hat, and tried to smooth his hair back into place—a futile effort. His hair stood out in all directions like the quills on an angry porcupine. Turning the hat around, he put it back on with the bill in front. The hat read "LA." The rider gave them a big grin, and David's first impression of the man was all teeth, eyes, and hair.

"Hi, I'm Cal Yoshida," he said, holding out his hand to David. He shook hands so vigorously that David's teeth rattled.

"Andre, I've never seen you wearing anything but that

gray suit. Why don't you loosen up and enjoy yourself
here? There's no one around but us."

"Good afternoon, Cal, it's always a pleasure. You've
made quite an entrance," LeBearc said, shaking his head
and climbing onto the golf cart. The motorcycle idled at a
very slow speed, shaking with a vengeance. As each cylin-
der fired, it sounded as if a pistol had gone off inside the
exhaust.

"David, you want to ride back with me? It's a lot more
fun than that silly Japanese golf cart," Cal said. Considering it further, he added, "On the other hand, maybe not,"
and he made a show of leering at the woman sitting behind the wheel, smiling back at him.

"No, I think I'll take the slow way back and enjoy the
scenery," David said. Cal lifted up the hat exposing his
spring-loaded hair, turned it around again, and pulled the
clutch. The transmission *clunked* into first gear. Cal took
off with a roar, a puff of blue smoke from the exhaust
pipes, and a slight chirp from the back tire as he released
the clutch. He leaned into a sweeping 180-degree turn and
roared off down the taxiway in the direction he had come.

The cart passed through the steel door David had seen
earlier and down another ramp into a cool air-conditioned
tunnel.

About a mile away they emerged in an underground
loading area, not dissimilar to the one in Orlando. Workers moved carts of boxes and tools in every direction.
LeBearc, David, and the woman in shorts entered an elevator. LeBearc got off first and said, "I'll see you in Cal's
office in an hour." With that he turned and was gone.

Then up on the elevator several more floors, David and
the woman walked down a short hallway and into a luxurious suite.

"I'm Krickett Hansen," said David's escort. "I'm a social consultant. I help entertain guests and make sure that
they enjoy their stay here. Anything that you need or that I
can do for you at all, of course, is my pleasure." She

handed him something that looked like a credit card. "My communication card," she said. "Put that in any phone and it will connect you to me wherever I am."

"I suppose someone will tell me where I can get something to eat. I didn't bring any money with me," David said.

"You can't use money here. Just ask for whatever you need. It would take you quite a while to learn your way around, so whenever you want to go somewhere use that communication card, call for me, and I'll come and take you there. It's best if you don't go wandering on your own, because there are a number of areas where guests are not allowed except with special permission. The best idea is to just ring me." Her accent was mildly Scandinavian with a hint of British and more than a hint of flirtation.

A knock at the door interrupted them. A man entered carrying one of the suitcases that had been on the airplane. He left the suitcase and departed without a word.

"I'll be back in forty-five minutes to take you up to Mr. Yoshida's office," Krickett said, walking to the door. Looking over her shoulder at David, she flashed another smile at him and was gone.

He looked around the sitting room and into the adjoining bedroom, furnished all in pastels from the drapes to the thick plush carpet. The small kitchen area included a bar and a selection of wines. David opened the drapes to reveal a garden even larger and more exotic than the one in Orlando.

David flipped on the television and surfed the channels. It was a satellite hookup. There was no radio. He took the suitcase into the bedroom, opened it on the bed and unpacked the array of clothes and various accessories. The shaving kit included familiar brands—again, as with the underwear, David could not shake the sense that this was not a coincidence.

Back at the bar he selected a white wine. Someone was a connoisseur, or expected that the guest would be. He poured a glass and settled into a large soft chair, kicked off his shoes, and propped up his feet. He glanced at the array of magazines in several languages on the table. David picked up a copy of a golf magazine and leafed through it without really paying attention. Before he knew it, Krickett had returned.

"Hi, I see you found the wine," she said, bouncing into the room. She helped herself to a wineglass and poured a small amount. She swirled the wine around, sniffed it, and then took a taste. "Mmmm—I like that," she said. She had changed into a white low-cut sundress that revealed considerable cleavage. David realized that he was staring and so did Krickett, who broadened her smile and tilted her head slightly to the side.

"Maybe we should get on to Mr. Yoshida's office," she said, and set her glass down.

The elevator ascended ten more floors. They stepped out into a glassed-in room with a breathtaking view. For the first time David could see the entire facility. In one direction was a building about ten stories tall, several hundred yards wide, and at least three miles long. Its square footage would equal that of all the buildings in a medium-size city. David had never heard of any such structure anywhere, although it reminded him of a giant version of the steel mills of Pennsylvania. The design had breaks and protrusions, corners and towers. Constructed of concrete, the structure had no windows that David could see.

By comparison, the building he was in seemed more like a resort hotel, or fancy office building, surrounded as it was by gardens. He could now see that there was a golf course along one side, and rows of tennis courts, a number of swimming pools, and several lakes on the other side. In the distance he could just make out the beach. He turned slowly around taking it all in. On the side away from the large building, he saw the airport where he had landed, with the ocean beyond; in between, there was nothing but scrub plants and sand.

"Come in, come in," Cal Yoshida said. David followed him into the office, but he couldn't take his eyes off the panoramic view, particularly the building complex. LeBearc sat on an Early-American-style couch in the office, and Cal gestured vaguely to a chair for David. Cal had changed into black linen slacks and a golf shirt with a small but elaborate pattern of white and silver splashes and check marks. His hair had not changed, however. He observed David closely, and when David noticed, Cal averted his eyes and with a sweeping gesture of his arm turned around his office.

The office looked like an antique store. A Wurlitzer jukebox rested against one wall, with a skateboard leaning against it. Cal also had a 1930s barber chair, and even his carpet was an Early American hooked rug.

"Take a look around. I've got some marvelous things here." David got up from the chair and, following Cal, walked over to a long glass display case. He could see a random collection of objects, all old and U.S.-made.

One of the small items was a plywood paddle with a little red rubber ball attached to it by a rubber band three feet long. Cal took out the toy and began bouncing the ball on the paddle. The ball sprang back on the rubber band and Cal moved it around, first hitting it upward and then outward, enjoying himself. "Here, you want to try it?" he asked.

David took the paddle, bounced the ball three or four times and then missed. He tried again, quickly getting the hang of it. He handed the thing back to Cal. "You learned to do that quickly," Cal said. He then reached inside the display case and handed David a 1911 model Colt .45 automatic pistol. David looked at it and handed it back. "We'll shoot it later, if you like," Cal said.

David did not know how to respond to this, so he simply tried to grin in a cordial way.

"Everything here is uniquely American," Cal explained. Cal closed the case without taking out any of the dozens of other items. He walked to the corner of the room where a golf bag leaned, pulled out one of the clubs, and handed it to David. "I understand you're a golfer. Maybe there will be time for a game before you leave. That's a Ping Eye, one of the original prelitigation square-grooved models," he said. The clubs were the first high-tech design in golf, and had revolutionized club manufacture. The originals were outlawed—because they worked too well.

David knew that Cal's clubs were worth more than a new car. Cal moved to his desk. "Let me show you a couple of things over here," he said. On his desk sat a large gray plastic box, as thick as it was tall, but when he swiveled it around David saw that it was an old-fashioned computer. Small electronic fish swam from one side of the screen to the other. Every few seconds a bizarre image would appear, a toaster with wings. It moved across the screen along with the fish. The computer dated back to the days before superconductors and the consolidation of the computer industry. Cal then picked up the receiver of an old black plastic telephone on his desk and handed it to David who listened and heard a normal dial tone.

"That old U.S.-made telephone cost the company over five thousand dollars," LeBearc said. "Electrical engineers had to rebuild the entire inside circuitry to make it work with a superconductor telephone system, but he insisted on having it regardless of the cost." Cal's grin widened.

The contrast between the surrealistic concrete structures outside and the hodgepodge of antiques inside, separated only by a wall of glass, left David with the same feeling of unreality he had experienced while watching the IORC transplant in Orlando.

"You have a lot to see while you're here. But I want to go over it with you first. We have cleared you for everything related to transplant organs. You'll find that this place is like nowhere else in the world, like nothing you've ever seen or even imagined. I designed most of it." His persona had changed instantly, from grinning eccentric to serious professional.

"I've never seen anything like this, that's for sure. What's that large building for?" David asked.

"It's really several dozen interconnected buildings. A tunnel from the basements below leads to the airport. All our activities are housed in that group of buildings. We fabricate production unit containers, we manufacture pharmaceuticals, and we do genetic and organ work there. It's like a city. Kitchens, warehouses, everything, within that building. The building we're in now is not only for guests. It contains all the administrative offices, stores and shops, movie theaters and indoor recreation facilities for the employees. Employees' apartments are located a couple miles away from the work areas on the other side of the island."

"Is the research you were talking to me about done here?" David asked LeBearc.

"Oh, no. What I was talking to you about was research on surgical procedures for transplants. That's done right at our regional facility and the other regional facilities around the world," LeBearc said.

"This is a production facility," Cal said.

"What do you mean by production?" David asked.

LeBearc looked at Cal and then Cal said, "The 'bottom line' to this place—to use an American phrase—is that this is where we produce the organs that we transplant." There was silence in the room. David's mind attempted to process this information.

"You mean you actually manufacture the organs? How could you possibly do that? I thought the organs you used were from donors in your organ program. Do you use stem cells?" Theoretically, embryo cells before they differentiate into specific organs could be used later to produce an organ for the individual. After early interest, however, research had supposedly come to a halt years before. David felt even more confused, as if he were in a dream.

None of this made sense. It seemed as bizarre as the flying toaster.

"We don't use donated organs anymore, except for research. With genetic engineering we've been able to produce organs with a much higher probability of successful transplantation. Using donated organs is a haphazard process at best. As I told you, quality control is our primary goal," LeBearc said. "As for embryo stem cells, it's not a practical alternative on a large scale. Only the very rich could afford to store their cells for life to have custom organs produced. Then there is the delay factor while an organ is grown and shipped. We've used some of the science, but we've got a much better system that works for millions of people."

"David, don't worry about this right now," Cal said, grinning. "You asked the question and I wanted to give you a straight answer. Don't even try to understand it until we show you around. Then you'll see what we mean, and I'm sure you'll agree it's a much better way. I'm an engineer, and the solution seemed obvious to me. You're a doctor, and I think it will be just as obvious to you."

Could this be another of Cal's jokes or eccentricities, David wondered? Then he looked back outside at the sprawling building and he knew it wasn't.

"What I like about all these American things," Cal said in an apparent non sequitur, "is that they're more like ordinary human hearts than modern machines. All these old things have personalities. They're each different. Basically, they're idiosyncratic, even inconsistent, inefficient, ineffective, and crude. My designs are exactly the opposite: simple, elegant, and efficient. The beauty of my designs and of our system is not in the objects that we use but in the results they achieve. My job is to furnish the best possible organs with the highest possible quality, and, given those constraints, in the largest possible numbers in order to save as many lives as possible and to improve the quality of life for our patients. We save hundreds of thousands of patients a year."

"What have you done, modified some primates so you can use their organs?" David asked.

LeBearc smiled and Cal roared with laughter. "We're not running a zoo here, David. Don't be impatient. We're going to show you the whole setup, and I think you'll find it very exciting." David, of course, couldn't be patient now. They had intentionally created this suspense. He had no choice but to wait until the next day to find out the answer, but that didn't stop him from speculating; nothing could stop that now. He looked back at the building stretching into the distance.

Cal leaned back in his chair and took a cigarette out of his shirt pocket. From his pants pocket, he produced an old Zippo lighter, flipped open the top, and spun the wheel with his thumb in a single practiced maneuver. Holding the four-inch flame under the end of his cigarette, he took a deep drag and blew the smoke out in obvious enjoyment. He snapped the lid closed and then, with what was becoming a familiar grin, he said, "I can't get any lighter fluid, so I have to use aviation gas. You've got to be careful or you'll singe your eyebrows," he added, and cackled. David looked at Cal's hair again and thought that his eyebrows would not be all that got singed if he weren't careful.

"Cal has seen our statistics on lung transplants. Under the circumstances I can't understand why he persists in that foul habit," LeBearc said. He wrinkled his nose, and held his hand in such a way as to try to deflect the smoke that hovered in front of him.

"Japanese don't get lung cancer or emphysema. Didn't you know that, Andre?"

"However that may be, it doesn't help the other people who are nearby, does it?" LeBearc said, disgusted.

"When you live out here like I do, you tend to look for any pleasures that are available. Speaking of which,

David, feel free to use any of the services that Ms. Hansen has to offer while you're with us." Cal winked at him.

"There is one nice thing about Cal's obsession with things American," LeBearc said. "He has a boat at the marina that is his pride and joy." David sensed that LeBearc might be trying to placate Cal in some way. The exact relationship between them was not clear but it was evident that LeBearc, while he might make some superficial comments uncomplimentary to Cal, still respected him.

"That's right. In fact, I thought it would be pleasant to have dinner aboard. I'll have it set up. You should plan to leave about seven. Krickett will transport you there. And for God's sake, Andre, wear something besides that suit. Skipper's orders: no ties aboard." Then Cal stood up, stubbing out his cigarette. He herded them toward the door; before they were out he had turned back to his desk. As the door closed behind them, David saw Cal pick up the phone. A panel in his desk slid open, exposing a modern computer and communications console.

David was in a daze from a combination of jet lag—*could there be jet lag if the time zones didn't change? Had they changed?*—and disorientation from all the strange things he was seeing and learning. A strong sense of danger swelled within him. *I'd better get myself together*, he thought.

# 12

Krickett stuck her head around the door when David didn't immediately answer her knock.

"Hi, are you ready?"

She still wore the same sundress, much to David's delight, but she had added jewelry.

"Yeah, I'm ready. We're going to Cal's boat?"

"Yes, it's marvelous. But I'll let Cal tell you all about it. He'll be disappointed if he doesn't get to do that himself."

They rode the elevator down to the underground transportation center and drove off in a green golf cart.

Coming up a ramp into the fading afternoon sunlight, they followed a trail through scrub. After traveling about five miles they emerged at a marina. At the head of the dock was a huge sailboat with a mast towering more than a hundred feet in the air.

Krickett drove the golf cart directly onto the dock, where several stewards wearing white jackets were unloading food from a van. David saw a dozen or so people on the deck drinking cocktails. Cal caught sight of David and hurried down the aft gangplank onto the dock.

"Hey, David, check it out. What do you think of my boat?"

"That's some boat, all right."

"Do you recognize it?" Cal asked, so excited that he could hardly stand still.

"I don't know that much about boats, but the paint scheme looks familiar."

"Well, it ought to! Photographs of it have appeared everywhere, even on a U.S postage stamp. This, my friend, is the defenders' boat from the 1992 America's Cup. You know, the first one after they put in the new formula," he said, expecting David to know about such things, and he puffed out his chest with pride.

"That's where I've seen it. How did you get a copy?"

"It's not a copy, my friend. This is the boat, the one and only boat," Cal said ecstatically. "The only thing we've done is finish out the inside so that we can use it. As a racer, it was just a shell, so we've made it more comfortable. Other than that, it hasn't changed. It's an absolute bitch to sail, though. One mistake and you can shear the mast off or even capsize. Come on, let me show you around."

Cal took David below deck to see the accommodations, which included a full galley, several staterooms trimmed in exotic woods, and a luxurious bath with a full-size tub. The opulence of the furnishings further emphasized the vast wealth those employed by IORC seemed to possess.

Back on deck, Cal introduced David around. The medical director, an American woman in her early forties, had a degree from Johns Hopkins in, of all things, pediatrics. But the guests seemed to talk about everything but their work.

The dinner, a combination of Polynesian and Cajun, and the wine, a superb vintage sake, left David's memory blurred and disconnected the next morning. He remembered Krickett popping spring rolls into his mouth, leaning toward him to expose her cleavage. He remembered getting an erection that everyone found humorous and that seemed to last forever, and Krickett taking him back to his room, then slowly undressing to the accompaniment of

Middle Eastern music. He recalled being so aroused that the more aggressive Krickett became, the better he liked it.

He also remembered her leaving before daylight and telling him that she would pick him up at eight-thirty. Last night he didn't really care one way or the other, but now he had an entirely different opinion. His head hurt beyond anything in his memory. His groin ached and he felt nauseated. It was already ten minutes to eight; he had to get ready, but if he tried to get out of bed he knew he would never make it to the bathroom before throwing up.

He lay very still and tried to make his head quit spinning and his stomach settle down by pure force of will. He was due to leave in a half hour with people he might publicly accuse of murder. He needed all of his capacities. Instead, here he was with a hangover—something he hadn't experienced since college—and God only knew what sort of reputation to live down from the party the night before. This was all bad. And it wasn't an accident. Obviously he had been set up—maybe drugged even—and seduced. It seemed as if everything going on around him had been planned to keep him off balance.

David swallowed a half-dozen times and breathed deeply through his mouth, trying to increase the oxygen to his brain. He slowly sat up to the accompaniment of a new, even more severe shot of pain in his head, above the bridge of his nose. He swung his feet onto the floor and held his head in his hands.

"God, I'm really screwing up by the numbers," he said out loud. When his head had cleared a little, he stood up, steadying himself on the table next to the bed, and waited for the latest wave of nausea to subside.

He decided to make a monumental effort to reach the bathroom in one try. He started for the door, and after his fourth step realized that he was going to be sick. He moved unusually quickly for his condition and was able to make the toilet before he vomited. There, staring back at him, was a partially digested head of a Cajun shrimp, and that made him renew his efforts to empty his stomach. David sat on the floor gripping the toilet for five minutes. Finally, he managed to pull himself up to the lavatory, turn on the water and wash his face. Amazingly, he felt much better. He climbed into the shower and turned it on as hot as he could stand and decided to ignore the time. He'd rather face the consequences of being late than show up in the condition he was in now.

David braced himself against the front of the shower and let the hot water stream over him. He realized then that he had been in bed, naked. He thought again of the events of the night before. Krickett had said to him it was definitely not part of her job to go to bed with the company's guests, and she had been quite angry when he asked the question. He would never have done such a thing under normal circumstances, but then, having a woman come into his room and undress was not a normal circumstance—for him, anyway—nor was the sex like any he had experienced before. They had been animal-like, uninhibited, compulsive. Still, looking back on it now, it all seemed so staged.

He got out of the shower and, dripping, walked back into the other room and looked at the clock: twenty after eight. He used the electric razor, brushed his teeth, and was stepping into his underwear when Krickett came into the room.

"Davey boy, you're going to be late. You're due at the infirmary for a physical in about five minutes. And God, you don't look to me as if you'll pass," she said, laughing at him and tossing her hair. "What in the world happened? You look as if you were up all night." He ignored her.

Trying to get himself together, he reached into the closet for a shirt, gray flannel slacks, and a blazer. He dressed awkwardly, the shared intimacy of the night before gone now in the glare of morning. "If I'm going to have to undress again there's no point in a tie. What's the bit about a physical, anyway? No one said anything to me about it." He didn't want to tease her or engage in any banter. He was embarrassed, and at any moment he might be sick again. "Let's just go," he said.

"Now, don't take it personally. All the guests must have a physical before they can go into the main complex to make sure that they don't have any communicable diseases. And I certainly hope *you* don't have any communicable diseases." She smiled mischievously, and skirted out the door.

Krickett took David to the infirmary where a technician took blood and urine samples. David then took off his jacket but kept on the rest of his clothes and lay down on the exam table. A scanner ran down his body from head to toe. David welcomed the chance to lie down. "Looks like you had some of the QC's sake last night," said the technician. "Hold on a minute, I've got something that'll help you." He left the room and David slowly and carefully sat up on the table, holding his face in his hands. He promised himself that if, in fact, he managed to survive this he would never, and he emphasized the word *never,* drink sake again. He probably would never *drink* again.

The technician brought in a paper cup that contained something brown, thick, and heavy like oatmeal. The sight of it sent his stomach into convulsions again. He glared at the man with disgust.

"I didn't say it was pretty, just that it would work. Give it a try," offered the technician, and David put the cup to his lips. It felt like drinking wet sawdust and tasted like unsweetened oatmeal but, to David's surprise, his stomach didn't reject it. Actually, it seemed to settle him a little. He tried a second gulp and then a third, and his stomach responded favorably. What the hell, he thought, and drank the rest of it down in three more swallows. He felt better immediately.

"Whatever else you may do here, you certainly make a world-class hangover tonic. What is that stuff?"

"Nothing special. We've got tons of it around here. I add a pinch of this and a shake of that and it seems to work."

"Do you think I'll live?" David asked.

"Nope, you're gonna die," he said. "At least you will if you keep drinking the QC's sake like you did last night. That stuff is like lacquer thinner. It'll burn a hole right through your stomach. As far as your exam is concerned, other than the hangover, you're okay. No infections. You're healthy. I'll post it on the computer and you'll be cleared into the main complex," he said, holding the door for David.

"You're quite a partyer, Davey," Cal said, ushering David into his office. David couldn't understand where they got "Davey." No one had ever called him that. Someone must have started it the night before.

Neither Cal nor LeBearc showed any signs of being the worse for wear from the night before. After David started drinking the sake he had paid no attention to how much anyone else was drinking.

Cal stood in front of his desk leaning back against it. "I want you to indulge me for a few minutes. I think we need to tell you some more about this place."

Cal Yoshida returned to the serious demeanor of the previous day, showing no sign of the colorful character from the night before.

"Soon after organ transplantation began, more people needed transplants than there were organs available. We knew we had to have a more prolific source of organs in order to utilize the rapid and continuing advances in medical technology. What's the use of knowing how to transplant hearts or kidneys if ninety-five percent of your patients expire waiting for the death of an accident victim who has agreed to donate?

"It's sort of like searching for the fountain of youth. Once we had perfected the techniques, and had achieved a success rate of ninety percent, people began to dream of a time when even if the heart they were born with failed, they might still be able to have a normal life span. We tried mechanical hearts, of course, but still haven't perfected a small reliable mechanical heart that would enable a recipient to lead a normal life. Mechanical hearts will get better, and maybe someday they'll be a viable alternative, but we're still a long way from it.

"We also made an effort to use animal hearts. But tissue differences and blood dissimilarities doomed them to failure as a practical alternative. With a monumental effort, we did achieve success with hearts from primates and were able to keep a patient alive for a few years, but it required extensive pharmaceuticals and heroic measures.

"Genetic research has made it possible to understand and even control many of the diseases that have plagued mankind for all of history. Pharmaceuticals to supplement some genetic defects work reasonably well. But social and legal constraints have inhibited open research into genetically engineering humans to make their hearts better. So it occurred to the founders of IORC, after these other areas of research were unproductive, that maybe genetic engineering could be used to aid organ production. That's what we've accomplished."

David was fascinated. "Why have you kept this such a secret?"

"The founders of our company made that decision, and Central Management has continued to support it. We don't want any interference. We won't tolerate it," LeBearc snapped.

"Recently, the Justification Factor system itself has taken on a life of its own. Society, through its political institutions, churches, advertising and marketing, and almost every other arena enforces its values through the J Factor system—with our help. The establishment that has developed around the world has a vested interest in perpetuating the J Factor system as a means of influencing the beliefs and controlling the actions of the public. We provide the glue that holds the entire system together. Society doesn't need or want to know the details. That would only confuse things." LeBearc savored his own words.

Cal ignored the interruption and continued. "We must maintain our complete independence and our ability to conduct our activities without any government's interference; otherwise, we would have to change our procedures at the whim of whatever happens at the moment to be politically correct in a given locale.

"We've already spent billions of dollars and are continuing to spend billions more in research and development to maintain our system and to improve it, to make it more efficient. The organs we produce are healthy and strong, and result in success rates in excess of ninety-nine percent.

"We have earned the legal right to our independence. We produce the best product possible at the lowest reasonable price. I don't see that this is any different from any other engineering exercise. That's how we've developed this system and it's been very successful."

Even though David's head was still throbbing, and his eyes burned as though he were in a room full of smoke, everything that he heard etched indelibly into his consciousness.

"Enough talk," Cal continued. "Let's go take a look."

Once everyone passed through the security check, the group entered the main complex.

Cal directed them toward the first section, which resembled a large, multistory factory. Inside, on the ground level, workers put together two halves of an opaque white plastic sphere two yards in diameter. The bottom half rested on rollers mounted on a base surrounded by electrical wires and piping. A small overhead crane lowered the top half into place. Workers bonded the two halves together to form a single sphere. And these complete spheres were then nested into square frames made of steel girders, with the wires and pipes attached.

"Let's go on to the genetic center," Cal continued. They headed for the tunnel in the basement, got into one of the ever-present golf carts, and drove for nearly fifteen minutes inside the building, arriving finally in another large room.

Several dozen people worked at computer screens there. Cal spent over an hour explaining all of the nuances of computerized genetic research. David's head pounded again, so he missed some comments about early research projects, but something reminded him of his own genetic analysis that was done in med school. The gentech that did the study had repeated it three times because he thought there was an error. The results showed amazingly exceptional combinations that usually did not occur in one individual. But David lost the thread of his thoughts in Cal's lengthy explanation mired with jargon.

Apparently Cal sensed his waning interest. "Are you feeling all right?" he asked, staring at David.

"Yeah, I'm okay. I need a couple of minutes to sit down and have a cup of coffee. That sake . . ."

"I think we'll cut the tour short since you're not feeling well. We'll show you the main production area and then get some lunch, and you can have the afternoon to yourself."

"I'm sorry. Maybe that would be best. Whatever you think." David assumed that he was experiencing the aftereffects of the sake, but it felt much worse than a hangover.

LeBearc watched David carefully and did not seem particularly pleased with what he saw.

For David, the day—indeed, the whole trip—had turned into a quagmire. First, he had made a fool of himself at the party. Now, supposedly sane people were calmly discussing the legal right to protect genetic research and justifying it as an international, social, and political stabilizing influence.

"All this must have cost an enormous amount of

money," David said, trying not to fade out entirely. He needed time to think.

"You mean the building and everything you've seen so far? That's a small part of the cost. The majority of our expenditures are tied up in the inventory. We've done everything we could to reduce the production time without loss of quality, but the expenses are still very high for each unit, and we have more than a million units here."

They went through the ever-present security check, but this time it also included decontamination and a change of clothes. They each put on a disposable coverall similar to an operating room gown.

David had a sinking feeling, as if he were descending a mine shaft. He had come here in a windowless airplane to a place whose location he could only guess. Slowly he had been progressing through what was surely the largest building in the world. He had passed through several layers of security. He felt out of control and trapped. He feared he already knew what he was about to see. But what could he do? He knew it would be naive to assume that any individual, including himself, could be of the slightest consequence to this company. At this point, however, he could do nothing but go along with the tour as planned, keep his thoughts to himself, and hope to get out alive.

When everyone had changed into the coveralls, Cal led the way into a different area, the vastness of which overwhelmed David's already overexpanded consciousness.

"We have twenty-six of these chambers," Cal said. "We just added the last one this year."

David looked around. The room rose many stories high. From floor to ceiling, hundreds of feet above, and into the distance for hundreds of yards ahead, he saw row upon row of the square-girded boxes containing the opaque white plastic spheres he had seen being assembled. Tens of thousands of them, stacked one upon the other. He recognized the hum of air pumps and motors running smoothly and quietly like fine machinery. Metal walkways constructed along one side of each of the rows of boxes and at each of about twenty levels stretched upward. An elevator opened onto each level. Looking down an open aisle, David could see the overhead forklift that provided access to the boxes. He watched as it slid one out from the back and moved it along the aisle.

High above them, in the center, at ceiling level, David saw a glass control room, with dozens of people moving around next to a wall of computer screens. The elevator, inside a glass enclosure, ran from the floor level up to the control room.

The glossy white floor, indeed the entire area, appeared as clean as an operating room.

A worker walked along one of the catwalks four stories above the floor. Stopping at one of the girded boxes, he removed an electronic meter from his pocket, plugged it in, and made some adjustments with his screwdriver.

"We designed the containers to last for the duration of the production of the units, but sometimes we have minor malfunctions," Cal said. "We want to make all the parts reliable, but it would be just too wasteful and expensive to overdesign them to last twice as long as they need to, since we replace all of the mechanical components anyway when we overhaul the containers. The room you saw earlier was our overhaul and test area. These particular ones in here are some of the oldest we have. When they were made, our quality control and the damn water pumps were not as good as they are now. We could never be entirely sure how long they would last. Actually, it was more of a human error than a mechanical one. Our statistician at that time calculated average pump life within two standard deviations. We are now paying the price for those two standard deviations with a lot of extra labor and a lot of new pumps that will be wasted. That statistician is no longer with us." David shuddered; he couldn't be sure what Cal meant.

David could hear no sounds coming from the spheres, nor could he see what was inside them. "Everything's so quiet," he said.

"Let's go up to the control room and we'll show you how we monitor the area." They boarded a glass elevator, and David's stomach fell away as they shot up into the base of the control room. When the elevator stopped, the doors opened onto a panoramic view of what David had seen from below: hundreds of computer consoles, each having nine CRT displays. He couldn't make out the images on screen from where he stood.

"Look, they're running a color recognition experiment now. David, you'll be interested in this," Cal said as he hurried toward the pediatrician who had been at the party the night before. David watched both the screen and the pediatrician. Lights flashed on an image on the screen in green, blue, yellow, and red. "She's installed some panels that can be lighted in colors. The row of colored buttons is responsive to touch and changes the colors. It's sort of like interior decorating." Cal let out a hoot, enjoying his private joke. It seemed both irrelevant and distracting to David as he glanced at the screens.

"Where are those kids?" David asked.

"What kids?" Cal looked puzzled.

"Those kids on the screen there," David said. He pointed at the images of four children, two boys and two girls, apparently in their early teens. All the children were nude. The girls' breasts had begun to develop and the boys had pubic hair. Something about them seemed strange, however. The shape of their heads was abnormal. And then David realized where the organs came from. It was like being struck by a bolt of lightning. "Those are teenage kids. What's wrong with their heads?" He didn't know what else to say. He could only stare at the screens.

"Actually, they are six-year-old GECs. They look older because of the growth hormones. One of the side effects is that the brain develops abnormally. It's an advantage, since most of them never develop an IQ much above sixty, which doesn't matter because we haven't learned to transplant brains yet," Cal said, and this time he roared with laughter, throwing his head back in what appeared to be a sick private joke. Several of the technicians turned and smiled. They were used to Cal's humor.

Stunned, unable to move, David watched the screens. As a light flashed on, a child would place his hand on the button and then look around in fascination, watching the overall color change.

Something about the scene reached down inside David to a level he never knew existed in himself. He watched in fascination as one might watch an impending accident, knowing he was helpless to change the inevitable outcome and yet unable to stop looking, even as something inside screamed for him to turn away. He felt himself trembling, yet he couldn't take his eyes away. He looked at other monitors and saw several spheres turning. What he saw were children tumbling and rolling inside their spheres as water sprayed in. They weren't playing; instead, they were desperately trying to stabilize themselves as the spheres rotated, but to no avail, since they had nothing to grab onto. The children's faces were panic-stricken. Several spheres had just stopped and the children curled up at the bottom and peered around, afraid that the tumbling would start again.

David looked back at the screens with the flashing colors. One of the children, a boy, looked directly into the camera lens. It was not a coincidence. His eyes registered intelligence. He had figured out that the camera lens could see him. He stared at it, refusing to play the color game. "Give it a shock," the pediatrician directed. A technician touched a spot on the screen and the boy writhed in pain and fell down. His expression changed to one of anger, of defiance.

"Schedule that one out for the next transplant shipment," she said, and switched her attention to another screen.

David felt himself getting dizzy. His vision began to close in so that he could see only directly ahead. Suddenly, his stomach began to heave.

"Look at that, David. She's put in a new variable. When they touch the right color, food comes out of the dispenser. Watch!" Cal said, fascinated. He leaned forward, looking at the screen over the shoulder of the pediatrician.

David followed his view and what he saw turned his stomach again. One of the boys who had touched the right colored button was holding his hand out below a stainless steel pipe that slowly extended into the sphere several inches. Out of the pipe came several teaspoons full of the brown oatmeal-like substance that David had taken as his hangover remedy. The boy quickly licked the substance from his hand and tried to get more out of the pipe by sucking on it like a straw as it withdrew into the wall. David's head swam with nausea.

"It gets the right color a lot quicker if it hasn't been fed for about twenty hours. After that, it seems to get too impatient to be able to match them up correctly," the pediatrician said.

Before she could finish, David felt his knees giving way. He lost his balance and as he started to fall he vomited violently.

"Sh-iit!" One of the technicians jumped back. He had been too close to David, and vomit covered him from the knees down.

"My word!" LeBearc said.

"What the hell," said Cal.

The pediatrician leaned down to check David, who had fallen to his hands and knees. She put her hand on the side of his face and turned it slightly so she could see. "What's the matter? Are you okay?" she asked.

"My God, they're just children," David said, and he

shook his head, trying to clear it. He was trembling violently.

"Get somebody up here to clean up this mess and take him to the infirmary," Cal ordered. He looked down at David, shaking his head with revulsion. He and LeBearc headed for the elevator, leaving David kneeling in his own vomit and muttering wordlessly to himself.

# 13

The last place in the world David wanted to be was the IORC infirmary. He felt more caged and vulnerable than ever. He lay on an examination table, gathering his wits as a medical technician drew another blood sample. He watched the scanner slowly pass over his body, which made his skin crawl. Then the technician started to give David an injection.

"Hold it. What is that? I don't need anything," David said.

"It's something for your nausea and to help you relax," the technician said, and again reached for David's arm.

"No, thanks," David said, and he grasped the technician's hand. "I'm a doctor. I don't need any injection. Bring me some ginger ale and ice and then I'll go back to my room and take a shower. I'll be fine."

The technician hesitated. David's grip convinced him to forestall any injection. The technician left the examination room rubbing his hand. In a few minutes he returned with the ginger ale and a cup of ice.

David's sense of self-preservation had kicked in. He didn't want any injections from anybody at IORC. He would have to use all his abilities if he was to have any chance of getting back home. Now that he had seen everything, he posed a threat to them. These people had no regard whatsoever for life. He couldn't fight back until he got off this damn island—that is, if they let him go.

He walked into the infirmary reception area, projecting as well as he knew how an air of confidence and control. "I need directions to my room; I've gotten turned around." The technician had been speaking to the receptionist and they both looked up at David, not knowing what to do.

"At least give me a hint. Do I turn right or left when I go out the door?" he asked as he started for the door.

"Hold on, there."

David stopped short of the door and turned around, not knowing what to expect but ready for anything.

"I'd better go with you," the technician said. "It's against the rules for visitors to be wandering around in the halls, and you're my responsibility." David unclenched his fists and took a deep breath.

Back in his suite and refreshed by a shower, he went into the living room. As he was reaching for the telephone, it rang. Was someone video-monitoring his room? Given everything else here, undoubtedly. He picked up the phone and answered it as if he had received a call at his own office. "West," he said.

"This is Krickett. I heard you got sick. Are you okay?"

David figured that she would report to the others whatever he said. "Yeah, I looked like a real idiot. I suppose I've ruined any chance of getting a position with the company. I'm about to call Cal and let him know I'm feeling much better, and see if he'll give me a second chance. I really want to see the rest of the operation here. I want everyone to know that I don't normally walk around with a hangover. The last time this happened to me I was in college, and I thought I had learned my lesson."

"Why don't you ring for something to eat and have it brought up to your room? I'll check in with Cal and get back to you."

"Great. Thanks."

*Would people care if they understood where their replacement organs came from? Or would they simply be glad to get them and ignore their source? If they did care, would they want to actually stop the IORC, or were people already too addicted to their products?* These questions troubled David as he nodded off on the couch.

David snapped awake, but had no idea how much time had passed as Krickett knocked on his door and, without waiting for an invitation, came in. The ivory silk blouse she wore did nothing to mask her figure. It contrasted nicely with a pair of white slacks. Her one piece of jewelry, a tennis necklace, had stones that looked like—but because of their size couldn't possibly be—real emeralds.

"You're to come to Cal's office at three o'clock. I take it now that it's over he thinks the whole thing is rather funny. At first, he thought you'd had an adverse reaction to seeing the production operation. I don't know exactly what LeBearc thinks. You know, he's very reserved." She raised her eyebrows and rolled her eyes upward to one side. The gesture conveyed her real meaning.

"The food I saw coming out of a tube upset me," David said. "The medical tech this morning gave me some of that stuff to relieve my hangover, and seeing it again was more than my stomach could handle."

"I'm sure they'll understand."

"I'd like to see the garden if there's enough time before my appointment," David said.

"We've got time if we leave right now."

With a bounce in his step and his voice, which took a monumental effort, he said, "Let's do it then."

Krickett linked her arm through David's and turned to him and said, "Doesn't it bother you about all those children or GECs or whatever they are, all to make more and more money?"

"I'm sure there's more to it than making money. I think I have to know more about everything here to really decide how I feel about it. One thing I do know: It works, and it saves a lot of patients' lives." *And costs a lot of lives, too,* he thought.

He hoped he had passed her rather obvious test. He couldn't decide if his speech had convinced her.

They made the full tour of the garden and then took the elevator to Cal's office.

A frown crossed Cal's face. David watched Cal's eyes and saw that he had glanced at Krickett. A look passed between them and he immediately glanced back at David.

"Are you feeling all right now? We got your exam results and there's nothing wrong beyond what's left of a slight hangover."

"It was a hell of a lot more than 'slight.' Anyway, I apologize."

Cal's smile had returned. "I've been there myself. Sake is something of an acquired taste."

"I've learned my lesson."

LeBearc appraised David. He was now on trial.

"You look much improved. I guess it's understandable that you would have an adverse reaction when you first saw the production process."

"I think everybody got the wrong impression. I was surprised when I saw those video screens, but I think you're misinterpreting my reaction. This morning, during my physical, I mentioned to the technician that I had a hangover, so he brought me some of that food I saw coming out of the dispenser on the video screen. When that . . . GEC licked it out of his hand, my stomach couldn't take it. No matter how hard you try, you have only so much authority over your stomach, and in this case I didn't have enough." David hoped this explanation sounded convincing. It contained just enough truth so that he hadn't had to grope for words—a sure sign of dissembling.

"We thought it was your reaction to how human our GECs appear," LeBearc said, unconvinced.

For a moment, David paled. "Yeah, I was surprised," he said, recovering. "If I hadn't felt so sick, I would have realized that human-compatible organs have to come from similar organisms."

Cal perched on the arm of his sofa and said, "They are similar, but they're not human by any proper definition. I mentioned this back in the genetic center but you looked a little green around the gills, even then." Both he and LeBearc still watched David very closely, measuring his response to everything they said. David knew that more was on the line here than whether he would be offered a job.

"I do think my level of concentration was reduced," David said, smiling at his deliberate understatement. "If you wouldn't mind, maybe you could hit the high points again. I promise to listen better this time."

"I never mind talking about my work," Cal said. "The humanlike figures that you saw are GECs, genetically enhanced clones. They are the result of our genetic research. We've had good success with simple gene splicing, computer-aided fertilization, and cloning. It takes time, but it's largely predictable insofar as the traits we are trying to emphasize are concerned.

"Initially, we did a great deal of research to find individuals—that is, individual humans—who had particularly strong organs of one type or another. We then carefully analyzed their genetic structure and were able to isolate certain gene groups for each of the various organs that concern us. For example, we found that certain Asians are less likely to have heart attacks, even factoring out environmental considerations, and so the basic gene splice for hearts is largely from a group of Japanese. We also found that it was more efficient to produce smaller-sized hearts. The somewhat smaller size tended to adapt to the various body sizes of recipients better, and kept the organs gender neutral.

"We have sources for the purchase of the base human

sperm and egg material from groups that are compatible with our activities. Utilizing that basic material, we splice in the genes that we want, manually fertilize the eggs, and grow the embryo to the point where we can do an actual genetic analysis of the tissue. If an embryo passes our testing, we allow it to mature. Those embryos, however, are no longer human in any fair sense of the word, because of the various gene splicing we've done. We alter the basic genetic structure not only to improve the quality of the organs, but to modify the organism itself to make it more adaptable to the environment we provide here. Once we have a good prototype—and we use dozens of prototypes to reduce the risk of an unforeseen genetic catastrophe—we can clone an unlimited number of duplicates."

"What else do you change besides the organ genes?" David asked. He wanted to know more, despite feeling ashamed of his aroused interest.

"Well, for one thing, they are all immune deficient, so that the organs are more readily accepted by their recipient's body. Our organs are adaptable to any recipient; no need to match tissue. We've tried to allow some of these GECs to grow to full maturity, but because of their immune deficiency, none of them has survived past about age ten. The units you saw are six years old, but with the growth hormones we administer, they appear more like fourteen. Even with our extreme efforts to maintain non-infectious conditions here, it's virtually impossible to control the environment to the point where the laws of probability won't catch up. GECs die of cancer unless something else intervenes. All our efforts have ended in the unpreventable demise of the units. If any of them tried to survive outside of the controlled environment we provide here, they would live only a few weeks at best. And this would be true even without the various growth accelerators we use.

"We try to limit exposure to infections by using the growth rate modifiers, which reduce the cost of production and generally increase efficiency. These growth rate modifiers have significant side effects, however—most notably, limited and impaired mental capacity and brain development. This is probably an advantage for the GECs, since at their level of intelligence they certainly don't perceive any sense of boredom, claustrophobia, or entrapment from the environmental constraints that we have to impose on them. Their level of consciousness is very low, lower than that of a pet dog, for example." David discounted this claim, recalling the haunting expression on the boy he had seen looking at the camera, and the panic in the eyes of the children in the spinning capsules.

"Physically, however, as you can see, the GECs are strong, and despite their immune deficiency they generally stay healthy. They get exercise—mental and physical stimulation—and scientifically perfect nutrition. All of the GECs are surgically rendered deaf after the early genetic testing confirms their viability. We found that they tolerate their confinement better if they can't hear. Once we've committed to growing a unit, a very significant effort goes into maintaining top quality until time for harvesting."

"These GECs are actually alive, then, when the organs are removed? If it's soon before transplant, what do you do about the presence of anesthesia and the other medications in the organs?"

"We use succinylcholine as a muscle paralyzer before the surgery. It's quick acting, and flashes out of the blood without leaving any significant residue in the tissue itself. The drug prevents involuntary muscle contractions during surgery."

The unfortunate creatures would be cut up alive, unable to move, but conscious, at first, of the pain and terror of being dismembered. David wished he could lash out against the vile and immoral information coming at him from Cal, but such ghoulish pragmatism as his host displayed could mean only one thing: IORC could just as easily dispatch him, and it would most certainly be in a horrifying way.

They left Cal's office, and resumed David's tour of the huge building. Inside, David was outraged as he learned more and more about the GEC-growing process, but he struggled for outward composure, knowing it was his key to survival. As he moved through the building, he saw spheres containing GECs of progressively younger and younger ages, down to ones just beginning to stand up.

He saw the genetic splicing areas where computer-controlled operations were conducted on the microscopic chromosomes of the eggs that would become GECs if they met all the tests and criteria. He was told of the use of virus to modify genes. He saw what they called the nursery, where individual embryos from only a few weeks to nine months old matured in environmentally controlled tanks.

Finally, thankfully, the afternoon ended. He begged off on Cal's dinner invitation, explaining that his queasy stomach and lack of sleep made a quiet evening in his room a necessity. He ate alone, and planned.

He watched the sunset and determined the north-south layout of the buildings. It wasn't quite dark yet, so he decided to implement the scheme he had been working on. Even though he knew little about astronomy or maritime navigation, he did know that some people were able to accurately determine their location simply by seeing the position of the stars. David needed to know where he was. He would have to compose a mental picture of the position of the stars, and fix it indelibly in his mind, since the idea of making any notes or diagrams was out of the question. First he would test the limits of their surveillance of him, find out if he could get off the island by taking an airplane or boat, before deciding what else he could do.

He looked in the closet and found some athletic shoes and sport clothes that could pass as a jogging outfit. He changed into these and left his room.

David walked casually in the direction of the golf course. The moon had risen in the darkening sky. He scrutinized the moon, trying to estimate how many hand-widths it rose above the horizon.

He could now begin to see the first stars, and he sat down on the edge of one of the sand bunkers to complete his mental calculations. Patterns of stars seemed vaguely familiar. And although he was concentrating on his task, he still sensed movement behind him.

"It's beautiful, isn't it?" David said. Krickett, who was almost invisible in the darkness, had approached silently.

"You're actually supposed to call me to go with you, because of all the restricted areas," she said, surprised that he had detected her presence.

"I didn't intend to go to any restricted areas. I only wanted to take a walk out to the golf course." He now knew that they were watching him very closely, so there was little chance of escaping.

"It doesn't really matter," she said, and sat down next to him, dangling her feet over the edge of the sand trap. She slipped off her shoes and ran her toes through the sand. "It is rather nice out here. I've never seen it at night before."

"That building is amazing, even in the dark," he said. He stood then and looked toward the building, ready to return to his room. "Anyway, it's time for me to hit the sack. I'm completely exhausted."

When they got back to David's room, Krickett made no move to come inside. "I'll see you at seven and we'll go to a breakfast meeting before you leave," she said, and walked away before he could even say good night.

David went straight to the bar in his room. He took out a thin towel, spread it on the counter, and wet his fingers under the faucet. Imagining that the towel was the section of sky he had observed, he tried to visualize the largest stars' locations. Using his wet finger, he made dots on the towel to indicate their relative positions. As he worked, he poured himself a soda to cover his actions and gazed at the towel for several minutes until he was satisfied that he had the positions of the stars memorized. Then he held the towel under running water, wrung it out and laid it on the countertop to dry.

He lay awake for hours. Every time he would begin to doze off he would see the image of one of the spheres or one of the children inside. He could almost smell the perfectly engineered food. He fought off several waves of nausea until finally, in the early hours of the morning, he managed to drift off into a fitful sleep.

He awoke at five o'clock, more refreshed than he would have dreamed possible. He showered and shaved, and by six-fifteen had time to spare. He sat in the living room ready to go. It was now full daylight, and David made a mental note of the time he had first noticed dawn breaking. His internal clock told him that he had traveled west through several time zones.

While David was waiting, a meeting took place in Cal's office. Cal held a cup of steaming coffee and lit a cigarette. LeBearc moved as far away from him as possible. Krickett had been telling them about David's walk on the golf course the night before.

"As far as I could tell, it was nothing more than it appeared to be. He went for a stroll after dinner, probably to think over everything he had seen during the day. I can't imagine anything else that he could have been doing. It looked innocent enough to me," she concluded.

"I keep telling you both not to underestimate him," LeBearc said. "None of us has any experience dealing with an individual with his abilities."

"We all know his background, Andre, and have seen how smart he is, but that doesn't mean he's up to something," Cal said. "I think he's overwhelmed by what he saw. You have to admit our system is pretty astonishing when you first learn about it. We've gotten used to it because we've seen it develop over the years. I don't see anything unusual in the way he acted, considering."

"I'm not so sure," said LeBearc, "but I still have orders to persuade him to work for us. His unconventional approach to medicine is fascinating. What we don't need is for him to decide to interfere. The other one, Janette Compton, has already done that. It's my view that it's still too dangerous to allow all of our methods to become public. Maybe we shouldn't have told him. And maybe now, we should not take him off the island. Maybe we should keep him here long enough to be certain how he really feels."

"Keeping him here would be useless," Krickett said. "If you force him to stay here, you'd lose any chance of gaining his acceptance."

"If he leaves, we can't control him. Either he goes back now and we take our chances, or he doesn't ever go, is that it?" LeBearc asked. He knew then the decision wasn't up to him, and that it had already been made.

David and Krickett joined Cal and LeBearc in Cal's private dining room a few minutes later and had a sumptuous breakfast. From there they all went to the airstrip.

"This was a short visit, David," Cal said. "But I hope that now you understand why we don't permit our organs to be retransplanted."

David didn't reply, although apparently they had expected him to.

The jet that they had arrived on, or one like it, was sitting on the ramp waiting, with the door open.

Krickett smiled at David. "I'll certainly never forget this trip," she said, stretching up to kiss his cheek. She smiled a little broader.

Cal reached behind his back and removed the Colt .45 automatic from his belt. He jammed a clip of bullets into it and cycled the slide, loading a round.

David stared at the gun, mesmerized, then glanced sideways to find an escape. Too late, he thought. He had been sloppy and it would cost him his life.

"Krickett likes to do the shooting," Cal said, handing her the gun. The "social director" persona was gone. David locked his eyes on hers and caught a glimpse of another person altogether, one with a deadly, ice-cold stare. She whirled around, crouched, and in three split-second pairs of shots sent three quart-size oil cans exploding off the airplane service cart fifty yards away, hitting each one twice and splashing oil everywhere. They had been impossible shots.

She turned back around, locked the safety, and handed the pistol to David, grip first, holding the hot barrel. "Want to try?" she asked. "You're a shooter, aren't you?"

"No, thanks," David said. How did she know he was an accomplished handgun shooter? David had acquired his shooting skills as part of his golf training program, to develop his eye-hand coordination. Then at graduation his father presented him with a pistol, along with a warning that he should always be prepared to protect himself from physical attack. This had come at a time when his father seemed more and more obsessed with the idea of David abandoning golf as a profession and making his own life choices "regardless of the consequences."

For a moment Krickett looked at him in a way that made him shudder, then she smiled and winked, leaving the unmistakable warning that it could have been his head that exploded instead of the oil cans.

"See ya," she said and walked away.

David climbed aboard the plane and stood looking

through the door's tiny thick plastic peephole. It distorted his view, but then everything on the island was distorting in one way or another. LeBearc had gone immediately into the aft private room before takeoff. Over the PA system a voice said, "Would you please take a seat, sir? This will be a maximum performance departure."

David sat down and swiveled the chair forward just in time. The plane made a turn onto the runway and immediately began to accelerate, far more rapidly than it had done when it left Orlando. David knew that the engine's deafening sound would greatly exceed the noise control limits of any commercial airport in the world. The plane lifted off, climbing at an alarming angle.

David looked around, but found no magazines or anything to read, and with no window except for the small one in the door there was nothing to see, nothing to do but sit and review in his mind all that had happened.

Clearly he had seen only a small part of what IORC did. There also must be other facilities, other islands, and other technologies. He already knew that they had extensive capacities in pharmaceuticals; hints here and there suggested a much greater involvement than was publicly known. The sophistication needed to create the GECs was sure to have spun off other unimaginable genetic projects, all secret.

Shaken out of his thoughts, he felt the plane slow, begin its descent, and finally touch down. While the plane was still rolling on the runway, LeBearc came through the cabin and said to David as he passed, "I hope you found the tour interesting and will decide to join our company. Let me know." And with this, he left in his own private car before David could even descend the plane stairs.

David checked back through IORC, changed into his own clothes, and was driven back to Orlando Government.

He felt relief after climbing out of the IORC car at the

front door. He went inside—back to reality and still alive—but now determined to act.

First thing, he checked the messages on his voice mail: one was from Janette.

Suddenly Martinez's death came back to him in a flood of memories, reemphasizing the danger and disorientation he had felt on the island. David remembered that when he had returned from North Carolina, he had left the autopsy papers on the backseat of his car and the modules in the glove compartment. Had anyone taken them? He bolted through the reception area and breezed past the secretary with only a wave, heading for the parking lot.

He found his car and fumbled for a few seconds with his keys, trying to get the door open. When he did, he slipped into the driver's seat, turned around, and reached onto the backseat to move his overcoat. The file was still there. He opened the glove compartment and, sure enough, the foil Alka-Seltzer wrapper that contained the modules was there. He put them into his sports jacket pocket and exhaled in relief. He had gotten lucky.

David drove back to his apartment and took the file inside. He saw immediately that some of his furniture had been moved and became suspicious. Then he remembered that the cleaning man had been scheduled to come and probably had moved things around. He wasn't, after all, still at IORC. He was home now, and safe.

He had received a fax—a handwritten list of names and addresses. A date, and a type of organ such as heart, liver, or kidney, followed each name and address. No explanation or signature accompanied the list.

He put the fax into an envelope and wrote Janette's name on the outside. He wanted to make sure that it didn't fall into the IORC's hands, so he decided to take the envelope himself to Janette's office. He didn't want to talk to her yet, not until he decided how much to tell her about what he had seen, and thus how much danger to expose her to.

He drove downtown to the UNILAW office. He gave the envelope to her, saying, "I can't talk now. I've seen so much in the last few days that I have to process everything. I'll call." He also handed her a folded note.

David still carried the foil envelope with the modules in the pocket of his jacket.

Janette stared after him as he left, then read the note.

This is all much more complicated and dangerous than I thought. We have to be very careful. We'll meet tonight at the Pizza Palace at 7:00 P.M.

# 14

That evening they met at the Pizza Palace a few blocks from Janette's apartment, and ordered a pizza and some beer. Even though David hadn't shaved and looked haggard, his hands were so steady that the stream of beer he poured into the mug looked like it was molded from plastic. He had a sense of purpose and resolution in his bearing that Janette had seen only hints of before.

"Look, Janette, IORC is much worse than we thought. They're much bigger and more powerful. They made me sign an agreement not to disclose anything I saw on my trip. I can't talk about the details of what I saw—and that's for your own protection."

"In that case, why did you want to see me?"

"My trip didn't have anything directly to do with the case, but I can tell you that Mike's heart didn't fail of natural causes. They deliberately caused it to fail somehow, and I intend to see that they don't do it to anyone else."

"Can you prove it?" she asked.

"I don't know. Maybe. But I'm sure that's what happened, and we'll have to work together to get the evidence to prove it. When they find out what we're doing, it's going to get very, very dangerous; more than you could imagine. What have you done with the list I gave you?"

"I gave it to Warren immediately. He'll find out what's happened to those people."

"Their lives are in danger. We have to guard that list," David added.

Janette stared at David. She clenched her jaw and her skin paled. "I'll call Warren right now." Janette rummaged through her purse for her address book. She went outside to a pay phone and called UNILAW. She returned to the table two minutes later. She looked more relaxed.

"Warren had already figured out how important security was on the list. He put the names in his computer in a secured file and then shredded the paper. After doing that he went back up to my office, got out my case file and shredded my copy. He also managed to work in the fact that he would collect his reward from me later.

"Anyway, what I had started to tell you on the phone this afternoon was that Warren also found out more about the autopsy. I got Mrs. Martinez to sign an authorization and then sent an investigator over to pick up the lab tests from the autopsy. Warren came up with the name of some sort of medication that was in Martinez's blood. It was called 'succinctline,' or something like that."

David began to chuckle.

"What's so funny?"

"No one has made 'succinct' medicine yet. I wish they would. I could use some. I think you mean succinyl-choline."

"Frankly, I'm not impressed. I could use several dozen legal terms that you wouldn't be able to decipher." She refused to acknowledge the humor, drilling holes in him with her glare.

"Don't get your feelings hurt."

"Anyway, that medicine, that—whatever you call it— was in his blood."

"Succinylcholine paralyzes the smooth muscles during

surgery so that there is no involuntary movement. It's not actually an anesthetic; it doesn't put the person to sleep or make him unconscious. He would be completely aware of what's going on if all he were to get was succinylcholine. The IORC uses it in their transplant process. Why would it be in Martinez's blood?"

"Is that something that could still have been in his blood from your surgery?"

"Oh, no way. It dissipates in only a few minutes. The anesthesia that accompanies it stays in the blood far longer and is also in the tissues longer. What other chemicals did he find?"

"There weren't any others that seemed unusual."

"That's really not possible, and I don't want to get into the possible-probable debate again. The report must be wrong. If succinylcholine was present, then traces of anesthesia should have been there also."

"Whether it's possible, or probable, that's what was in the report. If it were true, what would you make of it?"

"It's possible to use succinylcholine alone, but it's never done medically—except . . ." David flashed back to his conversation with Cal on the island. "It would be terrifying for the patient. His muscles would become paralyzed, yet he would remain fully conscious. It would immediately disable someone because the drug's action is almost instantaneous."

"What are you thinking?" Janette asked.

"I think IORC might have used succinylcholine to restrain Mike Martinez—not actually restrain as much as disable. It would have scared the shit out of him. If this drug showed up in the autopsy, something tells me Martinez must have been resisting—and died almost immediately."

The IORC had checked Dr. Byrd's fax list, electronically acquired through the tap on David West's telephone line. LeBearc was now reviewing the list. Of the forty-four people on the list, fourteen had already been discovered through channels similar to the discovery of the Martinez case and terminated as Code 6.

"Well, something has come out of this mess. At least we have identified even more Code 6 candidates," LeBearc grumbled to himself. He was angry. Even though they had already terminated some of the people from Byrd's group, this list proved what LeBearc already knew: Too many people were gaining access to IORC organs through improper sources. Illegal transplants placed IORC's quality control, for which he was directly responsible, in jeopardy. His duty was now clear to him. He telephoned the security director at home.

"Update the whereabouts of everyone on the list I just sent you," LeBearc directed, "and their doctors."

"Yes, sir. I thought you'd want to know that someone from the UNILAW office came here with a release and got a copy of the autopsy on the Code 6 we had here. That lawyer, Compton, signed the request. We also found out that her office has been hacking our computer again and asking questions around engineering departments at several universities concerning our serial number modules."

"Tell no one else about this, and get on that list right away." LeBearc jabbed the phone disconnect button. He then seethed as he waited for Hoffmeister, who was at the symphony, to be summoned to the phone. The sound of the orchestra in the background added to his fury. Finally Hoffmeister picked up.

"What's the matter, Andre?"

"Compton is causing trouble again. She's nosing around in our business, and her staff is involved in computerized snooping of our operations and some of our proprietary electronics. Try as I may, I can't see any excuse for this. I can't understand why she is still interfering after you told me that the matter had been resolved."

"I thought it was. I spoke to her boss and told him we didn't want to be harassed any longer."

"Whatever you thought, it's not taken care of, obviously. I don't see any excuse for this kind of harassment and I don't intend to put up with it. If you can't take care of it, I'll find someone who can." LeBearc disconnected without waiting for a response.


When Janette arrived at work that morning she got a sinking feeling in the pit of her stomach. She was immediately summoned to the U.S. Attorney's office—a call that promised trouble in her near future. Her former boss, Charles Henderson, was waiting, and so was her new supervisor, Ms. Moss. It got worse a few moments later when Wilson Hoffmeister arrived. He glared at Janette, yet said nothing and remained standing. It appeared he didn't intend to be kept waiting.

As Compton, Moss, Henderson, and Hoffmeister were led into a large, well-appointed office, the U.S. Attorney, Bob Collins, came around from behind his desk and shook Hoffmeister's hand. The two were clearly well acquainted.

"Wilson, it's good to see you. How's your family?" Collins asked.

"Bob, the family is fine, but I'm afraid I'm not here to make small talk."

"Have a seat, everyone," Collins directed. "Go ahead, Wilson, what's the problem?"

Hoffmeister recapped his displeasure with Janette's behavior for ten full minutes.

"Is there some investigation going on?" Collins asked Janette.

Janette hesitated. The others looked at one another and

looked at her, obviously unaware of any such investigation. Their expressions said it all.

"Yes, sir, there is an investigation under way. I'm handling a compensation claim. We had a hearing and the arbitrator gave us an opportunity to gather more evidence to show that there had been a medical failure. That's what I'm doing."

"What has an arbitration concerning a medical failure got to do with the number of heart transplants that IORC does, or the engineering background of our electronics devices?" Hoffmeister demanded in a condescending tone.

"Yes, what?" Collins asked Janette.

"I'd rather discuss that privately," Janette said.

"Nonsense, you can answer the question now, if you please," he said.

"We have reason to believe that the husband of my client may have died as the result of a deliberate act sanctioned by IORC." Janette hadn't wanted to say it but they gave her no choice.

"What! That's the most absurd thing I've ever heard!" sneered Hoffmeister.

"What evidence do you have to back up such an accusation?" the U.S. Attorney asked.

"We're doing a preliminary investigation to try to rule out certain things," she said.

"I asked you what evidence you *had*," Collins said, glaring at Janette.

"Well, actually, we're trying to get that evidence right now. That's the whole point of the investigation."

"That's what I had warned her about before, and the reason she got transferred," Henderson piped up.

"Did you authorize any investigation?" the U.S. Attorney asked Ms. Moss.

"Janette's a good lawyer. She is representing her client, and in my opinion she has a lot of leeway to do that. She is entitled to investigate such a death and its possible causes."

"I didn't ask you to give me a lecture on the duties of attorneys in this office. My question was, did you authorize it?"

"I didn't know about it in advance, but I support her decision."

Turning to Janette, he asked, "In your investigation, have you come up with anything that supports your theory?"

"The doctor who transplanted the man's heart thinks that's a possibility," Janette answered.

"Does he have any evidence for that opinion?"

"That's the reason for the investigation," she replied again.

"The doctor is a personal friend of Compton's," said Hoffmeister. "It looks to me as if she's trying to find an excuse so he won't be blamed."

"That isn't the point!" Janette flared. "An IORC doctor found nothing wrong with the surgery."

"Look, this is ridiculous," said Collins. "Accusing an institution such as IORC of intentionally causing a patient's death is totally irresponsible. Conducting an investigation without authority, particularly this kind of investigation, was bad judgment the first time. The second time, after having been warned, it's totally unacceptable. Ms. Compton, consider yourself on suspension until formal discharge proceedings can be held. I would recommend that you consider tendering your resignation to UNILAW before that. You have three days' notice as of now. Meanwhile you are to terminate any investigation in which you are engaged, and you are not to utilize any of the facilities of this office for any such investigation. You got me on all of that?"

"This is wrong. We're supposed to represent our clients the same as private attorneys would. It's wrong to have the attorney for someone who may be responsible for the death of our client's husband come in here and use political influence to get the lawyer fired," Janette said. She realized right away that she had gone too far.

The U.S. Attorney stood up at his desk, his face boiling red. He leaned over the desk toward her. "Don't you accuse me of bending to political influence! This hasn't anything to do with politics. You obviously don't understand the limits of your authority in this department. This discussion is over."

When they went out into the hall, Janette had an overwhelming urge to cry, but she refused to give in to it.

"I'm sorry you raised the issue of politics," said Ms. Moss. "I might have been able to do something to work this out until you said that. Now, I'm afraid it's too late. It's too bad. You're really a fine lawyer. If I can help you with a recommendation, let me know."

It wasn't fair. She hadn't done anything wrong. She had worked her butt off to do what she was supposed to do, what she had been taught to do in law school: represent her client. How could this be happening? As she was thinking these thoughts, Hoffmeister came out of the office, accompanied by the U.S. Attorney. "Wilson, I'm sorry all this happened. Please assure your client that it's not our intention to harass them."

"Thank you," Hoffmeister said, still projecting outrage. He turned and walked by Janette without so much as a glance in her direction.


Janette was a survivor. She immediately began thinking about what she could do for Mrs. Martinez and what she had to do to protect herself and her friends. First she went directly to Warren's office to warn him.

She tapped on his glass wall. Looking up, he waved her in.

"I've been fired, Warren."

"What—what happened?" He immediately became serious.

She explained, concluding, "That's why I came here right away. I'm sure you'll be getting a call any minute. I've gotten you in trouble again, only this time it may be much worse." She blinked back tears.

"You're in trouble and that doesn't seem fair, but I'm not in trouble. I have an authorization form, remember? Hold it just a minute," he said and turned back to his computers. He pushed a disk into the drive on his console and his fingers began flying over the keys. The screen flashed as a whirring sound emitted from the disk drive.

Then he handed the disk to Janette.

"That's the only copy of the list of names you gave me. I've taken the other one off the mainframe. You've also got the only copy of my notes and conclusions, too. I don't know what's going to happen, but you need to keep the disk, anyway. Too much work went into this to be wasted, and I'm convinced something bad is happening at IORC.

"I think you should take the disk right now and get out of the building. Come back for your things later."

"You're making me scared."

"Maybe it's time we all got scared," Warren said. "I think we can prove they killed Martinez, and I don't think he's the only one. I don't like what I see. You're probably safe, but still I want you to get the hell out of the building now, while you can, and take the disk with you."

She hesitated and stood, staring at him.

"Get the hell out, now!" he snapped. She had never heard him talk like this before, and it got her attention.

Without another word she turned and left. She took the elevator directly to the lobby, rather than to the basement parking garage, and walked straight out through the front door.

Janette didn't know where to go. She wanted to get her car, but decided not to go into the parking garage while she still had the disk. She was at a loss as to what to do with it. She stepped into a café down the street and ordered a cup of coffee. She sat at a table at the front of the room and stared out the window, more or less in a daze. Then she noticed a FedEx office across the street. Rummaging through her handbag, she found her address book and tore out one of the note pages. She wrote a note to Parker Ross, a retired attorney friend who had done legal work for her father.

> Dear Parker: I need to talk to you. I have enclosed a computer disk. It contains privileged communications and attorney work product. Don't call my house. My phone is probably tapped. I'll get in touch with you as soon as I can. By the way, I'm getting fired. —Janette

She walked across the street to the FedEx office and sent the disk and note to Parker.

She then walked back to the UNILAW building and went directly to her office. As she passed through the main room, several of her coworkers turned and stared at her. When she got to her office she could see why. A uniformed security guard blocked the door. She reached around him for the doorknob, and he stopped her.

"Are you Ms. Compton?" he asked.

"That's right. What's the problem?"

"I have orders that you are not to remove anything from the room until it is inventoried, and that you are not permitted to remove anything except your personal property," he said with a smirk.

"I haven't the slightest intention of removing anything from my office," she said, pushing his hand aside and going in.

The walls of her office were glass. The security guard started to follow her in, but she stopped him. "You can watch me through the glass and make sure I don't steal any of the silverware. I'm still an attorney here and I'll not have you in my way." He hesitated, and she slammed the door in his face.

She went around behind her desk, sat down, and began shuffling some papers, not really knowing what she was doing. She saw the security guard walk over to the nearest desk in the main room, pick up the phone, and dial a number. In a few moments he hung up, walked back over next to her door, and stood on the other side of the glass wall watching her.

*So be it, you son of a bitch. You can stand there all day as far as I'm concerned,* she thought. She looked at him and went back to shuffling papers. A few minutes later, Ms. Moss knocked on the door and walked in.

"Janette, technically you are still an attorney here. There's nothing Bob Collins can do about that until the review board meets. But you can't check out any files or work on anything, so you're just wasting your time by being here."

"It's my time to waste, isn't it?" Janette snapped.

"Janette, I'm as sorry as I can be about this. There's absolutely nothing I can do. I tried to call in some favors, but it's out of my hands and beyond my control. I'm sorry."

"I know it's not your fault. I'm sorry I snapped at you. It's all just so unfair."

"Why don't you take the next couple of days and think through your options. Maybe you should resign, rather than force them to go through all of the steps. It would probably look better on your resume."

"Are you telling me I have to leave?" Janette asked.

"No, you can stay here but, in fairness, it's pretty disruptive to have a guard standing out there staring at you. It certainly isn't doing anyone any good, least of all you. You do what you want, though." She turned and left.

Janette looked around her office. She had few personal items and in fact there weren't a dozen pages of papers and materials in her office that belonged to her. She tried to remember if there was anything in the Martinez file that shouldn't be, or anything that she would need later. She concluded that the file was harmless.

She would not—she *could* not—give up the efforts to find out what had happened to Michael Martinez; she couldn't give up her obligations to Betty and Jorge Martinez. Maybe she would go into practice for herself and represent Mrs. Martinez as her first private case. She thought about that for a while and realized that she had no idea how much it would cost to go into private practice, or how much she could hope to earn, if anything, by practicing law. Without the support of one of the few remaining large private law firms it would be virtually impossible to find paying clients.

She had saved enough to live on for several months and, though she really didn't want to do so, she could call on her father for help. Ultimately, though, she would have to get another job.

She had purposely left her purse sitting on her desk unopened so that the security guard wouldn't have an excuse to search it. She walked around from behind her desk and held her hands up and turned them back and forth, showing the palms and then the backs and then the palms again to the guard, who glared at her. Picking up her purse, she opened the door, walked past him without a word, and headed for home.

At around six o'clock that evening, Warren called Janette at her apartment.

"As you were leaving, I got a call summoning me to Bob Collins's office. He told me to make a printout of all my research. I took a bit of an ass-chewing."

"What did you say?"

"Name, rank, and serial number. But really, I did find a lot of coincidences, you might say. Even though the investigation is officially over, I think we still need to talk about it."

"I want to get David in on this." She arranged a meeting for that night.

At eight o'clock, as she pulled into the parking lot of the Pizza Palace, she saw David and Warren walking in together. By the time she parked they had gotten a table and were comparing their pilot ratings and experience. She came over and sat next to David, interrupting their conversation about flying.

"So, that's how it is," Warren said in mock jealousy. "Actually, there's some advantage to your sitting over there instead of next to me." He removed an imaginary cigar from his mouth, Groucho Marx–style.

"It's also safer," Janette teased back.

"I think I resent that," David said.

They ordered a pitcher of beer and a pizza, and Warren told David about his own airplane, a Cessna 172; old but serviceable. Then the conversation turned to Martinez.

Janette and Warren recapped the events of the day for David's benefit.

"I'm sorry you got fired. That's unfair."

"Very unfair. But that seems to be common when IORC is involved."

"Exactly what have you found out?" David asked.

"Mostly coincidences—and you know how I feel about coincidences. I've run down the names on the list. Of forty-four people, fourteen are now dead, which is statistically impossible in relation to long-term transplant studies. In twelve out of the fourteen cases, death was reported as resulting from the failure of the organ that had been transplanted. I was in the process of checking the doctors who signed the death certificates to find out if they were IORC doctors. The rest I hadn't completed yet. Incidentally, my investigation is officially terminated. Those are my orders."

"Somehow we need to check the autopsies on those deaths," David said, "to look for succinylcholine. But now

I'm even more certain they killed him. What I don't know is how they did it."

"Are you willing to testify? I mean, would you say that in court?" Janette asked, turning to look at him.

David hesitated. He knew what his answer had to be. "Yes, I'd testify. I believe it and I'd testify to it but I still don't know how we would get the evidence to prove what we know."

Janette realized that she had decided to do the Martinez case as a private lawyer, based on her idea that the IORC treaty, while preventing claims for negligence, did not prevent suits for deliberate misconduct. Immediately Warren agreed to continue his computer research at home.

"We can meet this weekend. How's that with you?" She looked back and forth and they both nodded.

"From now on we have to be careful," David said. "No phones unless we watch what we say. We're dealing with an organization that plays for keeps—never forget that."

# 15

Janette met Betty and Jorge Martinez on Sunday at a small, anonymous café in downtown Orlando.

"There have been some developments in your case. First of all, it's now Dr. West's opinion that your husband did not die of a medical failure."

"What's the matter, did he chicken out?" Jorge sneered.

"It's nothing like that, Jorge. In fact, it's just the opposite. He thinks your father didn't die of natural causes."

"You mean he was killed?" Jorge asked.

"That's exactly what I mean."

Mrs. Martinez began crying. Jorge slammed his fist down on the table, rattling the dishes and causing several people who were sitting nearby to turn and stare.

"Take it easy, now. David thinks IORC did it. Not only that, but IORC may have done this before to other people who received one of their organs without the right J Factor."

Janette explained her theory to them, and then told them she was going to resign from UNILAW.

"Can you do the case, even if you resign?"

"That's exactly what I would like to do. I have planned to open a small, temporary office and take care of your case before I make up my mind about what to do permanently. What do you think of that?"

"Well, Janette, that's fine, but . . . you know, how are we going to pay you? We don't have very much money."

"I can do the case on a contingent fee, which means you don't owe me any fee unless we get money from IORC, and then you pay me a percentage of that."

Mrs. Martinez began to cry again. "Everybody is being so nice to us. Why did this have to happen? Why would they kill Mike?" She shook her head back and forth. Jorge tried to comfort her but he didn't know how. He was as upset as she was.

"There's another thing. If we file this suit, the newspapers and television will want to know everything there is to know about both of you and Mike. They'll probably—at least in the beginning—act as if we're all crackpots, bringing a suit like this. IORC will put a lot of pressure on you, and you need to understand that before we get started. You will lose your privacy and there's not one thing we can do about it."

"We're not crackpots. If they killed my husband, I want them punished for it, and I don't want them to do it to anyone else. I don't care what the newspapers or television say."

"It's not quite that simple. IORC will try to embarrass you and make you feel like a fool for bringing the suit. It could even be dangerous. I don't know. They're bad people. We don't want to start unless we are willing to follow through with it. I don't want you to answer now. I want you to think about it. Let me check on the arrangements and you call me up whenever you're sure what you want to do."

"I don't need to wait. I'm sure now. I want you to handle the case and I don't care about the television people or the newspapers or any danger. Jorge and I can deal with that. It can't be as bad as what we have already been through. No, I don't have to wait. That's what I want you to do. Don't you think, Jorge?"

"Damn straight. If they killed my father, there's nothing anybody can do to make me back down."

On LeBearc's orders, the IORC security department had already located and were maintaining surveillance on three of the people on Dr. Byrd's list who were geographically close to Orlando—a heart transplant recipient in Jacksonville, a kidney recipient in Gainesville, and a liver recipient in Tallahassee.

The heart transplant recipient in Jacksonville was a copy machine salesman who lived with his family in a residential neighborhood a few miles south of the city. LeBearc sent two technicians in a van jammed with electronics to his neighborhood with instructions to wait for further orders.

By four o'clock on Monday afternoon, the technicians had parked the van in front of the next door neighbor's house. They waited as commanded.

After delivering her resignation on Monday morning, Janette spent the afternoon doing research. Although her decision to leave made her anxious, she was completely committed to the task at hand and quickly dug into her work.

Law libraries, though imposing in size, are the simplest and most carefully organized and cross-referenced of all libraries. It is possible to find any court decision since the Middle Ages in any appeal court in any country. Many trial court cases are also reported. Janette had at her fingertips the ability to access cases from a computer database, by subject or by selecting a group of words that come together in a decision such as "IORC, intentional conduct, negligence."

Janette found many cases where suits had been brought in the early days of the IORC, and the cases had been dismissed because of the treaty. But none of these suits involved intentional misconduct, so at least there wasn't a case contrary to her legal argument.

Finally she discovered a case that had occurred in Israel, in which the suit claimed that the IORC had acted intentionally and wasn't exempt. The decision came on a Motion To Dismiss in a trial court, not the highest court, but on this legal point the ruling had been in the claimant's favor. Janette could find no indication that the case had been tried, appealed, or ever referred to by another court anywhere else. She got a printout of the decision, which included the names of the lawyers who had handled the case eight years before. She decided that she would call the claimant's lawyer and ask him some questions.

According to the court papers the lawyer, Ben Masckowicz, had a New York address. A call to that firm got her his phone number in Israel where he now lived, retired. She decided to take a chance and placed a call to him.

A woman answered the phone speaking Hebrew, and Janette asked to speak to the lawyer. In a voice that was heavily accented, she asked Janette to wait a moment. A moment turned into several minutes and Janette was about to hang up, realizing for the first time that it was late evening there, when a raspy voice came on the line.

"This is Ben Masckowicz." The accent was pure New York City.

"My name's Janette Compton. I'm sorry to disturb you but it is rather urgent. I'm an attorney in Florida. I've been doing some research and I came across your case, *Arrow v. IORC*. I can't find out exactly what happened, and I'm interested in the legal theories that you used. Can you tell me anything? Why was there no appeal?"

"I'm retired now," he replied sharply.

"But do you remember the case? It had to do with a claim against IORC for intentionally killing a man. Surely you would remember that. It's the only case I can find anywhere in the world that has been brought on that basis."

"Of course I remember it," he growled. "I'm not senile, just retired." He seemed mad at the world and probably at Janette for interrupting his evening or his sleep.

"I am sorry to bother you, but I have a case like this and I need to find out what happened."

"My advice to you is forget it and do something else."

"I'm not going to do that. I want to know what happened. How did the case come out?" Janette had experience in dealing with grumpy lawyers. She had no intention of giving up.

"My client decided to settle, and that's all I'm able to say. The settlement specified that there would be no appeal and that neither my client nor I would discuss the settlement. We can say only that the case is resolved and that the terms of the resolution of the case are confidential. Much as I hate to, I'll have to abide by that."

For a moment, there was silence on the other end of the line. Then, "Ms . . . , what did you say your name was, again?"

"My name is Janette Compton."

"My best friend, Sid Arrow, got an illegal heart transplant. He had a low J Factor and he paid a doctor to illegally transplant a heart from an industrial accident victim—the heart was originally from IORC.

"Then Sid moved to Israel and went to IORC for a physical in order to qualify for our National Health program. He died right there. I sued IORC on behalf of Sid's family and alleged that they murdered him to protect their monopoly. They denied it, of course, and claimed that the treaty prevented the suit. But the judge denied a motion to dismiss. Then they settled. Like I said, though, I can't disclose the details of the settlement.

"Ms. Compton, I wish I were young enough to come over there and help you, because that is exactly what I would do. I can say this. You're right and it's about time somebody did what you're doing. I hope that you're successful."

"Thank you," she said.

Upon hanging up, Janette knew that this was a strong beginning: a precedent.

The copy machine salesman in Jacksonville arrived home a little early that evening. As he turned into the driveway he had to stop, get out, and move his daughter's tricycle from in front of the garage door. While he was outside, the technicians in the green van pointed a microwave scanner at him and got a clear response from the module attached to his heart. The telltale series of sixteen numbers registered on the portable computer screen.

The salesman stepped back in his car and drove into his garage.

Before the door even closed, one of the technicians was on the satellite phone to IORC Orlando. Then they continued to scan the subject. The signal had broken up when he got inside his car, but when he got back out of the car inside the garage the signal cleared.

They reported the details to LeBearc. He gave directions for them to meet him at Craig Airport in Jacksonville the next morning at five o'clock.

Inside the house, the copy machine salesman relaxed in front of the television. His four-year-old daughter sat on the floor beside him playing with her coloring book and crayons while he ate a sandwich and watched the news. His wife sat across the room reading. She looked up at her husband and daughter, realizing how close they had become as a family because of all they had been through.

Later in the evening, after their daughter had gone to bed, she kissed her husband on the cheek and he wrapped his arms around her and pulled her onto his lap. They kissed and necked for a while. One of the best parts of the heart transplant for them was that he didn't have to abstain from sex anymore. He picked up his wife, and she protested, so he put her down and they walked together into their bedroom. After making love, and quietly talking about their plans to get a nicer house soon, they drifted off to sleep.

A few minutes after four A.M., Andre LeBearc stepped on board an IORC jet in Orlando. Before he could sit it began taxiing, immediately took off, and twenty minutes later landed in Jacksonville and taxied up to the general aviation terminal. Fortunately, the technicians in the green microwave-equipped truck were cautious when it came to dealing with LeBearc. They arrived at the general aviation terminal early and had just pulled in when they saw the green business jet pull up in front. They hurried inside the terminal so it would appear that they had been waiting. Even before the engines shut down, LeBearc walked off the plane, dressed impeccably in his gray pinstripe suit, white shirt, and maroon silk tie. He glanced at the technicians wordlessly, headed straight through the terminal, and walked directly to the green van parked out front.

A metal partition with a door separated the two front seats from the rear. The windowless back contained two chairs anchored to the floor, a portable toilet, and a small refrigerator, along with an array of electronic gear including digital indicators and CRT screens.

LeBearc stopped at the back door of the van and waited while one of the technicians entered the combination on the keypad lock and then held the door open for him. He stepped inside and pulled the door closed behind him. The two technicians exchanged a glance and, without comment, went around to the front of the van, got in and drove away.

They knew without being told where they were supposed to go. A few minutes after five they pulled up in front of the copy machine salesman's house. LeBearc tapped on the partition, and the two technicians came into the back of the van.

From the van, the three men saw a light go on in the kitchen through the video surveillance camera.

One technician in the van turned on the microwave scanner and swung the machine back and forth trying to get a response. The readout was not clear, and only some of the digits were showing. They flickered, and the signal grew weak.

"I thought you said this thing worked," LeBearc said.

"It does. He may be in the bathroom where there could be metal pipes. Let's keep tracking him for a minute."

In the house, the salesman dressed for work. He had an important appointment at a doctor's office at seven to sell a new copy machine, and he needed to get there before any patients did. He planned to be early. He then walked into the kitchen, kissed his wife on the cheek, and sat at the breakfast table.

Outside, someone pounded on the back door of the van; all three of the men inside jumped. They exchanged glances. One technician opened the door an inch and peeked out. A neighbor in a jogging suit stood behind the van, his dog tugging on the end of a leash. The man's breath made a fog that hovered around his face.

"I saw this truck out here yesterday when I came home from work; now you're here again this morning. What the hell's going on?" he asked.

"We're from the satellite TV company," said the technician. "We've been getting some interference in this area, and we're trying to pin it down so that we can take care of it."

The man tried to look inside the van. He couldn't really see much since it was dark, but he did see the computer screens with the numbers flickering on and off.

"Why don't you have your name on the truck, then?" he asked, still suspicious. His dog pulled against the leash impatiently, ready to run some more.

"You got me, pal. I just work for them, I'm not the boss. Now, if you'll excuse me, we've got things to do," and he started to close the door. The man held it open.

"I'm not sure I buy that. I'm going to call the company and find out."

"That's fine with me. My dispatcher ought to know I'm out this early, anyway. I don't think he always believes me." With that, the technician pulled the door out of the man's hand and slammed it shut, locking it.

The jogger backed away a couple of steps, read the license plate number, and jogged away.

"There, the signal's steady and strong now. He's not moving around." The technician motioned to LeBearc, who had already seen the same thing.

LeBearc compared the number he saw on the screen against the one he had written down on a piece of paper. The numbers checked out.

"You two go up front. I'll let you know when I'm ready to go." They moved up front and closed the door to the rear. They knew better than to speculate on what LeBearc was up to.

LeBearc had done a Code 6 only in his own hospital, never in the field. He didn't intend to wait for this man to go to an IORC center by chance; he intended to act immediately and get this mess over with. Of course, since the signal to disable the organ could be transmitted by satellite like any other microwave signal, he could deactivate an organ literally anywhere in the world right from his own office—a useful feature. But this delicate work was fraught with risks, so he wanted to see to this first case personally.

To ensure security, it was essential to have a positive confirmation that the subject was who and where they thought he was. LeBearc checked the numbers again, then entered another series of numbers into the computer that was linked to his office. He pressed the "enter" button on the keyboard. The prompt on the screen said "Are you sure? Y/N." LeBearc hit the Y key. For a moment he hesitated, then pressed the "enter" button. A beam of microwave energy in predetermined digital groups was sent from Orlando to a satellite 23,000 miles above Florida and back to Jacksonville, penetrated the roof of the house and the chest of the copy machine salesman, and triggered a circuit in the module attached to his heart.

At that moment, the salesman was taking a sip of orange juice. He jerked and spilled the juice all over the front of his shirt and the table and dropped the glass, clutching his chest. The man's body convulsed again. This pulse straightened both of his legs, and caused his body to arch backward, lifting the table partly off the floor, sending the dishes crashing to the ceramic tile below. His wife ran to his side and his daughter screamed. His face pulled into a contorted mask of pain, and he clutched his chest with both hands. In a few seconds he fell sideways out of the chair and onto the floor. His body hit with a loud cracking sound; then he was completely still except for his right leg, which twitched for several moments. His wife gathered up her daughter in her arms, ran for the telephone, and dialed 911. She knew it would be too late; the blood that had at first run out of his nose and down his chin had stopped.

By the time the woman in the house was making the call, LeBearc was satisfied that the signal had not been interrupted. He got up from the chair, tapped on the partition, and sat back down, clearing the computer screen. He folded up the paper, put it back in his shirt pocket, and closed his eyes, leaning back slightly in the chair. The IORC ambulance that was waiting several blocks away had already pulled up as the van sped off.

In less than two hours, LeBearc was back in his office in Orlando. The copy machine salesman had been taken to the IORC clinic and pronounced dead, all in accordance with established procedures. LeBearc now knew that he need not be present in the future. The Code 6 procedure worked perfectly by satellite. It was necessary only for his team to confirm the location of the victim to facilitate the body pickup.

The thought of such power exhilarated LeBearc—especially when he considered that theoretically every IORC organ in the world could be disabled by a few simple keystrokes. But that was all part of the elaborate system.

At ten minutes to nine, Janette Compton walked into the clerk's office of the Circuit Court and handed the original and two copies of the lawsuit papers to one of the clerks, along with the filing fee. The clerk took the original complaint, stamped it showing the time that it had been filed, and then sat down to enter the details for a summons.

The clerk's job required him to read enough of the papers to be able to make appropriate entries in several places on the computerized docket. He began reading, stopped, reread several of the paragraphs and then looked at Janette. He rolled his eyes and looked up at the ceiling, shook his head and proceeded as any overburdened government employee might who knew that he was completely wasting his time. The very idea, with the courts as crowded as they were, of filing this sort of case was ridiculous.

He finished his entries and printed out a summons. He walked back to the counter and handed it to Janette.

"What law firm are you with, anyway? I don't think I've ever seen you before," he said.

"I'm in practice for myself. I'm not with a law firm."

He turned to the last page of the complaint, looked at the signature line, and saw that she had put down her apartment number.

"This is an apartment. We need to have your office address." He smirked.

"The law doesn't require that I have an *office* address, only that I have *an* address. That's *an* address. All I want you to do is process the paperwork, so you can mind your own business."

"Well, yes, ma'am, whatever you say, *ma'am*," he said, sarcastically, and stamped the papers and tossed them on the counter. She grabbed them and left the clerk's office to go to the sheriff's department, to arrange for the papers to be served on the IORC.

# 16

The next morning, after seeing the newspaper headlines about her lawsuit, Janette was ready for the inevitable call. But when the phone rang, it was the same reporter who had already left six messages. She cut him off with a "no comment" and hung up. The phone immediately jangled again.

"Ms. Compton, this is Wilson Hoffmeister. Of course, I'm calling about this suit that you have filed. I want to notify you about a hearing that has been set for next Monday at ten o'clock before Judge Cooper. We've made a Motion for Judgment on the Pleadings, which you should be getting by courier in a few minutes. I'll have my secretary call yours and get your fax number for the future." Professional but condescending, the unspoken message was that she was about to get a taste of playing lawyer in the big leagues.

"Don't you think it's premature to have a hearing for Judgment on the Pleadings?" she asked.

"Had I thought so, Ms. Compton, I certainly wouldn't have filed the motion and asked the court to take its valuable time on an emergency basis. Frankly, I find the entire matter completely preposterous. It's just another example of your abuse of the system. But I didn't call to argue with you."

"Why did you call, then?"

"Actually, the reason for my call is to give you an opportunity to exercise good professional judgment and dismiss this lawsuit before any more damage is done. It's possible that my client would be willing to forget the entire matter if the case is dismissed right now."

"That's not going to happen."

"I should tell you that I feel compelled to report this to the Bar Association. I intend to ask them to take immediate action concerning what you've done. I'm telling you right now that if you want to take the opportunity to dismiss the case now, all of this can be avoided; otherwise, I will do everything possible to protect the IORC and to put a final and permanent stop to this harassment and these irresponsible and baseless accusations. I suggest you think about it and discuss it with your client, if she really *is* your client, and get back in touch with me by four today."

"You do whatever you have to. We're not dismissing the lawsuit, not today, not next Monday, not at all. I have more evidence than you could possibly imagine. We'll quit when the decision of the highest court that can consider the case is final." She hung up the phone without waiting for a reply.

Just moments later, her doorbell rang. A courier from Hoffmeister's office handed her an envelope.

She tore it open. Inside was a notice of the hearing, a several-page motion, and a long printed and bound brief citing various laws and case decisions supporting the IORC argument that it was immune from suit. Her heart pounded and she felt as if she couldn't breathe. All of this had been done overnight.

She would have to read all of the cases cited in the brief and prepare her own brief and argument before Monday. She had only five days, counting the weekend.

Janette sank into her chair, clutching the papers. Maybe

she had acted too hastily in filing the suit. Maybe she should have done more preparation, more research, been more sure of herself before she sued IORC. She didn't have a staff to fall back on, or long years of experience to carry her through. She had taken on a totally one-sided fight. But it was too late for self-doubt now. She had made her decision. It would be nice to have some help, though.

She typed a notice changing her address and telephone and fax numbers to the temporary office she had rented. She also typed a change-of-address letter to the Bar Association.

Janette went into town and filed the notice with the clerk of the court, walked across the street to the Bar Association office, handed the letter to the receptionist, then walked the short distance to her temporary office. The receptionist there gave her a message to call the Bar Association office immediately.

"Ms. Compton, I'm glad that you finally notified us of your new address. We've been trying to reach you by telephone at the number you put on the papers that you filed in the lawsuit *Martinez* v. *IORC*. The reason for my call is to let you know that a hearing has been set concerning your case in the Bar Association office at nine o'clock on Friday morning. The chairman of the Grievance Committee has directed that the hearing take place on short notice."

"What hearing are you talking about?" Janette asked.

"The hearing on the ethical grievance that has been filed against you. A copy of that grievance was hand-delivered to the address that we had." The executive director treated her like a convicted criminal, not a lawyer.

"I'll tell you what, how about just hitting the high points for me. What is this about?" Janette asked.

"A grievance has been filed against you for solicitation of a case."

"Who filed the grievance?" she asked.

"That's confidential."

"What case am I accused of soliciting?" Janette asked.

"Have you solicited more than one case?" the director asked.

"Listen, ma'am, I don't appreciate your attitude. I'm an attorney."

"So I understand. It's about the *Martinez* v. *IORC* case. If you want to know any more about it you will have to read the grievance. I was required to call and give you notice by phone and that's what I've done. The hearing is at nine o'clock at the Bar office."

Things were moving too fast. Janette seemed out of phase with the events going on around her, yet trapped by them as if she were caught in a line of cars on a highway so that she couldn't slow down, couldn't go faster, and couldn't turn off.

She needed to do research on the Martinez case at the law library. Now, she also needed to review the rules on case solicitation, so that she would know where she stood for the hearing on Friday morning. The idea of a grievance in a case like this amounted to harassment. Hoffmeister was trying to rattle her—and it was working.

She skipped lunch and went to the Bar office again. She asked for a copy of the papers concerning her case. Finally, after several requests, a secretary brought out a document and made her pay a copying charge to get it.

She then spent the rest of the afternoon in the law library looking up and reading the cases cited in Hoffmeister's brief. She had read about half of them but her mind kept wandering. She kept coming back to the grievance hearing and the rules on solicitation. Finally, she gave in and looked them up.

The rules made it a disbarable offense for a lawyer to directly solicit a potential client to hire her or him to make a claim for an accident in which the client or client's family had been injured or killed. This was the method called "ambulance chasing." She was accused of doing just that.

According to her research, it appeared that she really

was guilty of violating the rule. The more she read, the more she squirmed in her chair and doodled on her notepad. She could see no loopholes, no exceptions or provisos that might help her. At the time she had thought she was doing the right thing. But now . . . Janette's eyes burned and her head pulsed with a dull ache.

It was time she got some advice—some legal advice. The only lawyer she trusted completely was Parker Ross, the man to whom she had sent the Martinez disk. Now seventy and retired, he had been her father's advisor since she was a child—even before: He had done the legal work for her adoption. He had guided her and made the all-important calls when she applied to law school.

Parker Ross was famous among lawyers. He had built his reputation by taking on anybody that his clients needed to sue, regardless of how important or rich they might be. Many of his cases had therefore attracted public attention.

And once people met him, they never forgot him. He seemed to have an aura about him. His white hair had a mind of its own, and his bushy eyebrows stayed in constant motion. He spoke in a slow, deep southern voice that exuded casual power and confidence.

Parker Ross answered Janette's call after half a dozen rings. "Have you really been fired?" Parker asked Janette. "I know a few people. I could make some calls if you want me to."

"It's too late. I plan to go out on my own. I've filed a suit that I couldn't have done if I had stayed. That's one of the things that I want to talk to you about."

"What in the world is going on?"

She told him about Martinez's death and her ordeal. "I lost my temper and told the U.S. Attorney that he was caving in to political influencee."

"And he fired you. What do you expect when you confront a politician with the truth?" Parker asked. "Whenever there's political influence it's probably best not to

mention that fact to the 'influencee.' That's just for future
reference," Ross quipped but Janette was having none of
it.

"I'm not about to give up, Parker. I want to talk to you
about the lawsuit. The widow is claiming that the IORC
intentionally killed her husband. I have read the IORC
treaty—it exempts them from lawsuits for negligence, but
it doesn't say one word about intentional misconduct."

"Well, that's certainly an interesting theory. I don't
think I've ever heard of a case like that." The wheels were
apparently turning in Parker's head. "Actually that's quite
brilliant. I think you're right. The theory is legally sound."
He was silent for several minutes and Janette waited. Then
he boomed, "Brilliant!"


In the early afternoon of that same day, Hoffmeister reported back to LeBearc, notifying the QC that Janette
Compton refused to drop the suit and that she claimed to
have damaging evidence. This information was met by
LeBearc with barely controlled anger.

That afternoon the QC had also received a report from
the electronics van that the woman in Tallahassee who had
received an unauthorized liver transplant had been located
and scanned. She worked the night shift in a pediatric
medical center. LeBearc called up the codes to implement
the Code 6. Then he hesitated. A remote Code 6 was risky,
very risky. A mistake could be made and the body taken to
somewhere other than IORC. If so, an autopsy would reveal the module as the site of organ failure. He deleted the
codes. It would have to wait.

LeBearc needed to know about the "other evidence."
He decided he would have to make a trip to Asheville and
confront Dr. Byrd, the probable source. He had also
learned that Dr. Byrd's kidney condition had deteriorated,
and that he was now receiving dialysis three times a week.

Janette called David. "Let's get away from here this week-end, and get Betty and Jorge Martinez away from the press. The TV people have camped out on Betty's lawn and are following Jorge to school. They are under a lot of pressure. We can go to Lake County. That'll give me a chance to talk further with Parker Ross about the Monday hearing."

"Sounds good," David said. *Safer, too, away from IORC,* he thought. He started calling to get his patients covered for the weekend. A few minutes later, he was summoned to Administrator Long's office.


When Janette called her, Betty Martinez offered to have her son bring her husband's boat along to Lake County. Boating had been Mike's main love in life.

Lately she watched her son go out in the afternoons to work on the boat, which sat on a trailer in the yard beside their house. He would climb inside the small cabin and polish and shine everything, even though it was already polished and shined. He changed the oil and spent hours tinkering with the boat, just as his father had done. It served as his connection with happier times.


Administrator Long compressed his lips into a straight line and furrowed his brow as he faced David across the huge desk. "This lawsuit is a big problem for the board. Also, you are spending more time away from your professional duties than appropriate. Your attention is on the wrong thing, and the hospital is suffering for it."

With considerable effort, David held his tongue.

"The board has directed me to suspend you until this suit is resolved and until you are ready to devote yourself to your professional responsibilities. The decision is not mine to make, but I must admit I don't entirely disagree. Politics aside, you can't expect to be away and distracted and still do your job effectively. Do what you have to, but the hospital must stay out of it."

"I see. Am I barred from the hospital, then?"

"Not barred, just relieved of your regular duties until you can devote your attention to medicine. We want you back. We need you. But without the lawsuit."

Janette's Friday morning Bar hearing was a fiasco. Due to attorney-client confidentiality, she was prohibited from testifying about what she and Betty Martinez had discussed. Without that testimony, she couldn't defend herself—a catch-22. She demanded another hearing in which she could call Betty Martinez as a witness. The Grievance Committee nearly decided that pending new evidence, she should be disbarred. But, over the grumbling objections of Hoffmeister, who was present at the hearing, she was given ten days to ask for another hearing.

Janette drove back to her apartment and began making notes of everything she could remember about the hearing, in preparation for her talk with Parker Ross. She was still stunned, but thinking on her feet nonetheless. Before she knew it, it was noon, time for David to pick her up. She rushed into her bedroom and began packing a suitcase. But before she could even get started, David rang the doorbell. She let him in and said, "I'll be ready in a minute."

While flinging clothes into an overnight bag, she told David about the Bar hearing.

"They claim that I solicited Betty Martinez into filing

this lawsuit. And I guess they're right! I want to talk to
Parker Ross about it."

"You're putting it all on the line in this case, aren't
you?" he asked.

"Aren't we all? That's the way it works. If you're going
to do something, you have to be willing to face the consequences. I'm not sorry. I did the right thing and I'll make
sure that the suit continues, one way or the other. If they
uphold my disbarment, I'll ask Parker to take over the
Martinez case for me."

"I've been suspended myself because of the suit. Political pressure."

Janette didn't know what to say to try to comfort him,
but she could tell he was trying to deal with the setbacks.
Things were moving too fast for them ever to have a
chance to contemplate the consequences of the cascade of
events.

LeBearc slipped into his overcoat and adjusted his hat before stepping out of his jet. He turned up his collar and
looked with distaste at the slush that had built up on the
ramp at the Asheville airport. LeBearc walked briskly
across the ramp and through the general aviation terminal.
He waited while a driver opened the back door of a company car. LeBearc rode silently, looking out the window at
the freezing rain falling around him.

Arriving at Asheville Hospital, he asked to see Dr. Byrd
and waited patiently while the receptionist called the
pathologist.

"Dr. Byrd, you have a gentleman here to see you. A Dr.
Lee Berg? I may be saying that a little wrong." She looked
up at LeBearc and smiled. He stared at her without comment. Withering under LeBearc's glare, she wiped the
smile from her face and gave him directions to the pathology department.

As he walked, LeBearc took off his overcoat. He turned it wrong side out so that he would not get his suit wet, and then draped it over his arm. Following the receptionist's directions, he found himself in the basement of the old hospital in a dimly lit hallway that smelled of disinfectant. On one door an emblem read "County Medical Examiner." LeBearc opened the door and walked in. Inside, he saw an old gray metal desk, the top piled high with papers and files. On one side was a telephone and on the other were half a dozen photographs of children of indefinite age, a picture of a cat asleep in a shoe box, and a snapshot of two people in their early twenties standing in front of a small house. As LeBearc looked at the pictures, a woman wearing fire-engine-red slacks and a flowered blouse came into the room carrying an insulated mug of coffee.

"Can I help you?" she asked, as she moved behind the desk and pulled out the chair and sat down, staking out her territory.

"I'm here to see Dr. Byrd. My name is Dr. Andre LeBearc."

"Is he expecting you?" she asked, turning around and looking toward the open door that led into Byrd's obviously vacant office.

"They called him from upstairs. It's about a matter in Orlando."

"He's probably back in the library trying to catch up on some paperwork. I'll get him."

She picked up her coffee and walked through the doorway that led out of the office. LeBearc looked back at the pictures again and saw that she was the woman pictured standing in front of the house. He judged that the picture must have been taken fifteen or twenty years before, when she was still reasonably fit. He walked over to the doorway of Byrd's office and looked inside. It was less cluttered than the rest of the area, but seemed to LeBearc's way of thinking a total nightmare. As he turned and stepped back to the secretary's desk, she came inside, followed immediately by Byrd, who wore a sharply pressed white lab coat.

He studied LeBearc over a set of half-glasses. Without offering to shake hands, he said, "I'm Dr. Byrd. Maybeth said you came here about some case in Orlando. What did you say your name is again?"

"I'm Dr. Andre LeBearc. Is there somewhere we can talk? I have some papers I need to show you."

"What case is this about, anyway?" Byrd made no move to go anywhere, and Maybeth was watching.

"I'm actually here to talk to you about several things. One of them has to do with your Justification Factor."

"You work for the IORC, is that what this is about?" Byrd asked, locking LeBearc in an unwavering gaze.

"I'm the quality control manager for IORC Southeastern Region. I may be able to help you with the problems you have been having concerning your Justification Factor, but I want to talk to you about it privately."

Byrd's glance darted to Maybeth. She, like most of his friends there, knew about his avid involvement in Equal Access and that he had J Factor problems that he thought were the result of his activism. She understood his discomfort when it came to the IORC.

"My daddy told me when the IRS comes a knockin' and tells you they're here to help you, look out, 'cause you're in big trouble. Is the same thing true for the IORC?" Byrd's attempt at humor relaxed Maybeth, and she turned away from the conversation and began shuffling some of the files on her desk, but Byrd could see that she still listened intently.

"Let's go somewhere and talk." LeBearc walked through the office toward the door at the back wall, knowing Byrd would follow. The library was vacant.

"Now that we're in private, what's this all about?" Byrd asked, afraid to hear the answer.

"Dr. Byrd, we have a copy of the list you sent to Dr. West in Orlando." LeBearc handed over a photocopy and watched the devastating effect it had on Byrd. Byrd collapsed into a chair, holding the copy and looking at LeBearc, shaking his head.

"We've had the list for quite some time now. We received it as soon as Dr. West did. He's helping a woman bring a suit against us concerning the death of a patient, Martinez. You supplied the heart. I don't think I need go into details. What I want to know now is, what else have you given to Dr. West? What other evidence do they have besides the list?"

"Why should I tell you anything? You've done everything to me you can do—that is, unless you intend to kill me like you did that man."

LeBearc smirked at Byrd, otherwise ignoring the accusation. "To answer your question, the reason why you should tell me is because if you do, you can make up for the fact that you illegally took one of our organs. I can't promise anything, of course, but if you are very cooperative, I can cut through a great deal of J Factor red tape. I'm prepared to do that for someone who is willing to cooperate. Now, I know West was here and he has other evidence. I just don't know what it is. I want to know and I expect you to tell me. I'm in a hurry, so I want you to tell me now." LeBearc had not sat down and Dr. Byrd was leaning forward, his face in the palms of his hands, his elbows resting on the table.

"What are you planning to do to all of those people on the list?"

"That's none of your business. Anything that happens to those people would have ultimately happened with or without the list. All of them are examined regularly, and eventually it would have come to our attention that each one had an unauthorized organ. You and your Equal Access group should know what happens under those circumstances, even if you don't know the details of it. It is inconceivable to me that you would keep encouraging the illegal transplantation of organs when you know the inevitable result of doing so. What you do is against the law and it's also cruel to those poor people who get the organs. What you think is humanitarian is not at all."

"*You're* the one who's inhumane and cruel," Byrd said, glaring at him. "You and your damnable J Factor."

LeBearc reached for Byrd's arm and pulled it away from his face. Pushing up the sleeve, he exposed the plastic shunt attached to the blood vessel on the inside of Byrd's left arm. "Dialysis isn't very pleasant, is it, Dr. Byrd? You get cramps, you're sick between sessions, and it makes you feel like a slave to a machine—which you are. Think about it. But don't think about it for long. Either you tell me now—right now—or I'm going to turn around and walk out of here and your J Factor will never be changed. You'll never get off dialysis . . . and you'll suffer a slow, painful death, a little at a time."

Byrd stared up at him. He looked down at his arm and back at LeBearc. "I'm not going to help you, that's for sure. No matter what you do to me. Can't you just forget the people on the list this time?"

"Did you give him some kind of evidence?"

"Go to hell."

LeBearc stared back at Byrd. "It was a module, wasn't it. You gave him a module. It's the only other thing that would help him prove the case."

Byrd dropped his eyes to his feet and made no reply.

"I intend to teach you and Equal Access a lesson. No one takes you seriously, but you've been a nuisance and a financial drain far too long. I'm going to stop you people once and for all." With that, LeBearc swept out of the library and slid into his overcoat as he walked down the corridor to the elevator.

Once back in his airplane, he placed a call to the managing director, who was currently in Singapore, to update him on the situation.

He then called Krickett Hansen, and asked her to come to Orlando immediately.

Dr. Byrd stayed in the library at the hospital in Asheville for several hours after LeBearc left, lost in his thoughts until almost quitting time. Finally he nodded his head once to himself and the muscles in his jaw hardened. He stood up and walked back to his office and closed the door. He picked up the phone and called David at Orlando Government, but got voice mail. Afraid to leave a message, he hung up. Then he thought about sending a fax to David's home number, but decided that was probably how IORC got the list, and he didn't want this message to fall into their hands, too. Finally he wrote out a note:

> They have the list. Doctor LeBearc also figured
> out that I had given you a module and that you
> planned to use it to stop him. I shouldn't have
> used their organs. I did it for the best of inten-
> tions. Now they're going to kill everyone on the
> list. You've got to try to stop them. It's wrong.
> Make them stop killing people.

He signed it "Byrd." He folded the paper, put it into an envelope, sealed it, and told Maybeth to send it FedEx to Dr. West at Orlando Government immediately, for Satur-day delivery.

"Are you all right?" she asked.

"You go along. It's okay. I'll be in the laboratory work-ing. Hold my calls," he said, and smiled at their private joke. He got almost no calls. Even with the humor, Maybeth knew that something was wrong. The meeting with the other doctor had clearly upset him.

Byrd went back into his office and sat for a while look-ing at his surroundings. He thought for a moment that he might gather up some books or finish a few things that he should have done. But they didn't seem very important now. He took one final look around and then briskly walked out, through the reception area, into the hall, and down to the laboratory where the autopsies were performed.

Everyone who worked in the lab had gone home. He went to his instrument table and picked up a set of blunt-nose surgical scissors. He took a swivel chair from the desk and rolled it over to the autopsy table. He pulled up his left sleeve and looked at the dialysis shunt attached to his artery. Made of surgical tubing, it was taped down so that it wouldn't snag on anything. Using the scissors, he tried to snip the shunt, but the tough tubing resisted his efforts.

He sat down in the chair, leaned forward over the autopsy table, and braced his elbow on the edge. He inserted the scissors under the tube near the tape and snipped off the end of the shunt. Blood spurted out. He laid the scissors down and leaned forward, watching his blood flow onto the cold steel table.

He knew the physical symptoms he was now experiencing. First, he felt a chill as if the windows were open. He noticed that his heart rate was increasing, but he had no sense of pain. He then began to feel drowsy. It seemed to be getting dark in the room, due, no doubt, to the reduction in the blood supply to his optic nerves, which were very sensitive to oxygen deprivation. His respiration began to increase, but mostly he felt overcome by tiredness. He laid his head down on the edge of the table and closed his eyes, letting sleep take over.

Maybeth came back down the elevator from the FedEx box, and as she walked down the hall she saw the lights on in the laboratory. She wanted to say good-bye to Dr. Byrd for the weekend, but decided against it since he had asked, in his way, not to be disturbed. She gathered up her purse, snapped off the lights, locked the door, and took the elevator back upstairs, dreading the drive home through the sleet.


LeBearc ordered a minute search of David's apartment to locate the module. If security didn't find it there, then he ordered them to search his car and the room at the motel to which he had been followed in Lake County. LeBearc had asked Krickett, who arrived shortly after noon, to take over the security detail. "That module has to be recovered."

This time the search team made less effort to conceal the fact that they had been to David's apartment. They checked every book, every cassette tape, every dish, every appliance, and every thread of clothing and pair of shoes in the apartment—first with a portable microwave receiver that could detect the module's signal, then, when that failed, they searched manually. They even vacuumed the carpets and combed through the residue. By seven o'clock in the evening, the search team reported that the module was definitely not in the apartment. Another team stationed at the motel was ordered to search David's room. They were told that the woman who arrived with an assistant in a white Volvo wagon was in charge.

# 17

After dropping their bags at the motel, Janette and David went straight to Parker Ross's condo.

Janette rang the doorbell, and from deep within the condo Parker Ross shouted, "Come on in." She tried the door and found it unlocked. In the cluttered foyer an old coat rack stood to one side with a couple of disreputable-looking hats hanging from it. A fast-moving ball of fur greeted them, sniffing Janette's foot and then circling her three times at high speed before standing up on its hind legs and putting its front feet on her knees. Janette reached down to rub the fur out of the dog's eyes. The dog, a mix of Schnauzer and unidentified terrier, groaned with pleasure and licked Janette's hand. They obviously knew one another. Suddenly the dog jumped down and at full speed disappeared around the corner of the foyer into the hallway, only to reappear seconds later at the feet of Parker Ross.

"Janette!" he shouted. "There you are, and just as gorgeous as ever." He walked straight to her and gave her a hug.

"I heard the news about the Bar Association problem already. You're causing quite a stir, according to the media sharks," Parker quipped as he led his guests into the den and guided them toward the sofa.

"Parker, I've gotten myself into serious trouble. I've got to make sure Mrs. Martinez has a good lawyer. That's why I'm here. I want you to take the case."

"Now, hold on just a minute. I'm retired. I'm too old and decrepit to be handling a case like this."

"They're going to disbar me for soliciting the case. I won't be able to handle the suit. She really needs your help. I'll do all the work—all you'll have to do is make the argument in court," said Janette, clinching her teeth.

"Let's take it one step at a time. Be calm. They claim you solicited this case from Mrs. Martinez, but I thought you already represented her."

"I did represent her at UNILAW, but I resigned from UNILAW."

"You missed my point, Janette. Did you resign from UNILAW before or after you asked her this?"

"I talked to her on Sunday night and filed my resignation Monday morning. I guess I talked to her before I officially resigned. So what?"

"Janette, you aren't thinking like a lawyer. She was already your client and you were her lawyer. You had a duty to tell her what you thought was best for her, as long as you were her lawyer. *She* hadn't fired you. You still worked for UNILAW. There was absolutely nothing wrong with your suggesting that she do the case. In fact, that was your job." Parker sat back a moment to let Janette process what he had just said. As Janette's eyes brightened with realization, he continued.

"You should have told me this when we spoke on Tuesday. Don't ever represent yourself. You know the tired old cliché made famous by Abraham Lincoln—a lawyer who represents himself has a fool for a client. It's corny, but it's all too true."

"Are you willing to represent me now? I don't have much money."

Parker Ross fixed her with his gaze, and his white eyebrows moved up and down so fast that it looked as if he was trying to take off and fly with them. "I would represent you on anything, anywhere. But I don't work for free. I never have. My fee is ten dollars, and I expect to be paid promptly."

Before Janette could respond, Parker picked up the telephone. Within five minutes he had the Bar committee chairman on the phone. After a heated discussion, Parker brought the conversation to a close, saying, "I expect Hoffmeister was behind this. It's typical. Anyway, Compton already represented Mrs. Martinez when she advised her to file the suit, so there could be no violation. Check it out. Besides, if she hadn't, why wouldn't you let her testify due to attorney-client confidentiality? We'll expect a public statement dismissing the charges. Otherwise, I'll file suit against the members of the committee. I'll be listening for the statement." Parker hung up before he got a reply.

It all happened so fast Janette had to process the result. Then she said, "Parker, would you be my cocounsel for the case itself?"

"Janette, I told you I'm retired. I don't handle lawsuits any more."

"I know that, and I understand. But would you at least meet Mrs. Martinez, talk to her about her case and meet her son?"

"I'd like to meet Mrs. Martinez and her son. I hope to do that on Monday. I plan to come and watch the fun."

"They're coming up for the weekend. They may already be here."

Before Parker could stonewall any further, Janette called the motel and spoke to Betty. They arranged to meet at the motel snack bar in thirty minutes.

Suddenly Parker's dog, Jingle Bells, let out a growl, a deep rumble in her throat. She stood absolutely still, and only the tip of her tail quivered and her lip curled exposing her teeth. Then the dog rushed toward the front door. The effect on David and Janette was electric.

"Now, what the hell. She doesn't do that." Parker got up and walked to the front door. Janette and David followed him. Something was very wrong. Jingle Bells stopped her growling for a moment and wagged her tail when Parker came up beside her, but then resumed her vigil. Parker looked out the window. A woman stood a few feet from the steps of his condo, consulting a piece of paper. A man sat in a white Volvo station wagon nearby. David peered over Parker's shoulder; the scene outside looked suspicious. His self-defense warning system was screaming at him. His muscles tensed, ready for something that he couldn't define.

Parker opened the door and as he did the hair on Jingle Bell's back stood up and she snarled. Parker nudged her back with his foot and asked through the crack in the doorway, "May I help you?" The woman had long black hair and appeared to be in her fifties.

"I guess I'm lost. I got a map from the office but we took a wrong turn, I suppose." She had a strong Spanish accent.

"The numbers are right there on the building." He opened the door the rest of the way. Jingle Bells started to go out and he turned around and sternly told her to get back. He pulled the door shut and walked down the two steps to the sidewalk.

"What unit are you looking for?"

She looked him over, as did the man in the car. Now Parker too felt uncomfortable. Maybe it was the dog's growling, which was so unusual. Normally she loved everyone.

"It's six four zero," the woman said.

"That's back near the office, over there." Parker pointed.

The woman hadn't moved when he got back to the door. He turned, and only then did she begin walking toward the car. David and Janette watched through the window. Parker went back through the front door.

"Strange, usually the office gives people good directions. It's awfully hard to get lost here. Jingle Bells, what in the world is the matter with you?" Only then did the dog stop growling and begin wagging her tail. Parker looked out the window one last time and saw the car driving away.

The woman seemed oddly familiar to David, not her appearance but the way she moved, a fluidity that made her much more agile than her age would suggest. David knew as one knows when the weather is about to change that there was going to be trouble, and somehow that woman would be involved.

Thirty minutes later the strategy session began at the snack bar. Parker and Betty hit it off immediately. Jorge caught sight of a strikingly pretty teenage girl, who had just come into the clubhouse from the tennis court. She was having an iced tea with a woman who looked like an Italian movie star. Jorge tried unsuccessfully to pay attention to the conversation around him.

Janette noticed Jorge staring across the room and followed his gaze. She tapped Jorge on the arm and told him in Spanish to come with her and she would introduce him. He smiled broadly at Janette. She had made a friend for life. He ambled along with her, in his huge shoes and oversized shorts and shirt, to the counter where the women sat. Janette introduced Jorge to Paola and Tammy Jeffries, Warren's wife and daughter. Janette explained that Warren had to work late, so he wouldn't arrive until the next day. A few minutes later Jorge and Tammy left the counter, went to a table, and were immediately lost in conversation.

Parker invited Betty to dinner, and suggested David and

Janette go to a festival scheduled for that evening in the nearby town of Mount Dora.

Jorge announced that he and Tammy wanted to go in the boat to the festival, if it was okay with his mom. She said it was all right if Paola Jeffries agreed, provided Jorge gave Janette and David a ride, too. Jorge looked disappointed but then, remembering who had introduced him, smiled at Janette and said, "Uh, OK." They agreed to meet at the marina at six-thirty.

As David and Janette were driving to the marina, he reminded himself not to take off the sport coat he was wearing. The modules were safely in the inside pocket. Somehow those modules were important beyond proving that IORC could identify its organs. Somehow they were related to the deaths. He had to get them tested before the trial.

David and Janette took their seats in the rear of the cockpit of Jorge's boat, and Tammy sat on a pedestal seat in front next to Jorge, who faced a large instrument panel. The array of levers, switches, gauges, and dials would have done justice to an airplane. Jorge pulled away from the marina carefully. David welcomed the chance to be on the boat, away from the IORC and with Janette, but the overwhelming sense of foreboding that had plagued him wouldn't go away.

They rode for a half hour, then saw a sight that was very unusual for Florida, which is mostly flat. Ahead of them an entire hillside glowed with the lights of condominiums and houses and hundreds of booths erected along the streets that led down to the waterfront. They saw a miniature working lighthouse at the end of a jetty, and boats tied up along several piers. Approaching the docks, Jorge used a large spotlight to see what lay ahead. Boats passed them from all directions, so it seemed impossible that anyone could come into the small harbor without having a collision.

"I don't want people's boats banging up against mine. If you don't mind, I'll pull up to the dock and let you two off, and then we'll go over there to the last pier and tie up. When do you think you'll be ready to go?"

"How about a couple of hours?" Janette said. "We'll be back here at, say, nine-thirty."

Janette and David walked up the hill from the dock toward the booths of arts and crafts, from fine oil paintings to horseshoes mounted on weather-beaten wood. Costumed musicians wandered throughout playing music. They also heard a jazz band and mariachi guitarists.

They walked among the booths, looking at everything and sampling ethnic foods. Thoroughly enjoying themselves, they almost forgot all about IORC.

The boat Krickett rented moved along at a brisk pace. It could make a little over twenty-five knots, but doing so pegged the battery discharge needle, so the driver backed off. He didn't want to run out of power halfway home. Krickett scratched her head with both hands, nails extended, and shook it violently. "I hate wigs!" She had shed the black hair and had dressed in a fashionable jogging outfit. She was back to her own youthful look.

At the marina, which by that time was deserted, two backup men pulled into the parking lot. First they checked the outside of David's car with the microwave scanner and found nothing. In less than thirty seconds they managed to get into his car, bypassing the alarm.

The two IORC men drove David's car to a town five miles away. They spent a few minutes looking for a good place to stop so they could search the car uninterrupted. Finally they settled on an automatic car wash, ran the car through, and pulled around back as if to vacuum it out.

The men began a methodical search, making fast work of it, actually sliding the seats off their tracks and removing them so they could take out the carpet. This attracted some stares from other people using the car wash, but no one said anything to them. In fifteen minutes they felt confident that the module was not in the car unless David had hidden it inside one of the mechanical parts, which was highly unlikely and thus not worth a search. They put the carpets and seats back in, drove the car back to the marina, and then went to the room the team had rented as their base of operation to report to the Orlando headquarters that the search had been unsuccessful.

As this call took place, Krickett and her driver arrived at the Mount Dora pier. They pulled up among the jumble, stepped across two other boats, and walked up the hill to the festival.

After half an hour she spotted David and Janette. They had stopped at a Cajun food booth. Krickett edged closer and motioned to her partner to follow. David and Janette talked as they waited for their food. Krickett's partner took a microscanner, which to be less conspicuous looked like a portable CD player, from his belt, put a small earpiece in his right ear, and pointed the scanner in David's direction. It immediately emitted beeping sounds.

He turned the machine off, nodded at Krickett, and put the earphone back in his pocket. She decided to have her partner divert Janette's attention while she approached David. They couldn't use too much force in public, but recovery of the module was paramount, and if she had to risk a scene she would.

Krickett reached inside her windbreaker and took out a high-voltage stun gun—a Taser identical to those that police once carried but that had long been outlawed. She palmed the Taser in her left hand.

The two, putting pleasant expressions on their faces, walked briskly toward David and Janette, who had just left the Cajun food stand and now stood in front of the next booth, which sold baskets. They were both eating steaming stew out of paper cups. The IORC couple walked directly toward them. Saying, "We need to talk," the man took Janette's elbow and led her away before David or Janette knew what had happened. Krickett did the same with David, heading him in the opposite direction.

Janette tried to pull her elbow elbow out of the man's grasp. He had maneuvered her several yards away, back to the Cajun food booth. Janette's back was to David, so she was unable to see Krickett guide him away.

Krickett said, "David, you have some property that belongs to the IORC. I've been asked to get that property back from you. I hope you'll make this easy for both of us."

"I don't know what you're talking about," he said, turning to walk away.

"Don't lie to me, David," she said, grabbing his arm again. "We're talking about an electronic module. I have a scanner and I know you have it now."

David froze. He looked at Krickett, trying to decide what to do. He couldn't get the picture of the exploding oil cans out of his mind. Though smaller than David, she certainly had been well trained.

Meanwhile, Janette was getting irritated by the man who was holding her elbow. Finally she dropped her cup of stew on the street and jerked her arm out of his hand. She whirled around and gave the man a push. He lost his balance but caught himself, and as she started to turn away he grabbed at her. It was a big mistake. She lunged and kicked him in the groin as hard as she could. He doubled over and staggered sideways, bumping hard into the counter of the Cajun food booth, spilling dozens of cups of stew all around, to the accompaniment of a wave of steam and a lot of cursing from the cook.

The commotion attracted David's attention. Krickett reached toward him with her left hand and he saw the

Taser. He wasn't sure what it was, but he knew it was dangerous. In a split second, having seen what Janette had done, and what was apparently about to happen to him, he acted decisively. He swept his right leg around, taking the legs out from under Krickett just as she pressed the button and the electricity arced between the poles of the Taser. Shocking herself for a fraction of a second, she lost her balance and fell onto her side, tumbling into a pile of baskets. David's action had been so swift that it surprised him as much as it did her.

Janette caught up to David and took his arm, and they quickly merged with the crowd walking down the hill, both of them fighting an overwhelming urge to run. The crowd gawked at the man who was trying to get up while the cook raised hell with him. Krickett lay among the baskets, rubbing her leg where she had been shocked.

"What was that about?" Janette asked. "Did you know that woman?"

"It was about the modules."

"What modules?"

"Dr. Byrd gave some modules to me when I was in Asheville. They're the serial number devices. They've been in my pocket since I got back. I'm keeping them for evidence. They prove that IORC puts an identifier on organs—and they may have other, more important uses as well. I'm now certain I need to show them to Warren right away and see if he can figure out how they work. We'd better get the hell out of here. They won't give up that easily, and next time they'll be better prepared. We got lucky."

David looked at his watch and saw that it was only eight-thirty. The harbor was filling up with brightly decorated boats and he saw no sign of Jorge or Tammy.

"Let's walk around to the far end of the harbor where Jorge said he was going. We can get there in five or ten minutes, and if we miss him we'll still get back here before nine-thirty," David said.

They walked on around the shoreline where several people had already put down lawn chairs between the docks to watch the fireworks and boat parade. David expected that Krickett and her partner would show up at any minute—this time with some help.

Krickett limped away, and soon the people who had been watching lost interest in her. Her assistant paid the cook for the spilled stew and the excitement died down. Krickett called the team at the motel and ordered them to the marina to watch for David and Janette.

The feeling had returned to her leg and it hurt. She knew she had been incredibly lucky. By rights, she should be unconscious. She could be dead, having underestimated David. He had moved so fast that she had been unable to respond. That had never happened to her before. She couldn't afford such mistakes in her job.

"Let's find them," she said. She touched the .15-caliber split-system pistol under her jacket. It used C-4 plastic explosives encased in small bits on a one-eighth-inch Mylar roll, and plastic composite projectiles that fed into the chamber separately. Looking like a small dictating machine, the weapon would fire quicker and more accurately than a conventional automatic pistol. It was also much lighter and the bullet traveled faster than a rifle bullet, thus reducing the ballistic drop and greatly increasing its effective range and accuracy. Its drawback was noise, not from the propellant, which was muffled, but from the sharp crack of the projectile exceeding the speed of sound as it left the short barrel.

Krickett swept her eyes around, trying to locate David. She couldn't shoot in a crowd. They would have to try to stop the boat or, failing that, catch him at the marina.

David saw what he thought was Jorge's boat at the very last dock.

"Come on, I think that's it. Let's go." They stepped up their pace, now running across a wet launching ramp. Janette slipped and almost fell into the lake, wetting her shoes and slacks. Her ankle immediately ached, but she managed to keep her balance.

They ran up the ramp, onto the dock. It was indeed Jorge's boat, but Jorge and Tammy were nowhere to be seen. David and Janette jumped on board. The key was missing from the switch. At that moment, Jorge opened the cabin door a crack and peered out.

"What's happening? You're early," he said, looking back over his shoulder. He came up carrying his coat and closed the door behind him. David looked around and was about to ask where Tammy was when she came through the doorway, buttoning her coat. She blushed, but David and Janette were too distracted to notice and couldn't have seen it in the dark anyway.

"Jorge, we've got to get out of here fast. A couple of people are after us. We had a fight up the hill there. One of them has a stun gun. I've got some electronic gadgets in my pocket that have something to do with the case. They tried to take them from me. If they catch us, it'll be bad news. Plus, Janette kicked the guy in the balls and I doubt he's too pleased about that."

Jorge looked at Janette who grinned sheepishly and shrugged her shoulders.

"Come on, Jorge, let's haul ass. I'm not kidding."

Jorge went into action. He fished the key out of his pocket. "Cast us off. Just unhook the line from the boat." When David had released it, Jorge began maneuvering the boat away from the dock. As Jorge turned on the spot-light, he swept around so that he would avoid hitting any other boats. He ran the spotlight across the harbor to the dock and around to where the boats were lining up for the parade. Just then the fireworks began.

"Hold it, Jorge. Shine the light back on the main dock again," David said. "That's them. Those two over there, getting into a boat. We have to move it. We can't let them catch us out here."

"Okay, everybody sit down and hang on," Jorge said.

He moved the throttle forward and the boat began picking up speed. People shouted at him, waving and tooting their horns. The disturbance got Krickett's attention, and her partner turned at full speed to an angle to intercept, oblivious to the shouting that followed their speeding. Krickett still held the split-system pistol.

"Jorge, it looks to me like they're going to cut us off. That boat's faster than yours and they've got a better angle."

"The hell they're faster," Jorge said, and he continued on course. "Give it a minute." Suddenly the windshield shattered; an instant later they heard a loud crack that sounded entirely different from the fireworks exploding overhead. Someone was shooting at the boat. Jorge slid back the cover on a compartment below the throttle, reached inside, and flicked two switches. The other boat was closing fast. Clearly, they would be caught. They all crouched down.

The engine made a hissing noise for a second or two and then a low-pitched hum began, rising slowly in frequency. In a couple of seconds the noise evolved into something that they felt rather than heard. The entire boat pulsed.

"Here we go," Jorge said. He jammed a lever forward. As he did, it was as if someone had put everyone else into slow motion. The noise that had been a rumble turned into the deafening scream of a turbine engine. The boat lunged forward, rising up in the water with only the back three feet of the hull touching the surface. David quit watching the speedometer as it passed through sixty knots. The speed continued to climb and David could only estimate their speed at over a hundred knots as they passed through a narrow channel of the lake and around the bend, out of sight of the harbor. Jorge had the spotlight focused forward, watching for obstructions. David looked back. Krickett's boat was no longer in sight. Jorge kept up his high speed for another minute and then began easing off the throttle. The boat gradually settled back into the water.

Jorge looked at David, grinning from ear to ear. "I've always wanted to do that. I don't think we hit anybody, did we?" They slowed down through thirty-five knots as they approached the mile-long Dora Canal. Jorge turned off the turbine engine and the boat settled firmly into the water, silently passing through the canal using its electric motor.

"What in the world did you do?" Janette asked.

"Just something my dad and I put together—a little extra juice," Jorge said in a feigned tone of casual swagger. Tammy looked at Jorge with total adoration. David considered the boat anew. He had never seen anything like it. He thought of Cal Yoshida, and how much Cal would want to own this boat if he knew it existed.

They came out of the Dora Canal into the adjoining lake on which the marina was located. No doubt another IORC team would be waiting at the dock for him and the modules. He really couldn't go back there while he had the modules.

"Jorge, you'll have to drop us off somewhere else. We can't go back to the marina now. I've got to get these modules to Tammy's dad before these people can take them from me." His attempt at finding safety out of town had failed miserably. He should have expected as much.

"I don't know this lake except what's on the chart," Jorge said.

"There's a tavern just around that bend," Janette said,

pointing ahead. "We could probably get a ride to Orlando from there."

"Where is it?" Jorge asked.

Janette pointed again at a group of lights on the shoreline.

Jorge spun the wheel around and the boat made a sweeping turn toward the lights.

"Jorge, you have to be careful when you go back to the marina. Some IORC people will be waiting. What I want you to do is tell them that we got off, but don't tell them exactly where. Just tell them you dropped us off somewhere in the canal.

"When you can, call Tammy's father and let him know that Janette and I are coming to his office. He's working late at UNILAW, isn't he?" he asked Tammy.

" 'Til two or three in the morning, he told us."

"If they start giving you any real trouble, if they try to hurt you or anything like that, don't try to be heroes. Go on and tell them what we're doing. It won't really make any difference. We'll be ready this time. Just get the message through to Tammy's dad." David was sorry he had involved them.

"Be careful," Janette said, and they climbed off the boat onto the dock outside the tavern.

Jorge eased the boat away from the dock and steered for the marina across the lake.

Janette and David went inside the tavern. They saw a waitress leaning against the bar talking to a lanky middle-aged man. Janette walked over and stood next to the waitress.

"Can I help you, honey?" the waitress asked.

"Yeah. My friend over there and I, we just got hassled by my old man. We had to catch a ride over here on a boat so nobody would get hurt. We need to get to Orlando. Is there some way we can get there from here?" Janette asked.

The waitress looked Janette over and noticed the algae and mud on the bottom of her white slacks.

"There's a car rental place a couple miles up the road. Have you got any money? You can rent a car there if you do." Janette looked at David, who nodded his head.

"Okay, then, come on and I'll give you a ride up there. Lou, I'm gonna be gone for a few minutes. Be right back," she said to the bartender who nodded. They went outside and got into her rusty old Chevy station wagon and bumped through the potholed parking lot out onto the highway. She drove them down to the car rental office without saying a word. When they got out, David reached into his pocket to get some money for her.

"Honey, you don't owe me nothing. You just do a favor for somebody someday and that'll pay me back," she said, and with a puff of smoke from the exhaust pipe, the car turned and chugged away.

They rented a car and soon thereafter were on their way to Orlando.

Krickett's boat came out of the canal at full speed. Wake waves washed along the banks as it emerged. It moved away for a few seconds. Then the driver spotted Jorge's boat and turned back.

Jorge, watching the approach of the other boat, decided to play with them a little. He opened the panel to the turbine controls and started the engine again. Jorge pushed the throttle for the turbine fully forward and the boat leaped ahead. He made a long sweeping turn in the middle of the lake. The pursuing boat first began to turn after him and then, realizing how fast he was going, gave it up and turned toward the marina. Jorge pulled in behind the boat, shined his spotlight on them, and went by ten feet to the left.

Amazingly, the wake didn't capsize the other boat, but

the driver jerked the wheel away, almost turning it over. That would teach them to shoot out his windshield. Jorge made another sweeping turn and headed back toward the boat again, this time straight on. Krickett steadied the split-system pistol and took aim at Jorge. Tammy began to scream and Jorge decided that they'd had enough excitement for one night. He veered off and headed to the marina, just as Krickett was about to shoot.

As he pulled in and tied the boat at the dock, Jorge saw two people sitting in a station wagon nearby.

He took Tammy's arm and helped her out. They walked along the dock toward his four-wheel-drive pickup. When he got to it he unlocked the door and Tammy slid in from his side. "Uh-oh," Jorge said. One of the men from the station wagon walked over.

"Where's Dr. West?" the guy said without any preamble.

"Who's Dr. West?" Jorge said, as he slid behind the steering wheel, closed the door, and started the engine.

"If you don't answer us we're going to take that boat of yours apart and make sure that West didn't leave anything in there," he said.

The man's companion walked up beside Jorge and jerked open the door. "We can make this easy or we can make it hard. Have you ever seen one of these?" He held out a Taser.

"I don't know what the hell you're talking about," Jorge said, putting the truck in gear.

"Let me show you." He held the Taser out in front of him and pressed the button. There was a blue arc of electricity and a crackle from it. "Now turn off the motor." Jorge did so.

"In about ten seconds I'm going to hold that right next to your balls and I'm going to press the button. When I do, it's going to lift you right out of that truck. You'll piss your pants and you'll hurt worse than you thought it was possible for anybody to hurt."

"You can kiss my ass," Jorge said, and he tried to close the truck's door. The man reached the Taser toward Jorge, and Tammy began to scream, "Tell him, Jorge, they said it was all right to tell them. Go on, tell them. We dropped them off. They're going to Orlando."

Krickett and her driver had arrived. She was limping and he still could not stand up straight.

"He had the module. It showed up on the scanner. Where the hell did he go?" she demanded.

"The kid says they dropped them off. They're on their way to Orlando. I'll check the boat with our scanner to be sure."

"Check the kids," Krickett ordered.

The man turned on the scanner and swept it over Jorge and Tammy. "No, it's not here."

"Where were they going in Orlando?" Krickett asked. Neither Jorge or Tammy said a word.

She walked around the front of the truck to Tammy's side and tapped on the window. Tammy looked at her and didn't move.

"Open the damn door," Krickett said. Trembling, Tammy reached up and pulled the lock. Krickett yanked the door open and held up her Taser. "I've had enough of this. We don't have long and I won't waste any more time. Now listen, tough guy. Start talking or your date gets zapped." She pulled Tammy's arm out and pressed the button on the Taser. The electricity moved toward Tammy's arm.

"They're going to UNILAW!" Jorge shouted, and he reached across and grabbed Tammy and pulled her away from Krickett. Krickett slammed the door and without another word limped to the parked Volvo.

Jorge, with Tammy now crying, drove back to the clubhouse.

"You go call your dad and tell him Janette and Dr. West are on the way—and that the IORC guys are following them. I'll take care of the rest. Don't be afraid."

"I'm not afraid anymore. We've got to pay them back."

"Damn straight, and that's just what I'm going to do." Jorge pulled out his wallet and took a card from it. He went to one of the other phones in the clubhouse and dialed an emergency number that connected to Fusion Electric's Special Services Group in Cocoa Beach. When he got through, he asked for Captain Stapleton and was connected in less than ten seconds.

Krickett, knowing she could never reach Orlando in time to intercept David, dispatched an Orlando team to UNILAW with orders not to allow the module to slip away again. The three-person team included Marvin Park, who had been a college defensive tackle from the University of Pennsylvania. He had dropped out of college after his junior year because of a knee injury that made further football impossible, but he was not the least incapacitated for duties like this. Normally he interrogated employees accused of theft from the company; his very appearance and manner usually elicited a quick confession. He was accompanied by his partner, Chuck Hayward, a wiry, fearless man, and a woman named Pauline Birch.

The trio used the security manager's Mercedes instead of a green company car to reduce the chance that West would recognize the car and bolt.

The three IORC security people were in place in the UNILAW parking garage within minutes of Krickett's command. Marvin stayed in the car, and Chuck and Pauline waited near the elevator. Though it was late, there were still quite a number of cars in the dingy garage.

During the hour they waited, most of the cars left but several others came in and the drivers stayed inside, apparently waiting to pick up a spouse or friend who had worked late.

David and Janette turned into the parking garage cau-

tiously, looking for anyone who might be waiting for
them. David drove around the inside of the garage, then
pulled several spaces beyond the Mercedes, turned into a
vacant parking place, and shut off his engine. He saw
nothing specific that was suspicious, but he was uneasy.
There were people in cars nearby, so he decided they were
probably safe enough. They had to go inside—even if it
was a great risk. As they started walking toward the elevator the Mercedes pulled out, turned toward David and
Janette's car, and slowly moved forward until it was
nearly between them and the door to the elevator. Chuck
and Pauline began walking toward Janette and David.
Pauline, who had a microwave sensor on with the earphone in her ear, nodded at Marvin in the Mercedes.
David and Janette were trapped.

The Mercedes suddenly screeched to a stop directly in
their path, and Marvin opened the driver's door in front of
David and climbed out. He literally towered over David.
He was every bit of six feet six inches tall and weighed
close to three hundred pounds, all of it muscle. He closed
the driver's door behind him, leaving the engine running,
and turned toward David. David would be no match for
him in a fight. Chuck and Pauline were now heading directly for Janette. They would never make it to the elevator without being caught. They would lose the modules,
and maybe worse. David and Janette began to run for the
elevator, weaving around two cars and trying to avoid the
Mercedes. The man and woman blocked Janette who
stopped, ready to fight.

Marvin moved fast considering his size but missed in
his grab for David who sidestepped him and shoved, causing Marvin to stumble. He turned back on David and
rushed him. David jumped aside and chopped Marvin's
neck as he passed—with no apparent effect. The encounter
was not going to turn out very well for David if he stood
and fought. He started to run but then saw that Janette
was caught and hesitated a little too long.

Marvin grabbed David by the coat lapel, actually lifting him off the ground. David struggled to free himself, and Marvin punched him in the face with his giant fist. David saw flashes of light, and he had to shake his head to clear his vision. David knew it was all over. Marvin started for the car, still holding David who was stunned and couldn't resist. Chuck and Pauline pointed to the car and motioned Janette to get in. She wouldn't abandon David so she let herself be guided to the Mercedes. She would bide her time and fight when she was in a better position—if she ever was.

Then David saw movement to his left. During the commotion, a man had gotten out of one of the nearby cars and started toward them. He was tall, looked to be in his late forties, and was wearing a white sport shirt.

"I say, what's the problem, here?" he asked. He had a British accent and an air of authority, and although he appeared fit, David decided he was no match for the huge man who had an iron grip on his coat.

"This ain't your business, pal," Marvin said. "Get the fuck away."

"Well, actually I think it is my business. You see, these are friends of mine, or at least, to be more precise, they're friends of the family of one of my shipmates." He kept walking toward the group, now almost beside Janette.

Chuck unsnapped a Taser from his belt. He spoke for the first time. "He told you to leave. Do it."

"I'm not alone, you realize. Some of my mates came along for the ride. They insisted when I told them that one of you threatened a sixteen-year-old boy and his date with one of those silly electric boxes that you've got."

"You won't think it's so silly in a second." Chuck stepped toward the Englishman. Janette began to struggle and Pauline slapped her. Janette smashed her in the stomach and pushed her to the floor. Chuck spun around, distracted. The stranger raised his arm.

"Steady on." The voice came from behind them. Chuck froze.

"Maybe we should show you what a real electric box does, before you make up your mind," the Englishman said. Another man had come from yet another car and stood about five feet to his right. Two other men were now standing behind Janette and Pauline, and one other was almost behind the Englishman. These four men looked very formidable, although none was as big as Marvin, who still had his grip on David.

Without any warning, there was a pop from the Mercedes that sounded as loud and hollow as a balloon bursting. It startled Marvin and he hesitated. The driver's door of the Mercedes had been the source of the noise. A small flame expanded outward from a hole burning the paint. The laser had burned completely through the driver's door, the rolled-down window, the driver's seat back, out through the rear floorboard, and then eight inches into the reinforced concrete floor of the garage. The Englishman held what looked like an old-fashioned fountain pen. The other three also held similar "pens." A tiny red light shone on the middle of Marvin's chest. It looked like a miniature flashlight beam. Marvin suddenly released David.

"These little jewels are pulsed lasers. They hit roughly where the red dot is, although they cut a straight line instead of a round hole. The temperature is about five thousand degrees Celsius. They pulse for a hundredth of a second but they can pulse four times in a second, so by moving them just a fraction, as my First Mate here did, they can actually cut a good-size hole through most anything. The one on the large chap's chest over there will probably just about cut the Mercedes engine in half after it passes through him. Now why don't you put out that car fire before the alarms go off."

Marvin pulled off his coat, opened the car door, and began beating on the seat with his coat to put out the flames. Pauline scrambled up from the floor and went to the far side of the Mercedes. Chuck, who was facing the Englishman and still holding his Taser, wasn't convinced. He was by far the dimmest of the three IORC agents.

"I think you should give me that thing." The Englishman held out his hand. David thought the Brit had lost his mind; he expected Chuck to fire the Taser at any second. The IORC man looked down at his hand holding the Taser, trying to make up his mind, and saw two red dots on his wrist.

"Don't even think about it. Before you could press the button, your hand and that thing would both be on the floor." The Englishman continued holding his hand out. Chuck took his finger away from the trigger on the Taser and handed it to the Englishman.

The IORC group put out the fire on the seat and the back carpet and got into the car. The Englishman walked over to Marvin's open window.

"I want you to take a message back to your company: Don't bother these people again. Mike Martinez was my crewman. The sixteen-year-old boy that your people threatened is his son. Don't do it again."

Marvin glared at him. He put the car in reverse, backed up, spun around, and left the garage.

The Englishman came over, smiling, and held out his hand to David.

"Good evening, Dr. West. I'm Captain Ian Stapleton." They shook hands.

"Would your man there have shot him?" David asked, rubbing his bruised face.

"You answer one for me, Doctor. Did they kill Mike Martinez?"

"Yeah, they killed Mike," David replied. He watched the captain, who made no further comment. He just clenched his jaw.

The other four men stood in a semicircle surrounding Janette who trembled, not from fear but from anger.

"Those are pretty powerful fountain pens," she said.

"Fusion Electric developed these toys for our Special Services Group. Actually, they're not quite so powerful as I led those chaps to believe. Carl there used up the entire charge with his demonstration on the car door. Of course, he carries several spares. I should very much appreciate it if you would forget about this, particularly about our little devices. No point in causing some sort of incident. Sometimes your government evidences an absence of understanding of the exigencies and so forth."

"No problem. Are these crew members?" David asked.

"After a fashion, they are. They're not much for sailors, I'll tell you that. Prefer to swim, I think. They're Special Services Group." He looked at them and they all smiled. "Actually, we have to be more careful of security than even the IORC. We have to ensure against any hijacking of our boats or any trouble at our master power control platform. These lads lend a hand here and there on the boat, but mainly their job is to protect all of us. When I told them what Jorge Martinez told me, in two minutes the whole lot were in their cars and on the way here. I had to threaten others to be sure a contingent stayed with the ship. Now that we're here, maybe we can go with you to wherever it is you're trying to go and turn over your evidence. What were they after, by the way?"

David showed him the modules. "We're not sure what they do. One like this was attached to Martinez's heart. It gives off a signal when it's scanned. It's also a pacemaker and we believe it has some other connection with what happened to Mike, since they are so interested in getting them back."

"Let's take the modules up to Warren and get out of here," Janette said.


When they got back to the parking lot, Captain Stapleton escorted David and Janette to their car. He held the door for Janette and then walked around with David to the other side.

"I want to thank you for what you did," David said. "We may be in over our heads."

"It was a pleasure to help. I only wish I could do more."

"Now that you mention it . . . I visited an IORC island and I would like to know where it is," David said.

"The ocean's a frightfully big place," the captain said, smiling.

"I memorized the position of some stars, position of the moon, times and so on," David said. He had duplicated the star chart he had memorized, and put sunrise and sunset times on a scrap of paper.

"I'll see what I can do," Stapleton said.

An IORC man had watched from his parked car, as was the standard procedure for company security whenever an action was implemented. His job was not to intervene but to watch, record, and report. He scanned David and Janette when they returned from seeing Warren, and so he knew they no longer had a module. He reported to Krickett, who was en route to Orlando. She went directly to the UNILAW building.

After saying good night, Stapleton returned to his ship. After working at his computer console for quite a while, honing David's crude map, he located the island and printed out a high-resolution color satellite photo of it.

Then he accessed the Special Services Group information database, highlighted the information he was searching for, and activated the ship's communications.

In Singapore, the telecomputer of the IORC managing

director bleeped, disturbing his breakfast. "What the hell?" He had left directions not to be disturbed.

"What," he demanded after punching the answer button.

"This is Ian Stapleton."

"Who the hell is Ian Stapleton and who are you calling?"

"Check for yourself. I'm sure I'm listed in your computer. I'm calling IORC's managing director. Are you not he?"

"How in hell did you get this number?" the managing director demanded as he punched keys, trying to find Stapleton's name.

"You're on your balcony at the Williamson Hotel in Singapore. Have you found my name yet?"

The managing director stared at his computer screen. Stapleton was head of the SSG of Fusion Electric, and not only a member of FE's board but one of the company founders. "What can I do for Fusion Electric?" he asked with a more restrained tone. One did not speak with disrespect to a person of Stapleton's stature and reputation.

"I'm calling for myself, not for Fusion Electric. Someone in your company apparently killed one of my crewmen because of an inadvertently unauthorized heart transplant. That was a serious lapse of good judgment, for which legal steps are being taken. The courts will sort that out presumably; make it public and so on.

"My call is to advise you that if any other FE person or family member suffers a similar fate, you and every member of your board will answer to me for it with your life. I expect the public would not like such conduct but may be powerless to remedy it. However that may be, I will not permit such violence when it affects those I am responsible to protect."

"How dare you threaten me!" the managing director shouted, but he was already talking to a dial tone.

# 18

After getting home from work at two in the morning, Warren Jeffries had trouble going to sleep. He had the jitters because of all he knew and all that had happened. He was a technician, not a spy. His confrontations were limited to intellectual ones where he could calculate his risks. Finally, he decided to trek through his backyard to his associate's garage-shop several houses away, where their after-hours project to develop an innovative computer chip was housed. He stashed the modules inside a box on the workbench there, returned home, and tried for another hour to get to sleep. He kept thinking he heard noises in his house.

It had taken Krickett several hours and some force to convince the security guard at UNILAW to divulge the identity of the person David and Janette had visited. Now, Krickett checked the Jeffries house from across the street, using the microwave scanner. She got no reading, but she didn't trust the thing and besides, if the module wasn't there, she intended to make this guy Jeffries tell her where it was. Her driver was down the block as a lookout. She picked the lock on Jeffries's front door, then eased the door open and closed it behind her while holding the doorknob turned all the way to avoid any sound.

She swept the room with the scanner and still got no signal. She could see surprisingly well in the house as her eyes adjusted to the dark. She slipped the scanner into her pocket and removed a Walther .380 automatic pistol with a silencer.

Warren's heart pounded as he lay still awake in bed. He thought he heard someone breathing. Then he saw a shadow cast by the streetlight shining into his living room. The shadow moved across the hall wall. *Someone really was in the house!* He picked up the phone and dialed 911 and got an immediate answer. When he didn't speak to the operator, she instructed him to touch 1 if he was in danger and couldn't talk. Warren touched 1. She said to lay the phone down and hide; help was on the way. They had traced his address from the phone call.

Warren eased out of his bed and squatted down beside the chest of drawers. He knew someone was there and he felt terrified. *Where the hell were the police?* A figure holding a gun slipped through the doorway. Thank God his wife and daughter were away. The figure moved slowly to the bed and poked the pile of covers with the gun. Finding no one, the figure dropped to one knee and swiveled its head around checking the room.

"Come out of there," Krickett said, pointing the gun at Warren. "Hands on your head."

The female voice surprised Warren as much as anything else. He stood up, hands raised.

"Sit on the bed," Krickett said, shining a penlight on his face. She held the gun in her right hand, aimed at his face. Warren could see nothing else. The tiny penlight blinded him.

"Give me the module," she coldly commanded.

"It's not here," Warren said. No point in denying his involvement now. They were obviously way beyond that stage.

"I already know that. Where is it?"

"I'm not giving it to you. I—" He didn't get to finish what he had planned to say. She hit him in the side of the head with the gun and the world exploded into red flashes. The shock and the unimaginable pain made everything seem unreal. He lost his equilibrium and slumped over. She put the silencer in front of his ear and pressed it hard into his face.

"You'll give it to me or I'll shoot you. Do you understand that?"

"If you do, you won't get it anyway. I'm the only one who knows." She hit him again. This time he drifted off, and although he didn't think he was actually unconscious, he felt as if he were somewhere else. The pain subsided, but he lost interest in what was happening.

She sat down on the bed, pulled him partway up, and poured the glass of water from the bedside table over his head. It stung the cut on his face and the pain started again.

Then Krickett's radio crackled in her earphone. "Bug out. Now! There are cops coming out of the woodwork. I'll pick you up at point alpha."

Then she noticed that the phone was off the hook.

"We'll see you again. Soon. So we can have a more intimate and revealing chat," she whispered into his ear. Krickett disappeared, blending into the shadows.

In less than two minutes, floodlights came on outside the house and someone on a loudspeaker ordered everyone to come outside with their hands above their heads. Warren got up, but had to sit back down from dizziness. Then he got up again, went to the front door, and walked outside with his hands high.

"Did you catch her?" he asked the officer with the loudspeaker.

Four police officers had responded to Warren's call. One came from the side of the house; two ran inside with their guns drawn. Everything was confused. Warren identified himself, and someone checked his face and said it wasn't serious but offered an ambulance, which he declined.

In fifteen minutes things had settled down. Of all the neighbors who came outside to gawk, no one but Warren had seen anyone.

"It must have been a burglar," one cop said.

"I suppose," Warren said. His head hurt too much to try to explain the whole story to the police, who would neither believe him nor be able to catch the woman, who was now long gone. It was a waste of time. Besides, he only wanted to lie down.

Within the hour he was back in bed.

David and Janette had left the parking garage just after Captain Stapleton drove away. Now they drove in circles throughout deserted downtown Orlando in the middle of the night. "I'm ready to go home and sleep for twelve hours," Janette said.

"Bad idea. It's not safe."

"They know we don't have the modules now. Why isn't it safe?"

"I tried not to get you further involved in this for your own good. I was the biggest danger to them. Now they'll assume I've told you everything, so I might as well."

"You mean there's more?"

Sighing, he described what he had seen on the island. She stared at him in silence. Finally she said, "That's impossible."

"No, it's not."

David knew how bizarre it must sound to her. He hadn't been able to believe it when he saw it firsthand;

how could he expect Janette to grasp it? "I saw it all on the island. I guess they think nobody would believe me without proof, or care if they did know. But I must be more of a threat now that I have the modules. That must be enough to make them worry."

"Are you just giving me a line to get me to spend the night with you?"

"I should have thought of that sooner."

"My ankle hurts, and your face looks like someone hit you with a brick."

"I'll take care of yours if you'll take care of mine," he offered.

They stopped at a drugstore and bought toothbrushes, a razor, gauze, antiseptic, and tape. They checked into the Airport Hilton. Janette registered, using her father's address and her mother's maiden name. She paid in cash and said her purse had been stolen.

Janette showered and washed the mud out of her white slacks. She emerged wearing the hotel bathrobe.

There wasn't another bathrobe, so after he showered, David wrapped a towel around his waist. When he came out, Janette was sitting on the bed.

"Come here and let me work on your face," she said. She looked closely at the bruise and cut below his eye. David stared into Janette's eyes. "Stop, you're distracting me," she said.

"What?"

She put antiseptic lotion on a pad and pressed it on the cut. "Ouch." He jerked away.

"I bet that hurts, doesn't it," she said, unsympathetic. She taped the pad in place. "It's already turning blue, but there isn't much swelling. I don't think he hit you as hard as he could have."

"I bet he did."

"I got a good shot in on the broad that held me. Did you land any punches?"

"He dropped me before I got a chance."

"Uh-huh."

"Let me check yours, now." David reached for her foot.

"Wrong ankle."

"Sorry." She leaned back extending her legs. The robe opened and she pulled it together over her thighs. David felt her swollen ankle. He massaged it, moving her foot around. He saw no serious damage, but he knew it hurt; still, she didn't flinch.

David began rubbing her calf, moving his hands up her leg.

"Is this a doctor trick?" she asked.

"Right," he said, starting on the other leg. Goose bumps formed, and she leaned back on her elbows. David moved over beside her and leaned over to kiss her. He touched his face to hers and winced as he felt a sharp pain from his bruise.

"Sorry," she said and kissed him. She lay back as David kissed her again. He slipped his hand under her robe and found her breast. She twisted toward him and stroked the back of his head.

"I'm scared," she said.

"Why? We know each other well enough."

"I mean I'm scared of the IORC."

"I know what you meant. Me, too. We've been lucky, but we can't keep depending on luck." Maybe together they had a chance. Together they would be hard to beat, even by the IORC. They were so alike, yet they complemented each other and gained strength from each other.

David kissed her again and opened her robe completely. She pulled off his towel and threw it to the floor.

They explored each other's bodies, prolonging their arousal. They made love, gripping each other and indulging themselves in their pleasure. For that brief time, their lovemaking was a jeer in the face of the danger posed by IORC.

Afterward, they lay on their backs, holding hands and

looking out the window at the runways. On the other side of the airport stood IORC, but it was beyond their view.

Without a word Janette turned toward David, took his hands and put them on her breasts, and kissed him gently.

Despite the danger, David was as happy as he had ever been.

All Warren could think about were the modules in the workshop down the street. At daylight he got out of bed, pulled on an old pair of blue jeans and a sweat-shirt, slipped his feet in some almost-worn-out Topsiders, grabbed a Diet Coke out of the refrigerator, gulped down three aspirins, and ducked out his back door.

When he saw the door to the workshop standing open he had a sinking feeling. Without even thinking that the intruder might still be there, he rushed in.

Nothing appeared to be disturbed. He opened the box where he had hidden the modules; to his great relief, they were still there. Only then did he realize that Frank, the engineer who owned the workshop, was sitting at his workbench behind a pile of boxes, so absorbed in his work that he hadn't noticed Warren's entrance.

Little wisps of smoke were being drawn into a small filter box by a fan in front of the circuit board that Frank was soldering. Frank glanced up and finally saw Warren. "What happened to you? Your wife catch you flirting?" Frank knew Warren's habits.

"Frank, I've got something I need help with. It's urgent, and I think you'll find it interesting," Jeffries said. Frank swiveled around in his chair and looked up at Jeffries. He made a gesture with his hands inviting Jeffries to explain what he wanted.

"I've got some electronics here. One of them has been opened. We need to figure them out; reverse engineer them." Jeffries poured the modules into Frank's hand.

Frank put the modules in a four-inch plastic tray. He moved them under his magnifying glass, adjusting it back and forth, and then moved the modules around with a nylon-tipped probe.

He rolled several feet down the aisle in his chair, carrying the plastic tray, and set it down on a counter below a small digital television macrocamera, which he turned on. He began zooming in on one side of the opened module, increasing the magnification of the camera lens.

"What the hell is this? It's the most miniaturized chip I've ever seen." Frank looked at it with fascination and continued to increase the magnification.

Frank looked up and asked, "Is this thing classified?"

"You mean by the government? No."

"It's a microprocessor. I have no idea what it does." He kept moving the camera around, looking at various parts. "Look over here, that's a microwave transmitter. Actually, it's a transponder. It gets a signal and then gives off a signal."

"Is that all it does?" Jeffries asked.

"No, that's just a small part of it. I'm only guessing now, but it looks like some sort of servomechanism. There's a superconductor battery. It could power this microprocessor for a hundred years and not run down. Even with a transmitter." He moved the camera around, increasing and decreasing the magnification.

Leaving Frank lost in his work, Warren went to his computer and called up the list of names from the disk Janette had returned to him. The Bureau of Vital Statistics database was open to anyone with a proper password. Warren logged on to it and began running the names on the list. Then Frank called him over.

"I think I've got this thing figured out. It's definitely a microwave transponder. It gives off a sixteen-digit signal when it receives a microwave inquiry signal. This other part pulses an electrical charge through the probe at some very low frequency, something on the order of one pulse per second. All of that's relatively simple. What's fascinating is this other part. When it receives a signal, it reacts." Frank was excited, but Warren understood only part of what he said.

"The idea is that it senses the signal and then sends out exactly the opposite signal. If the signal is positive, it sends a negatively charged pulse. It exactly nullifies or cancels whatever signal it receives. This is the kind of circuitry that you see on stealth airplanes. When the plane is hit by a radar signal, it beams back another signal in exactly the opposite frequency. The result is that one blanks out the other and fools the radar."

"Frank, make a video. Then let's see if we can make one of them work," Jeffries said.

Jeffries returned to his computer. The list of names had been checked. Jeffries looked down them, suddenly chilled. The man in Jacksonville who received a heart transplant had been alive and well when Jeffries had run this list before. Now it showed that the man had died this past Wednesday from heart failure. Warren got up and closed and locked the outside door. He then stared again at the screen. He felt certain that IORC had killed these people—but how did they do it? How could you *make* someone have heart failure?

"All right, I've finished the video. Let's fire up one of these puppies," Frank said.

Frank began twisting dials on some instruments; in a few seconds, they heard a screeching sound. Then he adjusted a dial until the screech became a warble and the lines on the oscilloscope jumped.

"Okay, I found the frequency that activates the transponder. Let's turn that into numbers." He clicked several more switches and a line of sixteen numbers appeared on a small LED screen.

"It broadcasts those numbers when you hit it with a certain frequency microwave. Now we know what frequencies it likes. Apparently it uses sixteen-digit numbers as a code to activate the other part," Frank said.

Frank scratched his head for a moment, then swiveled his chair around and flipped on a personal computer. He typed for a few seconds, writing a short program requiring the computer to try all possible sixteen-digit combinations.

"For the hell of it, let's check for a microwave output signal." Sure enough, something was being broadcast from another part of the module. Frank reset several switches, and on the computer screen, the words, "Are you sure? Y/N." appeared.

"I'll be damned, just as simple as that," Frank said. "It's not as complex as it looks."

Warren reached over and typed "Y" on the keyboard, and pressed enter. Nothing happened.

"Now what did we do wrong?" Jeffries asked.

"You're too quick on the trigger. It's a servomechanism. It's got to have a signal coming in so it knows what signal to put out." Frank explained as though talking to a dull child. He connected a wire to the probe and turned a dial. For three pulses, they saw peaks on the oscilloscope; three more pulses peaked below the center line, and then, with a few ripples, a straight line.

"Now what happened to it?" Jeffries asked.

"It's working. That's the whole point. There it is. It's working perfectly. We're pulsing at sixty cycles per minute positive, and it's pulsing at sixty cpm negative, exactly in phase. It's canceling the signal." Frank scratched his head looking at all the instruments and wires strung all over the workbench. "Are you going to tell me about this?" Frank asked.

"You don't want to know, Frank, believe me, you don't want to know. I'm not sure exactly what these things are capable of, but I know someone who can tell me. Can you set up some sort of portable package that I can use to make this thing work?" Jeffries asked.

"Now that we know how it works, sure. I can give you

something the size of a briefcase. If you use a portable computer, you can turn it off and on and make it sing songs."

"Will you put something like that together for me, Frank?"

"Sure, I can do it next weekend, no problem."

"No, I mean today, right now. I have to have it before Monday morning," Jeffries said. Frank's jaw dropped, and he looked at Warren with more than a little irritation.

"That'll take me all day. What about the project?"

"Frank, this is really urgent. No kidding, it really is or I wouldn't ask you. It may even be a matter of life and death, as corny as that sounds. Will you do it for me?"

"You don't give a person any choice, do you? I'll have it ready by tomorrow—that is, if you'll get out of here and leave me alone." Frank started unhooking wires.

"Hold on just a minute, Frank. We only tried one of those. The broken one won't work. Let's check the other one." Frank shrugged his shoulders. It was easy enough now.

Frank picked up the other module with some tweezers, put it in another tray, and hooked up the wires to it just as he had hooked up the first one. They went through the process again, allowing the computer to find the code number. This time Warren waited until Frank had hooked up a wire to the lead that was giving off a pulse, and then typed "Y" on the computer keyboard. They heard a loud bang. The computer screen and several of Frank's instruments went blank, followed by a puff of acrid smoke and the smell of burning insulation.

"What in the hell did you do?" Frank asked, rubbing his eyes. One of the lead wires lay on the floor, still smoldering. Warren stomped on it as Frank turned off all the various instruments. He looked at the module. He saw a black mark where the right probe had been. It was completely burned off, and the wire that was hooked to it had been melted. Frank disconnected the other wire from the module after it cooled down. He ran the recorded readings back to the point where the module had burned out. At exactly that point, a reading that went completely off the scale indicated that the module had released a huge electrical charge.

"Unless I miss my guess that entire battery charge dissipated in a fraction of a second as soon as you typed 'yes' on the keyboard. Everything was working fine before that. I don't think we had any short circuits. I know we didn't. Something you did made that little bugger put out thousands of watts of power. I'm sure glad my face wasn't too close."

They both stared at the module that was lying in the tray. The plastic tray had a melted spot and the smell was strong.

"Were all of these supposed to be identical?" Frank asked.

"I don't have any idea, Frank. Did we make some sort of mistake? Or maybe that's what the thing is supposed to do." Jeffries considered all possibilities.

"I'm afraid we're not ever going to know, because this little guy's toast," Frank said, holding the remains of the module with his tweezers and looking at it as if it were a dead roach.

"We've still got the other one. Make me that portable tester. Be careful. Lock the door when I leave—you don't want a visit like I had last night. And, keep this to yourself. I'm going to Lake County. I'll see you later. Oh, and Frank—thanks."

David felt groggy as he squinted into the sunlight shining through the partially closed blinds. It took him a moment to orient himself to the foreign-feeling room. He saw the back of Janette's head, hair in disarray, across the pillow on the other side of the bed.

Then it all came back to him in a flood—the boat chase and the confrontation in the parking garage at the UNI-LAW building and the more pleasant events shared once they reached the hotel.

David looked at Janette again and she stirred slightly. He could get used to waking up beside her.

He must have dozed off; Janette was gone.

In a few minutes, she came back into the room, dressed in the clothes she had been wearing the evening before. She looked as fresh as if she had spent an hour back at her own apartment getting ready.

"Last night was crazy. But maybe Captain Stapleton got through to those thugs. Anyway, I refuse to let them scare me away from my home. I'd like to go there, get a change of clothes, and then go and see what Parker thinks."

"I've been thinking the same thing. I guess I'd rather find out together now what kind of real danger we're facing."

They drove to David's apartment first. They agreed to be silent and leave as quietly as possible. Maybe the apartment was simply bugged, not under video surveillance.

David's apartment fascinated Janette. She browsed, looking at his photographs, his CD collection, the books on the shelf, the layout of the kitchen, and the view from the window. She made her observations with the air of a vaguely interested inspector, pacing around slowly and taking it all in with her hands behind her back, without touching anything.

David watched her for a minute, then went to his bedroom to get some clothes for the next several days of court hearings. He put the 9mm Baretta pistol that his father had given him for graduation into the nylon case with his clothes.

He could tell that his apartment had been searched by someone who had been less than careful in replacing things. *Well, what did he expect?*

"Why that expression? Did you see something up there?" Janette asked, when they got back in the car.

"Someone's been through my apartment. They've probably done the same thing at your place, too." He paused, thinking. Then his pager buzzed; the message was that he had an urgent FedEx envelope at the hospital. David showed Janette the message on the pager. "Let's go by and get this. I wasn't expecting anything—it could be important."

"Good idea."

The receptionist handed him the FedEx envelope that had come for him only a few minutes before.

Seeing it was from Dr. Byrd, he quickly read Byrd's note. He was stunned.

"What's the matter?" Janette asked. He held out the note to her. She read it over. "All those people, their lives really *are* in danger, aren't they?" she asked.

"Come on." He took her into a dictation cubicle. He dialed the number for Asheville Hospital. It was eleven o'clock.

When the operator answered, he said, "This is Dr. West in Orlando. I need to speak to Dr. Byrd. It's very urgent."

"Dr. Byrd doesn't work on Saturday, sir. His entire department is closed for the weekend, unless there's an emergency."

"Could you get in touch with him? This is an emergency."

"Please hold." The operator put David on hold to the accompaniment of country music, and came back on the line in less than two minutes. "No one answers at his house, sir."

"Would it be possible for you to check with someone to see if he's out of town? I know I keep my hospital advised where I can be reached in case of an emergency."

"Dr. Byrd's not a staff physician here—he works for the medical examiner—so we don't have him on our schedule list. I guess I could call his secretary. She's a friend of mine. Maybe she would know what his plans are for the weekend. Please hold a minute."

David started to hang up and redial when the operator came back on the line again. "I talked to his secretary. She says that as far as she knows he'd planned to be home all weekend. He rarely leaves town. The fact is, he had an appointment for dialysis this morning here at the hospital. I checked, and he hasn't come in. Maybe he's on the way. Our weather is bad and the roads are really slick, so that may be what's delaying him. I'm sorry I couldn't do any more."

"I'll call back. Would you please leave a message that I need to talk to him? And please ask him to leave a number where I can reach him."

"Yes, sir, I'll do that. I'm sorry."

Something had happened; David knew.

As they entered Janette's apartment, she looked around as someone might when trying to locate the present whereabouts of a large spider that had suddenly disappeared.

David did much the same sort of inspection of her apartment that she had done of his. He saw several golf trophies used as bookends and noticed a NordicTrack exercise machine in one corner.

"They've been here, too, I think. It's harder for me to tell, though. I don't keep my place as neat as you do," Janette said once they were back out on the sidewalk, and out of range of any microphones.


At five o'clock Saturday morning, LeBearc had become more frustrated and had contacted the team monitoring the pediatric care worker from Byrd's list. They had kept her under constant surveillance from the green IORC van parked across the street from the medical center. At five-thirty, LeBearc, while sitting in his office, punched in the proper code to a satellite which then had beamed down a signal. The electronic module attached to the woman's liver pulsed out a several-thousand-watt arc of electricity that made a small, soundless explosion deep inside her abdomen.

The woman screamed, clutching her stomach and waking several of the children, who began to cry. She doubled over, still clutching herself, and finally fell to the floor curling into a fetal position. She thought she would faint from the excruciating pain. In a few minutes the pain began to ease off slightly, as her stomach became numb. After five minutes she could straighten out her legs and push herself up into a seated position. The children had gradually fallen back to sleep.

The woman felt a knot forming in her abdomen, and a growing warmth that began to spread. She decided that she must have had a sudden cramp near the surgical site. She pulled herself to her feet and supported herself by leaning on one of the children's chairs. Finally, after fifteen minutes, she walked very slowly into the office, hugging the wall. She told the manager that she was ill and would have to go home.

The hemorrhaging in the woman's abdomen continued. She felt sleepy, and she still noticed a feeling of warmth but very little pain by the time she got in her car.

At home, she went only as far as the bedroom, deciding to wait for her shower until she had rested. Without removing anything but her shoes, she lay down on the bed, turned sideways, drew her knees up and went to sleep. She never awoke.

David and Janette's room at the motel in Lake County had been ransacked. All their clothes were piled on the bed, and their suitcases had the lining ripped out. The calculated message that they were not safe anywhere was very clear.

Quickly gathering their things, they drove to Parker's house. When they stopped in front, one of Stapleton's men from the night before walked out through the front door and down the steps toward them until he recognized them. Then he waved, smiled, and motioned them into the house, saying as they walked, "The captain thought it might be a good idea for me to hang around here a couple of days to make sure everything is okay."

"*Very* good idea. Thanks," David replied as they entered the foyer.

Jingle Bells lay on the rug at the foot of the stairs quivering slightly, the tip of her tail wagging. The man moved his fingers almost imperceptibly, and Jingle Bells dashed to Janette.

"It looks like you've accomplished something Parker has failed at for years," she said.

"It's not so complicated. All you have to do is let them know you're in charge." The guard leaned over and snapped his fingers; Jingle Bells immediately jumped down from Janette's leg, ran over to him, and sat down facing him. He reached down to rub her face. Then he walked over to a chair he had pulled into the foyer, sat down, and picked up a book. Jingle Bells trotted over to her rug and lay down, without taking her eyes off the man.

A few minutes later, Jeffries arrived. When they saw his bruised face—his bruises were much worse than David's—everyone spoke at once. Jeffries calmly gave the details of the beating in the same emotionally detached way as he might explain a new piece of software, except that he mentioned he had flown his Cessna to Lake County to stay out of their reach.

"We tested the modules this morning. They're complex. Not only do they contain the serial number, they can also give off an electrical pulse. The module first receives an electrical impulse, and then puts out a charge in reply, but of the opposite polarity. A positive charge is answered by a negative charge of the same intensity, duration, and frequency. It cancels or actually blocks the signal it receives."

"Would the electrical pulse of a heart set it off?" David asked.

"It's possible."

"Then that's how they do it. They install a device that can either be a pacemaker or a pacemaker blocker. It's like an on-and-off switch. IORC can turn off one of their hearts just that easily," David said, snapping his fingers.

"Could they really do that?" Warren asked.

"Absolutely," David said.

"One of the modules exploded when we sent a code. Why would it do that?"

David frowned for a moment. "Other organs, I expect. A heart wouldn't require such a drastic means to make it fail. I think they attach one to every organ they transplant, except maybe eyes or joints, and they can disable any major organ they supply any time they want to."

"What I can't understand is why they would do such a thing to an innocent person," Betty Martinez said.

"To raise their profits," Warren said.

"I don't think it's that simple," Parker Ross inserted, looking at David.

"No, it's not that simple, and profits are only part of it. It's about power and control. They claim that they're better at transplanting organs than anyone else, and they want to enhance that image. They don't want to lose the public's confidence. They want everyone dependent on them. They want to ensure their monopoly. I think that's a more accurate explanation," David said.

Speaking to Betty Martinez, Parker said, "We're not trying to stop them from transplanting organs. The reason for this suit is to get you and Jorge compensation because of what they did to your husband. A by-product of the suit is that we can make them reluctant to kill people in the future." He had lowered his eyebrows to their maximum as he leaned forward looking directly at her. She nodded her head. She understood Parker's point. "There's more, though, isn't there, David?" Parker asked, redirecting his gaze.

"You know more about the IORC than you've told us, don't you?" David replied, surprised at Parker's comment. This wise old man was trying to tell them something.

"Some, yes. I know they manipulate Justification Factors. I know some important people have gotten organs when they shouldn't have, and some have been improperly denied transplants. I also know something about their adoption program."

"What adoption program?" David asked. Now he was afraid he knew what was coming.

"They put infants up for adoption—very expensive adoption. A client came to me about it years ago. It's how they originally financed their organ transplant business.

"They charge several million for babies having special abilities; they had the most success with children who excel in music or athletics. Most of the the adoption fees are secured by mortgages on the adoptive parents' assets. The adoptive parents pay part at the time of adoption, and annual payments until the child reaches majority. Then a subsidiary of IORC gets a contract to control the child's career and to receive a percentage of the earnings. The adoptive parents must follow a prescribed program to train the child and facilitate the child's career.

"If the parents don't follow the program and assure that the child pursues the chosen path, or if the child refuses, the mortgages can be foreclosed and the parents' assets taken to pay the balance on the original charge, plus huge penalties.

"But problems arise as these children grow up. Some of the children excel at other things in addition to sports and music, and many of them are extraordinarily independent. Some have refused to follow their prescribed careers. Then IORC invokes its mortgages and penalties. As this became common, the IORC began to pressure the parents with J

Factor reductions if they didn't force the children to conform, and even threatened to harm the children."

David's mind was reeling. Undoubtedly he was one of the special adopted babies. That would explain his father's debts. David's independence and his father's support of it would also explain his father's low J Factor. It would even explain a lot of the things his father and mother had told him, for example, how important it was to do what he believed in. They had paid a heavy price to assure he could do that.

If he had been adopted from the IORC, then who were his biological parents? What about his "special abilities"? Then it all hit David—the same feeling he had when seeing the children on the island. He knew. And he knew also that, like the GECs on the island, he was alive at the pleasure of the IORC. The IORC was intertwined in his life— as in all of society—manipulating everything to achieve its goals.

He had often thought in his pensive moments that he was different from other people, and that the world around him was only a stage set for his benefit while unrevealed forces watched and controlled him. He had fought that perceived control his entire life. Now he could identify the IORC as the source of the problem—the unseen enemy.

David studied Parker Ross's face as Parker's eyebrows moved around, punctuating his thoughts and observations of David and Janette. David frowned; Parker lowered his eyebrows and nodded slightly at David's next unspoken realization. *The client Parker had described was Janette's adoptive father.* But Parker was sworn to silence by his confidentiality oath. It was for David to tell her—that was Parker's message. Janette's father had forbidden Parker to tell her.

David was angry, but quickly regained his perspective. He must tell Janette. Parker wanted that and so did

David—but in private, so she could have time to deal emotionally with the revelations.

David decided he must tell everyone assembled about IORC's island. They were all in danger now, and it would be safer for them if they knew just how deep all of this went. Then he would talk to Janette privately.

Besides, if he were killed it was important that others know the secrets. So, he told them everything he had seen. But he said nothing about himself and Janette. The others looked at him, stunned to silence by his revelations.

"Janette, let's take a walk while they process all this," David said.

They went out the back entrance of Parker's condo and walked along the lakeshore. They stopped and watched a great blue heron poised at the edge of the lake. It suddenly stabbed its beak into the water, coming out with an unsuspecting fish that had mistaken the heron's spindly legs for reeds. The fish had not seen the lurking danger, which, like most danger, was hidden in plain sight.

"Janette, I'm not quite sure how to begin, but there's something you need to know," David said, stopping and taking her hand.

"I've already figured it out. I'm the 'adoptee' Parker was talking about. That's why my dad made such a secret about my biological parents. It's why I haven't been able to locate them myself. It explains a lot of things." Janette stared out across the lake, lost in her own thoughts and memories. David squeezed her hand and she turned to look at him.

"Me, too, Janette. It's my background, too." She frowned for a moment, then hugged him tightly as tears ran down her cheeks.

As quickly as they started, she wiped them away, pulled away from David, and smiled. "I've wondered about myself for years. Now I know. And when I met you . . . well, I knew there was a connection there. We're just too much, oh, alike for it to be coincidence. Good. Now we know what we have to do." Then she took his hand and they walked back to Parker's.

David called the hospital in Asheville, reaching the same operator that he had spoken with before. "This is Dr. West again. I called several hours ago for Dr. Byrd. Were you able to reach him?"

"I'm sorry, Doctor, that won't be possible now," she said.

"Why not? I told you this is an emergency."

"Dr. Byrd has passed away."

"When?" David asked, his heart sinking.

"Sometime late yesterday afternoon. He lives alone, you see, and so no one knew that he didn't come home. It's all so terrible."

"I knew he had kidney problems, but I didn't think he was anywhere near terminal."

"It wasn't his kidneys, sir," the operator said.

"Then what happened?" David asked.

"I'm not able to discuss that, sir."

"Listen here, I'm a friend of Dr. Byrd's. I practiced medicine with him in Orlando. A lot of strange things have been happening here recently, and Dr. Byrd knew about them. I want to know what happened to him because it might be connected."

"I'm sorry, sir, I have my orders."

"Could you give me the number of the secretary you mentioned? Maybe I can talk to her about it."

"I guess I could do that." She gave David the number. He thanked her, hung up, and dialed the new number. A woman answered.

"My name is Dr. West; I'm from Orlando. I'm a friend of Dr. Byrd's. I understand that he has died. I wonder if you can tell me what happened?"

Maybeth recognized David's name. "They discovered

his body an hour ago, locked in the lab. His shunt was cut. He killed himself late yesterday, soon after the man from IORC, a Dr. LeBearc, left."

"LeBearc was there. . . . Suicide. Are you sure?"

"I'm afraid so."

"I'm sorry. Thanks."

He turned to the others. "Dr. Byrd apparently killed himself right after he wrote this to me." David showed them the note.

"Even if it was suicide, that doesn't mean LeBearc didn't cause it," David said and sat down at the table and stared out the window. "I think we should call the FBI or somebody."

"Before you do that," Parker Ross said, "think about it for a minute. If you call the FBI and tell them you've got a list of names of people that the IORC is systematically killing, they're not going to believe you. They'll think it's a publicity play because of the lawsuit. Finally, in several days or a week, maybe even longer, they might start seriously looking at your evidence. By that time it'll probably be too late for some, if not all, of those people. I think we'll have better luck doing what we can at the hearing tomorrow, and hope that the press picks up on it. If not, then we can tell the FBI."

"I'm not sure there's anything more we can do about the people on the list except to contact them directly. But they probably won't believe us. Warren, how do you activate one of these devices? I mean to say, can someone press a button a hundred miles away and activate it?"

"It's possible in theory, I suppose. They could do it by satellite even, although it would require a lot of power. Satellite fees are based on the power required. A single signal would cost many thousands in satellite charges. I imagine they use a microwave transmitter on the people when they are in an IORC hospital."

For several minutes no one spoke. "It's not my nature

to sit here and patiently wait for the legal process to take its course." David walked back to the telephone.

"What are you going to do?" Janette asked.

"I'm going to call LeBearc and try to put a stop to this," David said.

David quickly reached LeBearc's secretary but then met with opposition. "I need to speak to Dr. LeBearc right away. This is extremely urgent."

"He's not in at the moment," she said.

"Then reach him. I'll hold."

"I'm not sure that's possible, sir. This is Saturday and Dr. LeBearc is not in."

"Listen to me," he rasped, "if you don't find him right away he'll read about it in the paper tomorrow, and he won't like it."

"I'll try," she said, and she put David's call on hold. Classical music played at a soft volume in the background. In less than a minute, LeBearc answered.

"Dr. West, what exactly is all this about?" LeBearc snapped.

"I think you know perfectly well what it's about. We know you saw Byrd. Did you kill him?"

"What are you talking about? You may be distraught, but be careful about making accusations. I saw Dr. Byrd on Friday afternoon. He seemed well, aside from a chronic kidney problem. He answered some of my questions, and when I left his office he was very much alive."

"You, apparently, were the last person to see him."

"You, of all people, should understand that we're trying to save lives, not terminate them. You need to get hold of yourself, Doctor. You're acting irresponsibly."

"Don't give me that," David snapped. "I know you have the list, and I know you've been killing the people on it."

"I have no idea what you are talking about," LeBearc said.

"Like hell you don't. We've had your electronics analyzed. We know now how you do it. Didn't count on that, did you?"

LeBearc paused. "We want our property back," he said coldly. "Do you understand? If you don't return it to us immediately, you know what will happen. You won't be so lucky next time."

"LeBearc, I'm asking you not to kill the rest of the people on the list. These are real people with families, jobs, lives. They're not some creatures that you can kill without any consequences. They're not your GECs."

"This is none of your business," LeBearc hissed.

"I think it is and I intend to do whatever is necessary to stop you—in court and out. The more people you kill, the easier it will be for us to prove it and expose what you're doing. If that doesn't work, I'll try something more direct. You'll have to contend with *me,* then."

David had hung up on LeBearc without waiting for a reply. Furious, but determined to contain his emotion, LeBearc drummed his long fingers and frowned. West was becoming a dangerous liability. He punched some buttons on his console to call the managing director.

"Director, I want approval to conclude David West and Janette Compton. Their lawsuit is extremely dangerous. *They're dangerous.* I told you when you ordered me to hire West that we wouldn't be able to control him. Every one of these adoptees that we try to use turns out to be so independent-minded that we lose all control of them. West and Compton know about our process, and now they have a heart module in their possession. Even with Krickett Hansen's help, we haven't been able to recover it yet."

"LeBearc, this entire matter is becoming an inconvenience and an embarrassment. I expect you to be able to handle the company's problems in your district without having to bother me. If you can't, I'll send you some help."

"But, Director, without approval . . ." But the managing director had already disconnected.

"All right, I will," LeBearc said to himself. He jabbed a key on his console to call Krickett Hansen.

While Janette spent the afternoon preparing for the hearings on Monday, David called the people on the list.

He didn't tell them what he feared, because he didn't want them to panic. Instead, he told them that he was doing a study on transplant patients. Since IORC only provided transplant doctors, he urged each of them to have no further contact with the IORC until they had talked to their personal, non-IORC doctors.

He also asked each of them to have their personal doctors contact him as soon as possible, so that he could give them urgent information he had discovered in his study. When these UNIMED doctors called him, he would tell them what he knew, if they hadn't already heard it on the news. He told everyone on the list that some of the IORC's tests could harm them.

He reached all but three of the people, and they all said they were willing to accommodate his request.

After dinner that evening, David and Janette returned to her office and began trying to reach the remaining three people. One of them was the woman in Tallahassee. Her sister answered the phone. She explained that the woman had suddenly become ill on Saturday morning at work, gone home, and died of internal bleeding.

Slowly David replaced the receiver. He realized how difficult it would be to stay alive in the coming days.

# 19

Sunday night, Warren Jeffries had tried out the demonstration setup for the module in his kitchen. The working module lay imbedded in foam in the top of a medium-size aluminum case, with a small computer and several instruments inside that activated the module.

When he dressed Monday morning, he put the envelope containing the cracked module in his shirt pocket. As he opened the garage door, a nearby IORC operative with a scanner picked up a very weak signal from the module in the case.

The technicians in the van called Krickett who, along with her driver in a rented white Chevrolet, waited two blocks from Jeffries's home.

Warren did not actually see the car as much as sense it from a shadow that crossed his peripheral vision: something very large and very close, moving fast. As he turned his head to look, the Chevrolet sped through an intersection, ignoring the stop sign, and slammed into his left front fender, forcing him off the road. His car bumped up over the curb and blew out a tire as he tried to put on the brakes. He knocked down a bus stop sign, smashed into a large bush, and came to rest with the bumper against a palm tree.

To Warren it felt like watching some stunt on television, in which he was an observer rather than a participant. The seat belt prevented him from being seriously hurt, and the air bag had not deployed, but glass covered him and the radio blared.

The Chevrolet skidded to a halt. Krickett jumped out of her car and headed for the broken-out driver's window, while her driver opened the passenger door and turned off the radio.

Still stunned, Warren nevertheless noticed the gorgeous woman wearing a low-cut purple sweater and an emerald necklace who leaned toward him through the window.

"Hello, again," she said. It was not a friendly greeting. The hair on the back of Warren's neck stood up as he recognized the voice of the woman who had assaulted him on Friday night. "Give me the module."

"Go to hell," Warren muttered. He glanced up at her face, then back down her sweater.

"You like these?" she asked, throwing back her shoulders and thrusting her breasts toward his face. Warren's eyes locked on, so he didn't see the needle that Krickett jabbed into his arm, injecting him with succinylcholine. He tried to struggle out of the seat belt and grabbed for her. She backed away from the window and patiently waited while the drug took effect.

Warren knew he was in big trouble. Within a few seconds, he felt his arms go weak and his muscles go limp. He slumped forward and hit the horn, but Krickett immediately pulled him away. Warren's arms and legs felt heavy. He wanted to move them, but the effort seemed too great to try.

The driver sat on the passenger side of the car. He pulled the aluminum case onto his lap and snapped it open. "It's only a computer and some instruments. He probably has the module on him." He closed the case and tossed it into the backseat. He went through Warren's pockets, found the envelope, and gave it to Krickett. She poured the burned-out module into her hand and smiled.

Krickett lifted the shoulder harness and pushed Warren over on the seat. Unable to resist, Warren allowed himself to fall. She leaned inside, giving Warren one more view down her sweater, kissed her fingers and touched the bruise on his face. "See ya," she said.

He tried moving his toes and found that he could, if only slightly. But when he tried to lift his arms, he couldn't make the effort.

Just moments later he heard some kids coming. Three boys rode up on their bicycles and stopped to look in the window.

"Hey, man, I think he's dead. Somebody go call the cops. Tell 'em a guy's dead out here."

"Noooooo," Warren heard himself say.

"Hey, no, man, he ain't dead, but he's hurt. Go over there to that house, knock on the door, and ask the lady to call the cops." One of the boys hopped back on his bicycle and peddled furiously up to the house, dropped his bike, and banged on the door.

The corner of Warren's lips twitched as he tried to smile. *They hadn't gotten the module that worked.*

Going to court is a humbling and awesome experience. Courthouses have a unique atmosphere, even a characteristic aroma, just as hospitals do. Courthouses are cold in all senses of the word. The extra-large doors, high ceilings, and tall windows make people feel small, subservient to the government whose power is symbolized by the scale of the building itself.

The bailiff opened the courtroom at exactly eight-thirty. A crowd of reporters rushed inside and took most of the seats not reserved for witnesses. The clerk and court reporter arranged their materials. While people continued to mill around, a large black man carrying a small brown envelope came in and walked up the aisle to the railing that divided the courtroom. "Excuse me," he said, looking at the clerk who sat at the table in front of the judge's bench.

"Yes, what can I do for you?" she asked.

"I have an envelope here for delivery to attorney Compton. Can I leave it for her?" he asked.

"I guess so," the clerk answered. She took the envelope and the man left.

Burrows had seen the TV report of the suit. The woman lawyer needed his help, so he decided to give her the tape. He owed her that much, after the Thomas hearing. Besides, he didn't like what he saw on the tape, or the IORC itself for that matter.

A few minutes later, Wilson Hoffmeister and Andre LeBearc entered, followed by two associate lawyers carrying briefcases; except for LeBearc's inevitable gray suit, they all wore blue pinstripes.

David had come in and now sat in a witness seat in the second row. Several of the newspeople asked him who he was, and he gave them his name. When they asked for a comment, he told them he had nothing to say. They didn't like it, but apparently this wasn't an unexpected response, since they accepted it and left him alone.

A few minutes later, Parker, Janette, and Betty and Jorge Martinez came into the courtroom, and Parker led them down the aisle, through the gate and to the table on the right side. Parker, wearing a dark blue suit and white shirt, placed his small portfolio on the right end of the table. Janette, also wearing blue, sat down in the chair on the left, closest to Hoffmeister. She was less than pleased to be even that close to her opponent. Parker dragged a chair from the exhibit table to the end of the counsel table where he had put his papers. The bailiff frowned at him and started to say something, but thought better of it. Perhaps it was Parker's white hair or his piercing eyes that dissuaded him; something about his bearing silenced the bailiff.

Parker walked over to Hoffmeister and with a big smile held his hand out. "Why, Wilson, it's good to see you."

Hoffmeister felt forced to stand up and shake hands with Parker. "Good morning, Parker. I thought you had retired. Here you are back again, complicating my life."

"I'm having the most fun I've had in years. This gentleman must be the IORC representative," Parker said and held his hand out to LeBearc.

LeBearc stood, gave a slight bow, and shook Parker's hand. "I'm Dr. LeBearc."

Parker nodded and smiled. He turned around with his hands behind his back and ambled slowly to his chair.

Krickett came in through the public entrance of the courtroom, still wearing the purple sweater and necklace. She attracted plenty of attention from the reporters. Walking forward to the railing, she tapped one of the associates on the shoulder and pointed to LeBearc. LeBearc saw her and rolled his chair back. She handed him a foil envelope without saying a word. LeBearc cupped his hand and poured the burned module out of the envelope. She turned to leave and saw that David had seen the envelope. She walked over to him and sat down. Smiling, she put her hand on his shoulder and leaned against him. "Nice to see you," she said.

"Yeah. The last time you shot at me."

"Not me. It was my driver. He was aiming at Compton. He doesn't like his love life jeopardized. I hit his hand so he missed. All we wanted was the module. Besides, you've seen me shoot. I don't miss."

"Did you hurt Warren?"

"Nothing permanent."

"Now what?" David asked.

"I was called in to recover the module. I did that. My job's over. As soon as I finish my report, I'll be on my own for a few days' vacation. Thought I might check out Orlando, maybe go to a basketball game or something. Want to come?"

"No, thanks," David said. Janette turned in her seat to watch David and Krickett.

Krickett flashed a huge smile, tilted her head a little, and said, "Too bad." Then she left. David knew it would not be that simple.

LeBearc whispered to Hoffmeister, "We have recovered the missing module."

Hoffmeister nodded. LeBearc had not told him the truth. As far as Hoffmeister knew, Mrs. Martinez's claim was completely unfounded. LeBearc had told him only that the module, a trade secret of IORC, might be used in a misguided attempt to prove the allegations of the lawsuit.

Janette shuffled her papers nervously and struck through parts of her notes for the opening statement she had planned. In reading it this morning, it seemed too stiff and too long, even melodramatic.

The clerk remembered the brown envelope and took it to Janette. "You attorney Compton?" she asked.

"Yes."

"Someone left this for you a few minutes ago." She handed Janette the envelope.

She took the envelope and opened it. Inside were a video minicassette and a note that said, "I owe you a tape. Burrows." She placed the tape on her legal pad and looked at it. It had no label. No one had borrowed a tape from her. Who was Burrows? The name seemed familiar. Then she remembered: It was the cop. It was too late for the Thomas arrest tape to make any difference. Why would he send it now? She put the tape back in the envelope along with the note, and dropped it in her briefcase. She didn't have time to think about old defeats now, but she was a little curious—Might the tape have changed the outcome of that case?—and intended to take a look at it as soon as she could get to a VCR.

Judge Ralph Cooper entered from behind the bench, and the courtroom quieted immediately.

"All rise," the bailiff said in a loud voice, and conversation ceased as everyone stood up. "The Circuit Court in and for Orange County, Florida, is now in session, the Honorable Judge Ralph Cooper presiding. All those having business before the Court draw near, and you shall be heard. You may be seated." By the time the bailiff had finished his litany, Judge Cooper had taken his seat and was looking at the file in front of him, as if attempting to determine what matter had come before him today.

Judge Cooper had spent seven years in the U.S. Attorney's office, followed by ten years in private law practice before he became a judge. Though no legal scholar, he had a reputation for being fair-minded and honest. His fifteen years as a judge made him the second most senior justice in the Circuit. He enjoyed the status of his position, and he also enjoyed the work. Parker Ross and Wilson Hoffmeister had each tried several cases before him.

"Ladies and gentlemen, the case before the court this morning is Martinez versus the IORC. I see that we have some attorney acquaintances of mine appearing today, and also attorney Janette Compton. Good morning, everyone. I understand that the unfortunate matter with the Bar Association has been completely resolved. I'm glad that's behind us now. With the preliminaries out of the way, let's proceed."

The experience of being paralyzed but fully conscious is not something the human psyche can accommodate with equanimity. Warren Jeffries kept telling himself that the effects would wear off in a few minutes and that he had to remain calm, but the drug made him feel claustrophobic. He could now move his toes and the tips of his fingers, but he could not move his body enough to change the awkward position Krickett had pushed him into. With his face pressed against the seat, he could hardly breathe.

*How long,* he wondered, *will it take for the effects to wear off?* Perhaps the paralysis built up for a while, and it would get worse before it got better. He could still hear the children outside the car. He had exerted a monumental effort to tell them that he wasn't dead, and now he couldn't summon enough energy to make another sound.

The ambulance arrived before the police.

"He must have broken his neck. He can't seem to move or talk, but all of his vital signs are pretty much okay. There's no shock. It's got to be his head or neck. Let's get him on a board."

"Sir, your neck may be broken, so we're going to immobilize you. Then we'll take you out of the car and get you to the hospital where a doctor can do X rays." The paramedic looked into Warren's face but saw no change in his expression. The paramedic thought he saw fear in Warren's eyes, but decided he had imagined it.

They slipped the board behind Warren's back while he was still lying across the seats and strapped him to it. Then they put him in the ambulance and left.

The police and wrecker had arrived and were carrying out the task of impounding the car.

"I make it a couple of fishing rods and a white metal briefcase," the policeman said. The wrecker operator initialed the police inventory. The police left all property with the car and in the wrecker company's custody unless a crime was suggested. The wrecker operator, following his rules, took the briefcase out of the car, put it on the front seat of his truck for safekeeping, and hauled the car away.

Somewhere between the accident scene and the hospital, Warren noticed that he could move his entire foot, not just his toes. He thought he could turn his head if it weren't strapped to the board, and he found he could

THE J FACTOR 307

move his fingers like a piano player exercising before a recital. The paramedic noted the movement on his chart.

"Isszkay," Warren said, trying to tell the paramedic that he was all right.

"Take it easy, now. You've been in a car accident."

"I, icky, okay," Warren managed to get out.

"Yes, you're gonna be fine. Please lie still."

"No. I, I'm okay. I-am-okay." Warren forced the words out slowly and distinctly. He found that he could raise his forearm, which he did to demonstrate, and he also moved his feet around. He licked his lips and grimaced; his face was still numb.

Warren tried to relax as much as he could. Now that he could move his feet and hands and talk a little, he knew he would be all right.

"Succ . . . s . . . ," Warren tried.

The paramedic smiled in spite of himself. "Yeah, I guess it does, and I don't blame you for feeling that way after having a wreck like you had, but I think you're gonna be just fine."

Warren smiled at the man, catching on to what he meant. He decided to relax for a few more minutes, and maybe he would be able to explain, to say the word.

The paramedic took Warren into Orlando Government's emergency room.

Chaos reigned as people in various stages of distress waited for help. The triage nurse checked Warren's vital signs and looked into his pupils with a penlight. She asked him, "How do you feel?"

"I'm okay. Succinylcholine, succinylcholine."

"What's that? You've had an automobile accident and you must have hurt your head," she said.

"No, given succinylcholine," Warren said.

The nurse looked at his chart. "No, you weren't given anything. You had an accident. I don't think you're in any immediate danger, so relax as much as you can until we can x-ray your head and neck," the nurse said. She laid his chart on top of the blanket that covered his legs and left.

Warren raised his left arm high enough to see his wrist-watch: 9:25. He was missing the trial. Then he remembered his briefcase. *My God, it's still in the car,* he thought. *I can't let them get the briefcase.* He squirmed and thrashed his legs and forearms. He was strapped down. The metal clipboard the nurse had laid on him clattered onto the floor. He tried to call for help, but his effort sounded more like a croak. No one came for several minutes, until an orderly strolled by, picked up the clipboard, and laid it back on Warren's legs without saying a word. Warren tried to get him to listen, but the orderly either didn't understand or was so used to the unintelligible complaints of people in the emergency room, he paid no attention.

Each time someone passed Warren, he asked them for help, but they either looked away, pretending not to hear, or said something intended to be reassuring and walked on.

Twenty minutes passed before an orderly finally came and took Warren to radiology. By then, the drug had completely worn off.

After the tests, back in the holding area, the orderly told Warren that the doctor would see him in a few minutes to explain what he had found. Warren saw a clock that registered 10:55. Twenty minutes later, the radiologist walked over and said, "Are you Warren Jeffries?" Rather than take Warren's word for it, he looked at the plastic arm-band on Warren's right wrist.

"Yes. I wasn't really hurt in the accident," Warren said.

"Well, I don't see anything on the X rays, CT scan, or MRI, and I wanted to tell you so. You could have a concussion, but your neck is not injured." The doctor released the Velcro straps across Warren's forehead, but left the chest and arm straps on. Warren thankfully turned his head back and forth to relieve the tension in his neck muscles.

"I've been trying to tell everybody that I wasn't hurt."

"The report here says that you were paralyzed when the paramedic arrived, that you couldn't move and you couldn't talk. En route to the hospital you regained partial use of your extremities and said a few words, which they thought were incoherent. It's most likely that you've had a concussion," the doctor said. "Or it's from whatever happened to your face."

"No, I don't have a concussion. The accident wasn't that bad."

"But you were paralyzed after the accident, so something must have happened," the doctor reasoned.

"Something did happen. I was given succinylcholine," Warren said.

"What?" The doctor looked at the chart again, leafing through the several pages that had built up since Warren had arrived.

"There's nothing in here about any medication. You wouldn't have been given succinylcholine. That's used in the operating room. How do you know about succinylcholine?"

"The woman who caused the accident gave it to me. She's the one who did this to my face, Friday night. She ran me into the tree and then injected me with succinylcholine. It's all an IORC scheme to get a secret module that I have. But it's in my briefcase and I have to get it back." Warren struggled against the straps. "Now take these damn straps off."

The doctor looked at Warren and puckered his lips. Looking first at his records and then back at Warren, he wrote on his chart:

Paranoid delusions, psychotic, perhaps trauma-induced. Psychiatric consult, admit for Baker Act evaluation.

He signed his name.

"Mr. Jeffries, we'll have another doctor take a look at you before we can remove the straps. Is there someone I can contact and let them know you're here at the hospital? The police usually take all day before they get around to calling. Would you like me to call for you?"

"Yes, I'd appreciate it if you would call my wife." Warren gave him her name and telephone number.

The doctor went to the nurses' station in radiology, and ordered a strong sedative for Jeffries and his transferral to psychiatric holding, pending the Baker Act evaluation and commitment. This order got immediate attention. The nurse filled a syringe with Demerol and injected Warren, while he asked what it was. She had experience with psychiatric patients, and as far as she was concerned the sooner they were knocked out, the better. Warren could feel immediately that he had been drugged, and he began to protest. Slowly, a warm feeling spread through his body, and his protests seemed less and less important. He decided to wait a few minutes before he protested any more. He could always get around to it later.

"Mr. Hoffmeister, it's your motion, so you may proceed," Judge Cooper said.

"May it please the court, I'm Wilson Hoffmeister and I have the privilege of representing the International Organ Replacement Corporation. As I think everyone here knows, among their many endeavors the IORC is engaged throughout the world in the transplantation of various organs. Many thousands of people owe the prolongation of their lives and the improvement of their quality of life to the IORC.

"Starting as a small research company in a field fraught with uncertainty and failure, IORC has advanced the science of organ transplants to the point of everyday occurrence. As a point of interest, I would like to remind everyone present that the President of the United States has an IORC heart, and that the heads of state of several other countries have also received IORC transplants.

"The IORC administers the Justification Factor system, which is in effect in all of the world's countries. IORC maintains medical records for most of the population, and it engages in research and development encompassing all of the sciences, not medicine alone.

"During IORC's development, it became clear that for such an organization to operate effectively, it could not submit to interference by various local authorities. While we in the United States might not object to our government's involvement, and while such involvement might, at least theoretically, not be counterproductive to the goals of the IORC, we cannot say the same for all governments. As a result, the IORC has entered into the same treaty with every country in which it operates. These treaties provide certain basic legal rules for the interaction of the IORC with the people and the governments of those countries.

"These rules expressed in the treaties must by their own terms be enforced by the countries in question. Ultimate enforcement of these rules lies not with any single country, but rather with the International Court of Justice. Under the law in this country, and every other country where the IORC has a treaty, the courts as well as the other branches of government are obliged to abide by those treaties. It benefits everyone that these rules be inviolate. Without the enforcement of these rules, the IORC would have no alternative but to withdraw from any country where such rules were not in effect, and withhold its services and its organ transplants from the people in those countries.

"One of those rules," and Hoffmeister picked up an imposing-looking book and opened it to a marked page, "provides in Section Two, and I'm quoting, 'The IORC shall be absolutely immune from any claim for negligence in connection with any of its activities. IORC and its employees shall not be subject to regulation of its business or professional activities in any way.'

"Your Honor, it's difficult to see how anyone could conceive of language clearer than that which I have just read.

"A claim is made in this case that the IORC took some action or other to cause the death of a heart transplant patient. As inconceivable as any thinking person might find such a notion in light of the very purpose of the IORC, that is not really the legal issue or the important matter before this court. Instead, the question is whether this court will enforce the treaty that gives IORC absolute immunity from any such claim as the one being brought here. If the IORC were required to go to court and defend itself every time a medical complication arose that in any way involved the IORC, then the situation would deteriorate to the point that the IORC would have to adjust the way it performed its operations, not to accord with the best medical and scientific methods, but to be legally defensible or acceptable to the changing whim of juries. Such action would cripple the company.

"Your Honor, courts and juries are not qualified to determine the proper techniques for organ transplants; they never have been and never will be.

"The claim presented to this court is made by the family of a patient who received a heart transplant not at IORC but at Orlando Government Hospital. The heart in question belonged to IORC and could be transplanted lawfully only by IORC. The transplant was, therefore, illegal.

"Under the treaty between the IORC and the United States, this court is completely without power, authority, or jurisdiction to even consider the claim, and it is our position that the claim must be dismissed. The claim itself is, of course, utterly absurd and irresponsible. It is based upon the opinion of a doctor whose first patient died after he performed an illegal transplant, and it is argued by a lawyer who—for some reason that totally escapes us—is on a vendetta against the IORC. She attempted to prosecute one of its doctors although she had no evidence to do so, and then she proceeded to unlawfully investigate IORC operations, which are immune from such investigation under the treaty. This she did in violation of directions from her superiors. As a result, UNILAW discharged her."

"Your Honor, I object. I was not discharged. I resigned," Janette said.

"Excuse me, Your Honor, let me correct that. She resigned pending proceeding to discharge her. I know, because it happened in my presence. In any event, for reasons known only to her, this attorney managed to convince the widow of the poor unfortunate man, who died from medical complications of an inferior transplant, to bring a claim against the IORC because he happened to be there for a checkup when the complications occurred.

"Your Honor, it is cases like this that the treaty is intended to prevent. The IORC would have to devote a significant amount of time and resources to defend every crackpot claim and charge made against it. Organ transplants and serious medical problems are always highly emotional, particularly when family members die. The concept that every time a medical procedure doesn't work out as everyone hoped it would, someone must have been negligent, or even worse as is alleged here, that such complications are the result of intentional misconduct, is an entirely incorrect and unacceptable premise.

"We contend that this case should be dismissed on the law, right now, before any more time is wasted—time of the court, of the IORC, and of the public." Hoffmeister sat down, straightened his sleeves, and looked at Janette. He intended his speech for rebroadcast on the six o'clock news.

"Ms. Compton, what's your response?" Judge Cooper asked.

Janette had prepared, edited, corrected, reduced, expanded, and then reprepared her statement over the last few days. What she had intended to say had been nothing at all like Hoffmeister's statement. Instead, she had planned to make a short, purely legal argument. Given Hoffmeister's approach, however, she couldn't make her planned argument. It would leave an entirely wrong and inadequate impression. She decided to argue the case as well as she could and hope that it was enough.

"Your Honor, the quotation that Mr. Hoffmeister read is not disputed. It is the basis of our argument, too. The treaty says 'The IORC will be absolutely immune from any claim for negligence . . .' and so on. This is not a claim for negligence. The IORC killed Mr. Martinez intentionally."

There was a stir as members of the media began talking among themselves; several of the reporters left the room. The judge frowned.

"I don't make such charges lightly, Your Honor, but for purposes of the Motion to Dismiss, the allegations are that the actions of the IORC were intentional, not negligent. Legally, for purposes of considering this motion, the court is obliged to accept the truth of those allegations. If it's true, then there's no exemption under the treaty. That's our legal argument. It's that simple.

"As for the rest of it, this is not a crackpot claim. We are prepared to present testimony from a board-certified heart transplant surgeon that in his opinion the death of Michael Martinez was from intentional actions of the IORC. We have research that will back up these allegations. Most important, we will be able to prove to the court exactly how the IORC's actions were accomplished. We have an example of their electronic device, and we are prepared to demonstrate how the device can disable a transplanted heart."

This time there was more than a stir in the back of the room. One reporter tripped over the tripod of a television camera as he tried to get to the door. Judge Cooper banged his gavel and glared at the people in the back of the courtroom. The man stopped where he was on the floor, and there was silence.

"We ask the court under these exceptional circumstances to allow us to have discovery and to require the IORC to answer questions. I believe when all the evidence is in, the court will be convinced that we have proved our case." Janette sat down.

"Mr. Hoffmeister, I suspect you may have some rebuttal," Judge Cooper said wryly.

"Yes, indeed I do, Your Honor. To begin with, IORC categorically denies everything that has been said. It is, as I said earlier, totally absurd. As far as some mysterious device is concerned, we object to any reference to that until and unless it is actually produced. It's very easy for a lawyer to make a claim and pretend to have evidence because newspeople are listening to what's being said. It's another thing altogether to actually produce the evidence.

"She made reference to discovery. By that I assume she means trying to force the IORC to produce volumes of records so that she can go through them. Article Four, Section Two of the treaty between the IORC and the United States provides, and again I quote, 'The records of IORC of whatever nature shall be exempt from any requirement of disclosure.' We will oppose any effort whatsoever to require IORC to produce any records. I hasten to say it's not because we're trying to hide anything, but because it is the universal precedent throughout the world that our records are not subject to disclosure.

"If this weren't so, our records would be continuously under review by all manner of claimants and all levels of administrations, insurance companies, UNIMED, et cetera. We would be doing nothing but producing records. That's particularly so because of the Justification Factor procedures. No, Your Honor, we will not agree to any discovery. As the court well knows, the precedent in this regard is universal. We are ready to try the case today

They can produce no evidence to back up their case. But again I say that the case should be dismissed on the law." Hoffmeister sat down.

"Ms. Compton, do you have any case authority for the distinction that you are trying to draw here?" Judge Cooper asked her.

"Yes, Your Honor, as a matter of fact, I do. The case of *Arrow* v. *IORC,* decided by the court in Israel, has recognized the distinction that I am making here," Janette said. Hoffmeister huffed.

"Your Honor, the case Ms. Compton is referring to is a trial court case decided many years ago in Israel, and it involved only a motion to dismiss, no trial, no appeal. The case is not recognized as authority anywhere. It was a total anomaly, a situation in which a local judge ruled for an out-of-town attorney on a preliminary issue in order to avoid any appearance of favoritism. Your Honor, we think this case should be dismissed right now, before any more time is wasted and any more damage is done," Hoffmeister concluded.

"Your Honor, may I say something?" Parker Ross asked.

"I object. Ms. Compton's handling this hearing, and I object to a second lawyer," Hoffmeister snapped.

"Well, now, Your Honor, there are two parties here, two plaintiffs, Mrs. Betty Martinez and Mr. Jorge Martinez. I want to enter an appearance right this minute for Mr. Jorge Martinez. I believe he is entitled to have his own lawyer," Parker said.

"It's all right, Mr. Ross. I was going to let you say anything you wanted to, anyway. I don't know of anyone who has ever had any success silencing you. Please, proceed." The judge gestured.

"Thank you, Your Honor. Judge, maybe I can add a little historical perspective to this issue of negligent versus intentional conduct. The law recognizes a distinction between the two types of conduct. For example, intentional misconduct is necessary to commit a crime. It's the intent that's punished, along with the misconduct, by the criminal law. While this is a civil case, the additional element of intent colors the conduct and changes the rules.

"Long ago, when these concepts were in their formative years, you might say, a private person wasn't allowed to sue the king. That started in England, where the law said that the king could do no wrong. The same sovereign immunity applied to the employees of the king and of the government. But long ago, the U.S. courts decided that in our country, when misconduct occurred, a government could be called to task for that misconduct. When an individual was a victim of a government's misconduct, such as an unconstitutional law, for example, well, then, that person could sue the government and straighten out the injustice. The early days of the United States Supreme Court were *filled* with such claims, and it struggled with the issue of whether the judicial branch of the government could review the conduct of the other branches. The conclusion was that when conduct was wrong—and I should say here in this context, intentionally wrong, not simply a mistake—then the courts could consider it and correct the injustice.

"Now, the IORC has become almost like the government—in fact, in most ways, exactly like the government. It probably has more money than our government right now, and maybe does more things in more fields, since we have reached the point where we're devoting most of our government's attention to paying for medical care, and creating jobs and other benefit programs. Their in-house airline works more efficiently than the Air Force, and if you can believe Mr. Hoffmeister, they are taking care of all of our medical records and our Justification Factors, and doing research in all the fields of medicine and science—and have sovereign immunity. Under our legal system, the government couldn't engage in intentional wrongful conduct without being called into court for it.

IORC may be as powerful as our government—but not more powerful," Parker concluded. He sat down.

Judge Cooper picked up directly after Parker's conclusion. "This is a very interesting question. The court will rule that the Motion for Judgment on the Pleadings be denied. I do think there's a legally recognized distinction between intentional conduct and negligence, at least in the context of a claim such as this. However, don't misinterpret my decision as an agreement that this is a legitimate claim on the merits.

"The allegations made here are frankly very hard to accept. In every case, the plaintiff has the burden of proving the truth of what is alleged. That certainly will apply in this case.

"I should also comment on the question of pretrial discovery. Even though no specific motion for discovery has been made, let me tell you what my ruling will be right now. Under the treaty, no discovery—that is, no court-ordered production of records or information from the IORC—will be permitted. I'll not allow this case to become any more of a circus than it already has. I'm obliged legally to deny the Motion for Judgment on the Pleadings, but I want to get this case resolved as soon as possible. If there's merit to it, fine and good, but if there's not, then the case should be finalized, so that the public is not alarmed by any unfounded accusations." Judge Cooper began making some notes.

"Judge," said Parker, "my esteemed colleague, Mr. Hoffmeister, said earlier that he was ready to try the case immediately. I wonder, was that just rhetoric, or did he really mean it?" Janette turned to Parker with a look of pure panic. He leaned over and whispered, "He's not going to allow discovery. The quicker we get the case to trial, the better."

Hoffmeister spoke a few words to LeBearc. "The IORC is ready to proceed as soon as the court has time. We want this case finished. We are prepared to have the trial as soon as possible."

"Ms. Compton, what do you say to this?" Judge Cooper asked.

Janette looked back at Parker again, swallowed several times, licked her lips, and stood. "If we cannot have discovery, then we'll proceed as soon as the court has time available."

"All right, then, just a moment." Judge Cooper picked up the phone on his desk and spoke quietly for a few seconds, then looked up. "I have some hearings set this afternoon. In fairness to the parties, they can't be canceled now; some of the people involved are already here. Since everyone seems eager to get the case tried, I will treat it like a temporary injunction hearing. I will give the parties overnight to make their preparations. I have canceled all my other obligations for tomorrow. The trial will begin at nine o'clock in the morning without objection of any of the parties." He looked at each of the attorneys and they all nodded. "Let the record reflect that the attorneys for the parties agree. Court is now adjourned until nine o'clock in the morning." Judge Cooper stood. A mad rush for the doors and the TV cameras ensued. Camera operators hugged their tripods to keep their cameras from being knocked over. The crowd kicked loose several cords, but in a few seconds all the reporters had made it through the doors without hurting anyone.

As the courtroom cleared, Janette sat stunned in her seat. "Parker, that's really a risky thing you agreed to. How can we possibly get ready for trial by tomorrow?"

"We're as ready now as we'll ever be. We have all the evidence we're likely to get. All we would do if we waited would be to give them more time to find more ways to hurt us. This way, we know what the evidence is going to be. We also need to remember the people on that list."

David waited at the railing. "I hope you can come tomorrow. Unless you have another engagement," Janette said raising her eyebrows, referring without saying so to Krickett.

"Oh, I'll be here tomorrow, don't worry. My concern, though, is Warren. Krickett caught him and took the modules. She gave them to LeBearc. There's no telling what she did to him. I got the impression that he's hurt. He's probably somewhere at the hospital. She said he would be okay, but I don't trust her."

"Neither do I," Janette said, frowning.

"I think the first order of business is for us to find our star witness," David said. He looked across at LeBearc who smiled contentedly. Janette had a horrible sense of foreboding. It wasn't just winning the case that bothered her. What would IORC do to *all* of them, win or lose? She looked at her watch. The time was 11:45.

They had to fight their way through the TV cameras as shouting reporters pushed and shoved and closed in on them for a quote. Janette and Parker both played their cards close to the chest with the press, but wore game faces that exuded more quiet confidence of a victory than they actually felt. Once through the gauntlet of frenzied reporters, David and Janette headed straight to Orlando Government to look for Warren.

# 20

For most people under UNIMED, the emergency room had replaced the doctor's office. A visit to a clinic involved many hours of waiting. But now, apparently, so did a visit to an emergency room.

David got nowhere with the ER receptionist. He had no official standing there; he was no longer on the staff. Finally, as a favor, David's secretary found out through the unofficial secretary's net that Jeffries had been moved to the psychiatric ward. Paola Jeffries waited there, absently leafing through a magazine.

"Have you seen Warren yet?" David asked her.

"No, but one of the nurses told me they x-rayed him and he's not hurt. That's what worried me. Now they have him going through some sort of psychiatric evaluation. He doesn't have any psychological problems—except flirting, which is normal for him. It's all just a mistake, I'm sure, and will get resolved soon. Don't you think?" she asked David. Trim and fit, the short dark-haired woman appeared half her actual age. She spoke with a cultured Italian accent.

"I'll try to find out what's going on."

David entered the ward through doors that said "No Admittance" and tapped on the glass for the clearance clerk, who jerked to attention. "Sir, you're not supposed to be in here," she said.

"I'm Dr. West from Cardiology. I want to see your chief right away." She escorted him to the office of the head of psychiatry.

"What can I do for you, Dr. West?" the psychiatrist asked.

"You have a patient who was brought into the emergency room this morning, Warren Jeffries. There's nothing wrong with him."

"I'm not familiar with his case, just a minute." He punched several buttons on his computer and skimmed through several pages of records.

"Dr. West, you know the rules. I can't discuss the details of a psychiatric patient. He had an automobile accident but no serious injury. The paramedics thought he had paralysis but he progressively overcame it. The tests showed negative for any physical deficit. Then he started insisting . . . well, I guess I shouldn't go into it."

"This man is an important witness in a court case that I'm involved in. He has to be at the trial tomorrow."

"He certainly won't be in court tomorrow. He claims his paralysis resulted from his being drugged by a beautiful blonde with big boobs, driving a phantom vehicle that he claims ran him off the road. He claims the IORC developed some sort of a device that can stop people's hearts, that he had the device, and that they were after it. He keeps telling us he wants to get his briefcase. We sedated him and he's calmed down, but he hasn't changed his story. Can you believe this? We really hear some strange ones here, don't we?" The psychiatrist chuckled.

David kept his cool. "What he's telling you is the truth. We're in the middle of a lawsuit about it. This man is a computer expert, and he has analyzed an electronic pacemaker. Haven't you been reading the papers?"

The psychiatrist stared, dumbfounded. West pushed on. "A blonde did try to get that device away from him, and yes, she is well endowed. Let me guess what kind of drug he said she used. I'll bet it was succinylcholine."

The psychiatrist stared at David for a few moments, then looked back at his computer screen. "How did you know that? You're the doctor who was suspended because of the IORC suit, aren't you?"

"That's irrelevant—and temporary. I'm still a doctor. I want him released immediately."

"It's not that simple. The man's been committed under the Baker Act for evaluation, and it will take three days to release him. Not only that, but it takes a court order."

"Like hell. He's leaving. You work it out somehow."

"The only other way he can get off this ward is if the administrator will sign release papers. Do you mean there's really a device that can shut off a heart?"

"Not all hearts, just IORC hearts. They install an electronic module on all of their organs. It has a code. For the hearts, you put in the code, it short-circuits, just like that." David snapped his fingers.

"Have you actually seen one of these things yourself?"

"Not only have I seen one, but one killed my patient," David said.

"Jesus." The psychiatrist was beginning to believe him.

"I want to see Jeffries."

"All right, you can see him, but don't get him upset. Give this note to the woman at the desk and she'll get an orderly to go with you." He scribbled the pass.

David walked over to the desk and handed the note to the receptionist.

A white-coated orderly waited at the heavy double swinging door until the receptionist released the lock, then led the way for David.

The orderly showed David into a small room barely larger than the bed inside. A tiny window overlooked a parking lot, but the window was too small for a person to pass through. A bathroom in one corner had no door. Warren lay on the bed, apparently asleep, tied down with

Velcro straps across both wrists, both feet, his waist, and his chest.

"Why is he restrained?" David asked.

"He's sedated and he might try to get up, plus he's an evaluation patient, and until his initial evaluation is done he has to be restrained," the orderly said. He went out into the hall, leaving the door half open. David removed the straps from Warren's arms but left the chest strap in place so he wouldn't fall.

"Warren?" David said quietly. "Warren, are you awake?" Warren's eyelids fluttered open for a moment and then closed.

"Yeah, I guess I'm awake. They gave me something to calm me down. It makes me feel sleepy. I may have dozed off, but I'm awake now anyway." He slurred his words but was able to open his eyes and, after blinking several times, focus on David. "Can anybody hear us?" Warren asked.

David looked around. "The orderly is out in the hall. But a TV camera is monitoring the room and probably taping the sound as well. I don't really know. Why?"

"I didn't have an accident. They came after the module," Warren said. The effort to talk and keep his thoughts together sapped all of his energy.

"I know all about it," David said.

"I keep trying to tell everyone it was no accident. They ran right into me, and then the same woman who broke into my house injected me with succinylcholine," Warren said, his eyes fluttering as though he were drifting off to sleep.

"Warren! Don't go to sleep. I know what happened."

"I'm not asleep. I'm not asleep. I don't know how to tell you about it. The point is that I'm trying to think how to say this since somebody's probably listening. You remember I told you about the little explosion we had? Well, they got what was left out of my pocket, but not the setup for court. I didn't make it to court today, did I? Anyway, the setup is in a briefcase in the car. I don't know where the car is now, but you've got to find that briefcase." Warren strained against the strap, trying to sit up. "Why am I strapped down?"

"Where's the car now? Don't worry about the straps. They'll keep you from falling out of the bed while you're sedated. Try to relax."

"It was in the car when she rammed me. The woman didn't take it, so it must still be there. I don't know where the car is now. We've got to find it. We've got to find the briefcase." Warren again struggled against the straps.

The orderly returned. "Doctor, you have to leave now. You're upsetting him, and I've been told not to let him get upset. Why did you unstrap him?" The orderly tied down Warren's arms.

"Find the car," Warren said. "Find the briefcase."

"Don't worry, Warren, we'll find it."

David returned to the psychiatric waiting area. He sat down between Paola and Janette and gathered his thoughts before he began. "I saw Warren; he's sedated. He did not get hurt in the accident, which IORC staged as an excuse to get some very important evidence."

"He did have a case that Frank brought over," Paola said. "He took it with him this morning—one of those big aluminum cases, a little bigger than a briefcase, actually."

"That must be the one he told me about, then. He said it may still be in the car. Do you know where his car is?"

"No, I haven't any idea. I haven't thought about the car."

"Janette, why don't you see if you can find out where the car is and whether the briefcase is still in it. I'll get Warren released."

He went to Administrator Long's office and said to the secretary, "I must see him. Now."

"The administrator is in a meeting with UNIMED and the chief of nursing, working out an agreement for a policy and procedure manual change." His secretary seemed unconvinced that anything David might want could be sufficiently urgent to interrupt Long's meeting.

"Tell him I have to see him, please."

In a few seconds, she looked up at David, nodded her head, and hung up.

"He says you can come in, since the matter is so *urgent*," she said sarcastically.

Virginia Pruitt sat in a chair pulled up to the administrator's desk, looking at a file. The chief nurse sat beside her.

"Dr. West, I don't like to have my meetings disturbed. What is it?" Long asked.

"I need to speak to you privately," David said.

"Will you two please excuse me? It would be a good time for a coffee break, anyway." Pruitt glared at David. She slammed the file together and picked it up, reached down, and retrieved her leather portfolio.

"I thought he was on suspension," Pruitt said as she stalked out. The chief nurse followed, grimacing at David. Long pushed the door closed.

"This better be good," the administrator said sitting back down at his desk.

David told Long the whole story and urged him to sign a release for Warren. After thinking it over, Long called the head of psychiatry, who confirmed that succinylcholine was actually in Warren's blood. Then he signed the release.

"Thank you," David said.

"Don't thank me too fast. I'm taking the responsibility officially, but you're taking the responsibility unofficially. I'm relying on your judgment. If anything happens, both of us will be looking for a job. Your suspension will become a termination. It's your responsibility to see that this man is back here by five o'clock on Wednesday to complete his official evaluation."

David gave Warren a drug to offset the sedative, and then took him and Paola home where he administered several cups of strong coffee to his patient. Janette went to work trying to find the briefcase. Overcoming considerable resistance, she finally convinced the dispatcher at the wrecker service to contact the driver and ask him to call. Surprisingly, he agreed to bring the briefcase to Jeffries's house. They all sat in the kitchen waiting for him to show up. Without the module, David figured the judge would never believe him. He had to do whatever was necessary to get it back.

The tension of waiting translated into silence. No one knew what to say. Janette took to pacing back and forth, checking her wristwatch every few minutes. Paola mixed up some brownies, and Warren scribbled on a notepad.

The doorbell rang. A red wrecker truck had parked in front of the house. Warren opened the front door.

"I'm looking for Warren Jeffries." the driver consulted a piece of paper and then looked at Warren.

"I'm Warren Jeffries. Did you bring the briefcase?"

"First, I need to see some ID." Warren took out his driver's license and handed it to the driver, who looked at the license and then back at Warren. "Since I'm turning this over instead of the office doing it, I need you to describe what's inside, and sign a receipt," the driver said.

Warren explained the contents in great detail.

The driver, back at his wrecker, opened the briefcase and compared the description to what he saw. Then he brought the briefcase back to Warren's front door.

"If you'll sign this here receipt, you can have the briefcase." He held out the clipboard. Warren signed, and the driver turned to leave.

"Wait a minute, we need to pay you for your trip over here. Let me get a check," Warren said.

Looking back over his shoulder, the driver said, "Ain't no charge. The lady said this was real important, and I wasn't that far away. Ain't no big deal," he said, and walked to the wrecker. He got inside and crunched into gear. The engine, a large powerful diesel, had been idling the whole time. He drove away in a mighty clatter, chased by a trail of black smoke from the exhaust pipes.

Warren took the briefcase back to the kitchen table, afraid to open it. He lifted the lid and moved the foam aside. The module was still in place, still connected to all the wires. Warren breathed a sigh of relief as David and Janette looked over his shoulder. He turned on the computer and the other instruments and typed for several seconds. Rows of numbers and diagrams appeared on the computer screen as Warren's fingers flew over the keyboard. "It all checks out, everything's working just as it did before. No harm done."

"We don't want any repeat of what happened this morning. I think all of you should stay at the hotel with Janette and me until this is over," David said.

"That's a good idea. Let's do go to the hotel," Paola said. "Tammy will be home any minute."

Knowing that Jorge would be staying there, too, Tammy instantly approved the plan, and she packed in less than ten minutes.

Later that night, Janette reported to Parker everything that had occurred. He sat listening with his eyes closed, leaning back with his fingers laced together behind his head. From time to time they wondered if he had gone to sleep, but an occasional grunt or "harumph," accompanied by rapid eyebrow action, evidenced that he absorbed every word.

"We have the module. With what Warren has found out and with David's opinions, do you think we have enough?" Janette asked.

"To tell you the truth, I'm not sure. I'd like to build up your confidence and say absolutely that we do, but I think everything depends on how tomorrow goes. We have to go in there and lay it on the line, win or lose. That's what makes lawsuits interesting." He sat forward, slapped his hands on his knees, and stood. "The best preparation I can make is to get a good night's sleep."

# 21

At breakfast, Parker's stories kept everyone entertained and helped settle their nerves before court.

As they left the hotel, David took custody of the briefcase. But when he tried to enter the courthouse, the security guard refused to allow beyond the metal detector a briefcase containing a device that looked disconcertingly like a bomb. David consequently refused to give up the briefcase, so they had a standoff. David decided to wait at the checkpoint with the briefcase until Janette and Parker came, and sent Warren ahead. The courthouse had several entrances, but he hoped they would pass through this one.

Flashing her security identification card, Janette came in through the lawyer's side entrance, but Parker had to go through a time-consuming full security check. The entrance they had used was not the public one where David waited. Now late, they walked into the courtroom. Everyone else was present, and the judge sat at his bench reading over some papers.

"Well, I'm certainly glad you two decided to come this morning. Do you think we can get started now?" Judge Cooper asked.

"I think we can dispense with opening statements and

treat the statements of the attorneys from yesterday as such, if there is no objection," the judge said.

"Plaintiffs have no objection," Parker said.

"The defendant agrees," Hoffmeister said.

"All right, the plaintiffs will call their first witness."

Janette grabbed her notes and announced, "The plaintiffs call Dr. David West." She looked in the audience for David, but couldn't see him anywhere. This couldn't be happening. Where the hell was David? Then she realized that he may have been hurt and the briefcase stolen.

"Where's your witness, Ms. Compton? Bailiff, call in the hall for the witness."

The bailiff walked into the hall and shouted David West's name. Warren motioned to Janette. Trembling, she walked to the railing and asked him what had happened.

"They wouldn't let him through with the briefcase and he wouldn't leave it, so he's still down at the security checkpoint. Didn't you see him when you came in?"

"No, we came in the side door. I'll take care of it." She turned to the judge and said, "Your Honor, Dr. West is with security at the front entrance. I'm told they refuse to allow him to bring a briefcase containing evidence into the courthouse."

"Ms. Compton, this trial is not starting off very well. I want the bailiff to go down to security at the front entrance and bring Dr. West to the courtroom immediately. We'll take a recess while we wait."

It was only a matter of minutes before the bailiff returned with David in tow and deposited him immediately onto the witness stand. The bailiff, really a deputy sheriff, offered to arrest and handcuff David if he continued to refuse to check the case with security and go with him to the courtroom. He would not even be permitted to leave. There was nothing he could do but comply.

"Your Honor, this is Dr. West, our first witness."

David was sworn in.

"Would you give us your name and your profession, please."

In an almost identical order of questioning as their first experience in front of the arbitrator weeks before, Janette ran David through the case history, up to and including Martinez's death.

"Dr. West, have you formed an opinion as to the probable—not possible, but probable—cause of Mike Martinez's death?"

"Yes, I have an opinion. I believe—"

"Your Honor—wait a minute, Dr. West. Your Honor, we object. There is no foundation for the question, and we'd like to voir dire the witness in private, that is, outside the presence of the news media, for reasons that will become clear to the court," Hoffmeister said.

"Counsel, approach the bench," Judge Cooper ordered. He waited while the three lawyers walked up to the bench. Leaning forward, he said, "I'm not going to conduct this trial twice in two places. I know this is a controversial matter, but it's my intention to make sure that the news media don't think we're trying to hide anything here.

"I'm going to rule that the doctor can state, as I think he already did, that he has an opinion, then I'll allow him to state his opinion. Now, Dr. West, I want you to give the attorneys an opportunity to object before you answer."

"Okay," David said.

"What about my voir dire?" Hoffmeister asked.

"I'm satisfied that the doctor is qualified and competent to give an opinion. The rest of it goes to the weight of his testimony. You save the other questions you have for cross-examination. I want to get this trial moving," Judge Cooper answered dismissing the lawyers back to their positions.

"Dr. West, you said that you have an opinion as to the

actual cause of death. Would you tell us now what that opinion is."

"Yes, it is my opinion that Mike Martinez died as a result of heart failure, intentionally induced by the IORC as a part of a company policy—"

"Your Honor, I must protest. The court ruled that the doctor could answer the question, not that he could editorialize or go beyond that without giving an opportunity for objections. He started to blurt out something about an IORC policy. I don't even know what he meant to say, but it's beyond what the question called for."

"Dr. West, you have answered the question as to the cause of death. Any comments you have concerning the policy of IORC, as you see it, should be given in answer to specific questions, and you should wait before you answer until the lawyers have had an opportunity to object," the judge said.

"Dr. West, why would the IORC intentionally induce heart failure?" Janette asked.

"Your Honor, we object. She is asking for the doctor to draw a conclusion about a corporation's motivation. It's speculative, and there's no proper predicate to show that the doctor knows the company's motivation. It's also in violation of a confidentiality agreement he signed with IORC," Hoffmeister objected.

"Objection sustained."

"Dr. West, are you aware of any other occurrences similar to what happened to Michael Martinez?"

"Your Honor, we object. It calls for speculation on the part of the doctor. It also calls for, at least it seems that it calls for, hearsay, unless the doctor has personal knowledge of any other events. The other events, if any were to exist, would also be irrelevant and immaterial to this case," Hoffmeister said, and with an exasperated look he glared at Janette.

"Objection sustained."

"Dr. West, do you know the actual mechanism by

which Mr. Martinez's heart was made to fail?" Janette tried.

"Your Honor, we object. This now calls for hearsay evidence."

"Ms. Compton, before I'll permit the doctor to testify on the exact mechanism, you'll have to establish a proper foundation to show that he knows what it is and how he knows."

"Dr. West, did you personally see the electronic module that was attached to Mr. Martinez's heart?"

"Yes, at the end of the surgery."

"Have you since seen another module similar to the one attached to Martinez's heart?" Janette asked.

"Yes, I have," he said.

"Your Honor, we protest again. The doctor is answering the questions without giving us an opportunity to object. We do object to the testimony, or certainly to any testimony that follows, until it's shown that this isn't information the doctor obtained while under a confidentiality agreement, because of its trade secret nature," Hoffmeister said.

"I don't think she has asked anything that asks for trade secrets. Besides, the witness has already answered the question. Dr. West, please wait a moment before you answer each question so that the attorneys can object. It's part of our system. I know it's not normal conversation, but the rights of the parties and of the public here are very important."

"I wasn't trying to cut off any objections," David replied.

"May I have a moment?" Janette asked. She turned to Parker and whispered, "I'm not getting anywhere, Parker. I've come at it from every angle I can think of. It doesn't look as if the judge will allow David to testify about what really happened."

"You have to keep plugging until you find a way to get the testimony admitted. Hoffmeister's tough and he won't give up, but you're doing fine. Tell you what, maybe you should let David tell how he got the modules from Dr. Byrd, and about the list. With that kind of foundation the judge might let him say more," Parker suggested.

"Ms. Compton, please proceed," Judge Cooper said.

"Dr. West, were the circumstances in which you saw a similar module in any way related to an IORC location or facility, that is, did you see it there?"

Hoffmeister stood up, then thought better of it and sat back down. David looked at him for a moment and then at the judge who nodded to David to proceed.

"No, it wasn't at IORC that I saw the other modules, plural," David said. LeBearc's head snapped around, and he stared at David.

"Tell me the circumstances, then, when you next saw one of these modules?"

David recounted his meeting with Dr. Byrd in North Carolina and his acquisition of the modules. Repeatedly, Hoffmeister's objections were thwarted.

"Have you subsequently found out anything about those modules?" Janette asked.

"Your Honor, we object. Now we *are* talking about trade secrets. Those modules have been identified as IORC modules, and we object to his testimony. Also, he obtained them unlawfully. They were at the time and still are the absolute property of the IORC, not subject to discovery, and we want them returned."

"Dr. West, how did Dr. Byrd come by these modules, do you know?" the judge asked.

"Before his recent death, Your Honor, Dr. Byrd was the assistant medical examiner in Asheville, North Carolina. He obtained the modules during autopsies while performing his duties as a medical examiner. He gave them to me to try to determine their function and how they might be related to the deaths of certain people."

"I'll overrule the objection. As to the first part, the doctor is not prohibited from testifying about objects simply because their design includes trade secrets. If he begins getting into technical details that might endanger the confidentiality of the module's design, then that may be a different matter. As to the illegality, I think a sufficient foundation exists for the doctor to be allowed to testify about the modules, based upon his having received them from an official source, to wit: the medical examiner's office of Asheville, North Carolina," Judge Cooper said. "Also, they are not the result of discovery, so they are not barred by the treaty."

"But, Your Honor, that's all hearsay," Hoffmeister said.

"On the contrary, it's not hearsay. The doctor told us where he got the modules. He's here to testify as an expert on this issue. Your objection is overruled. Let's get on with the trial."

"Dr. West, what became of the modules?" Janette asked.

"I kept them in my coat pocket for a while."

"When did that change?" Janette asked.

"After someone from the IORC approached me while I was at the Mount Dora festival and tried to force me to give them to her."

David's testimony continued and recounted the story of his run-in with Krickett Hansen, and his refusal to give up the modules.

"Did you give them up?"

"No, fortunately I escaped and was able to deliver the modules to your expert, Warren Jeffries, for testing."

"Did my expert later advise you as to what he had found in studying the modules?"

"Object, hearsay," Hoffmeister said, offhandedly.

"Objection is sustained."

"Your Honor, I think this is an exception to the hearsay rule. Dr. West is appearing as an expert witness, as the court observed earlier, and in giving his opinion to this court he is entitled to rely upon the opinions of other experts. The expert witness whose opinion is in question is present in the courtroom and will be called to testify in the case," Janette said. Parker winked at her.

"That point's well taken. The objection is overruled, and the doctor can answer the question, but the details of the analysis I think I prefer to hear from the expert himself."

"Your Honor, we object on another ground also. The expert is able only to give us hearsay evidence, and so it's double hearsay. Unless the expert actually has the module."

"Your objection is overruled as to this question. When it gets into the technical matters you may have a point, but I will take it up then," the judge said. He instructed David to answer the question.

"The next day, or the day after, I'm not sure which, Warren Jeffries reported to me what he had found in examining the modules. I won't explain the technical part, but in my opinion the bottom line is that, in addition to showing the serial number on a scanner, the module is capable of stopping a heart." He felt a stir in the courtroom.

LeBearc said to Hoffmeister, "Find out right now where the modules are."

"We'd like to know where the modules are located right now," Hoffmeister interrupted.

"That's totally out of order. Your client has used extreme violence to take these modules, including causing a car accident and injuring our expert witness—" Janette began but was then cut off.

"That's outrageous! There's no excuse for this shameless pandering to the press . . . ," Hoffmeister blustered.

"All right, everybody, I'll have no more outbursts. I don't want the attorneys arguing with one another. You will each address your comments to the court. Mr. Hoffmeister, you'll have an opportunity to cross-examine the witness later. Ms. Compton, you will confine yourself to questions and responses to objections and leave the testifying to the witness," Judge Cooper said.

"I have no more questions," Janette said.

"Mr. Ross, I think the proper order of business would be for you to ask any questions you have now, before the cross-examination by Mr. Hoffmeister," the judge said.

"Well, Judge, I think Ms. Compton has covered everything that I might have asked if I had been doing the questioning. I might have something to add in redirect testimony after Wilson's cross-examination, but I'm enjoying the luxury of just listening," Parker Ross said.

"Mr. Hoffmeister."

"Thank you, Your Honor. Dr. West, I take it that you are exceedingly angry with the IORC. In fact, it sounds to me as if you are to the point where you actually hate the company, isn't that true?"

"I disapprove of what the IORC did."

"Are you angry at the IORC because they didn't offer you a job?"

"On the contrary, IORC did offer me a job."

"Are you testifying here that the IORC's transplant procedures or methods are—you choose the word—negligent or wrong or somehow incompetent or incorrect?"

"No, I'm not. In my opinion they have deliberately, and as a matter of policy, caused hearts and other organs to fail, which killed the patients, including Mike Martinez. I find that reprehensible."

"You say it's a policy. Has anyone told you it was a policy?"

"Not in so many words, but I'm convinced it happened to Martinez and to other people on Dr. Byrd's list. I've spoken with some of the people on the list and urged them to stay away from the IORC."

"You mean to say, Doctor, that you're calling members of the public and telling them it's unsafe to go to the IORC?"

"That's exactly right. People who are on the list who

have received unauthorized transplants of IORC organs are dying, so you bet I've called to warn every one of them I could reach."

"And you feel that because a module is supposedly capable of—what did you say—'causing his heart to stop,' that IORC killed Martinez?"

"I suppose so, but I have considered other factors."

Hoffmeister began to solicit a list of other factors that might cause a heart to stop after a transplant: drugs, hypothermia, even excess radiation from X rays. His circuitous tactics slowly but effectively undermined David's allegations.

"Well, of course, almost anything is capable of causing the heart to stop if it's improperly used."

"That's exactly the point, Doctor. Even if the modules that you've been talking about were capable of causing a heart to stop, that doesn't prove that they were misused for that purpose, does it?"

"It's not that simple. That's not what I meant."

"Dr. West, Michael Martinez was your first transplant patient after you finished your medical training, was he not?"

"That's correct, but I had done dozens of transplants during my training," David said.

"You are trying to make an excuse for his death, aren't you."

"No. I'm stating the actual cause."

Abruptly shifting gears, "Dr. West, how many of the IORC's modules did Dr. Byrd give you when you went to North Carolina?"

"I don't think the modules belonged to the IORC anymore."

"Doctor, you're trying to argue with me, and that's not your function in this case. You are a witness. The lawyers are here to argue. How many modules did Dr. Byrd give you?"

"He gave me three: Two modules were intact, and one had been split open."

"Now, you claim someone took one of the modules from your witness, and I don't want to hear the details of that now, but where are the other two?"

"I don't know where the broken one is at the moment, although we have a videotape of it that we took through a microscope. The other one, which is still working, is here in the courthouse. Actually, it's in the briefcase being held at the security checkpoint at the front door."

Andre LeBearc glanced at his security manager. Parker Ross, who was facing LeBearc, noticed the gesture and watched as the security manager quietly left the courtroom. Parker stood, clearing his throat, and said, "Judge, excuse me, I really hate to interrupt this interesting cross-examination, but I must bring a matter to the court's immediate attention."

"Now, Your Honor, I object to Mr. Ross's involvement here. Ms. Compton did the direct examination, and I think she should be the one who makes objections," Hoffmeister said.

"Judge, Wilson misunderstands. I'm not objecting to anything. It's about the briefcase Dr. West just mentioned. Apparently the security personnel at the front entrance, in fulfilling their important responsibilities and I don't say that lightly, declined to allow that briefcase into the courthouse. Now, the importance of that briefcase has been disclosed in the testimony here, and I'm personally quite concerned about its security. It may be that the outcome of this case is going to depend on that briefcase and the module inside it. What I'd like to request is that the court make a call down to the security people at the front entrance and ask one of them to personally bring that briefcase up here to the courtroom now."

"Mr. Ross, the court is not in the habit of taking care of errands concerning evidence for the attorneys. Why didn't you go down during the recess and get the briefcase? Or even go down now?"

"Unfortunately, Your Honor, because of my retirement, my security card has expired. Now, I might go down there and try to get the briefcase, but I suspect those security guards are not going to be any more willing to let an old goat like me bring it into the courthouse than they were Dr. West. Besides, I expect he had to sign a receipt, and so unless the court orders that the briefcase actually be brought up here, it's going to have to lie down there on that table—from which it might disappear—until Dr. West and Ms. Compton can go down and get it. I must tell you, Your Honor, in light of all the ruckus those modules have caused, I would feel a lot more comfortable if the court directed the security guard to bring the briefcase up here now."

LeBearc glared at Parker, who smiled back at him. Hoffmeister, who was oblivious to what was going on, shrugged his shoulders and shook his head in an unconcerned manner.

The judge picked up the telephone on his desk and asked to be connected to the front entrance security. In a brusque manner, Judge Cooper ordered the delivery of the briefcase to the courtroom.

After hanging up, the judge said, "Ladies and gentlemen, we'll take a five-minute recess." And with that, Judge Cooper left the courtroom. LeBearc stood, glaring at Parker Ross, at David, and then at Janette, turned on his heel, and walked through the door, slamming it aside and causing it to bang against the doorstop.

The deputy sheriff and the guard with the briefcase were stepping onto an elevator as the door to another elevator opened and the IORC security manager stepped out. He walked to the checkpoint and told the woman who had taken over for the guard that he had come to pick up Dr. West's briefcase and take it to the courtroom. He flashed his IORC badge. She shrugged her shoulders, saying, "It's gone. The other guy got a call and already took it up to the courtroom." The security manager swallowed hard.

Upstairs, in the back of the courtroom, Cal Yoshida and Krickett Hansen watched from among the newspaper and television reporters.

The uniformed deputy sheriff escorted the rent-a-cop security guard into the courtroom by the arm. When the deputy saw that the court had recessed, he pointed to the corner by the clerk's desk and told the man to take a seat. The deputy wasn't sure what was going on, but given what Judge Cooper had said to him, neither the guard nor the briefcase was leaving his sight for a moment, and no one would get close to either of them until the judge said differently.

Judge Cooper returned a few minutes later and, while everyone scrambled to stand, he announced his presence by saying, "Be seated. Is the briefcase here yet?" The deputy motioned for the guard to come forward and he stood, holding the briefcase.

"I want to thank you for your diligence," Judge Cooper said. The security guard smiled and nodded at the judge. He and the deputy sheriff left the courtroom, leaving the briefcase on the table next to the court reporter sitting at the base of the judge's bench.

"Mr. Ross, would you please come take charge of this briefcase. I trust there's nothing further and we can continue with the testimony now?" the judge said, in a good-humored way.

"I want to thank you, Your Honor. We're all much relieved under the circumstances and with the court's permission, I believe I'd rather leave this briefcase in your custody until its use as evidence is over," Parker Ross said, and returned to his chair. The briefcase remained standing on the table below the judge.

"You hand that up here to me," the judge said to the clerk, who lifted the briefcase to him. The judge placed it on the corner of his bench. "Now, let's get on with the trial. We've all had enough excitement."

Andre LeBearc had not returned after recess, and Hoffmeister grew uncomfortable in his absence. "Your Honor, Dr. LeBearc hasn't returned yet. I would prefer to wait until he gets back. I don't know what might have happened to delay him."

"Mr. Hoffmeister, I'm sure you're capable of proceeding with your cross-examination even in the absence of your client's representative. The recess was for five minutes and it's been fifteen. Let's proceed, and if you need to confer with your client before actually concluding your cross-examination, I'll take that into consideration."

"I have no further questions at this time," Hoffmeister said.

"Ms. Compton, redirect?" the judge asked.

"No, Your Honor," she said.

"Mr. Ross, do you have any questions?"

"Not at this time, Judge."

"Dr. West, you may step down. Ms. Compton, call your next witness."

As he had been the first time he testified, David was frustrated. He hadn't been able to say what he wanted to say and had probably made the wrong impression, it seemed to him. He hated court procedures. Like most formalities, they seemed to inhibit getting to the desired end—in this case, the truth.

"The plaintiffs call Warren Jeffries as our next witness," Janette said.

When Jeffries had been sworn in, and Janette had led him through detailing his credentials, and his connection to the case, Janette asked, "What did you find when Dr. West asked you to check the list he had obtained from Dr. Byrd?"

"Amazingly, as of my first check, of the forty-four people who had received unauthorized transplants, fourteen were dead, twelve from causes relating to the transplanted organ. Statistically, the number of victims is several thousand percent greater than what anyone would expect on a list of transplant recipients."

"In your opinion, are they dying of natural causes?" Janette asked.

"Something untoward is happening to the people on this list," continued Warren. "Statistically it cannot be a coincidence."

"Mr. Jeffries, has anything occurred since you did the initial research that has affected your opinion?" Janette asked.

"Yes, as a matter of fact. A few days after I did the initial research, I followed up on the same list of names, and two more people had died. I did the recheck two days ago, and at the rate these people are dying, others may be dead by now."

"Now, Your Honor, I object. That's pure speculation by the witness," Hoffmeister said.

"Objection is sustained. Mr. Jeffries, I want you to confine your testimony to the things you've actually discovered, not speculation."

"Excuse me, Your Honor, I was being unscientific. Frankly, I'm very disturbed about this," Warren said.

"Mr. Jeffries, in addition to your computer research on this list of names, did you do other research?"

"Absolutely. On my own time I did follow-up research, as I mentioned earlier. In addition, a colleague and I reverse-engineered the modules to see how they worked."

"What did you find?" Janette asked.

Hoffmeister jumped in. "At this point, Your Honor, we object to this testimony on the grounds that the modules were illegally obtained and that their custody is illegal, and on the further grounds that the testimony that is being asked for here will require the disclosure of trade secrets that should not be disclosed."

"All right. Based on our earlier discussion, I think it is appropriate to have an in camera hearing on this matter. Ladies and gentlemen, because of the sensitive nature of the technical information concerning these modules, the court will hold a private hearing in chambers."

"Judge Cooper, Mr. Jeffries will need the briefcase during his testimony," Parker Ross said.

Hoffmeister looked for LeBearc, but he was nowhere in sight. When they got to the judge's hearing room, Warren first recounted the tests that he and Frank had done, outlining the way they had examined the module and made a video of it. Then he explained how they got one of the modules to work, and what David had concluded it could do to someone's heart. The judge allowed Warren to demonstrate the operation of the module, as everyone gathered around the briefcase.

"Judge, I object," Hoffmeister said. "This demonstration is prejudicing the court, and there's been no ruling that this evidence is admissible. All this proves is that someone who knows nothing about the medical use of this device has concluded that it could be misused. I think we're losing track of what's at issue. This is a case to prove that the IORC killed Mr. Martinez. Proving that one of these modules could do harm to someone is no different from proving that a gun can kill. You don't then conclude that because a person has a gun that he actually killed somebody. In fact, that analogy is not very good because a gun is designed to inflict injury. This module is a pacemaker. It seems to me that it's no different from, for example, an X-ray machine. That's probably a better analogy. Certainly an X-ray machine can be used—or I should say misused—so as to injure a patient, but it normally is used in a way that benefits a patient."

"No, Your Honor, we've proved more than that," Janette said. "We've proved that an unusually high number of people on Dr. Byrd's list have died. We have presented evidence that shows exactly how these people could be killed after having transplants." She looked at Parker Ross for help, but he said nothing.

"Ms. Compton, I have to think in terms of what's been proven and what hasn't. I don't think you have yet presented a sufficient basis to show that the module attached to Mr. Martinez's heart caused his death. I do think you've shown, at least arguably, that he didn't die of normal, natural causes. I also am convinced by the evidence I've seen in this hearing so far that there is sufficient basis to believe that one of these modules is capable of stopping a heart. I think Mr. Jeffries's testimony about the number of people on the list who have died is also persuasive, but I don't think it's all been tied together sufficiently to prove cause and effect, or to allow this evidence to be admitted at this point. There could be something else going on among people who have these transplants, a common disease maybe, and certainly there could be something going on that's not the result of a deliberate act of murder as you're suggesting. Before I will permit Mr. Jeffries to explain how these modules work, or allow him to demonstrate them in open court in front of the media, I'll have to see more evidence to show a connection between the modules and the death of Martinez. Otherwise, I think I would be acting irresponsibly in leaving it to the media to draw possibly unjustified conclusions. We'll break until one-thirty.

"The briefcase will stay in my chambers until this proceeding is concluded.

"I'll see everybody when we reconvene. Ms. Compton, you can proceed at that time with your next witness."

# 22

"Parker, what should we do? Are we sunk?" Janette was clearly in a panic, but hadn't given up.

"I told you last night that it would be a close question. The judge's ruling is probably correct. We have to come up with more evidence to convince him. You and David meet us at the snack bar for lunch—but lock everything up in David's car first."

David and Janette took the elevator to the garage. On the way down, she told him about the judge's ruling. She pushed the "B" button repeatedly as the elevator descended.

"They're too powerful. The whole system is designed to protect them. We have to break out of the system—do something they don't expect," David said.

Before she could reply, the elevator door opened and LeBearc was waiting. A green Volvo wagon with its engine running blocked their way.

"I won't let you ruin this company!" LeBearc said, jabbing at Janette's arm with a syringe. She reacted instantly, jumping back, then smashed him in the side with her briefcase as the needle ripped into her sleeve and scratched her skin. David grabbed for LeBearc's arm, but LeBearc turned and ran for the car as the driver began to get out.

"Let's go," he ordered and slammed the door, glaring at them as the car sped off.

*If he had left it to the professionals, we'd both be dead—or having our organs harvested, more likely,* David thought. Then another elevator door opened and Cal Yoshida stepped out.

"What's happening, Davey?" he asked, looking from one to the other. They both turned on him, ready for another attack. "Take it easy!" he said holding his hands up, palms toward them. "What happened, anyway?"

"LeBearc tried to inject Janette," David said. "I'm calling the police."

"Hold on. I want to discuss a settlement with Ms. Compton."

"Who the hell are you?" Janette asked, glaring at him.

"He's with IORC," David said sullenly.

"Then I won't talk to him. Only his lawyer. Let's get out of here. Forget the cops. We can take care of this ourselves."


"What on earth is the matter with you?" asked Parker Ross as he watched Janette burst into the snack bar and sling her briefcase onto a chair, tipping it over with a crash. People turned and stared at them.

"I got the same treatment Warren got—except they missed. I've never been so angry in my life."

"Want to tell me about it, David?" Parker asked, unflappable.

"Regardless of what we or the judge may think, the other side must think we're getting the best of them. LeBearc tried to inject Janette. He got bruised ribs for his effort." David chuckled.

"Is she hurt? Is she able to go back to court? We have to be back in less than an hour," Warren asked as Janette took off her jacket and looked at the torn sleeve.

"She'll be okay," David said. He reached out to check Janette's arm.

"I'm fine!" She jerked away and began to pace back and forth, glaring at everyone. Most of the other people now ignored her. Temper flare-ups were not uncommon in the courthouse.

"IORC has a new player. I met him on my trip to the IORC production plant. Now he's here in Orlando. He wants to talk settlement before the trial resumes. I suppose we won't have time now."

"We'll have to make time. Frankly, I can't come up with any ideas, and unless something happens, the judge will dismiss the case." Parker smiled at Janette despite what he had said. "You did a good job, Janette. I don't know anyone who could have done better. Let's go back and see what else we can do."

After lunch they all rode up on the elevator, together this time. When they got off, they saw Cal standing with LeBearc, who seemed to have regained his composure.

"Please, I'd like to talk to you about this case before court starts again," Cal said, approaching the team.

"You made a serious mistake, LeBearc," Janette said, glaring at him. He neither responded nor looked away, as if he didn't hear her.

"I'll ask the judge to give us a few minutes," Parker said.

Parker found Hoffmeister, who, not having seen LeBearc, looked very uncomfortable. "Wilson, there's another representative here from IORC. He wants to talk."

"What do you mean? How do you know this and I don't?" Hoffmeister demanded.

"Come on. Let's go ask the judge for a few minutes to discuss the case, then I'll introduce you to your new client." Parker Ross enjoyed every minute of Hoffmeister's discomfiture.

When they got to where the others were waiting in the hallway, Parker said, "Wilson, I'm told that this is your client's representative, Mr. Yamaha."

"Yoshida. Cal Yoshida is my name. I'm here to help Dr. LeBearc. Perhaps I can calm the waters, as it were."

"Who's in charge?" Hoffmeister asked.

"Dr. LeBearc isn't feeling well, so I'll fill in," Cal said.

"Maybe we should talk a few minutes in private first," Hoffmeister said.

"That won't be necessary. Can we all go somewhere to discuss this?" Cal asked. Hoffmeister pointed to a room across the hall, which had a large table, a VCR, and television screen. After everyone was seated, Cal stood as if he were addressing a board meeting.

"I'm here to make a settlement offer in behalf of IORC's Central Management. I personally feel that this entire matter has gotten out of hand and has been blown all out of proportion. It's not our company's desire to hurt anyone or drug anyone or do any of the things that apparently have occurred and of which we're accused. The publicity coming out of this trial is neither good for the company nor good for the public, who will lose confidence in the IORC. As a result, people who might otherwise get transplants won't trust us, and that may cost them their lives."

"And cost your company a lot of money," Janette added.

"That's right, Ms. Compton, it will cost our company, too, but that's not the point. We'll still make plenty of money. What we want to do now is offer a settlement to Mrs. Martinez to compensate her for the loss of her husband."

"So you're admitting that you killed him," Janette said.

"No, Ms. Compton, we're not admitting anything of

the kind. We want to settle the case. We want Mrs. Martinez compensated for what she's been through. We want an end to this case. We're not acknowledging that we are responsible, only that we want the case over with."

"No way," Janette said. "No way will we settle this case on that basis. You can't buy us off."

"Janette, let's listen to what the man has to say, and then we'll talk it over in private and with Mrs. Martinez," Parker said. He turned to Cal. "What do you have in mind, Mr. Yashuda?"

"Mr. Ross, perhaps you can learn to pronounce my name correctly. It's Yoshida. If not, you may call me Cal. Everyone does, and I don't take offense at such familiarity.

"IORC will pay Mrs. Martinez every month, for the balance of her life, an amount equivalent to what her husband made at the time of his death, with normal cost-of-living increases. In addition, we'll pay for his son's education, for as much schooling as he wants with a reasonable living expense allowance, plus a lump sum to get him started after he finishes college. In addition, Mrs. Martinez and her son will have the benefit of full IORC medical and transplant coverage as if they were company employees for the balance of their lives."

"Well, Mr. Yoshida—did I get it right that time?—I've written down your offer, and if you will excuse us now we'll discuss it," Parker Ross said. Janette now glared at Parker as if *he* were the enemy.

"What about your policy concerning retransplants, Cal? What about that?" David asked.

"David, we've made our settlement offer. The company doesn't concede that there *are* any issues involved here from a legal point of view. The company is willing to defend the case legally if we have to. We're trying to put an end to it. This is a lawsuit and it's the lawsuit we want to settle. We're not talking about company policy."

"We'll discuss your offer with our client, if you folks will excuse us," Parker said, standing.

Cal, LeBearc, and Hoffmeister left the room.

"Parker, Betty can't agree to this settlement," Janette said. "We won't have accomplished a thing. Nothing will change. The rest of the people on the list will die, and God knows how many others. And everything they do will remain a secret. The public has a right to know the source of IORC's organs, and a right to decide whether to permit the cloning of humans—or modified humans."

"Janette, we represent the Martinezes. It is up to Betty and Jorge to decide what to do, not us. Do you have any idea what the value of their settlement offer is? Betty and Jorge will have more than enough to take care of them for the rest of their lives. Even though we were trying to establish some principles here, don't forget that the judge will probably dismiss the case anyway if we don't settle."

David clenched his jaw in frustration. "I'll ask Betty and Jorge to come in," he said.

In a few minutes, Betty and Jorge Martinez arrived. "Dr. West said you wanted to talk to us."

"The IORC has made an offer to settle the case. I should tell you first—as we discussed at lunch—the chances are that the judge will dismiss the case when he finds out we don't have any more evidence. The IORC has offered to pay you the same amount that your husband was making when he died, plus cost-of-living increases, all Jorge's school expenses, and a nest egg to start him off. Also they've agreed to provide complete medical care and transplants to you and Jorge for the rest of your lives. That's a substantial offer, involving a huge amount of money. I think you must consider it very seriously."

"I don't want them to provide any medical care for me or my mother," Jorge said. "They provided enough for my father."

"That's not the point here, Jorge. What they're offering is what we started out to get for you and your mother to begin with. I think you should really consider the offer."

"If we were to accept, what about your fee and Janette's fee? How would we pay that?" Betty Martinez asked.

"Our fee is not the important thing, Betty," Janette said. "They'll literally get away with murder. They refuse to admit wrongdoing, or to make any changes whatsoever. So even though this might be a good settlement for you and Jorge, it won't have accomplished our objective in bringing the suit."

Parker, directing a firm stare at Janette to remind her of her duties, said, "The main reason we brought the suit was for you and Jorge. We hoped to accomplish more than that, and maybe we will indirectly, but we can't hope to resolve all the issues in one case. I've learned that small changes often have much greater results in the future. But this is your suit and you don't owe an obligation to anyone else. As far as the fee is concerned, I think we can demand that they pay our fees in addition to what they've offered you, and I expect they would agree. Money is not really the issue for them. They want the case over. I think if we don't settle, it's over anyway because the judge will dismiss the case. Then you will have given up the opportunity to receive the benefits they are offering."

"What does Dr. West think?" she asked.

"It really doesn't matter, Betty. This is your decision for you and Jorge."

"After all he's done, his opinion does matter to me. Can I ask him?"

"Of course," Parker said.

"Then Jorge and I will want to discuss this with each other, and we want to talk to Dr. West. We'll step outside and talk it over; then we'll let you know what we've decided."

Betty and Jorge left the room and found David.

David told Betty that he wished that others could be saved, and that he would be disappointed that all their goals hadn't been achieved, but the settlement was beneficial to her. Betty and Jorge left to discuss what to do.

When David came back, Janette looked dejected. She had poured everything from her briefcase out on the table and arranged the contents in neat piles. She began scribbling on a pad. Parker stood impassively gazing out the window.

"Betty wants to talk to Jorge about the settlement and then let you know what she has decided," David told them.

They heard a knock on the door and David opened it to Captain Stapleton's smiling face. "Excuse me for interrupting you. I have the satellite photo you asked for."

"Thank you," David said. The captain smiled, excused himself, and left for the courtroom.

As Stapleton left the room, he and Krickett saw each other. She glared at him. "Why, good day—Ms. Hansen, isn't it?" As top security officials, each had a dossier on the other—and both knew it.

"Captain," she replied, her eyes ice cold.

He looked her over as a street fighter might evaluate his opponent. "Although we haven't met, I believe we have a good deal in common, training and the like."

"So I understand. Our managing director sends his regards. I don't think he likes threats."

"A pity, I'm sure."

"If you interrupt our electricity, we have auxiliary generators."

"Which don't react well at all to electromagnetic pulses. I didn't mention electrical interruptions, in any case. Perhaps he misunderstood. I was speaking for myself. Personally, not for the company. But, I expect you understand quite clearly, don't you?"

"How did you locate him, by the way?" she asked.

"My SSG keeps track of your board, just as we do heads of state and the like. One never knows when it may be necessary to contact such people on short notice—or unofficially, as I did your managing director on his hotel balcony. He should mind his diet, by the way. Ham and eggs are deadly."

"Like the director, I don't like threats."

"A pity." And Stapleton smiled again and strolled into the courtroom.

Inside the conference room David opened the envelope Stapleton had given him.

The envelope contained a high-resolution color satellite photo showing the island. He could make out the huge building, the airport, the golf course, the tennis court, and even the golf cart paths; every detail.

"If she decides not to settle, call me back to testify," David said. "Now I can prove the island exists."

While David and Parker gazed at the photo, Janette, ignoring them, continued fidgeting with her papers. Absentmindedly, she pushed the tiny videotape back and forth with the tip of her pen. Finally she picked it up and, more from nervous energy than anything else, inserted it in the video viewer and pressed the play button. The screen lit up with a view of a man coming into the examination room and beginning to take off his clothes.

"Oh, yum, this is lovely," she said, not recognizing Martinez, as she reached to turn off the machine. David glanced at the video screen. The man on the screen was taking off his undershorts as Janette hit the off switch.

"Turn that back on!" David said.

"Oh, sure, that's just what we need," Janette said, and flipped out the tape, ready to throw it in the trash can.

"Turn that tape back on! That was Mike Martinez!"

Janette stopped, holding the tape, and looked at David to see if he was teasing her. She could tell that he wasn't.

She reinserted the tape in the video player, pressed the play button, and watched as Mike Martinez stripped off his undershorts and climbed onto the examination table.

David and the others watched silently, in horror, hypnotized by the video. They watched the scene unfold and the technicians immobilize Mike with the drug. Even though he could not move, it was clear that he was frightened out of his wits. Time passed slowly and nothing seemed to be happening on screen. Then Martinez started moving his fingers and his toes, and even rearranged his feet. He blinked a number of times and watched as a mechanical arm scanned him. Then he stared into the camera. David remembered the teenager on the island. His expression had been much the same. Suddenly, a set of numbers appeared in the box in the lower left corner of the screen, then another set, then the word "Yes," and a split second later, Martinez's body arched and twisted and began to shake and convulse.

"Shit!" David whispered. The cardiogram readout, in a small box on the screen, became a confused jumble of lines with declining amplitude, until in a few seconds the line straightened out flat.

"Back that up and rerun the last part again," David said.

Janette rewound the tape and replayed the portion beginning right before Martinez's body began to convulse. This time David watched the cardiogram and saw an impulse on the graph. For several beats it followed and then slightly preceded each pulse of Martinez's heart, but went exactly opposite the line representing the heartbeat. Each pulse became weaker and weaker, through twelve or fifteen beats, until they ceased altogether. David knew he was seeing a graphic display of one of the modules at work.

"Where did you get this tape? How long have you been carrying it around?" David asked in an accusatory tone.

"It was left at the courtroom yesterday with a note. Here, I still have it." She shuffled through the things on the table, came up with the note, and handed it to David. "I thought it was the Thomas tape."

"Who's Burrows?" Parker asked, reading the note over David's shoulder.

"He's the cop who switched the arrest tape of Dr.

Thomas. He now works at IORC as a security guard. Now I understand the note! What do you think of our chances with *this* evidence?" she asked, grinning.

"Improving. Definitely improving," Parker said. His eyebrows moved up and down and the wrinkles in his face outlined his smile and accentuated his eyes.

Betty Martinez tapped on the door and stuck her head in. "Is it all right if we come in?" Betty asked.

"Of course," Parker said, motioning her inside.

"Jorge and I have talked it over, and we've decided that we can make our own way without charity from the IORC. If they won't stop killing other people, then we won't settle. We'll take our chances, and if we don't win in court then we'll go on TV and tell what they did to Mike. We've made up our minds, so don't try to talk us out of it."

"That's right," Jorge said.

"All right, Betty, we'll abide by your decision. Why don't you and Jorge go back to the courtroom and let us talk to the IORC again and see what they have to say," Parker said. She and Jorge left.

"Doesn't she have a right to see that tape, Parker?" Janette asked.

"She has a right to it, but I don't see any need to put her through the process of watching her husband die unless there's no other alternative. Let's get those bastards in here and show 'em what we're going to do to them unless they do what we want," Parker said, finally enjoying himself.

David found the IORC group halfway down the hall, standing together talking. Krickett had joined the three men.

David asked them to come with him to the room.

"My client has made a very reasonable and handsome offer to settle this case," Hoffmeister said. "It wasn't intended as a beginning of negotiations. Either it's accepted or it's rejected."

"I'm not the lawyer, Mr. Hoffmeister," David said. "I have something important to show you. You'll want to see this before you threaten my friends again." David turned on his heel and walked back toward the room. The tone in his voice made them follow.

"Wilson, our client has declined your offer," Parker announced as soon as everyone was seated at the table. "But she does have a counteroffer."

Hoffmeister and Cal immediately started to leave. Krickett remained seated and Cal, seeing her, sat back down. David could tell that there had been a change in the relationships. Krickett now seemed in charge. "Let's hear what you have to say. That won't cost us anything," Krickett said.

"Well, actually it might. What we want in addition to what you've offered is the payment of our fees and the costs of the case," Parker said.

"How much would that be? If it's not totally unreasonable we might consider it," Krickett said.

"Oh, our fees and costs are reasonable enough. There is one other condition, though. In order to settle the case, your company must discontinue its policy of killing people who have a retransplant of your organs," Parker said.

"Mr. Ross, you're wasting our time. Dr. West brought this up earlier. We don't concede that's ever happened, and because of one lawsuit we certainly won't discuss changing the policies of a company that operates in several hundred countries and treats millions of people. You're being ridiculous," Cal said, and stood up to leave.

"Well, sir, I think there's one more thing you ought to know about," Parker said, and he motioned to Janette, who clicked the play button on the video machine. It showed a picture of Martinez a few seconds before the medical technicians came into his room. "What you see here, folks, is the unfortunate Mr. Michael Martinez on

the day of his death. Please watch for a minute or two,"
Parker said.

The tape continued to play as the technicians came in,
manhandled Martinez, gave him the injection, and put
him back on the table.

"Janette, fast-forward now to the other part." She did
as he directed, stopping at the point a few seconds before
Martinez's heart had been disabled.

"Now, watch this, and watch the cardiogram," Parker
directed.

The time clicked off slowly, and suddenly Martinez's
back arched and his body convulsed. You could see his
expression of fear and pain. When the cardiogram line
went straight, Parker told Janette to rewind the tape and
play it again, which she did.

"Thomas!" LeBearc blurted.

"Dr. LeBearc, perhaps you will explain to your attorney exactly what this shows. I believe the judge will give us
about five more minutes to conclude this discussion or
restart the trial. Wilson, would you like to use this room to
discuss with your clients what you plan to do?" Parker
asked as he clicked off the video player, took out the miniature tape, and slipped it into his shirt pocket. He motioned for Janette and David to leave with him. As they
were about to go into the courtroom across the hall, David
excused himself and walked back to the room. He tapped
on the door and stuck his head inside. Hoffmeister was
standing, and David's interruption caught him in the middle of an arm-waving gesture.

"We won't be blackmailed like this. You'll never be able
to get that tape into evidence. It's stolen property, just like
the modules," Hoffmeister said, glaring at David.

"Mr. Hoffmeister, I'd like to speak to them privately
for a minute," David said, indicating Cal and Krickett.

"Anything you have to say to them you can say in my
presence," Hoffmeister said.

"It's all right with me, but it concerns my visit to their

facility. I have a confidentiality agreement. If you're already familiar with that, it doesn't make any difference to me," David said.

"Mr. Hoffmeister, please excuse us and wait outside," Cal said. Hoffmeister, who was used to such treatment from LeBearc, had hoped that the new QC would be more pliable; he quickly learned differently. Without a word he walked into the hall and closed the door.

David sat down at the table. "Cal, you have to stop killing people, and there has to be some way to guarantee you won't do it in the future. The only way I see out of this is for IORC to publicly end its reclaimed organs program, and to publicly urge the donation of organs to government hospitals instead of to the IORC. You're not reusing those organs anyway, and we can use them to save a lot of lives.

"If you publicly announce the availability of J Factor points for donating organs to us, then several things are accomplished—most important, we can save more lives and prevent your company from killing people, which you never should have done in the first place. I don't want to debate your reasons for doing it, but we insist that you stop. I think you know we can win this case, Cal," David said.

"David, you're asking too much. We can't acknowledge that we've killed anyone, so we can't say it won't be done in the future," Krickett said.

"I'm not asking the company to acknowledge guilt, but only to change your organ donation program. Right now you give J Factor points to anyone who agrees to donate their organs to IORC. If you gave points to anyone who donates their organs to private and government hospitals instead, the problem would be solved. Then we could transplant these donated organs into people who don't have as high a J Factor as you require. Maybe someday you'll be able to supply enough organs for everyone—that s, if the public will accept your production methods, which we intend to disclose," David said.

"What do you mean? If you go public with what you saw at the island, no one will believe you," Cal said. "You'd be considered a crackpot, because we'll maintain a blackout on that. We will not tolerate any interference."

"Don't underestimate me, Cal," David said.

The bailiff knocked on the door, opened it, and told them the judge was ready to begin the trial.

Cal stood. "We're not changing our offer. Don't do anything foolish. If you violate your confidentiality agreement, you could end up losing everything you have, including your professional standing, and find yourself treating ingrown toenails at some clinic in the boondocks." He leaned forward, his hands flat on the table, glaring at David. Krickett looked at him the way she had at the airport before she shot the oil cans. David did not look back at them again as he left the room.

# 23

As Judge Cooper entered the courtroom from behind the bench, the buzz of conversation quickly silenced.

"Are you ready to proceed?" he asked.

"Yes, Your Honor," Hoffmeister answered.

"Yes," Janette agreed.

"All right then. Ms. Compton, you may call your next witness."

"Your Honor, the plaintiffs wish to recall Dr. David West."

"To which the defendant objects," Hoffmeister said. "Dr. West has already testified, and if there was anything that needed to be covered by his testimony, it should have been done while he was on the witness stand the first time."

"Your Honor, new evidence has come to our attention. It's a videotape, and it is necessary for Dr. West to testify in order to make a proper predicate for its introduction into evidence."

"To which the defendant also objects, Your Honor. This tape, which we saw for the first time only a few minutes ago, belongs to the IORC and was obviously stolen from IORC. Like the other evidence the plaintiffs attempted to introduce, and which the court declined to admit, this tape proves nothing except that Mr. Martinez died, and there is no issue in that regard."

"Mr. Hoffmeister, I think you're getting a little bit ahead of the question. The question is whether Ms. Compton is allowed to recall Dr. West to testify. I'm going to permit her to recall him."

David walked to the witness chair and sat down.

"Dr. West, I remind you that you're still under oath," Judge Cooper said.

"I understand."

"Dr. West, during the recess you had occasion to see a videotape, did you not?" Janette asked.

"Yes, I did."

"Did you recognize the person who was depicted on that videotape?"

"Yes. It was Mike Martinez."

"And in recognizing Mr. Martinez, was it possible for you to determine when the events depicted on the tape took place?"

"Yes. They occurred the day Mr. Martinez died. The tape is of his death itself."

"Your Honor, at this time the plaintiffs offer the videotape of Michael Martinez's death into evidence. We'd like to play the tape and have Dr. West explain some of the information shown on the tape."

"Your Honor, the defendant objects. We'd like an opportunity to question Dr. West concerning the tape before the court makes a ruling on its admissibility."

"All right, Mr. Hoffmeister, you may inquire," Judge Cooper said.

"Dr. West, where did you get the tape?"

"I didn't actually get the tape myself. Ms. Compton had the tape. I understand someone delivered it to the courtroom yesterday morning, along with a note that simply says, 'I owe you a tape.'"

Janette handed Hoffmeister the note. "Dr. West, do you

know 'Burrows'?" Hoffmeister asked. *He* certainly remembered Burrows.

"I don't know anyone named Burrows."

"Is it your testimony, Dr. West, that you have no idea where this tape was made?"

"I didn't say that. Of course I know where the tape was made. It's perfectly clear that it was made at the IORC at the time of Michael Martinez's death. In fact, the tape includes data from various sensors and monitors that recorded Martinez's vital signs as he was dying."

"Then you do know the source of the tape. It's from the IORC, is it not?"

"I'm sure it was made at the IORC."

"Dr. West, you've been to IORC. Based on those visits, would IORC permit removal of a tape of a patient like this?" Hoffmeister asked.

"Absolutely not. It's like a confession."

"So it was stolen? Your Honor, we object to the tape on the grounds that it was made at the IORC and is barred by the treaty. It was unlawfully taken off the premises," Hoffmeister said.

"Overruled," said Cooper. "I'm going to allow the tape into evidence and allow it to be shown. It was not produced by court order nor by any official action, so the treaty does not prevent it. IORC must keep better control of its records if it wants to keep them secret. The tape is relevant to this case."

"But, Your Honor—" Hoffmeister started.

"I've ruled."

Janette took the tape and inserted it into a large-screen video player. Before she pressed the play button, she looked back at Parker. He took Betty Martinez's hand and spoke quietly to her for a few seconds. Then he nodded at Janette. She pressed the play button and the image of Martinez as he entered the examination room appeared on the screen, life-size. A hush spread throughout the courtroom, as everyone except LeBearc watched the events play out on the screen. After a moment, Janette asked David to confirm that the man on the tape was in fact Martinez.

Finally the tape reached the point of Martinez's death. Several people in the courtroom gasped, and Betty Martinez began to sob. Jorge glared at the screen and tightened the muscles in his jaw. Janette let the tape run silently for half a minute. When the tape ended, Janette rewound it to the point at which someone gave the signal to stop Martinez's heart. She asked David, "Will you explain, as the tape proceeds, what we are seeing and what exactly is occurring?"

She pressed the play button again. In a few seconds, the row of numbers appeared on the lower left and the cardiogram readout appeared on the right. David explained all of the medical readouts.

"You may inquire," Janette said to Hoffmeister, smiling.

"Dr. West, what that tape actually shows, does it not, is the unfortunate death of Michael Martinez?" Hoffmeister asked.

"Yes, that's what it shows."

"There is nothing to indicate, is there, that Martinez's heart didn't simply fail, that what's pictured is not just a heart attack?"

"Oh, yes, indeed, the tape clearly shows that is not what happened."

"Dr. West, isn't it true Martinez's heart could have simply failed spontaneously just like your heart or my heart might? In fact, wasn't it even more likely to fail because it had been transplanted?"

"The answer is no. Without the intervention of the electronic module attached to this heart, it was less likely to fail than yours or mine, even though it had been transplanted."

"Dr. West, that's pure speculation, is it not?"

"No, Mr. Hoffmeister, it's not speculation at all. I'm basing my opinion on hard scientific fact."

"And what might that be, Dr. West? What is there that would make this transplanted heart less likely to fail than yours or mine? Upon what do you base such an opinion?" David saw Cal Yoshida tugging on Hoffmeister's coattail, trying to get his attention. Cal finally stood up and said something to Hoffmeister, who whirled and looked at Cal, frowning. No lawyer wants to be interrupted in the middle of his cross-examination, but it was now too late.

"Mr. Hoffmeister, I've seen how that heart was produced. I've seen it personally."

Cal looked at David. He shook his head. He had tried to get Hoffmeister to change the subject, but Hoffmeister had been concentrating on David's answer, and was operating at a significant disadvantage because he didn't know the facts. "Dr. West, you said the heart was *produced*? The heart had been transplanted before, is that what you're talking about?"

"No. The IORC artificially produces the organs they transplant, including hearts, and including this heart."

"Are you trying to tell this court that IORC organs are mechanical devices or animal organs?" Hoffmeister asked.

"They are not mechanical devices in the way you mean. Whether they are animal hearts, I suppose, depends on your point of view and your definition. Traditional definitions are inapplicable, and the distinction here between animal and human is blurred—if there is a distinction at all. The organs are harvested from GECs, genetically engineered humanlike creatures that the IORC raises from cloned embryos specifically for that purpose."

Everyone in the courtroom looked at one another, not entirely certain they had heard correctly, or whether they could give any credence to Dr. West's testimony. Cal and LeBearc glared at David, and he returned their stares without flinching.

"Dr. West, where is this supposedly done? Isn't this story a figment of your imagination?"

"The GECs are grown on an island, perhaps several

islands. I visited one recently. The IORC has hundreds of thousands of these 'production units'—as they like to call them—at various stages of maturity."

"A mysterious island, you say?" Hoffmeister asked, looking around at the audience and gesturing. The testimony sounded absurd. "What is the name of this island, Dr. West?"

"I don't know the name of it, or if it has a name."

In a voice loud enough for everyone to hear, Cal finally told Hoffmeister to sit down and be quiet.

"Mr. Hoffmeister, I have a satellite photograph of the island right here, if you'd like to see it." David held up the brown envelope Captain Stapleton had given him.

The judge blinked several times. "Dr. West, let me get this straight. You are testifying under oath here that Martinez's heart was taken from some genetically engineered creature. You also claim to have satellite photos of the island where this bizarre activity occurs, is that correct?"

"That's exactly correct, Judge, and that's why I said the heart seemed less likely to fail. These hearts are young, of extremely high quality, and virtually fault-free."

"Are these humans? Do you mean they raise people to produce organs?" the judge asked.

"Judge, as I said, I think that point is debatable. The IORC claims the GECs are not human, because they have been so extensively altered. They appear human, and of course it would be necessary that they be very humanlike for the organs to work. Frankly, I don't know enough about the genetic details to be able to express an opinion about their humanity or lack of it. It's also a question that involves a lot of different issues: spiritual, ethical, medical and biological, and certainly legal. The point is, the IORC produces humanoid organisms; actually, 'genetically enhanced' is their term. It raises them in solitary confinement for the express purpose of harvesting their organs. They've kept the process a secret because they don't want public interference." Shocked to the point of inaction, everyone in the courtroom was looking at David as the TV cameras zoomed in on his face. Then the courtroom exploded in conversation. David decided not to mention the adoption. There was such a thing as too much chaos. Besides, why let IORC know that he and Janette knew?

"Court is adjourned until tomorrow at nine-thirty," Judge Cooper pronounced, largely unheard.

The information had come too suddenly for anyone to process. Krickett and Cal approached David.

"You've made a terrible mistake," Krickett said. "It's better that people not know certain things for their own good."

"You aren't going to kill any more transplant patients if I can stop you. The rest isn't up to me, it's up to the public. I know what I think about it, and in the final analysis that's all I have a right to decide."

LeBearc glared at him. Then he said, "Enough," and stalked out of the courthouse.

David joined the others at the lawyer's table.

Janette retrieved the tape and put it into her pocket for safekeeping. The case depended on it; she didn't intend to let it out of her possession now.

"We've done all we can do here. Now we've got to stop LeBearc somehow," David said. "They're very powerful. We have to act unexpectedly to have any chance of beating them. Warren, what would he need in order to activate modules attached to organs by satellite?"

"Lots of money, which he has. Plus a large, powerful satellite antenna with a microwave transmitter."

"Then he's headed back to IORC. I saw a group of antennas in a fenced area beside the administration building."

"The police won't react fast enough," Janette said. "And even if they believed us, they might not be able to get inside. The damn treaty prevents it."

"And you think we could?" Warren asked rhetorically.

"They certainly wouldn't expect it," David said.

"You think they'll just let us in?" Janette said.

"Or back out, after your testimony?" Warren added.

"If we play by the rules, a lot of people will be killed. I've done my talking. Now I'm going to try something else," David said.

"I'm going with you," Janette said.

"You sure?"

"Absolutely. I have the same stake in this as you do," Janette said. "It's just as personal for me as it is for you."

"I guess I'm in, too," Warren added.

"It's too dangerous, Warren. You're not directly involved and besides, you've got a family," David said.

"So do some of the people on that list. You need someone who knows computers. I don't want to, but I'm going. He has a head start, though. We may be too late," Warren said.

"We'll have to use your plane, Warren. That will get us there much quicker," David said. David, Janette, and Warren rushed from the courtroom, followed by shouting reporters whom Parker Ross headed off. Hungry for something, anything, the reporters swarmed around Parker while Janette, David, and Warren slipped away.

Piling into David's car, they raced to Executive Airport, only five minutes away, where Warren kept his Cessna 172. En route David took the 9mm Baretta out of the glove compartment and shoved it under his belt. He handed Janette his cell phone. Given the traffic, LeBearc would take at least a half hour to reach IORC at International Airport twelve miles away.

"I'll fly, Warren. I know the place," David said. Warren directed him as they drove onto the flight line. Warren and Janette jumped out of the car to untie the airplane, as David scrambled into the cabin to start the engine. Then Warren and Janette climbed into the plane and David taxied it out of its parking space and immediately pushed the throttle wide open.

"Whoa! You're on the parking ramp—no clearance,

Oh, shit!" Warren shouted as David lifted off, turning sharply to avoid a plane that had just turned off the taxiway. They climbed directly toward International Airport.

"There goes my pilot's license," David said. "We missed the guy, though."

The control tower staff screamed into the radio, with everyone talking at once, trying to divert other traffic, and calling the police to report the rare incidence of a drunk flyer.

David kept the plane just above the rooftops, to avoid colliding with passing jets on their final approach. They would reach the IORC in another five minutes, about the same time they figured LeBearc would get there.

"Janette, call Burrows. Tell him there are innocent lives at stake. Tell him anything. Ask him to meet us at the main office parking lot as soon as he can get there." David figured if Burrows had gone to the trouble of stealing the Martinez tape, he might prove an ally now.

"How do we get to the parking lot from the runway?" Warren asked.

"We don't need a runway. A parking lot will do just fine," David said, grinning.

"Oh, shit."

"I hope you've got good insurance," David said.

"Wayne Burrows, please," Janette said to the receptionist. "It's an emergency. I'm his wife. Our child is injured. I have to speak to him immediately." The connection went through.

"Burrows? Compton. Thanks for the tape. We need your help right now. Your head man is on his way there to do the same thing to a number of innocent people as he did to the guy on the tape. Then I expect he'll come looking for you. No shit—there's no time to explain. Will you help?"

At the other end of the line Burrows hesitated. He had taken a huge risk to give her the tape. But he was, deep down, still a cop, and he didn't like murder. *She sounds like she's riding a motorcycle,* he thought, remembering that IORC monitored every conversation. He wasn't sure it was her. He said to Janette, "Was the earlier tape erased?" If she was on the ball, she'd know what he meant. And he'd know if she was who she claimed to be.

"No, it was a new tape. You can't erase those tapes."

"Right answer. How can I help?"

"Meet us at the main office parking lot—now."

"How will I find you when you get there?"

"Don't worry, you'll know. Be armed."

Ahead loomed the giant IORC facility, entirely fenced in. International Airport had David on radar, and controllers worked to divert planes until they could figure out what David was going to do. In the twilight, the runway lights turned on.

Meanwhile, Krickett urged her driver to terrifying speeds as he dodged traffic. She had called the managing director himself, and he had given her specific directions, which she meant to carry out to the letter.

Cal stayed far behind in another car, also heading to the IORC, but at a more sensible speed.

LeBearc stormed into the administration building as Burrows hung up and as Dr. Thomas was leaving.

"You there, guard," LeBearc said to Burrows. "Take this person into custody." He pointed at the open-mouthed Thomas, who looked around to see if LeBearc meant someone else. "And find somebody named Burrows." Then LeBearc said to Thomas, "I'll see you in a few minutes. You won't steal any more tapes, I promise you that." LeBearc hurried off to the elevator.

Burrows took Thomas's arm, and Thomas's eyes darted around like those of a trapped rabbit looking for an escape. "Recognize me?" Burrows asked.

"I thought I told you to throw that tape away."

"I only throw away one tape per person."

The light of recognition showed in Thomas's eyes. "The cop. You're the cop from the accident."

"Right. Burrows."

"He'll kill me. Didn't you just see it on TV? They played that tape in court. I'm dead. So are you."

"You want to help take that guy down?" Burrows asked.

"What have I got to lose?"

"Exactly. According to that woman lawyer, he's going to kill a lot of people, just like he killed the guy on the tape. Then he'll start on us. The lawyer is on the way to try to stop him. If you want to help, come on." Thomas followed him out the door.

Outside, they saw the Cessna headed directly for them, just skimming over the perimeter fence. It touched down at the edge of the parking lot, skidded sideways, barely avoiding a light pole and several parked cars and then, with tires screeching, slid to a stop only a few feet from them. Warren and Janette piled out of the right side and slammed the door as the plane spun around and roared away.

"Where's he headed? Is he going to take off?" Warren asked.

The plane turned back around and stopped, engine idling, about three hundred feet from the fenced-in antenna area.

David set the trim adjustments to keep the plane's nose down so it wouldn't take off. He opened the door and stepped out onto the pavement. The plane began to inch forward; he jammed the throttle wide open. When it shot forward, his coat pocket snagged on the door handle, and he tripped. The engine roared as the plane accelerated. David tried to regain his footing but was dragged along as the plane picked up speed.

He tried to reach inside to pull the throttle off, but he couldn't reach it. Helplessly, out of desperation, he pushed away from the airplane with all his strength. His coat pocket ripped away and David spun around, falling to the pavement. The plane's tail passed only inches over his head. He rolled, covering his head. Three seconds later the plane, now rolling at forty miles per hour, hit the fence, swerved, slid sideways, and careened into an antenna, chopping it to pieces. Then it spun the other way and reared up on one wheel, causing the propeller to shear off chunks of another dish. Finally the plane impacted the concrete base of a large antenna, broke apart, and exploded into a fifty-foot fireball, followed by a huge plume of black smoke and a spray of electrical sparks.

David was up and running.

"Is your flying as exciting when I'm not with you?" Janette asked him.

"Nothing is as exciting when you're not with me," he said.

"That's my line," Warren quipped.

People ran outside and alarms sounded everywhere. The three of them, joined by Burrows and Thomas, walked calmly into the administration building while everyone dissolved into chaos.

Several security guards rushed toward them, guns drawn. They stopped when they saw Burrows.

"QC told me to bring these people to his office," Burrows said.

"Then do it," a sergeant replied, and he ran outside with the others to see what had caused the explosion. Sirens wailed in the distance.

Burrows and his group boarded the elevator, and Burrows punched the button for the top-floor. Nothing happened. He jammed the button repeatedly. Still nothing happened. "What the hell?" he said.

"It requires a key," Warren said, pointing at a keyhole beside the top-floor button. Burrows punched the next lower floor, and the elevator quietly ascended.

"Now what?" Janette asked, as the elevator door opened.

"Let's find LeBearc."

Burrows directed them to the fire stairs and they

climbed to the top floor. The door leading out was, of course, locked.

"It's just a matter of time before they check the monitors and find us," Burrows said, looking at the camera mounted on the wall. David walked toward the camera, pulled out his gun, and smashed it. Following David's lead, Burrows pulled out his pistol and shot the electric box that controlled the door lock. Sparks flew, but the door opened. "This is the fire escape," he explained. "The lock opens if it malfunctions."

"We'll go after LeBearc," David said. "You two stop anyone who comes after us."

Burrows kept his machine pistol and handed his semi-automatic pistol to Thomas. "You know how to use this?"

"I've done some hunting."

"Here are some clips. You go down and prop open the fire escape door. I'll stay here at the top of the stairs. They should come directly to the top. You cover my back."

Thomas took the extra magazines and trotted down the two flights to the door below. Using the doorstop, he propped the door open and leaned against it where he could see the elevators a hundred and fifty feet away. Burrows turned up his radio and listened. So far, he heard no one talking about them. Everyone seemed occupied with the plane crash. Each witness had a different story, and the security guards argued in confusion.

Krickett's car skidded to a halt in front of the building, which provoked a response from the sergeant and his men. Weapons drawn, they surrounded Krickett's car. Then the sergeant saw Krickett's emerald necklace, and he snapped to attention. "Sorry, ma'am. Everybody, put your guns away. She's security."

"What happened here?" she asked.

"It depends on who's telling it. All we know for sure is that an airplane crashed into the antenna farm and exploded. Apparently the occupants got out before it hit. It landed in the parking lot and then went out of control and crashed."

"Has the QC come in?"

"I think so. I can check with the guard." He glanced again at the necklace, which identified Krickett as the overall head of IORC security, and, therefore, a member of Central Management. The sergeant had never met Krickett, but he had certainly heard of her and he didn't want her to be displeased with him for any reason. He called Burrows on his radio, but got no answer.

"What the hell?" he said, looking at the vacant security desk through the glass doors. Then he remembered having seen Burrows, and he hurried inside followed by Krickett, her driver, and his men. He looked at the monitors and typed on the keyboard. The picture showed the QC's floor outside the elevator. Someone stood by the fire escape door. The sergeant switched to the fire escape camera and watched as the picture went blank.

"There's no camera in the QC's office."

"Call him," she ordered.

He punched in a number, ringing the QC's phone. LeBearc answered.

"Andre, it's Krickett. Have you done anything yet?"

"No. The antennas are out. I am trying to route the code through New York, but all our technicians are outside watching the fire."

"Apparently some people are trying to get to you. I'm downstairs. Don't send any signals until I get there. I'm on the way."

To the sergeant she said, "I need three of your men and a radio. Leave someone on the console. You come with me." They ran across the lobby to the elevators, and the sergeant pressed the QC's floor. As with Burrows and his group, nothing happened.

"Damn. The elevator locks out the top floor without a key or a code from upstairs. LeBearc's secretary will have already gone home."

"Where's the key?" she asked.

"The security office."

"Lovely. Maybe you could send for it." Her voice was laced with sarcasm. She had removed her split-system pistol and turned on the electronic sight. The sergeant spoke on the radio, calling for someone to bring him the key. Burrows heard the call and shouted to Thomas.

"They know we're up here. Get ready."

Janette, David, and Warren were in LeBearc's waiting room. He had locked his door. David started to shoot the lock, then stopped.

He walked over to the secretary's desk and saw that the computer displayed a screen saver of the company logo. The last time he was here, the secretary had punched a key on the computer to open the door. He punched the shift key and a menu appeared. Item four said "door." He highlighted four and pushed the enter key; the door clicked open.

LeBearc sat in front of his computer console. Before he could move, David rushed him and tackled him to the floor. Warren sat down at the computer and studied the screen. It showed a connection to the New York IORC, and a block flashed, asking for the password.

"Have you sent the signal yet?" David asked.

"I have nothing to say. Get out of my office."

"Apparently he made the connection, and the password is all he needed. Dozens of different identification numbers are listed. He would have killed all these people. Who are they?" Warren asked. LeBearc sneered at Warren and remained silent. "Maybe I can enter a command to interrupt the uplink connection."

David sat on LeBearc's chest, pressing him to the floor. "Make it quick," David said.

"How long before the key will be here?" Krickett asked.

"Maybe four, possibly five minutes."

Krickett frowned. "Let's go as far as we can on the elevator, then go up the stairs." The sergeant pushed the button. The elevator rose quickly and the door opened. As the three guards burst out of the elevator, Thomas shot one dead and wounded one of the others in the upper leg. He emptied his pistol, then ducked inside the door to the stairs. The wounded guard and the third one saturated the area with automatic fire, deafening everyone and filling the hall with plaster dust. The lights went out and the electrical fixtures sparked. Krickett held her hands over her ears, shouting for them to stop.

"I got one! I got one!" Thomas shouted to Burrows. Krickett heard him and smiled menacingly.

Everyone in LeBearc's office heard the gunfire. "We have to do something, Warren, even if it's wrong," Janette said. LeBearc now sat on the couch, and David looked over Warren's shoulder with his gun on ready.

"If I hit the wrong key, I may kill these people," Warren said, and his hands paused above the keyboard. Automatic fire from below echoed up the stairs and down the hall.

David walked back into the waiting room, shot the secretary's computer, and returned to LeBearc's office, locking the door behind him. Time was running out.

Janette saw LeBearc reach under the couch cushion, and she sprang at him. Before he could raise his hand she had his arm in a grip that made him suck in his breath with pain. She removed the pistol from his hand and stood covering him.

David looked at the screen. "It's not logical that an accidental entry would activate the command, Warren. For God's sake, do something." Warren hesitated, then pushed the escape key. The screen instantly changed and a message appeared:

"Uplink is established. Command interrupted. Enter new command."

Warren typed "DIR" and pressed enter. The screen blurred with file names and finally stopped, giving a number of files. Warren typed "Cancel uplink" and pressed enter. The computer replied "Unable to execute command. Enter password."

Thomas glanced around the doorway as a hail of bullets tore into the wall and ceiling. He could not hear anything because of the ringing in his ears. He stuck the pistol around the corner and fired a clip of bullets as fast as he could without looking, then glanced around the doorway once more to see if he had hit anything. Someone looked around the corner of the elevator. The dead guard lay out of commission, and Krickett held her fire.

Thomas fired another clip of bullets and when he stopped, Krickett looked around the corner. She calmly braced her split-system pistol against the edge of the elevator entrance, turned up the magnification on the infrared sight, and waited. The sergeant fired another burst and, as expected, Thomas shot a clip without looking and Krickett waited. Then he stuck his head around the corner. Krickett aligned the dot that was visible only through her sight on Thomas's left eye, and fired. A loud crack erupted, and Thomas disappeared around the corner.

"Let's go back for the key," she ordered.

"What about him?"

"He's dead."

The sergeant shouted into his radio that they were returning for the key. Burrows heard the call and decided to check on Thomas, then move to LeBearc's waiting room to watch the elevators, where he would have a better shot.

He walked down the first flight of stairs and saw Thomas's body sprawled on the floor. The entire back of his head was gone; a pool of blood slowly formed beneath him. Burrows swallowed hard and ran back up the steps and down the hall to LeBearc's office.

"LeBearc, what's the password?" David demanded. LeBearc smiled and sat silently.

"I can fix that," Janette said and pointed the small gun at him. His smile broadened as he looked at Janette steadily.

"Wait a minute. I've got an idea," David said. "I hope you still have the Martinez tape." She tossed it to him. He inserted it into a video player and rewound the tape back to the point of Martinez's first convulsion. He stopped on a single frame of the video. It included all the data around the borders. "There, let's try that short group of numbers. We know the activation code is sixteen numbers, but this other one is six numbers. It appeared for only a second. Maybe that's his password." LeBearc remained perfectly still and glared at them.

Warren typed in the numbers and a box came up that said "Password accepted. Enter command." Warren grinned at them. David nodded his okay and Warren began typing furiously, pausing occasionally to view the screen. Throughout the procedure, a small box that said "uplink established," remained in the lower corner. Warren was afraid to try to deal with that. He worked on the other files. Janette retrieved the videotape and slipped it back into her pocket.

"This confirms it. There's a VIP file for the U.S. with hundreds of names. Each one has a code number after it. Dozens of people—including some government officials I recognize. He's entered the names of everyone on our list. Several names from the VIP list are highlighted, too."

Warren resumed typing.

David said to LeBearc, "What were you trying to accomplish?"

LeBearc glared at him.


The elevator started up again, and this time, Krickett had the key. The sergeant had pushed the top floor. She punched the floor below LeBearc's office. "I'm getting off on the floor below. I'll come up the stairs. Stay off the radio." As the door opened, she glanced around the corner and down the hall toward the steps. As she expected, she saw no one. She motioned the sergeant to go ahead, and then she retrieved the pistol from the dead guard's holster. She left his machine pistol. Anyone who needed more than two shots per target, Krickett believed, was incompetent.

She went into the stairwell carefully, checking before she entered. Only Thomas lay there. She paid no attention to his body. She eased up the steps.

The elevator door opened on LeBearc's floor and Burrows emptied an entire clip from his machine pistol into it, killing or seriously wounding everyone. The door closed and he reloaded, his heart pounding. Krickett heard the shooting and waited. Burrows heard someone on the radio calling the sergeant, but he heard no reply. Then the elevator began descending. Only seconds remained before security discovered the bodies and sent more people, this time better prepared.

Burrows decided to relocate, and he walked into the hall to look for a place. When he did, Krickett emerged from hiding and, to prevent the noise of a pistol shot, delivered a punch to the back of his neck. He staggered against the wall and collapsed. She kicked the machine pistol down the hall and took his radio. Because he was a big man, he had not died, but had merely lost consciousness from her blow. She saw his uniform and couldn't figure out why he had shot into the elevator. He must have been confused. She decided to let him live; he no longer seemed a threat.

She pressed the transmit button, advising security that she was outside LeBearc's office, and it was safe for them to come up.

They heard the shooting outside LeBearc's door. "How do you expect to get out of here alive? How do you expect to prevent me from sending the code once you are caught?" LeBearc asked, smiling again. "You can't get out of here with any proof. Did that occur to you?"

"David, open the door!" Krickett shouted. They all turned and stared at the door.

"Warren, could we reprogram the modules? Can we deactivate them?" David asked.

"There is a command 'Deactivate' listed here," Warren said.

"What do you think?"

"I guess," Warren said, and typed it in. The screen turned red and flashed the prompt "Are you sure? Y/N."

"Stop!" Janette said. LeBearc smirked. "Don't do it. It's not right."

"Woman's intuition?" David asked.

"Don't knock it if you don't have it."

Warren stopped. The door blew open in a burst of gunfire. Krickett leveled her pistol at Warren. "Step away from the computer," she ordered. Janette still held LeBearc's pistol. "Drop it. I can shoot you before you can raise your arm."

"Do it, Janette. She's good."

"Why, thank you, David. I'm glad you remember." She tilted her head, smiling. Janette laid the pistol on the floor. Krickett motioned and Janette knocked it away with her foot. Krickett pointed her gun at Warren. "Move it," she said, and he complied. "David, is that a gun you have, or are you just glad to see me?" David removed the gun from his belt and dropped it to the floor. She motioned for him to slide it toward her, which he did.

"Now, let's wait for the cavalry to come."

Janette dove at Krickett, taking her waist high and knocking the gun out of her hand. They rolled into a glass-topped table. Janette scrambled for the gun, but Krickett kicked her in the stomach and spun away.

LeBearc rushed to the computer as Janette grabbed Krickett again and they sprawled across the floor, struggling. David started for them as Krickett elbowed Janette in the head and reached for the gun that was lying beside her. "You're pretty fast," Krickett said to Janette. Then, from the floor, Krickett fired the pistol twice in rapid succession, so that it sounded like a single shot.

Everyone froze. LeBearc, sitting at his computer, looked puzzled as blood spurted from his shoulder. "Move away, Andre," Krickett ordered. He complied slowly. Keeping the gun on them, Krickett went to the computer, typed in a code with one finger, and pressed "enter." On the screen flashed a box that said, "Uplink disconnected."

She flipped open her satellite telephone, pressed a button, and said into the mouthpiece, "The deactivation is aborted." She listened for several long seconds. "Yes, sir." She clicked the phone shut. Pressing the transmit button on her radio she said, "Everything is under control here. Please send security to LeBearc's office, now."

"Krickett, what's happening up there?" Cal's voice crackled over the radio.

"Cal, where are you?" she asked.

"In the lobby."

"You're acting QC as of now. Take over, will you? I'm on overtime up here." She smiled at everyone. LeBearc collapsed in a chair, his head hanging, his blood dripping on the carpet.

Guards carrying rifles crashed into the room, shouting

for everyone to drop their weapons and freeze. Krickett raised her hands, dropping the pistol. Then the security manager moved forward, recognized Krickett's necklace, and began giving orders.

"You are all free to go," Krickett said to David, Janette, and Warren. "Arrange transportation for these people," she directed the security manager. "I think their airplane is broken."

"You want to explain what you're doing?" David asked her.

"The company doesn't want anyone killed that might spark an international uproar. If we did, they'd have been dead before LeBearc left the courthouse."

"That's it?"

"Isn't that enough?"

"No. Your whole program has failed to consider one thing, the human free spirit. Janette and I have an extra big measure of it. You can't genetically engineer that out. So, just agreeing not to kill some people isn't enough for us."

"Well, it'll have to do. See ya," she said, and motioned for the guard to escort them out. Cal entered as they were leaving, looked around at the mess, and frowned.

"Ms. Compton," he said, "tell your clients we will propose a new settlement."

The guards escorted them to a green Volvo wagon and drove them to Warren's house. When they arrived, David said, "You better tell me that you transferred the files."

With a wicked grin, Warren grabbed his portable computer, connected it to the telephone jack, and began typing. "Beautiful. Absolutely beautiful!" he said.

"What?" Janette asked.

"I copied all his files onto my office database by modem. I've retrieved them all. We can deprogram every module once I figure out the codes. Of course, we'll need a satellite uplink."

"I think Captain Stapleton can help us."

"Now what? What will you do?" Janette asked David.

"With Stapleton's help, maybe we can make some changes, and also convince people to take back their autonomy."

"You think we are still in danger?" Janette asked.

"We'll always be in danger. We're alive now only because they have some use for us." *I need to figure out whether they've put some sort of time bomb in us—something hard to find, maybe a genetic one,* David thought.

Cal and Krickett sat alone in LeBearc's waiting room, drinking Diet Coke. "It's fascinating isn't it, seeing those two together?" Cal said.

"They're amazing," Krickett agreed. "They don't realize their capacities and powers. We're just beginning to learn ourselves. She moved so fast I didn't see her coming. With training she would be truly formidable."

"You really think they don't know?"

"David obviously suspects part of it. You heard his comment. They both know they were adopted. I think they took their capacities for granted—their independence and intelligence, their coordination, even their golfing ability. They don't suspect anything beyond that. Unforeseeable events sidetracked Janette's golf career. David's father pushed David away from his program. Like so many of them, these two have vastly more abilities than we ever expected. At least that's what our reports concluded. And my encounters with David confirm it. Maybe it's for the best. Maybe we can profit even more by their developing their individual strengths in some way. It's an amazing coincidence that they even met."

"I expected that when Janette and David gave up golf as a career, their parents would have explained everything to them."

"A disclosure would have violated their contracts with us."

"But people violate contracts all the time."

"Not that part of our contracts. No one ever tells. They're told the consequences in advance."

"What about David? He revealed the source of our organs; what will you do about that?"

"Nothing. It's too late, anyway. He is absolutely off limits. They both are. No one is to touch them except on direct orders from Central Management. I have a feeling Janette and David will figure out what they are, if for no other reason than because we haven't done anything to punish them. Maybe it will end here and they won't do anything further."

"David is a Stage Four, isn't he, and Janette a Stage Five?" Cal asked.

"That's right. Very early complex gene enhancement, late Four, early Five, before the sterility gene was added," Krickett said. "We started with a high intelligence base and spliced aggressiveness and tenacity along with coordination and other special traits. We did far too much, too many variables for simple sports products. We were just learning then, experimenting. They're completely unpredictable and uncontrollable. Wouldn't it be something if they had a child? Their bases are different; an offspring would be viable, and the result might be a world-class golf or tennis champion, or something even more unexpected than the parents. Unfortunately, we wouldn't have a contract on the child!"

"We're going to the basketball game, aren't we? We do have a percentage contract on our two GECs playing tonight." Cal had been looking forward to the game all day.

"We have to deal with Andre first," Krickett said.

"Couldn't we wait a few days and see what develops?" Cal asked, but he knew the answer already.

LeBearc stood in front of the glass wall in his office. Rubbing his bandaged shoulder, he looked out at the airport and gardens below. He had no personal items to collect, no picture, no memorabilia. The office and his life were a shambles. He started when Cal and Krickett entered.

"Central Management has decided to expand the organ donation plan and to cancel all Code 6's. Allowing outside retransplants of our organs is necessary to be consistent and to help stop further inquiry. Now we have to do damage control," Krickett said, watching LeBearc as she spoke. His proud, erect bearing seemed to deflate with her announcement.

"What about my family?" he asked.

"We'll send them to Switzerland for the time being," Krickett said.

"I don't suppose the change in policy will solve my problem, will it?" he asked.

"Andre, the Secret Service and the U.S. Attorney will have questions. What would you do? Should we invoke the treaty?"

LeBearc silently looked out at the gardens for several minutes more. "I would like to work in the gardens, I think. I have always wanted to garden, but I have never had time for it."

"The gardens would be good, Andre. In Paris, perhaps," Krickett said.

"Paris, yes, Paris is fine. My wife likes Paris."

He walked to his communications console and pressed the button. "Advise neurosurgery that I will be down immediately. I have a severe headache." He released the button, and walked out of his office without further comment.

LeBearc checked into the neurosurgery department where the chief of the department waited for him, looking worried.

LeBearc said, "Doctor, I have a four-centimeter benign tumor in my right cerebral cortex that I want you to remove—now. Dr. Yoshida, the new QC, will be along in a minute to oversee the procedure. You are to follow his directions exactly. You are not expected to understand or to question your instructions. You will report that I have a tumor exactly as I have told you."

"Yes, sir. Please follow me and we'll get a CT and an MRI."

"Neither one will be necessary. The tumor is here." LeBearc pointed to a spot on a wall chart that depicted the brain, with parts and function labeled. The doctor's gaze followed LeBearc's finger to the area labeled "memory."

"Let's get on with it, Doctor. This is painful." LeBearc opened the medication drawer. He removed an injector and a vial of succinylcholine. Filling the injector, he said, "I understand that this drug is unpleasant for one who is conscious. Please don't delay."

The doctor did not move; he watched in stunned fascination as LeBearc climbed onto the surgery table, lay back, and injected himself with the drug.

At that moment, Cal Yoshida stepped into the room.

# EPILOGUE

Thursday morning, the following article appeared on the front page of the Orlando *Tribune:*

## IORC SUIT SETTLED

In a move that surprised veteran courthouse watchers, the IORC has settled the claim of Betty and Jorge Martinez for an undisclosed sum, on condition that the details of the settlement remain private. Mrs. Martinez had claimed that the IORC deliberately disabled a transplanted heart her husband received in an operation performed at Government Hospital in Orlando. IORC had denied any wrongdoing, but the settlement and other events cast doubt on that denial.

The plaintiffs' attorney refused to comment on the settlement, but did say that she stood by the arguments she made in open court, which included the accusations.

The doctor who performed the transplant, Dr. David West, said he was satisfied with the settlement. His testimony in court, along with a dramatic videotape of the actual heart attack and death of Martinez, may have been the deciding factor that led to the settlement.

Dr. West also testified that the IORC actually produces its organs from genetically engineered humanlike creatures, called "GECs" for genetically enhanced clones. Several medical experts discounted this assertion as "improbable." The IORC refused to comment on any of its activities. West claimed to have visited an unnamed island where he saw the organ production, and he also claimed to have a satellite photo of the island. The *Tribune* is attempting to obtain a copy of the photo.

The trial was adjourned Tuesday.

Later that day, the President held a press conference in which he announced that he would send a Bill to Congress to modify the treaty with the IORC, making it subject to governmental oversight of its activities involving pharmaceuticals.

The President also said that he had ordered a full investigation of the allegations made at the trial. He said, "I am certain that an institution such as the IORC would not engage in the activities charged. I am sure that the investigation will reveal that these actions were the work of a deranged individual."

In what some observers believe is a related announcement, the IORC has just implemented a new policy for organ donation, granting Justification Factor points for donations to private and government hospitals, when previously only donations to IORC earned points.

The effect of this change is not yet clear, but one thing is certain: There will be more organs available to patients who cannot qualify for an IORC organ transplant because of an insufficient Justification Factor. Officials declined to speculate on what this might lead to over the years.

The FBI was present at the trial and, after the settlement, took possession of a briefcase used earlier in the trial. The warrant states that the evidence is needed "as a matter of national security to aid investigation of a possible danger to the President and other high government officials."

The U.S. Attorney also held a press conference yesterday on these events. He stated that his office had attempted to question Dr. Andre LeBearc, local head of the IORC. However, IORC claimed that LeBearc was recuperating from emergency brain surgery to remove a tumor, and was unable to talk. The tumor reportedly has affected his behavior in recent weeks. LeBearc was expected to survive the surgery, but with severe mental impairment, according to an IORC statement.

"Our investigation began several weeks ago," the U.S. Attorney stated. "Our office is always alert to possible illegalities, regardless of who might be involved. No one is above the law, and we will not tolerate any cover-ups, even when an individual who becomes deranged is employed by a powerful and upstanding institution such as the IORC."

When asked how his office would pursue the investigation, he replied that the matter was being studied in Washington and he was awaiting directions from his superiors. "There are difficult legal issues involved," he said.

Ben Masckowicz, the retired lawyer in Israel whose case Janette relied upon, put down the newspaper clipping. No message or explanation accompanied it—only the handwritten word "thanks" at the bottom of the page. For the first time in eleven years, he smiled to himself. He thought of Sidney Arrow, and he smiled.

# ABOUT THE AUTHOR

Stephen Kanar has practiced law in Florida for thirty years, specializing in high-tech, aerospace, and medical-related Litigation. Simultaneously, he has pursued a part-time career in aviation, single-handedly building and test flying a high-performance experimental aerobatics airplane.

Steve and his wife divide their time between Florida and Maine. *The J Factor* is his first novel.